Pooches and Kiddies

The Further Adventures of Healing Weintraub

Todd Walton

Trenton, Georgia

Published by Under the Table Books, Mendocino, California 2023.

Print ISBN: 978-1-958892-71-8
Ebook ISBN: 979-8-88531-731-3

Library of Congress Cataloging in Publication Data
Walton, Todd
Pooches and Kiddies: The Further Adventures of Healing Weintraub
by Todd Walton
Library of Congress Control Number: 2023918971

Cover Design by Todd Engel.

Under the Table Books
P.O. Box 366
Mendocino, California 95460

Other Books by Todd Walton

Inside Moves

Forgotten Impulses

Louie & Women

Ruby & Spear

Open Body: Creating Your Own Yoga

The Writer's Path

Buddha In A Teacup

Under the Table Books

Little Movies

Oasis Tales of the Conjuror

Why You Are Here

Good With Dogs and Cats

Dedicated to

Sally Fletcher

Bill Fletcher

Wendy Mull

Doug Fields

Deb Kvaka

Peter Temple

Marcia Sloane

Contents

Pooches and Kiddies

The Further Adventures

of Healing Weintraub

I always feel like I'm on a quest to find a point of connection, a moment in space and time where the puzzle pieces fall into place and the conundrum is revealed to be an answer to a question far greater than the one that initiated the quest.

Healing Weintraub

Who's Who

Mercy, a town on the far north coast of California

The Mercy watershed was home to the Pomo people for thousands of years prior to the 1800s when European settlers arrived to log the redwood forests. In the 1930s, immigrants from Mexico began settling in and around Mercy, and in the 1950s and 60s Beatniks, Hippies, and Back-to-the-Landers discovered the area. Mercy today, population 2432, is a destination for tourists, retirees, and those who serve them.

Healing Weintraub, 70

The second child of Naomi and Ezra Weintraub, Healing was born in the little old farmhouse on two acres on Nasturtium Road at the south end of Mercy, and he has lived here his entire life. A promising actor in his youth, he chose not to pursue acting as a career and instead worked as a gardener until he was thirty-three when he became a grocer. He retired from the grocery business when he was sixty. For the last ten years he has occupied himself by giving accordion lessons, playing accordion in his band Mercy Me, growing vegetables and flowers, and continuing his lifelong work of helping cats and dogs resolve their conflicts with humans.

Naomi Weintraub, 92, Healing's mother

Born in Oxford, England, Naomi settled in Mercy with her husband Ezra when she was twenty and Ezra was twenty-four. They bought the derelict little old house on Nasturtium Road a few weeks after their arrival in Mercy and spent several years renovating the place, during which time they added a third bedroom. Naomi and Ezra lived in Mercy until they were in their sixties and inherited a house in Oxford, England where they then lived for fifteen years until Ezra died ten years ago, after which Naomi returned to Mercy and now lives in the cottage behind the little old house.

Jean Weintraub, 72, Healing's sister

Born in the little old house, Jean moved to England when she was sixteen. She has been married to Albert, an Archaeology professor, for fifty-three years. They live in Exeter and have two grown children. Ever since Naomi moved back to Mercy ten years ago, Jean visits Mercy every year for a month or so.

Jahera Weintraub, 64, Healing's wife

The child of an Algerian mother and Norwegian father, Jahera has been married to Healing for ten years. A professional photographer and calligrapher, Jahera lived in France for most of her life before moving to Mercy with her parents eleven years ago.

Tova Weintraub, 44, Healing's daughter

Born in the little old house, Tova is an actor and singer. Tova's mother vanished when Tova was eleven-months-old, leaving Healing to raise Tova with help from Naomi and Ezra. Tova lived in Portland Oregon for nineteen years where she was a veterinarian's assistant before returning to Mercy six years ago and marrying Jahera's son Lucien with whom she had the twins Raaz and Oz.

Raaziyah and Ozan Weintraub, 4, twins

Raaziyah a girl, Ozan a boy, they are known as Raaz and Oz, and they refer to Jahera as *Jadda*, which means *grandmother* in Arabic.

Lucien Dahl, 41

Born and raised in France, Lucien lived in Switzerland for several years before moving to Mercy six years ago. An art director for movies, Lucien relocated to Los Angeles shortly after Raaz and Oz were born. He returns to Mercy a few times a year for brief visits with Tova and the children.

Maahiah Dahl, 83, Jahera's mother

Born in Marseilles, Maahiah is Algerian. Her Norwegian husband Caspar Dahl died five years ago. An illustrator, baker, seamstress, and knitter, Maahiah lives across the street from the little old house in a cottage adjacent to the house where Tova lives with Raaz and Oz.

Darby Riley, 85

A close friend of the Weintraubs, Darby has resided in Mercy for sixty years after emigrating from Ireland, his antique shop a Mercy landmark for fifty years until he sold his building and retired to a house on the headlands.

Marjorie Kleinsasser, 83

A longtime Mercy resident and Darby's housemate.

Eliana Levine, 25

A superb violinist and Healing's longtime accordion student.

Justin Oglethorpe, 72

Healing's lifelong friend and the very tall owner of *Big Goose*, Mercy's largest pub.

Helen Morningstar, 70

A poet and Justin's wife, she, too, is Healing's lifelong friend.

Ruben Higuera, 61

The unflappable Sheriff of Mercy.

Ω

1. Raaz and Oz

On this last night of May, Raaz and Oz, four-year-old fraternal twins with olive skin and dark brown hair, are camping in the living room of the little old house on Nasturtium Road where Weintraubs have lived for seventy-three years.

Oz and Raaz usually spend the night in their house across the street, but while their mother Tova is in France making a movie, the twins and their great grandmother Maahiah are living on *this* side of the street where they feel safer and happier while Tova is away.

"Shafi?" says Raaz, calling from her sleeping bag. "I think Moosh *really* wants to hear a story."

"I *know* he does because he told me," says Oz, coming to the kitchen table where Healing is playing Scrabble with his wife Jahera, his mother Naomi, and his mother-in-law Maahiah.

"What did Moosh say exactly?" asks Healing, who is called *Shafi* by several members of Weintraub collective, *Shafi* meaning *healer* in Arabic.

Oz purses his lips as he concocts his answer. "He said he was waiting for a long time, but you never came."

"How like him to put it that way," replies Healing, smiling at his naked grandson. "Well translated."

"When *are* you coming?" asks Oz, impatiently. "So I can tell Moosh and Socrates who also wants to hear a story."

"I'll be there in a few minutes," says Healing, exchanging looks with Jahera. "Please ask the dogs to be patient."

"I'll try," says Oz, returning to the living room. "Only it might not work."

"Go on, Shafi," whispers Jahera. "You have no hope of overtaking your mother. None of us do."

*

Healing builds up the fire and settles into the rocking chair on the edge of Raaz and Oz's camp composed of air mattresses, sleeping bags, knapsacks, pillows, and flashlights. Raaz's knapsack contains clean clothes for tomorrow, an orange, an apple, and a small jar of nuts and raisins. Oz's knapsack contains these same items, minus clothes, because he refuses to wear clothing.

There are five dogs, medium-sized mixed-breeds, arrayed around the campers: Mendelssohn, eleven, known as Moosh, Socrates, ten, Puccini, six, and the siblings Tabinda and Kadan, both twelve.

"Moosh?" asks Healing, speaking to Mendelssohn, a handsome golden brown dog with black markings. "Did you have a particular *kind* of story you wanted to hear?"

Mendelssohn looks at Healing to say *The sound of your voice will suffice.*

"About Oziyah and Rozan," says Raaz, snug in her sleeping bag. "Solving a mystery."

"They use microscopes to get clues," says Oz, who has yet to lie down. "And telescopes."

"Do they have dogs?" asks Healing, as if he doesn't know.

"Of *course* they do," says Raaz, exasperated by the question. "Goosh and Plato and Govinda and Paganini and Nadak. They help solve the mystery."

"*Usually*," adds Oz, falling to his knees on his sleeping bag. "Sometimes they solve the mystery using special inventions."

"Where would you like this story to take place?" asks Healing, rubbing his chin to denote deep thinking. "Bulgaria?"

"Not Bul*garia*," giggles Raaz. "*All* the stories are in Mercy, only not *this* Mercy but almost."

"Their house is across the street like our house," says Oz, crawling into his sleeping bag. "Only they have a laboratory for experiments and inventing things."

"This wouldn't happen to be a story I've already told you, would it?" asks Healing, squinting suspiciously at his grandchildren. "Sounds *very* familiar."

"Not the *same* story," explains Raaz. "But *kind* of like the last one when they found buried treasure."

"Only *not* with a scary tunnel," says Oz, squirming in his bag. "Scary things are better for daytime stories."

"Got it," says Healing, clearing his throat. "Buried treasure, no scary tunnel."

"But still exciting," adds Raaz, closing her eyes to imagine the story.

"Maybe *you* would like to tell the story," says Healing, addressing both of them.

"I could *start* the story," says Oz, getting out of his sleeping bag and standing with his back to the fire. "But only the beginning."

"Please," says Healing, listening intently.

"One day Oziyah and Rozan were pulling carrots," begins Oz, miming the pulling of carrots, "when Goosh came running up to them very excited. 'What is it, Goosh?' asked Rozan, and then..."

Oz pauses momentously and Raaz says, "Now you tell the rest, Shafi."

*

Healing rises at dawn, dons shorts and T-shirt, and tiptoes down the hall to the open doorway of the guest room where Maahiah is sleeping in the queen-sized bed with Raaz and Oz on either side of her, the children having abandoned the living room floor in the middle of the night for the comfort of sleeping with their great grandmother.

Armed with a large basket, Healing opens the kitchen door and waits for the dogs to go out ahead of him before he crosses the deck and goes down the two wide steps into the large backyard where the vegetable garden is in full summer glory.

While the dogs wander about, Healing releases the fourteen hens from their coop into the scratch yard and sings *Oh What A Beautiful Morning* in Spanish.

Now Naomi, still spry at ninety-two, emerges from her cottage in her usual attire of long-sleeved shirt and corduroy trousers, her snow-white hair in a ponytail.

"Have you brought in the paper, dear?" she asks, looking over the tops of her wire-framed glasses at him, her British accent distinctly posh.

"No, but I heard a mighty thud on the front porch moments ago," he says, his accent a mild version of his mother's.

"Then I shall go straight in," she says, breathing deeply of the cool morning air. "Rather than go round to the front where the paper has been landing in the rhododendrons of late."

Now Raaz and Oz come charging out the kitchen door, Oz naked, his hair long and unruly, Raaz wearing a blue skirt and emerald green blouse, her hair in pigtails.

"You're just in time to help gather eggs," says Healing, which prompts the children to race across the yard to the coop.

"My goodness you are fleet," says Naomi, watching her great grandchildren run by.

"Gently now," says Healing, following the children. "Those eggs will get broken for our omelets soon enough."

*

Omelets consumed, Jahera and Maahiah and the children commandeer the kitchen table for drawing with crayons on butcher paper while Naomi and Healing walk to the pond and sit on the old wooden bench to confer about the current dilemma facing the family: Oz's refusal to wear clothing under any circumstances.

"Like it or not, we live in a society that frowns upon public nudity after infancy," says Naomi, shaking her head in dismay. "I fear Oz's obstinacy in this regard is verging on sociopathic. Do you agree?"

"At this point," says Healing, angrily, "I find Tova and Lucien's handling of the situation far more troubling than Oz's refusal to wear clothes, since it was *their* behavior that launched his career as a nudist."

"Are you referring to Lucien rarely being here?" asks Naomi, unaccustomed to Healing being so angry.

"I am referring to Lucien who, on those rare occasions when he's here, dotes on Raaz and either ignores Oz or is harshly critical of him. This inequity reached its zenith at the twins' third birthday party when Lucien was, as usual, showering Raaz with attention and ignoring Oz. So Oz took off all his clothes and immediately got *lots* of attention from Tova begging him to put his clothes back on and from Lucien threatening to spank him. And the brave little boy hasn't worn a stitch of clothing since. For fourteen months!"

"During which time Tova has repeatedly asked you not to intervene, and you have acquiesced to her wishes," says Naomi, who has unbounded faith in her son. "But now, at last, she *has* asked for your help, though it pained her greatly to admit that she and Lucien botched things. May I know how you plan to proceed?"

"I will take Oz into the wilderness," says Healing, gazing eastward at the forest ascending the coast range. "Where we will get to the bottom of things."

*

When the crayon masterworks are affixed to the wall next to the parrot cage in the sunniest corner of the kitchen, Jahera announces that she and Raaz are going shopping and then meeting friends for lunch at *Café Brava*.

"Not fair," says Oz, pouting. "Why can't I go?"

"If you wear shorts and sandals you can," says Raaz, nodding encouragingly. "But they don't let naked people into the café. Do they, Jadda?"

"No, they don't," says Jahera, shaking her head.

"I hate you," says Oz, storming out the back door.

"He did *not* mean that, Raaz," says Maahiah, pausing in her bread making. "He's having a difficult time and spoke out of anger. You know he loves you very much."

"I know," says Raaz, sadly. "If people would let him go places naked he wouldn't get mad." She shrugs. "But they won't."

*

Healing finds Oz at the pond with Mendelssohn and Puccini, the dogs watching the little boy throw rocks into the water, something he knows he's not supposed to do.

"I'm sorry, Shafi," says Oz, dropping the rock he was about to throw. "I just got *so* mad. How come *she* gets to go and I don't?"

"Why do you think?" asks Healing, sitting on the old wooden bench that has stood near the water's edge since Healing and his sister Jean helped their father dig the pond sixty years ago.

"Because you have to wear clothes," says Oz, snarling. "Stupid."

"I was thinking we could take a hike up Trout Creek to Kingfisher Pool and have a swim. Promising to be another hot day. Sound good?"

"Can we take a picnic?" asks Oz, climbing onto Healing's lap.

"A feast of hummus and crackers and apples and oranges," says Healing, putting his arms around his grandson.

"Can we take the dogs?" asks Oz, starting to cry.

"No," says Healing, gently rocking the little boy. "They're not allowed in that particular state park."

"Why not?"

"Their scent scares the wild animals, and their piss and poop is not good for the environment there, so we'll leave them here and take them to the beach later on."

"But *I* can go naked there," says Oz, defiantly. "Can't I?"

"Yes you can," says Healing, speaking quietly. "As naked as you want to be."

*

Wearing size-appropriate knapsacks, Healing and Oz walk seven blocks from Nasturtium Road to Onyx Lane from where they enter Mercy River State Park and take the trail that follows Trout Creek up a steep incline through a forest of redwoods.

"This is more fun than stupid *Café Brava,*" says Oz, leading the way, the soles of his feet as tough as leather.

"Certainly different," says Healing, dressed in shorts, T-shirt, sandals, and a broad-brimmed sunhat. "Though not necessarily better."

"But *you* like it better, don't you Shafi?" asks Oz, looking back at Healing.

"Today I do," says Healing, breathing deeply of the forest air. "Though some days I like nothing better than going to the café and meeting friends and having a scone."

"I like doing this better *every* day," says Oz, emphatically. "Much better."

*

When they get to Kingfisher Pool at the base of little Kingfisher Falls, they leave their knapsacks and Healing's clothes on the rocky beach and jump into the water, Healing as naked as Oz.

After a good long bathe, they sit in the sun and eat hummus and crackers and olives, their spirits exalted by the wilderness.

"Looking forward to going to school?" asks Healing, savoring a section of orange. "Making new friends?"

"I'm not going to school," says Oz, haughtily. "They make you wear clothes and I'm never wearing clothes ever again."

"Why not?"

"I hate them."

"*Hate* is a strong word, Oz. Why do you hate clothes?"

"They feel bad. They make me itch."

"Do they? Even a nice cotton T-shirt and cotton shorts? That's what I like to wear when it's warm, and then layers of cotton when it's cold. I'm a cotton man. Wool and polyester make me itch. But not cotton."

"Why are you talking about this?" says Oz, glowering. "You never do."

"I'm talking about this, Oz, because it's time for you to start wearing clothes. Not at home if you don't want to, but out in the world and at school and when you come on cases with me." He gives Oz a serious look. "I wanted your help with Helen's cat, but I couldn't take you with me because you wouldn't wear clothes."

"Why do I have to?" says Oz, trembling with rage. "Dogs don't wear clothes. Cats don't wear clothes. Only stupid people do."

"That's because we don't have fur covering our bodies. Moosh and Puccini and Socrates and all the dogs and cats wear coats every minute of their lives. If they didn't have fur coats they'd catch cold and be miserable."

Oz considers this. "Why don't people have fur?"

"It's a great mystery," says Healing, nodding sagely. "Our ancestors had fur, but for some reason we stopped having it except on our heads and in a few other places, and now the only way humans can survive in a climate like ours is to wear clothes."

"I don't want to," says Oz, despondently. "Please don't make me, Shafi."

"Tell you what," says Healing, handing Oz a section of orange. "I brought along a beautiful green cotton T-shirt Maahiah made for you, your favorite color, and some brown cotton shorts she made for you just like mine, and you can stay barefoot unless you want to go inside somewhere, in which case I brought along some sandals for you. If you'll gives these clothes a try, we'll go to the animal shelter and see if they have something you might want to take home with you."

"A puppy?" gasps Oz, who has been begging for a pup since he was two.

"If you'll give wearing clothes a chance, you can have a puppy."

"I'll try, Shafi," says Oz, starting to cry. "I won't like it, but I'll try."

*

In the animal shelter, Oz chooses a darling female pup, a mix of Border Collie and German Shepherd.

Healing nods his approval. "Excellent choice, Oz."

"I think we better get a puppy for Raaz, too," says Oz, beaming at Healing. "Or she'll be *very* jealous."

"How thoughtful of you," says Healing, taking the female pup from Oz. "By the way, how are those clothes feeling?"

"Okay," says Oz, giving a little shrug before going in search of another pup. "I'll get used to them."

*

When all the members of the collective are snug in their beds that night and the pups are sequestered in a small pen in the living room with the older dogs watching over them, Healing does some stretching on his yoga mat on the bedroom floor while Jahera sits up in bed reading *The People*, a novel about a small band of humans living in the Kalahari Desert thirty thousand years ago.

"The little boy will be naked in public no more," says Healing, rolling up his mat and stowing it under the bed. "And our dog population is replenished."

"These people were naked all the time," says Jahera, looking up from her book as Healing climbs into bed. "The women made beads from ostrich-egg shells and strung them on strands of leather to wear around their waists, and the men wore nothing at all."

"I seem to recall it was warm there most of the time," says Healing, closing his eyes to imagine the Kalahari. "When I read that book some years ago."

"No," says Jahera, putting the book on her nightstand and turning off her light. "The days were warm, but the nights could be very cold and the people slept close to each other by their fires, which was all that saved them from the lions, and sometimes even their fires didn't save them."

"No wonder we love having a fire."

"I feel such a strong kinship with these people, as if I'm reading about a life I once lived."

"I felt the same way when I read that book," he says, embracing her. "No wonder we get along so well. We both remember the old way."

Ω

2. Cassius

On a warm sunny morning in June, a week after Oz started wearing clothes again, Jahera, Healing, Raaz, and Oz are at work in the garden accompanied by Mendelssohn, Socrates, Puccini, and the two darling puppies Flora and Max.

Flora is a Border Collie Shepherd, her brown fur splashed with white, and Max is a Chihuahua Fox Terrier, his reddish brown fur streaked with black, both pups twelve-weeks-old.

"Shafi?" says Raaz, looking stylish in shorts and T-shirt as she picks snow peas. "Oz and I have a wonderful plan."

"My heart beats faster in anticipation of your revelation," says Healing, looking up from his weeding of the broccoli.

"Now that Oz wears clothes when we go somewhere," begins Raaz, glancing at her naked brother to see if he approves of her phrasing, "we should take the puppies in the wagon and visit people."

"Which people did you have in mind?" asks Healing, exchanging smiles with Jahera who is kneeling beside the carrot patch thinning seedlings.

"Helen and Justin," says Oz, picking snow peas, too. "Darby and Marjorie. And Rico and Sally. We will be in the wagon with the puppies and you will pull us."

"We could go *now*," says Raaz, munching on a snow pea. "Because the weather is good today for visiting."

"Alas," says Healing, joining the children at the snow pea vines, "today's docket is already full. However, tomorrow is an ideal day for executing your wonderful plan, assuming the people you named are available."

"What are we doing after gardening?" asks Oz, pouting. "I think those people would like to see the puppies *today*."

"I'm sure they would *love* to see the pups," says Healing, nodding in agreement. "However, I am scheduled to give two accordion lessons, the first of which begins any minute now. After the lessons it will be time for lunch, after which a man named Edgar is bringing his dog Cassius here for a consultation. I anticipate Jadda and I will be taking Cassius with some of our dogs to the beach. We hope you and Raaz will come along, though you're welcome to stay here with Naomi and Maahiah. Then after the beach walk Darby and Marjorie are joining us for supper, and then we will have the usual after-supper fun, teeth brushing, and bed."

"Can we come to the accordion lessons?" asks Raaz, who hopes to get a small accordion for Christmas, as does Oz.

"I believe Jadda and Maahiah have something else in mind for you between now and lunch," says Healing, lifting Oz high to pick peas at the top of the vines.

"The rec center playground," says Jahera, standing up and stretching her arms. "We're meeting Gina and Gustav and their mothers there at nine. Go wash up and get ready to go."

The twins race away to the house and Jahera and Healing have a sweet embrace before the twins come racing back, Oz wearing shorts and T-shirt, Raaz having added sandals and a small beaded handbag to her ensemble.

"Jadda?" asks Raaz, handing Jahera a length of red ribbon. "Will you please give me a ponytail?"

"I will," says Jahera, obliging. "Now lets puts snacks and a jug of water in the big basket and be on our way. Have you both used the bathroom recently?"

"I just did," says Raaz, running to the kitchen to ask Maahiah to fill the basket with snacks and water.

"I peed near the lemon tree," says Oz, matter-of-factly. "To give it nitrogen."

*

Accordion lessons over, Healing is waiting in front of the little old house when Edgar and his dog Cassius arrive. Edgar is thirty-seven, portly and bespectacled with thinning black hair, his default expression a frown, his attire baggy gray trousers, red moccasins, plaid socks, and an orange sweatshirt with complicated mathematical equations printed on the front and back.

Cassius is a large ten-month-old brown and white Springer Spaniel so strong and frantic Edgar has to use all his strength to control the overexcited dog.

"He's insane," says Edgar, yanking furiously on Cassius's leash. "What is his *problem*?"

"Calm down, sweetheart," says Healing, taking the leash from Edgar and speaking calmly to Cassius. "No need to panic. All will be well."

Cassius calms down just a little and gazes anxiously at Healing.

"Good dog," says Healing, holding Cassius close to him. "Sit."

Cassius obeys ever so briefly before resuming his frantic effort to get away.

Healing draws him closer. "Sit still my friend. Good things will follow."

Cassius obeys again and Healing slips him a chewy treat that mollifies him for a moment.

"I would like to introduce Cassius to my dogs," says Healing to Edgar. "Our yard is fenced so there is no way for him to escape. As I explained on the phone, his interactions with my dogs will be helpful in diagnosing the problem."

"What's to diagnose?" says Edgar, angrily. "He's deranged. I can't do this anymore. I've put up with this insanity for ten months thinking it was a puppy thing, but there's obviously something wrong with him. He never calms down. *Ever*."

"Let's see what happens when he meets my dogs," says Healing, leading Cassius through the gate into the backyard where

Mendelssohn, Socrates, Puccini, Tabinda, and Kadan are waiting on the path that winds through the vegetable garden – the puppies sequestered in the house with Oz and Raaz.

Once unleashed, Cassius hurries to give each of the Weintraub dogs a cursory sniff before racing away to the pond where he leaps into the water, swims in a big circle, clambers out, shakes himself, and rushes off to the far northeast corner of the property from where he sprints back to the pond, leaps in again, has another good swim, and races back to the house where he re-introduces himself to the Weintraub dogs before coming to Healing for another chewy treat.

"You see what I mean?" says Edgar, pointing at Cassius. "He's berserk."

"I'm still gathering data," says Healing, watching Cassius trembling at the sight of the chickens in their scratch yard. "To that end, I would like to take Cassius to the beach for further investigations. You're welcome to join us."

"How long is this going to *take*?" asks Edgar, irritably. "I have to get back to work. I'm *days* behind schedule because of this *insane* dog." He shakes his head in despair. "To be honest with you, I was about to take him to the animal shelter when our mutual friend Myra Goldstein begged me to bring him to you. But as you can see, he's impossible."

"Come back at four," says Healing, nodding assuredly. "I'm sure we'll have things sorted out by then."

"Great," says Edgar, striding to the gate. "See you then."

*

When Edgar departs, Healing and Jahera and the children walk with Mendelssohn, Socrates, Puccini, and Cassius to the beach at the mouth of the Mercy River, and while Jahera and the children play Frisbee and build sandcastles, Healing and the dogs walk two miles north to the end of the beach and back to the sandcastle builders.

"If you wish to wander," says Healing, addressing the dogs. "I beg you not go far."

Mendelssohn, Puccini, and Socrates lie down, and Cassius lies down with them.

"Can we go *way* out there now, Shafi?" asks Oz, pointing at the little waves lapping the shore. "With you and Jadda holding my hands and *never* letting go?"

"We can go way out there and never let you go," says Healing, taking off his shirt. "Then we'll come back in and go home to help Maahiah make supper."

"I don't want to go in the water today," says Raaz, sitting on the beach blanket eating an apple and musing about what color to paint her toenails. "It isn't very hot anymore today and the water is too cold when it isn't hot."

"You don't have to go in," says Jahera, stripping down to her bathing suit. "We won't be long."

Oz stands between his grandparents and grips their hands as the three of them step into the icy water and wade away from shore.

When the water reaches Oz's waist, he looks up at Jahera. "We're *way* out here now. Aren't we, Jadda?"

"Yes, we are," she says, smiling down at him. "Would you like to go deeper?"

"Not today," says Oz, shrieking as his grandparents lift him over an incoming wave that surely would have knocked him down.

*

When Edgar returns to the little old house at four-thirty, Naomi and Maahiah are in the midst of having tea at the kitchen table while Cassius and Mendelssohn snooze on the living room floor.

"Healing is in the backyard digging potatoes," says Naomi, ushering Edgar into the house. "I'm Naomi, Healing's mother, and this is Maahiah, Healing's mother-in-law."

"Hello," says Maahiah, nodding politely to Edgar.

"Hello," says Edgar, uneasily. "Um... where..."

"Tea?" suggests Naomi, smiling encouragingly "We just made a fresh pot of excellent Darjeeling my daughter sent us from England. A rather circuitous route to get here, I know, but such is the world."

"Is that my dog?" asks Edgar, pointing into the living room. "Cassius?"

"Himself," says Naomi, nodding. "Knackered from the beach walk. Tea?"

"Oh... sure," says Edgar, frowning. "Is he okay?"

"Better than okay," says Naomi, gesturing for Edgar to take a seat. "He's marvelous. The children and the pups adore him and so do I. Have you met the pups? Criminally cute. They're helping with the potato digging. Raaz and Oz call it a potato *hunt* because it reminds them of hunting for Easter eggs." She pours Edgar a cup of tea. "What is your line of work, Edgar?"

"Data mining," he says, sitting down and glancing into the living room where Cassius continues to slumber. "Do you know what data mining is?"

"I do," says Naomi, sitting down with him. "That's what I do."

"How so?" asks Edgar, his frown giving way to a curious smile.

"I mine data from the invisible dimensions," she says, gesturing to the sky. "Using Tarot cards. Remarkably accurate when one knows how to interpret them."

Edgar laughs. "I never thought of that sort of thing as data mining, but I suppose it is, with the success of the mining depending entirely on the accuracy of the interpretation."

"Precisely," says Naomi, sipping her tea. "Information is only useful if we're capable of understanding it."

At which moment, Healing comes in from the garden with a big bowl brimming with red potatoes, and a moment later Raaz and Oz enter, each carrying a puppy.

"*Edgar*," says Healing, as if greeting a dear old friend. "How are you?"

Edgar fights his smile, but can't quite make the shift back to frowning. "I'm okay. What happened to Cassius?"

"Ah," says Healing, setting the bowl of spuds on the counter. "Let's you and I confer in the privacy of the garden." He looks at Maahiah. "I promised the children olives and carrot sticks before supper. Would you mind feeding the potato diggers?"

"Love to," says Maahiah, rising in her effortless way.

"Have you two met Edgar?" asks Naomi, looking over the tops of her glasses at her great grandchildren. "He is Cassius's human."

"The puppies love your dog," says Raaz, bringing Max to Edgar. "This is Max. Isn't he darling?"

"He is darling," says Edgar, his smile expanding as he pets the puppy.

"Flora is darling, too," says Oz, setting Flora down and watching her toddle into the living room to bother Mendelssohn. "Shafi says Flora will be much bigger than Max, but right now she's only a little bigger."

"I guess you never know how a puppy will turn out," says Edgar, sadly. "Cassius certainly didn't turn out as I hoped he would."

"We love him," says Raaz, carrying Max into the living room. "He's *such* a good swimmer."

*

Standing on the garden path, Healing says to Edgar, "I'm happy to report that your difficulties with Cassius can be solved by taking him for three good walks a day."

"*Three*?" says Edgar, aghast at the number. "*Every* day? How long do these walks have to be?"

"A mile or so," says Healing, pleasantly. "Fifteen to twenty minutes."

"Impossible," says Edgar, shaking his head. "I don't have the time."

"You don't have an hour a day for your dog?" asks Healing, frowning. "Cassius is a young Springer Spaniel. He needs to walk and run and... *spring*. Springers are bird dogs. Hunting dogs. His frantic behavior was simply the result of not getting enough exercise. Easily fixed."

"Then I can't keep him," says Edgar, shrugging disdainfully. "I made a mistake. Thanks for your analysis. What do I owe you?"

"Surely Myra told you I help dogs and cats for free," says Healing, disappointed by Edgar's response.

"She did," says Edgar, impatiently. "But I want to pay you. I feel terrible about this. How about two hundred?"

"No," says Healing, with a touch of anger in his voice. "What do you intend to do with Cassius?"

"Take him to the animal shelter," says Edgar, sneering. "What else I can do?"

"We will take him," says Healing, infuriated by Edgar's behavior. "And we'll find him a good home or keep him."

"That's very kind of you," says Edgar, getting out his wallet. "I insist on paying you."

"*No*," says Healing, holding up his hand to say *Stop*. "We are grateful you brought him to us. Let that suffice."

*

After supper, Maahiah and the children go out into the twilight with the dogs, and when Cassius runs up to Raaz to be petted, Raaz touches her nose to Cassius's nose and says, "You so good Coosi."

To which the happy pooch responds by rolling onto his back and presenting his tummy to her.

And ever after he is known as Coosi.

Ω

3. Movie People

On a cloudy morning in late July, a week before Lucien and Tova are expected back from France, Naomi is sitting at the kitchen table speaking on the phone to her daughter Jean in England.

"So long as Coosi gets a good walk or two every day," says Naomi, smiling at the thought of the young Springer Spaniel, "he is as sweet as can be and not at all the anxious soul he was when he first arrived. And best of all, he's spending the night with me now." She laughs. "So lovely to have him on the bed with me while I'm sleeping."

"I can't wait to meet him, Mum," says Jean, pleased to hear her mother sounding so happy. "I'm arriving on September fourteenth and staying through Thanksgiving."

"I shall alert the munchkins and we will mark your arrival on the calendar," says Naomi, turning in her seat to look at the parrots Bogart and Bacall squabbling in their cage. "They are currently touring the town with their puppies in the wagon pulled by Healing and Jahera. Taking the puppies visiting is their favorite pastime these days, and their grandparents are amenable. They're visiting Justin and Helen this morning. Now if you'll excuse me, I *must* attend to the parrots. They've gotten quite fussy in their old age."

"Love you, Mum," says Jean, tearfully. "Would you tell Jahera I bought the calligraphy pen she suggested and I love it?"

"I will tell her," says Naomi, carrying the old landline phone to where it lives on the kitchen counter. "Love you, dear."

The parrots Bogart and Bacall, African Greys, are twenty-seven years old and have been squabbling lately, something they rarely did in their younger years.

"What *is* the matter?" says Naomi, opening the cage door and offering her arm to Bogart. "Come tell me."

Bogart steps out of the cage onto Naomi's wrist and she raises him up so he can step onto her shoulder where he bobs up and down in anticipation of a treat.

"Naomi!" shrieks Bacall, bopping the bell inside the cage with her beak.

"Patience, dear," says Naomi, laughing. "I can only handle one of you at a time."

Now Maahiah comes in from the garden carrying a profusion of pink and blue sweet peas.

"Maahiah!" screams Bacall.

"One moment," she says, placing the flowers in a vase before coming to get Bacall out of the cage.

"Here we are," says Naomi, smiling at Maahiah. "Two great grandmothers tending cranky old parrots while our children and great grandchildren parade around town with puppies. Did you ever imagine it would come to this?"

"I never did," says Maahiah, kissing Bacall on the beak.

"Shall we have a pot of tea?" asks Naomi, giving Bogart a sliver of dried apricot.

"Love some," says Maahiah, placing Bacall on her shoulder. "I'm making cookies."

*

When the cookies are in the oven and the parrots returned to heir cage, Maahiah sits down at the dining table to knit while Naomi stands at the kitchen counter musing over *The New York Times* crossword puzzle. Two cats are slumbering on the living room windowsill, two cats are snoozing on the sofa, and a fifth and sixth cat are drowsing in the sun on the stoop of Naomi's cottage on the other side of the vegetable garden. The elderly dogs Kadan and Tabinda, brother and sister, are napping in the living room, Socrates and Mendelssohn are on the deck contemplating the sky, Puccini and Coosi are running around the yard pursuing intriguing scents, and Bogart and Bacall are roosting in peace for the moment.

The phone rings.

"Weintraub menagerie," says Naomi, pleased with her choice of words. "How may I help you?"

"Good morning," says a young woman with a California twang. "I have Robert Engle calling for Healing Weintraub."

"Do you?" says Naomi, amused. "Where do you have him?"

"We're in Los Angeles," says the woman. "Robert Engle would like to speak to Healing Weintraub."

"Healing is not in right now," says Naomi, chuckling. "If you will give me your number, I shall have him return your call."

"Who are you?" asks the young woman, sounding annoyed.

"Naomi Weintraub. Healing's mother," says Naomi, wondering at the woman's irritation. "Who are you, dear?"

"Lisa Feldman," says the young woman, softening. "Robert's assistant."

"A pleasure," says Naomi, picking up her pen. "I am ready to take down your number and any other salient information you wish to divulge."

Phone call at end, Naomi returns the phone to its cradle.

"Self-importance tends to inspire sarcasm in me," says Naomi, resuming her perusal of the crossword puzzle. "I should be more forgiving."

"Movie people," says Maahiah, looking up from her knitting.

"How do you know she was a movie person?" asks Naomi, bringing the crossword puzzle to the table. "She made no mention of a movie."

"Caspar's book was optioned for the movies several times and I had many dealings with movie people," says Maahiah, resuming her knitting. "I knew it was movie people calling the moment you answered the phone."

"When was it you first realized you were clairvoyant?" asks Naomi, having experienced Maahiah's uncanny prescience on numerous occasions.

"I suppose I've always known," says Maahiah, musing. "I think many children are clairvoyant, though few retain the gift after childhood."

"Healing has the gift," says Naomi, nodding thoughtfully. "Tova to a lesser degree. What about Jahera and Lucien?"

"Jahera, yes. Lucien, no." She shakes her head. "Caspar was too harsh with him when he was young so he closed off that part of himself."

"I'm so sorry," says Naomi, getting up to make a fresh pot of tea. "He's a dear person when he's not in such a great hurry, which he so often is. I wonder why. And I wonder why he stays away from his family so much of the time."

"He's terrified of intimacy," says Maahiah, pausing in her knitting again. "I was amazed he could be intimate with Tova for as long as he was."

"You don't think they're intimate now?"

"No," says Maahiah, going to see if the cookies are done. "The babies frightened Lucien because they were helpless and needed so much attention, and he felt Tova's devotion to them as a rejection of him. So... he ran away."

"Thank goodness they have Tova as their rock," says Naomi, pouring their tea. "And you and Healing and Jahera and me."

"Thank God," says Maahiah, clasping her hands in prayer. "Blessings on our loving family."

*

In the evening, after Healing lulls the children to sleep with a bedtime story, Naomi, Maahiah, Healing, and Jahera gather in the living room for a game of Scrabble.

When letters have been drawn, Naomi looks over the tops of her glasses at Healing and asks, "May we know what Robert Engle wanted of you? I find the suspense is compromising my ability to efficaciously arrange my letters into lucrative words."

"Then I should keep you in suspense," says Healing, wryly. "So someone else might win tonight."

"I know you're dying to tell us," says Naomi, enjoying his teasing. "You were positively giddy when you got off the phone with him."

Healing laughs. "He wants me and Moosh to be in a movie he's producing."

"Where will the movie be filmed?" asks Maahiah, thrilled to think of Healing in a movie.

"My scenes would be filmed here," says Healing, placing five letters on the board to begin the game: RONDO. "The movie is entitled *Essentiel*, which Robert Engle translated as *Heart of the Matter*. The script calls for a man and his dog to appear at the beginning, middle, and end of the film. I would be that man thinking back over his life while Moosh and I wander along the shore."

"Will you do it?" asks Naomi, sensing her son's ambivalence.

"I think not," he says, studying his new letters. "I like the idea of punctuating a movie with scenes of a man and his dog, but the plot sounds painfully schmaltzy. Monsieur Engle is sending me the script, though I seriously doubt it will convince me to take the part."

"Nothing wrong with schmaltz if done well," says Naomi, seeing how she can use all her letters. *If only Jahera doesn't spoil the board.*

"Tell them why they want you, Shafi," says Jahera, who has taken thousands of pictures of Healing and finds him remarkably photogenic.

"You may recall," says Healing, lacking only a T to spell QUAINT, "that just before the twins were born, Lucien filmed me giving a lesson to a woman and her dog. He then sent that film to Daniel Tautou who shared it with Marianne Savoy, the director of *Essentiel*, and now she wants to use me in her movie."

"Marianne Savoy?" says Maahiah, gasping. "She's my great hero. Her movies changed my life. Oh please do it, Shafi. Then she will come here and we will meet her."

"When would she come?" asks Jahera, placing her letters on the board using the D of RONDO to spell ADAGIO, which causes Naomi to groan in dismay.

"October," says Healing, laughing at his mother. "When the light is most eloquent."

"Oh please do it, Shafi," says Maahiah, beseeching him. "It would mean the world to me."

"In that case..." he says, taking a deep breath, "I'll do it."

*

An hour before lunch the next day, Healing and Mendelssohn and Puccini accompany Maahiah and the children across the street to their beautiful old farmhouse, and while Healing tends to Tova's vegetable garden, Maahiah oversees the children feeding their cats Siena and Jose.

Pulling the rampant weeds, Healing ponders the mystery of Lucien moving to Los Angeles just a few weeks after the twins were born, though he and Tova were happy together all through her pregnancy. He said he was getting an apartment down there to make it easier to establish himself as an art director, and he would move back to Mercy once he could command enough money per film to only need to be away a few times a year. But now four years have gone by and Lucien rarely comes home, and when he does he only stays a few days.

And now, early this morning, Tova called from France to say she has agreed to Lucien's demand to move with the children to France where Lucien wants to establish a new base of operations.

"Not easy keeping my mouth shut about all this," says Healing to Mendelssohn who is nearby snapping at a pesky fly. "Not that I can do anything to change their minds, though I am sorely tempted to try."

Mendelssohn comes to Healing and nudges his hand to say *Gain solace from me.*

"I do," says Healing, scratching behind Mendelssohn's ears. "But there's something fishy going on here, Moosh. Lucien spends most of his time now in Los Angeles where he is scheduled to make several movies in the next few years, which means he will rarely be in France. So why would he want Tova and the children to move there and not to Los Angeles?"

Mendelssohn looks at Healing to say *I feel your uneasiness. Pet me and we'll both feel better.*

*

When Raaz and Oz have fed the cats, Maahiah says to them, "Now we'll water the houseplants so they'll be beautiful when your parents come home."

"We decided not to live here anymore," says Oz, using a step stool to stand at the kitchen sink and fill the watering can. "Because we like it more across the street."

"We'll come here *some* of the time," says Raaz, explaining further, "but mostly we'll stay over there."

"I don't think that's what your parents want," says Maahiah, opening a window to air out the house. "They want you to live here with them."

"We'll come visit," says Raaz, nodding complacently. "And they can visit us across the street."

"It's just better at Shafi and Jadda's," says Oz, making sure not to overfill the watering can. "Everyone wants us to live there."

"Who is everyone?" asks Maahiah, frowning.

"Jadda and Shafi and Naomi and you," says Raaz, opening the kitchen door and looking out at Healing pulling weeds.

"But I live *here*," says Maahiah, solemnly. "In my cottage."

"You don't need to," says Oz, carrying the watering can to the potted cacti in the living room. "You have your room over there and we sleep with you. Mama can sleep there, too, with Naomi."

"This is not for you to decide," says Maahiah, dreading the moment when the children learn they are moving far away from all the people they love.

"Why not?" asks Oz, thoughtfully pursing his lips.

"Because children don't decide where they live," says Maahiah, fighting her tears. "That's for your parents to decide."

*

Returning to the little old house for lunch, Oz and Raaz go outside to play with the puppies while Jahera and Healing make tacos and Maahiah recounts her conversation with the children about which side of the street they want to live on.

"Oh dear," says Naomi, frowning. "We must take immediate action to remediate the situation."

"What difference does it make?" says Healing, despondently. "They're moving to France in a matter of weeks."

"We'll make supper over there tonight," says Jahera, cheerfully.

"A big soup and salad," says Maahiah, setting the table.

"I regret to say I shall not be joining you across the street," says Naomi, smiling wistfully. "I am more at ease here after dark."

"This is madness," says Healing, frowning at Jahera. "Why should the children spend another minute across the street when Tova is moving them to France to accommodate Lucien who, by the way, spends most of his time in Los Angeles and is scheduled to be there for years to come?"

"Maybe Lucien will change his mind and they won't go to France," says Jahera, shrugging. "In which case the children must learn to live across the street."

"It won't hurt for them to spend a night in their own beds," says Maahiah, crying. "Bring your accordion, Shafi. We'll sing after supper and the cats will like having us there."

*

When the dishes are done and the children are asleep in their beds for the first time in a month, and Maahiah retires to Tova's bedroom to knit and read before going to sleep, Healing and Jahera return to the little old house – a cold wind blowing in from Mercy Bay, the stars obscured by fog.

"I can't imagine Raaz and Oz not being with us," says Jahera, taking Healing's hand. "How can we allow my wounded son to take them away from us?"

"Because they are not our children," says Healing, putting his arm around her. "They are Tova's children, and she will decide where they live. Not us."

"Can't you speak to Tova?"

"And say what? Don't let your false hope of saving your marriage ruin your life and the lives of your children and the lives of their grandparents and great grandmothers?"

"Yes. Say that to her. Maybe she will listen to you."

"No. My saying that will only harden her resolve to do as Lucien wishes."

"But this is so terribly wrong. The children will be devastated."

"How well I know," he says sadly. "But dear Tova is prisoner of her fantasy that Lucien will miraculously become the person she thought he was when they fell in love, so much so she's willing to move to France with the children and forgive him for abandoning them. And knowing her as I do, I know there is nothing I can say to break that will break the spell of her delusion. All we can do is have faith in her higher self and hope she comes to her senses and discovers the truth, whatever that turns out to be."

*

They find Naomi at the kitchen table studying an array of Tarot cards.

"What sayeth the unseen ones, Mum?" asks Healing, building up the fire.

"I have one more card to turn," she says with a heavy sigh.

"I'll put the kettle on," says Jahera, going into the kitchen.

"I'll take the dogs out and pick some mint leaves," says Healing, petting the dogs as they mill around him.

"Ah," says Naomi, sounding pleasantly surprised. "The Queen of Swords. I wasn't expecting to see her, but now I see she *had* to come. Of course."

"Meaning?" says Healing, stopping at the kitchen door.

"The veil will soon be lifted from Tova's eyes," says Naomi, tapping the card. "I believe we have reason to hope the truth may yet save the day."

Ω

4. Nasturtium Road

On July 27, the afternoon sunny and warm, Tova and Lucien are expected home any minute now after nearly two months in France making a movie.

In anticipation of their parents' arrival, Raaz and Oz are playing Frisbee with Healing on the driveway that curves up the gentle incline from Nasturtium Road to the farmhouse where Tova and the children live with Maahiah. Wearing their new turquoise Mercy Montessori T-shirts and knowing nothing about their parents' plan to relocate the family to France, the children assume they'll be living in Mercy for the rest of their lives.

"Shafi?" says Raaz, flinging the disk to Healing. "Can you make the Frisbee go *way* up and come back to you?"

Healing obliges by flinging the disk up into the breeze where it stalls and glides back to him.

"Now I'll try," says Oz, taking the disk from Healing and flinging it into the wind where it goes nowhere and flutters to the ground.

"Good try," says Healing, picking up the disk and handing it to Oz. "I had to do that *hundreds* of times before it came back to me."

Before Oz can try again, Tova's shiny blue car turns off Nasturtium Road onto the driveway, and Healing and the kids step off the drive to let the car go by.

"It's Mama and Poppy!" cries Raaz, waving as the car approaches.

"I don't see Poppy," says Oz, frowning as the car goes by.

"I don't see him either," says Healing, following the car to the farmhouse.

"Where's Poppy?" shouts Raaz, racing with Oz to greet their mother.

"He stayed in France," says Tova, kneeling to embrace her children.

"When is he coming home?" asks Oz, excitedly. "So he can see I wear clothes again?"

"You're a fashion plate," says Tova, kissing him.

"We have *four* Montessori shirts," says Raaz, beaming at her mother. "The other two are burgundy and we're saving them for the first week of school."

"We also got two puppies named Flora and Max and a new dog named Coosi," says Oz, bursting with things to tell his mother. "He *was* named Cassius, but then Raaz called him Coosi and he liked it better and now he sleeps on Naomi's bed at night."

"Let's go meet the puppies and Coosi," says Tova, giving Healing a look to say *I'm hanging by a thread.*

*

After supper, the children fast asleep in the guest room, Tova sits on the sofa between Maahiah and Naomi while Jahera makes a pot of mint tea and Healing stands with his back to the fire.

"We were about to shoot the first scene of the day," says Tova, shaking her head in disbelief. "Lucien was at another location. I was watching the crew move the camera into position when a beautiful young woman came up to me and said in English with a strong French accent, 'Hi Tova. My name is Jennifer Badeaux. Lucien and I have been living together for three years. He loves me, not you, and I'm pregnant.'"

"Goodness," says Naomi, frowning. "She just walked up to you and said that?"

Tova nods numbly. "She sounded like a little girl. It was very strange. So I waved to one of the security guards and asked her, 'Where do you live with Lucien?' And she said, 'In our house in Los Angeles and sometimes we stay in a hotel in Zurich.' Then the security guard arrived and she said to him, "Bon jour Felipe. I brought Lucien some chocolate. I gave it to Cheri to give to him.' And then Felipe smiled sheepishly at me and escorted Jennifer away."

"What did Lucien say about her?" asks Healing, dismayed though not terribly surprised.

"It was a crazy busy day so we weren't ever alone until we got back to our hotel room that night." Tova grimaces. "When I asked if he knew a woman named Jennifer Badeaux, he shrugged and said, 'Never heard of her. Probably just some crazy person.' And I said 'Why would you think she was crazy? I just asked if you knew her?' And he glared at me and said, 'Well she's obviously lying.' And I said, "Lying about what?'"

"Forgive me for interrupting, dear," says Naomi, taking Tova's hand. "But I must excuse myself. I'm exhausted and this is too much for me to bear right now. I'm so sorry this happened to you. I want to hear more, but not tonight. I love you dear. I'll see you in the morning."

"I'll walk you to your cottage, Mum," says Healing, helping her up from the sofa.

"Thank you, dear," says Naomi, taking Healing's arm. "Goodnight all."

*

"You okay Mum?" asks Healing as they make their way through the moonlit garden to Naomi's cottage.

"I'm fine," she says, glad for Healing's arm. "Just very tired and very sad. You suspected, didn't you?"

"I did," says Healing, nodding. "Did you?"

"Oh yes. The cards were explicit whenever I inquired."

"When did you first ask them about Lucien?"

"When he left so suddenly after the twins were born, and then he was gone for two months when he said he'd only be gone a week."

"The cards said he had a lover?"

"Plural," says Naomi, waiting for Healing to open the door and turn on the light. "Would you mind helping me to bed? I'm feeling a bit shaky."

"I'm happy to stay as long as you need me, Mum," he says, keeping hold of her.

"Oh... and would you call Coosi for me? I do so enjoy his company."

*

When Naomi is settled in bed with Coosi beside her, Healing returns to the house and finds Jahera putting on her shoes.

"Tova went to bed with the children in the guest room," whispers Jahera. "I'm going across the street with my mother."

"I'll come with you and walk you back."

"No, Shafi," she says, embracing him. "Stay here in case Tova needs you. My mother and I want to talk."

"Okay," he says, kissing her. "I'll wait up for you."

"Don't wait up. I'm going to sleep over there with my mother tonight."

So Healing builds up the fire and says to the dogs, "I know I should be sad, but I'm not. I'm thrilled Tove and the children are staying."

The dogs smile at Healing and wag their tails to say *Going outside would be just the thing. Don't you think?*

*

Healing wakes at dawn and follows the dogs out into the day, the sky free of clouds, the plants bedecked with dew.

Naomi opens her cottage door and looks over the tops of her glasses at Healing.

"I'm better now, dear," she says quietly. "I'll be over soon."

"I shall fetch the puzzle," he says, having heard the paper land among the rhododendrons.

Now the kids come racing out the kitchen door and dash across the deck and down the stairs into the garden.

"I'll pick zucchinis for breakfast!" shouts Oz, running along the garden path to a big zucchini plant. "I saw two *really* good ones in here yesterday."

"Two good ones is just what we need," says Healing, laughing.

"May I have a carrot?" asks Raaz, standing expectantly next to the carrot patch.

"Yes, you may," says Healing, looking skyward in gratitude to the universe for allowing the children to stay in Mercy. "Pull several, would you? We'll have them for palate cleaners before breakfast."

*

Tova sleeps until eleven, takes a long shower, and emerges from the kitchen onto the deck where Healing and Naomi and the kids are having a luncheon of avocado and cheese tacos with refried beans.

"We went to the beach after breakfast, Mama," says Raaz, smiling at Tova. "We saw *so* many whale spouts."

"Tomorrow we'll bring binoculars," says Oz, taking a bite of his taco. "To see their fins come out of the water."

"Sit thyself, daughter," says Healing, gesturing to an empty chair. "What can I make for you?"

"Toast and coffee would be lovely," she says, sitting down and gazing at her children and grandmother. "Hello everybody."

"Hello dear," says Naomi, touching Tova's hand. "Welcome home. I like how they cut your hair for the movie. Shows off your beautiful ears."

"Hi Mama," says Raaz, giggling. "You slept and slept."

"Shafi's giving Eliana an accordion lesson after lunch," says Oz, his mouth full of food, "and we're walking to school with Jadda to see how long it takes. And Gina and Gustav are meeting us there."

"So on the *real* day we won't be late," explains Raaz.

"Good plan," says Tova, yawning. "I might come, too."

"When is Poppy coming home?" asks Oz, taking another bite of his taco. "So he can see I wear clothes now."

"I don't know," she says, forcing a smile.

"But *you're* not going away again," says Raaz, shaking her head. "Are you?"

"No," says Tova, solemnly. "I'm home for the foreseeable future."

*

After two splendid accordion lessons, Healing lies down on the sofa and has a brief restorative nap, after which he puts the kettle on for afternoon tea – the kitchen clock telling 3:22.

At precisely 3:30, Naomi comes through the kitchen door with Coosi at her heels, and Maahiah enters via the front door with her dogs Kadan and Puccini.

"Here we are together again," says Healing, kissing his mother and giving Maahiah a hug.

"I hardly slept last night," says Maahiah, exchanging kisses with Naomi. "But I'm so relieved the children and Tova are staying I've already had two good naps today."

"I'm relieved, too," says Naomi, fetching cream and sugar. "So is Tova."

"I knew he was unfaithful to her," says Maahiah, bringing a plate of cookies to the table. "But I saw no good way to tell Tova."

"I held my tongue because I didn't think she'd believe me," says Naomi, sitting down. "I should have said something years ago."

"She must have known," says Healing, spooning Darjeeling into the teapot. "How could she not?"

"We only know what we allow ourselves to know," says Maahiah, sitting down next to Naomi.

"So true," says Naomi, nodding. "And fear is the great stifler of truth."

Now the front door swings open and Oz and Raaz rush in followed by Tova and Jahera.

"It only takes fourteen minutes to walk to school!" shouts Oz, triumphantly.

"And we only ran *part* of the way," says Raaz, dashing into the kitchen where Healing lifts her high into the air before gently setting her down.

"Since when is *all* the way only part of the way?" asks Tova, collapsing on the sofa.

"We tried the new swings," says Oz, speaking to Naomi and Maahiah. "I went higher than Gustav *and* Raaz. By this much." He holds one hand a foot above the other. "Maybe more."

"Because Jadda gave you a better push," says Raaz, coming to sit on Maahiah's lap.

"You know," says Healing, joining Tova on the sofa, "it's not so much about how *high* you go on the swing, as about getting into a salubrious groove *as* you swing."

"What's a sloobrious groove?" asks Oz, climbing onto Healing's lap.

"Salubrious means good for you," says Naomi, chuckling.

"Hence," says Healing, hugging Oz, "a salubrious groove is a jam what am."

"Now you're being silly," says Oz, laughing. "Isn't he, Mama?"

"Yes, he is," says Tova, fighting her tears. "Silly as ever."

*

At supper's end, Raaz asks, "Are we sleeping here tonight or going to the other house?"

"We'll be going to our house in just a few minutes," says Tova, smiling at her daughter. "We'll take the puppies with us so they can get used to being over there."

"Why don't we just stay here?" says Oz, glancing at Healing to see if he agrees. "The puppies love Moosh and Socrates."

"I know they do," says Tova, nodding, "but we want them to get used to living at our house, and you need to get used to sleeping over there again before school starts."

The children exchange glances and Oz says, "But we like it better over here."

"That's because you got used to being here while your mother was in France," says Jahera, clearing the table. "Soon you will be used to being there again."

Raaz makes a sad face. "Don't you *want* us to stay here?"

"Of course we do," says Healing, winking at Tova. "But there are extenuating circumstances that must be taken into account."

"What does *that* mean?" asks Oz, suspiciously.

"Come with me and I shall explain," says Healing, beckoning the children to follow him into the living room where he sits on the sofa and they crowd onto his lap.

Tova joins them on the sofa and gives her father a look to say *This I gotta hear.*

"There is a road between this house and the house across the street," says Healing, as if telling a story. "You know the road I mean. Nasturtium Road. Where we always look both ways before crossing. Now here's an interesting thing to know. If Nasturtium Road were not there we would say this house and your house were right beside each other with a little space in between. And *another* interesting thing is that we need *both* houses so we can all have our own rooms and never feel too crowded."

"I don't feel too crowded here," says Oz, shaking his head. "Do you feel crowded, Shafi?"

"Sometimes," says Healing, nodding.

"Why?" asks Raaz, puzzled. "You and Jadda have your own room and Naomi has her cottage and Maahiah can live with Naomi and we can sleep in the guest room with Mama."

"Yes, but that means we would have no room for guests unless I give up my office which I really need. And where would we put all your clothes and shoes and toys and books and school things?" Healing waits a moment for the extenuating circumstances to sink in. "And where would your mother put all *her* things? The fact is, you're both growing so fast you'll soon be as big as I am and won't fit onto my lap anymore, certainly not at the same time. Nor will the two of you fit into one small bed with your mother. And before long you'll each want your own room. That's why we need the house across the street *and* this house. So if we think of the houses as being close together with just a little space in between, then when you're over there you're really over here. And when you're over here, you're really over there."

The children exchange looks and Oz says, "What if we're over there and want to come over here? Can we?"

"If your mother says you may, you may," says Healing, reassuringly. "Sometimes you'll spend the night here and sometimes you'll spend the night there. Sometimes we'll have supper there, and sometimes we'll have supper here."

"What about lunch?" asks Raaz, giving her mother a worried look. "Will we still have lunch over here most of the time?"

"I would imagine so," says Tova, on the verge of tears again.

"What about breakfast?" asks Oz, urgently. "Especially pancakes on Saturday and waffles on Sunday."

"Fear not. Pancake Day and Waffle Day are sacrosanct," says Healing, giving Oz a tender squeeze. "On most school days you will wake in your beds in your house across the street, eat your breakfast there in your beautiful kitchen, and set off for school."

"But not by our*selves*," says Oz, shaking his head. "You or Mama or Jadda or Maahiah will have to come with us because we're still small children."

"Right you are, Oz," says Healing, nodding in agreement. "So every day until you are *much* older, one or more of the adults will walk you to school and come fetch you when school lets out."

"Until we're six?" asks Raaz, glancing at her brother.

"I think seven probably," says Oz, nodding. "Because six is only two more years and we might still be too small."

*

That night in bed, Jahera looks up from reading *The People* and says, "I think Tova is glad to be done with Lucien."

"Glad?" says Healing, looking up from a biography of Henry VIII. "I'll grant you *relieved*. Not sure about *glad*."

"Well *I'm* glad she's done with him," says Jahera, slamming her book shut. "He was a terrible husband and a horrible father. I'm ashamed of him."

"Don't be," says Healing, holding out his hand to her. "He chose to go away rather than stay and be horrible to the children and Tova."

"Then why did he demand they move to France with him and not to Los Angeles where he lives and works?"

"Because he was certain Tova would refuse."

"Are you saying he *wanted* her to refuse?"

"That is my surmise. He knew she might very well agree to move to Los Angeles, which is only a long day's drive from here, but he was *sure* she would refuse to move the children to the other side of the world, and he intended to use her refusal as grounds for divorce. Tova, however, foiled his plans by agreeing to move to France, and that's when he had Jennifer reveal the truth to Tova."

"Why didn't he just divorce Tova? Why torture her for four years?"

"I don't think Lucien ever wanted to torture her. I think his plan was to stay away until Tova couldn't take it anymore. As we've said many times, Tova was the mover and shaker of their relationship and Lucien went along with her so long as she left him alone to do his work. And I think he was fairly content being married to her so long as they didn't have children. But once the twins became the focal point of Tova's life, he found the relationship intolerable and wasted no time making a new life for himself."

"So are you saying he never intended to take the children away from us?"

"Never. He just couldn't shake Tova because she'd do anything to preserve the illusion that she was giving her children a family with two parents, the family she always wanted and never had growing up with her single father and grandparents. I think deep inside her are memories of those first eleven months of her life before her mother vanished, eleven months with two loving parents, after which her father was very sad, and she felt that sadness along with missing her mother."

"And it took Jennifer telling her the truth to shatter her illusion."

"No, not even that. It took Lucien blatantly lying about Jennifer, *obviously* lying, otherwise Tova might still be trapped in her purgatory of waiting for Lucien to come back to her."

Ω

5. Getting To Know You

Waking at dawn on August third, nine days before the first day of Kindergarten, Healing and Jahera snuggle for a while before getting up to let the dogs out.

"If Jennifer Badeaux was telling the truth and has a baby with Lucien," says Jahera, no longer angry, "their child will be my grandchild and I would like to know him or her."

"So would I," says Healing, tenderly.

"You're so good, Shafi. Thank God I found you."

"Wait a minute," he says with mock dismay. "I found *you*."

"No, I found you first," she says, getting out of bed and stretching her arms. "Remember? I called you from the post office to ask you to help me find my dog, sweet Harriet, and you jumped off a cliff to save her and I fell in love with you."

"I remember," he says, loving the sight of her in the morning light.

*

Every Saturday morning the collective gathers in the little old house for pancakes and sausages, and the gathering always includes Darby, eighty-five and Irish, and Marjorie, eighty-three and German, and they always bring their dog Pierre, a darling Jack Russell Terrier. Darby is hard of hearing, Marjorie is not, and when Darby isn't sure what someone says, he'll give Marjorie's hand a squeeze and she'll whisper a synopsis in his ear.

Over the scrumptious breakfast, talk is mostly of the sixty-sixth annual *Getting To Know You* Montessori Kindergarten mixer to be held this afternoon at Wampler's Farm adjacent to the Montessori School at the north end of Mercy.

But the moment the children go outside to play with Pierre and the puppies, Darby says to Tova, "I'm glad the blighter's gone. You're better off without him."

"Dar," says Marjorie, frowning at Darby. "Don't say that."

"Well he *is* a blighter," says Darby, never one to mince words. "If I he were here I'd give him a good one to the jaw. Don't think I wouldn't. What's the man thinkin' leaving such a fine woman and these glorious children? He should be ashamed of himself."

"I appreciate your loyalty, Darby," says Tova, gazing fondly at her old friend. "Unfortunately, the situation is more complicated than a good one to the jaw will fix."

"I apologize," says Darby, sighing in sympathy. "Just my way of saying I love you and I'm sorry for what happened." Now he riles again. "But you *are* better off without that blighter and I hope you know it."

"I've been mostly without him for four years now," she says soberly. "Though I convinced myself he was here in spirit, which was not the case. Now that I know he's not coming back... I'll carry on the best I can."

"The why of things is a mystery we only ever solve a tiny part of," says Naomi, taking Tova's hand. "So let us endeavor to inhabit this moment as fully as we possibly can. All else is conjecture."

"Amen," says Darby, nodding. "I've certainly done my share of things the why of which I'll never know."

"You have always been reflexively generous, Darby," says Healing, raising his mug to Darby. "And we are the grateful beneficiaries of your incalculable largesse."

Darby gives Marjorie's hand a squeeze.

"He's grateful for your generosity," she whispers.

"I heard him, dear," says Darby, raising his mug to Healing. "Just sharing my joy with you."

*

In the early afternoon, Healing and Jahera go with Tova and the kids to the kindergarten mixer on the edge of a pumpkin patch where a dozen wooden picnic tables are circled up like a wagon train at the end of a day's travel.

Upon their arrival at the soiree site, Raaz and Oz become bashful and attach themselves to their mother's legs.

"Why do I find this sudden onset of shyness implausible?" asks Tova, looking down at her children.

"What do you mean?" says Oz, clinging to Tova's leg. "I really *am* shy."

"Since when?" asks Tova, ruffling Oz's hair. "Not since I've known you."

"I'm shy, too," says Raaz, gripping Tova's other leg. "I've never *been* to a *Getting To Know You* mixer before."

"Oh look," says Oz, letting go of his mother's leg. "There's Gustav and Leo and Felicia and Gina."

"And Lisa and Jeremy," says Raaz, letting go of Tova's other leg. "May we go play with them, Mama?"

"Yes you may," says Tova, laughing. "Mix away."

*

A half-hour later a triangle sounds telling everyone to find a place at the picnic tables. When everyone is seated, sort of, Elias Wampler, plump and bald, rises to address the revelers.

"Welcome everyone," says Elias, a Mercy native who spent forty years in Seattle before moving back to Mercy a few years ago. "Believe it or not, I attended the very first Montessori Kindergarten mixer here sixty-six years ago. There were seven kids in our class including Healing Weintraub and Justin Oglethorpe who are both here today and haven't changed a bit except they're taller. In Justin's case, *much* taller. Healing's mother Naomi started the school with my mother Sheila and Justin's mother Monica. They hired the first two teachers,

Alice Veltfort who taught a combo Kindergarten and First Grade, and Myra Katz who taught a combo Second and Third Grade. Today we have ten teachers, a principal, two office administrators, a groundskeeper, and one hundred and seven students. I now give you Isadora Baumgartner."

"This is my seventh year teaching kindergarten at Mercy Montessori," says Isadora, a lanky gal with long raven black hair and a charming Oklahoma drawl. "I sure am happy to see y'all. We are gonna have *so* much fun and learn *so* many things, you're gonna want to stay in kindergarten for the rest of your life."

"Yay Miss Bumgarter!" shouts Gustav, who has yet to learn to raise his hand before speaking.

"Yay for you, too, Gustav," says Isadora, her eyes twinkling. "Why don't you and..." She scans the tables. "Felicia. Come out here and help me lead the singing."

Gustav, red in the face, his curly brown hair falling to his shoulders, and Felicia, her black hair in a ponytail, join Isadora in the center of the circle.

"Okay now," says Isadora, smiling around at everyone, "I know you grownups know this song, so help us out here."

"Yay Miss Bumgarter!" shouts Gustav again.

Isadora rests her hand on Gustav's shoulder and sings, "Getting to know you, getting to know all about you. Getting to like you, hoping that you like me."

*

At mixer's end, a man and his daughter approach Healing, the man handsome with longish brown hair, his daughter a little cutie pie with curly red hair.

"Hello," says the man offering his hand to Healing. "I'm Darvin Shapiro and this is my daughter Esther."

"Healing Weintraub," says Healing, shaking Darvin's hand. "I'm Tova's father, Tova the mother of Oz and Raaz who will be matriculating with Esther."

Esther tugs on Darvin's hand and he picks her up.

"Hello Esther," says Healing, smiling at her. "I love your name."

"And we love *your* name," says Darvin, holding Esther on his hip. "Elias tells me you help people with dog and cat problems. I'd love to get your contact info. We're having a *very* challenging time with both species at our house and we'd love your help and be happy to pay you whatever you charge."

"My dog and cat work is pro bono," says Healing, extracting a business card from his wallet, the calligraphic lettering courtesy of Jahera. "Accordion lessons, however, are another matter."

"Great," says Darvin, laughing. "I give piano lessons."

Now Jahera, Tova, Raaz, and Oz arrive.

"My wife Jahera, my daughter Tova," says Healing, introducing them to Darvin. "And Tova's progeny Raaz and Oz. This is Darvin Shapiro and his daughter Esther."

"Hi," says Tova, shaking Darvin's hand. "Welcome to Mercy. I say that because I've never seen you before."

"We've been here for three years," says Darvin, undisguisedly smitten with Tova. "I've seen *you* many times. Shopping at *Good Groceries* and walking on the beach with your dogs and pulling your children around town in a wagon."

"Nice to meet you," says Tova, blushing. "Hi Esther."

"Hi," says Esther, taking her thumb out of her mouth. "You're pretty."

"Oh thanks," says Tova, her blush deepening. "So are you."

"Darvin has a dog and cat case for us," says Healing, picking up Oz who has been tugging on Healing's hand. "Oz here is very good with dogs and cats. Aren't you?"

"*Very*," says Oz, nodding emphatically.

"So am I," says Raaz, tugging on Healing's other hand.

"So are you," says Healing, picking her up, too. "And very soon you will both be too heavy for me to lift, so enjoy the view while you can."

"I'll call you," says Darvin, winking at Healing. "Great to meet all of you. See you soon."

*

The next morning Tova and Maahiah and the kids migrate across the street to the little old house for the Sunday waffle feast. Oz helps Healing and Jahera make waffle batter and fry the bacon, Naomi, Marjorie, and Darby sit at the kitchen table kibitzing over the crossword puzzle, and Raaz and Maahiah go out to pick flowers while Tova walks to the pond to call Lucien.

"Oh," she says, startled when Lucien answers his phone. "I didn't expect you to pick up. I'm... I'm wondering if... have you given any thought to how we should proceed?"

"I have," he says tersely. "If you will engage a lawyer to handle the divorce I will pay his fee and give you full custody of the children along with my share of the house. And I'll send you a monthly allowance."

"Wow," she says, sitting down on the old wooden bench. "You really *have* given this some thought."

"Of course," he says curtly. "I can give you two thousand dollars a month?"

"I don't want any money from you," she says, shivering with unexpected joy. "The house will suffice."

"Are you sure? You have no steady work."

"I am beyond sure."

"Okay. If that's what you prefer."

"What would you like me to do with your clothes and the things in your studio? Ship them to you?"

"No, no," he says dismissively. "Sell them and keep the money."

"Your super duper computers and fantastic color printers? You don't want them?"

"I replaced them long ago," he says, impatiently. "You have my address here for any papers I need to sign. Anything else?"

"By *here* you mean Los Angeles?"

"Of course," he snaps. "Where else would I be?"

"Jennifer said you were sometimes in Zurich."

He makes no reply.

"So..." Tova takes a deep breath. "What would you like me to tell the children?"

"Tell them I love them."

"They'll want to know why you left and why you aren't coming back."

"Tell them I met someone else and my life changed so I won't be there anymore."

"Needs work," she says, smiling as Socrates and Mendelssohn come to her. "I'll send you whatever you need to sign."

"Thank you, Tova," he says, softening. "Have a good life."

"We had children. Was that where I went wrong?"

"You did nothing wrong. Things change. No one is to blame."

"How simple you make it sound."

He says nothing.

"To recap, I will engage a lawyer to handle the divorce and remove you from the deed to the house we currently own with Maahiah. And I will have sole custody of our children and tell them... something."

"Yes," he says, his voice suddenly loud. "Thank you."

*

Waffles on every plate, Maahiah intones a prayer in Arabic thanking God for their good food and the company of friends, after which Oz and Raaz lead the collective in singing, "Getting to know you, getting to know all about you. Getting to like you, getting to hope you like me."

Ω

6. Joe and Cleo

On the ninth of August, three days before the first day of school, the day muggy and verging on unpleasantly warm, Raaz climbs into the big red wagon in the backyard of the little old house and says to her brother, "Max first."

Oz picks up Max, the smaller of the two pups, and puts him in the wagon with Raaz.

"Now where did Flora go?" asks Oz, looking around for the larger of the two pups. "She always runs away when I pick up Max first."

"She's behind the comfrey bush," says Raaz, giggling. "She thinks we can't see her."

"There you are," says Oz, picking up Flora and carrying her to the wagon. "She's getting heavier and heavier. Shafi says she might be bigger than Tabinda and Kadan."

"But Max will always be little," says Raaz, holding the pups close as Oz climbs into the wagon.

"Because he's part Chihuahua," says Oz, frowning at the kitchen door. "Let's shout we're ready to go."

"Mama said not to," says Raaz, shaking her head. "She said it's annoying."

"Then why don't they come out?" asks Oz, glowering. "They better not do this for school or we might be late."

"If this was for school we can shout," says Raaz, nodding. "Today is just visiting Esther."

A moment passes and Healing and Tova emerge onto the deck.

"Come *on*, Mama," says Oz, impatiently. "They might be waiting for us to get there."

"Fear not," says Tova, crossing the deck. "We agreed on ten-*ish*, which gives us great latitude."

Healing makes an airy whistling sound that brings Mendelssohn and Socrates and Coosi out of the woodshed where they were lying in the shade.

"You'll be staying here Socrates," says Healing, leashing Mendelssohn. "You, too, Coosi. We'll have a beach walk later on."

So with Tova pulling the wagon and Healing walking with Mendelssohn, the four humans and three canines head for Cypress Lane at the northwest end of town where Darvin and Esther live.

"We assume Darvin has a partner," says Tova, still reeling from the denouement of her relationship with Lucien. "Yes?"

"A reasonable assumption," says Healing, gladdened by Tova's interest in Darvin. "Charming, funny, good looking. Surely the town gossips have much to say about Darvin."

"Are you suggesting I have ties to the town gossips?" asks Tova, feigning indignation. "How dare you."

Healing laughs. "Darvin's marital status notwithstanding, the case seems fairly straightforward. They have a seven-year-old cat named Cleo, a six-year-old cat named Alec who is Cleo's offspring from her only litter, and they have a big friendly two-year-old dog named Joe, a Chinook with a reddish hue to his otherwise golden brown fur. They got Joe as a puppy, and though Darvin was scrupulous about doing all the right things to acclimate the cats to the pup and vice-versa, Cleo has on several occasions viciously attacked Joe, and not in self-defense. When Joe was a puppy he was eager to befriend the cats, but Cleo would have none of him. Now Joe lives in Esther's bedroom at one end of the house and the cats rule the rest of the house."

"They've been living like this for *two* years?" says Tova, her sympathies with the dog. "Sounds awful."

"Darvin says things are tolerable so long as Joe stays in Esther's room or outside or in Darvin's studio, which is separate from the house. But with Esther about to start school, Darvin wants to do whatever needs to be done so they can stop living in fear of an altercation between Joe and Cleo."

"Enter Healing Weintraub," says Tova, smiling fondly at her father.

"And his witty daughter," says Healing, looking back at the children. "And her brilliant progeny."

"Why did the cat attack Joe?" asks Oz, frowning. "Our cats don't attack *our* dogs."

"Maybe the cats don't like Joe because he gets to live in Esther's room," says Raaz, thoughtfully. "And *they* want to live in her room."

"Except they didn't like him *before* he lived in Esther's room," says Healing, musing. "Though jealousy may lie at the heart of the matter."

"You'll know when we get there, Shafi," says Oz, confidently. "You always do."

*

"Oh *this* house," says Tova, as they arrive at a modern one-story home on a half-acre lot, the gently sloping roof covered with solar panels, the front yard a spectacular flower and vegetable garden. "Or I should say this *address*. Irene Purcell lived here in a falling down wreck with her mother Pearl who gave massages in the living room. The house was half-buried in blackberry bushes. I wonder whatever happened to Irene. She was ditzy, but very nice."

"What's ditzy?" asks Oz, frowning.

"It means... silly," says Tova, considering the word. "In an absent-minded sort of way."

"What's absent-minded?" asks Raaz, frowning, too.

"Absent-minded means distracted," says Healing, gesturing for the children to get out of the wagon. "When we're thinking about something else instead of focusing on the matter at hand. Speaking of which, please leash your puppies. We'll leave the wagon here and travel the rest of the way on foot."

As they approach the house, a deep-voiced dog in the backyard begins to bark, and a moment later Darvin and Esther open the front door to greet the visitors.

"Welcome," says Darvin, shaking hands with Healing and Tova. "Thanks so much for coming. Given our cat situation, we'd better have you bring your dogs around back and not through the house."

"Can I pet your puppies?" asks Esther, wrinkling her nose at the puppies.

"Sure," says Oz, holding Max's leash. "This is Max. He's little because he's part Chihuahua."

"This is Flora," says Raaz, holding Flora's leash. "She's going to be gigantic. See how big her paws are?"

"I love them," says Esther, snuggling the pups. "Joe will love them, too."

"This is Moosh," says Raaz, petting Mendelssohn. "Shafi says Moosh is the smartest dog ever."

"Who is Shafi?" asks Darvin, smiling at Raaz.

Raaz and Oz both point at Healing.

"Other people call him Healing," explains Oz, "but Jadda and Maahiah and me and Raaz call him Shafi."

"My wife Jahera and her mother are Algerian," explains Healing as the mob follows Darvin to the back gate. "*Jadda* means grandmother in Arabic, and *shafi* means healer."

"What does *Darvin* mean?" asks Oz, looking up at Darvin.

"It means *dear friend*," says Darvin, stopping at the gate. "In Old English. My mother was from England, my father from Detroit. They met at a shul in Philadelphia and named me Darvin Abraham Shapiro."

"My father was British," says Healing, enjoying this talk of names, "and my mum still is, both Oxfordian Jews."

"Which makes *me* British and Jewish and something else we're not sure of," says Tova, laughing. "Hence Tova Abigail Weintraub."

"Mazel tov!" says Darvin, opening the gate. "Here's Joe."

*

Joe, a big broad-chested dog, madly wags his tail as the entourage enters the backyard, and after cordially touching noses with Mendelssohn, Joe knocks the puppies over with his snout, something the children find hysterically funny and the puppies seem to enjoy because they keep coming back for more.

"Ooh a pond," says Raaz, running to the water's edge. "Not as big as our pond, but almost. Look at all the koi!"

"Who lives *there*?" asks Oz, pointing at a small adobe building on the far side of the pond, the red tile roof ablaze with blue Passionflowers.

"That's my recording studio and where I give piano lessons," says Darvin, smiling at Oz. "And where Joe likes to hang out during the day."

"Gorgeous here," says Tova, turning full circle. "Someone has a serious green thumb."

"Oh thanks," says Darvin, turning full circle, too. "My mother was a landscape designer and my father was a botanist. They told me my first word was *soil* and my second was *amendments*."

Tova laughs. "Are your parents still alive?"

"No," says Darvin, smiling wistfully. "They died six years ago. Two months apart. I was the great surprise of their middle age and their only child. My mother was forty-eight when I was born, my father fifty-two. And now *I'm* forty-eight."

"Does your property go all the way back to land's end overlooking Raskin's Cove?" asks Tova, finding Darvin alarmingly attractive.

"It does," he says, beaming at her. "Hence the sturdy fence to keep Joe and Esther from falling over the cliff."

"That must be Alec," says Healing, pointing toward the house where a large black tabby is inside peering out the sliding glass door. "Handsome fellow."

"Why did you guess he was Alec?" asks Darvin, frowning curiously at Healing. "I don't remember telling you what our cats looked like. Did I?"

"No, but you said Alec was six," says Healing, nodding, "and that is a six-year-old cat if ever I've seen one."

"He's a sweetheart," says Darvin, his voice full of love. "Not so Cleo."

*

Leaving the children outside with Joe and Mendelssohn and the pups, Darvin slides open the door and ushers Tova and Healing into the house where Alec rubs against Tova's legs and gazes up at her wanting to be picked up.

"Okay if I pick him up?" asks Tova, leaning down to pet the purring cat.

"Oh please do," says Darvin, sounding regretful. "I *never* pick up Cleo, so I've gotten out of the habit of picking up Alec, which is silly, but... there it is."

"This place is stunning," says Healing, recalling the ruin wherein ditzy Irene lived with her ditzy mother Pearl. "Did you design this?"

"I did," says Darvin, gazing around the beautiful high-ceilinged room.

"I love the tall walls and the gently sloping ceiling," says Tova, admiringly. "Makes me want to stretch my arms and shout to see if it echoes in here."

"Please do," says Darvin, blushing. "Nothing would make me happier."

Tova blushes, too. "So where's Cleo hiding? Under your bed?"

"No. Cleo is on the little covered deck we built on the roof for the cats," says Darvin, pointing to the far end of the living room where wooden steps ascend the wall to a cat door in the ceiling. "Before we got Joe, we made sure there were lots of places where the cats could feel safe from the dog. Sadly that didn't lessen Cleo's hatred of Joe, and it *is* hatred, I'm sure."

"Does Alec hate Joe, too?" asks Tova, setting Alec down. "I wouldn't think so."

"No," says Darvin, shaking his head. "Alec just avoids Joe, I think to placate Cleo, though I may be anthropomorphizing about that."

"I assume you have the cats' bowls out of reach of the dog," says Healing, gazing into the splendid kitchen.

"Yes. In the pantry on a high table," says Darvin, nodding. "I'm pretty sure this isn't about food. Cleo hated Joe the moment she saw him. Not that she's particularly nice to Alec or me or Esther. She's always been aloof and testy, to put it mildly."

"Is she mean to Alec?" asks Tova, exchanging glances with her father.

"Um... yes," say Darvin, embarrassed to say so. "She's mean to anyone who gets anywhere near her."

"How shall we meet her?" asks Healing, looking up at the ceiling. "Do we go up on the roof?"

"I will summon her," says Darvin, going into the kitchen and picking up a small brass bell. "Ready?"

"Ready," says Healing, his eyes fixed on the little door in the ceiling.

Darvin rings the bell and a moment passes before a large black cat pushes through the cat door and gracefully descends the steps, her yellow eyes fixed on Tova and Healing.

"She's a panther," says Healing, awestruck by Cleo's size and beauty. "Stunning."

Cleo lingers for a moment on the bottom step from where she surveys the room before jumping down and strolling into the kitchen where Darvin opens the refrigerator to get her a treat.

"You don't pet her?" asks Tova, watching Darvin drop the treat on the floor at Cleo's feet.

"Never," he says, shaking his head. "She'll attack anyone who tries to pet her."

"You've had her examined by a vet?" asks Healing, watching Cleo raise her paw to ask for another treat.

"Once a year," says Darvin, dropping another treat on the floor. "They have to come here. I couldn't possibly get her into a cage. And they sedate her before examining her." He sighs. "She's in perfect health."

"Would you mind if I try to pet her?" asks Healing, kneeling on the floor several feet from Cleo.

"I don't mind," says Darvin, wincing. "But beware."

Healing holds out his hand to Cleo and she gazes at him for a long moment before coming to sniff his fingertips. When she discerns he has no treat for her, she walks into the living room where she leaps up onto the sofa and begins to groom herself.

Healing follows and sits on the sofa a few feet away from her.

"Hi Cleo," he says quietly. "I'm Healing. Shall we be friends?"

Cleo shoots him a warning look to say *Don't even think about touching me.*

"Please?" says Healing, speaking softly. "I'll be gentle. I promise."

To which Cleo responds by displaying her fangs and hissing ominously.

"Okay," says Healing, getting up and making a wide berth around her. "I've seen enough. Shall we rejoin the children and the dogs?"

"Lemonade?" asks Darvin, nodding hopefully. "At the picnic table under the big blue umbrella? We made some especially for you."

"Love some," says Healing, opening the sliding glass door and stepping out into the muggy day.

"Can I help you schlep anything?" asks Tova, waiting for Darvin at the door.

"I've got it, thanks," he says, fetching the lemonade from the refrigerator. "Glasses are already out there."

"I love your house," she says dreamily. "I used to come here when I was in high school. Well... to this address. I was in plays with Irene Purcell. She lived here with her mother Pearl. Place was filled to the rafters with junk."

"We tore the old house down and started from scratch," he says, following her out, "though we did manage to salvage lots of gorgeous old redwood to build my studio."

"Who is we?" asks Tova, turning to him. "If you don't mind my asking."

"Esther and I," he says, laughing self-consciously. "True, I did most of the work, but she's a wizard at keeping track of my tape measure."

"Raaz is good at keeping track of things, too," says Tova, flustered by how much she likes him. "Oz not so much."

*

After lots of lemonade, Darvin turns on a whirlybird sprinkler and the children shed their clothes and run back and forth through the cold spray, shrieking with delight.

"So tell me," says Darvin, returning to the picnic table. "Can anything be done to make things better with Cleo?"

"Better for her or better for you?" asks Healing, laughing as the puppies chase the children through the spray, with Mendelssohn and Joe watching from the sidelines.

"Better for all of us," says Darvin, looking from Healing to Tova and back to Healing.

"I hate to disappoint you," says Healing with a heavy sigh, "but because you have catered to Cleo's every whim for seven years, she is habituated to a life in which you and Esther and Joe, and to some extent Alec, must sacrifice your happiness and freedom to mollify her, and it would be impossible to change her now."

"I'm guessing she was already problematic before you got Joe," says Tova, making a sad face. "In terms of biting and hissing and so forth."

"She's been a hellcat from the get go," says Darvin, nodding wearily. "A hell kitten. And then somehow she got pregnant at seven months, the week before she was to be spayed, and had two tiny kittens. One of them died a few hours after being born, the other was Alec, and Cleo wanted nothing to do with him. So I was his mother. And I kept thinking if we kept loving Cleo and giving her what she needed she'd eventually love us. That's what the animal behaviorist we hired told us to do. But she never changed. And I wanted Esther to have a pet she could love, so we got Joe. And now things are terrible for everyone except Cleo, and I'm at my wit's end."

"You may already know this," says Healing, choosing his words carefully, "but the technical term for Cleo is *mean cat*, and as I said, at her age she is irredeemable. Which means you have four options. You can maintain the status quo for another seven to ten years until she dies. You can have her put to sleep, which is something many people in your situation would do, nor would I fault you for making that choice. You can release her into the wilds where she might survive for a few days or a few months or even a few years before falling prey to a larger predator or disease. Or you can take her to the animal shelter where they will determine she is unfit to be adopted and *they* will euthanize her."

"So really only two options," says Darvin, grimly. "Maintain the status quo or end her life."

"In my opinion, yes," says Healing, sadly. "What does the vet say about Cleo? I assume you had one of our Mercy vets do the annual exam."

"Yes," says Darvin, fighting his tears. "Dr. Cisneros comes and shoots Cleo with a little knockout dart, and when Cleo's comatose she examines her, takes blood and stool samples, and leaves. I've never asked her what she thinks I should do about Cleo because I'm stuck in my habit of enabling her."

"I understand," says Healing, having guessed this was the case. "If you *do* want another opinion, I'm sure Dr. Cisneros would be happy to weigh in, though I'm also sure she will agree with me."

"I greatly appreciate your counsel," says Darvin, clasping his hands together. "I'll let you know what we decide to do."

"Good luck," says Tova, signaling the children it's time to go. "By the way, is Esther's mother still alive?"

"As far as we know," says Darvin, lowering his voice. "Last we heard she was living in Seattle. She and I divorced when Esther was two and I was given sole custody."

"*Quelle coïncidence*," says Tova, hoping not to sound glad, though she is. "I have sole custody, too." She points at her soggy children. "Of those two."

"You know," says Darvin, chuckling, "speaking of sole custody, when Shafi was enumerating my options vis-à-vis Cleo, it occurred to me that this situation is very much like the one we were in with Esther's mother." He waggles an invisible cigar and imitates Groucho Marx. "And getting ridda her woiked out just fine."

Healing and Tova howl with laughter.

"Why I didn't see the parallel until now," says Darvin, dropping the Groucho voice, "is a testament to my formidable powers of denial."

"Ooh another coincidence," says Tova, who hasn't laughed so hard in years. "I happen to have those same powers."

*

Home from Darvin and Esther's, the children go to the garden with Jahera to pull carrots and pick flowers while Maahiah makes avocado and cheese tacos for lunch and Naomi considers the particulars of The Case of Joe and Cleo.

"I see Cleo living in a big barn catching rats to earn her keep," says Naomi, looking over the tops of her glasses at Healing. "Surely we know someone with a rat-infested barn who would love to have a ruthless predator on the premises."

"Excellent idea, Mum," says Healing, giving a little shiver as he recalls Cleo baring her fangs and hissing at him. "I shall make a few phone calls to those we know with rat-infested barns."

"Darvin and Esther will be *so* relieved to be free of that cat," says Tova, filling a pitcher with water. "We used to get mean cats fairly regularly at the clinic in Portland and I was always amazed at how reluctant their owners were to euthanize them, despite living in constant fear of them."

"We had such a cat once," says Naomi, solemnly. "I'm sure you will remember Egypt, Healing. The enormous gray?"

"I wish I didn't remember him," says Healing, feeding the parrots pieces of apricot. "He was only here for a week and he killed three chickens and almost killed Beezo when he was a puppy. I was ten. We called Animal Control and they had to net him because he was so violent. What were you and Papa thinking when you brought him home?"

"We had gone to the shelter to get a kitten," says Naomi, sipping her tea, "and your father inquired about the animals scheduled to be euthanized that day, which he always did when we went there. That's how we got Phoebe the old poodle and Sigmund the one-eyed cat with a stub of a tail. Egypt was scheduled to be executed that afternoon, and despite the shelter people warning us of his violent nature, Ezra wanted to give Egypt one more chance, so we brought him home."

"I remember we cornered him in the woodshed," says Healing, the terrible scene etched in his memory. "Papa had a pitchfork and I had a rake. Egypt was all puffed up, his teeth bared, his eyes slits of fury, and then he growled a deep rumbling growl. The most terrifying sound I'd ever heard."

"You were upset for a long time after," says Naomi, gazing apologetically at Healing. "So was Jean. I'm so sorry, dear."

"When I was a girl in Marseilles we lived next door to a butcher shop," says Maahiah, pausing in her making of the tacos. "The butcher would throw meat scraps into the alley behind his shop and many cats would come to fight over the scraps. My brothers would watch from our window, and the sounds of those cats fighting terrified me, which is why I never had cats until now."

"They *are* little tigers, you know," says Healing, picking up the old tabby named Dickens and cradling him like a baby. "And there is nothing more terrifying than a hungry tiger."

Ω

7. Eliana

On a muggy afternoon at the end of August, Eliana Levine arrives at the little old house in her turquoise truck to have a Tarot reading from Naomi. The only child of her beautiful mother Conchita Ontiveros and her handsome father Zeke Levine, Eliana is twenty-five and wonderfully fit from yoga and modern dance classes at the Rec Center and from her daily work as a landscaper.

Having come directly from a gardening job Eliana is wearing blue jeans and a faded red T-shirt rather than one of the old-fashioned dresses she likes to wear for her weekly accordion lessons with Healing. Her long brown hair is in the usual two braids, and her beauty is accentuated today rather than muted by her uncharacteristically sorrowful countenance.

Naomi and Eliana sit at the small dining table in Naomi's cottage and share a pot of mint tea rather than black because caffeine makes Eliana uncomfortably jittery.

"It has been several months since you've had a reading," says Naomi, handing Eliana the well-worn Tarot cards, the Rider-Waite deck. "Though I do occasionally check in with the unseen ones about you. I hope you don't mind. I consider you a member of the collective and like to keep abreast of the cosmic potentialities as they present themselves to us."

"I'm glad you check in about me," says Eliana, shuffling the cards. "Makes me feel loved."

"I do love you, dear," says Naomi, glad to be saying so. "Your music and your company fill me with joy. What's on your mind today?"

"On my way here," she says, placing the Tarot deck in the center of the table, "I was trying to think of what to say, and I just kept hearing... *my father is chronically depressed.*"

"Let's begin with that," says Naomi, speaking quietly. "Say to me *my father is chronically depressed,* and then anything else that comes to mind. Don't worry about making sense. Just allow the words to come out as they will."

"My father is chronically depressed," says Eliana, crying. "He hasn't written a word or played his guitar in years and years. My mother races around all day showing people houses and making a fortune, and I still live at home though I've wanted to leave since I was sixteen. I say I don't have enough money to move out, but that's not why I don't."

"Why don't you, dear?"

"Because... I think I might be the only reason my father doesn't kill himself. I hope that's not true, but I think it might be."

"Goodness," says Naomi, turning over the top card: the Four of Swords. "No wonder you're plagued by anxiety. I would be, too, if I harbored such feelings about my father. And I must say I'm baffled to hear you say this because you always seem so happy when you're here, and your happiness feels entirely genuine to me."

"I *am* happy when I'm here with you," she says passionately. "Because I get to be who I really am and you love me even so." She looks at the Four of Swords. "What does this dreadful picture mean?"

"As often happens, the first card drawn recapitulates what the seeker initially shares with me," says Naomi, nodding. "The Four of Swords depicts you oppressed by a trio of swords, the unhappy trio that is you and your parents."

"The unhappy trio," says Eliana, nodding. "That's certainly who we are."

Naomi turns over the next card. "Ah. The Ace of Wands reversed. You will be happy to know this card predicts a wonderful new life is at hand if only you can overcome the inertia of your current situation."

"If only," says Eliana, laughing despite her tears. "The great *if only*."

"Easier said than done, I know," says Naomi, chuckling sympathetically, "but not impossible, especially with the Weintraub collective at the ready to assist you."

Naomi reveals the next card: the Knight of Cups.

"Don't tell me," says Eliana, amused by the image of a knight riding a regal steed. "I'm about to meet my Prince Charming if only I can escape my dysfunctional family. "

"Sorry dear," says Naomi, looking over the tops of her glasses at Eliana. "This knight, if you will look more closely, is a woman. You. Powerful and talented and well-equipped to embark on the creative quest that will free you forever from the emotional dynamic that has gripped you since childhood."

"How to begin?" whispers Eliana. "That is the question."

"You may spend the night here with me whenever you want," says Naomi, taking Eliana's hand. "Coosi sleeps on my bed with me now, but there's plenty of room for you, too, or you may sleep on my sofa, which both Jean and Maahiah tell me makes a fine bed. I would *love* for you to be here at night with me. I am often anxious about one thing or another these days, and having you here would be a great comfort to me."

"What if I wanted to spend *every* night with you?" asks Eliana, looking into Naomi's loving eyes. "And *never* go back to my parents?"

"That would be fine with me," says Naomi, smiling brightly. "The choice is yours."

*

Two nights later, after the children and Tova and Maahiah have crossed the street to their house, Eliana joins Healing, Jahera, and Naomi for a game of Scrabble as prelude to Eliana spending the night with Naomi for the first time.

"How's your father doing?" asks Healing, placing five of his letters on the board to spell ELOPE. "We see your mother all the time at the café or zipping around town in her snazzy convertible, but I haven't seen your father in eons. Still writing his novel?"

"No," says Eliana, frowning at her letters. "He's had writer's block for some years now and decided the solution was to build a studio separate from the house where my mother blabs on the phone all day. So he's been working on his studio for the last two years." She shrugs. "It's kind of ironic because when he was a landscaper, he wrote like mad every night, and now with nothing else to do he doesn't write at all."

"That happened to my father, too," says Jahera, spelling the word QUINCE.

"Oh goodie," says Naomi, gleefully. "I suspected you had the Q, dear. Thank you so much for placing it with space below so I may now spell QUAILS and snag that Double Word score."

"But your father was a famous writer," says Eliana, frowning at Jahera. "Didn't he write *lots* of books?"

"He wrote several books before he had his one great success," says Jahera, tiring of the game. "But after his one triumph he only managed to write two very short books, both pale imitations of his one success."

"I wonder why," says Eliana, spelling the word BOND.

"In my experience there are two kinds of art," says Healing, getting up to put a log on the fire. "Art fabricated by the intellect, and art created without forethought. The intellect, try as it might, cannot help but imitate, and imitation is the kryptonite, if you will, of creativity."

"That would go well on a T-shirt, dear," says Naomi, tittering. "Imitation is the kryptonite of creativity."

"I concede," says Eliana, returning her letters to the box and going to sit with the dogs by the fire.

"I do, too," says Healing, bowing to his mother. "Your reign as champion continues."

"My father worships Dickens and Steinbeck," says Eliana, petting Mendelssohn. "Reads them constantly. Steinbeck in the morning, Dickens at night."

"I certainly hope he doesn't measure himself against Dickens," says Naomi, pleased with her victory. "That would stifle anyone. Even Dickens."

"What *I* need to do is stop thinking about my parents," says Eliana, staring into the flames. "They hover over me when I'm with them and haunt me when I'm away from them. It's exhausting."

"Tonight is the beginning of your life without them," says Naomi, holding out her hand to Healing for assistance in rising from the sofa. "I suggest you declare your independence aloud to the universe."

Eliana jumps up and strikes a defiant pose. "Tonight is the beginning of my new life without my father and mother."

"Bravo!" says Healing, applauding.

"Bravo! Bravo!" shouts Jahera, giving Eliana a hug.

"Bravissimo!" says Naomi, holding out her hand to Eliana. "Walk me to my cottage, dear, which is now your pied-à-terre and where you shall sleep free of parental vapors whenever you want to."

*

The next morning, Saturday, Oz, Raaz, Maahiah, and Tova arrive at the little old house to find Eliana in the kitchen helping Healing and Jahera make pancakes, while Darby and Majorie sit at the dining table with Naomi who is manning the crossword puzzle and calling out clues.

"You're still here!" cries Raaz, rushing to embrace Eliana's leg. "Where did you sleep?"

"On Naomi's sofa," says Eliana, moved by Raaz's show of affection. "Every bit as comfy as my bed at home."

"I took naps there when I was a small child," says Oz, coming to hug Eliana's other leg. "But I don't take naps anymore because I don't need to."

"Tell me about it," says Tova, rolling her eyes.

"Naps are the elixir of life," says Healing, flipping the cakes.

"What's a lixir?" asks Oz, looking at his mother.

"An ee-lixir," pronounces Tova, "is something that revives you and makes you feel wonderful. Like a good nap."

"But I don't take naps anymore," says Oz, shaking his head. "Either does Raaz. And we feel just fine."

"That's because you are four-years-old and you sleep a deep healing sleep for ten hours every night," says Jahera, taking up her camera to photograph the children crowding close to Eliana.

"Nor are you troubled by the future," says Healing with a melodramatic sigh. "As some of your elders are wont to be."

*

Following the pancake feast, the dogs are leashed, and the collective minus Naomi walks to the beach at the mouth of the Mercy River where they head north along the shore, the wind minimal this morning.

"When I was your age," says Eliana to Raaz and Oz, "I was in a movie made right here on this beach." She smiles at Healing. "They showed the movie at the Surf Theatre when I was five, though I didn't get to see it until I was twelve because my parents said it wasn't meant for children."

"One of the best movies I've ever seen," says Healing, scanning the bay for whales.

"Gustav saw a movie about a man who can fly and shoots light out of his eyes," says Oz, holding Coosi's leash.

"Did you fly in your movie?" asks Raaz, holding Eliana's hand.

"No," says Eliana, remembering the thrill of being in that movie twenty-one years ago. "My movie was about a woman remembering her childhood, and I played the part of the woman when she was a little girl."

"What movie was this?" asks Maahiah, frowning at Eliana. "Might I have seen it?"

"*Isabella Remembers*," says Eliana, gazing out to sea. "Directed by Jason Randle Jones, though my Uncle Fernando directed the scenes they shot here in Mercy so I wouldn't have to go to England to be in the movie."

"*Isabella Remembers?*" says Maahiah, gasping. "*You* were that amazing little girl? Why have you never spoken of this before?"

"We don't talk about it at our house," says Eliana, smiling to keep from crying. "So... I'm not in the habit of talking about it. I only mentioned it now because I was the same age as Raaz and Oz when I was in the movie, and we filmed one of the scenes right here, so... it just popped out."

"Why don't you talk about it at your house?" asks Maahiah, horrified. "You were the heart and soul of that movie."

"I'll tell you later," says Eliana, glancing furtively at the children.

"What *is* a movie, Shafi?" asks Oz, taking Healing's hand. "Mama says we can't see one until we're older, but Gustav watches them all the time on their television."

"Movies are a kind of play," says Healing, gesturing for everyone to turn around and head for home. "Like the plays you and Raaz and Tova and Jahera and I put on sometimes. And a play becomes a movie when someone with a camera takes lots of pictures of the play, and those pictures are the movie."

"Oh," says Oz, frowning at Tova. "So why can't we see one, Mama?"

"Because most of the plays they make into movies aren't good for little children to see," says Tova for the umpteenth time.

"When I'm twelve I'll watch your movie," says Raaz, looking up at Eliana.

"I'll watch it with you," says Eliana, smiling down at Raaz.

"It's a masterpiece," says Maahiah, gazing in awe at Eliana. "I've seen it many times."

*

When Tova and the children go across the street to feed their dogs before supper, Eliana uses the old landline phone to call her mother.

"Hola Mama. I just wanted to let you know I'll be spending one more night with Naomi, and then I'll come home."

"I'll be right over," says Conchita, speaking Spanish.

"I'm fine, Mama," says Eliana, plaintively. "There's no need for you to come here. I'm just... hello?"

"What did she say?" asks Naomi, filling a kettle for tea.

"She's coming over," says Eliana, despondently. "She thinks there's something wrong."

"Do not despair," says Naomi, leading Eliana to the sofa where they sit side-by-side and welcome cats onto their laps. "You belong to you now, not to your parents."

*

"I have no problem with Eliana spending the night here once in a while," says Conchita, sitting with Naomi and Jahera at the kitchen table while Eliana helps Maahiah make supper. "But she's *much* happier sleeping in her own bed. She feels safe there. Don't you, cariña?"

"I feel safe here, too," says Eliana, sighing with frustration. "I'm twenty-five. I'm only three miles away from you and Papa when I'm here. I'm not an idiot."

"No one said you were an idiot," says Conchita, a fifth-generation Mercyite and Mercy's most successful realtor. "You have a chemical imbalance and you won't take meds. So you have to live at home. Of course you can stay here tonight if you want to, but why not sleep in your own bed so you don't have a panic attack and end up in the emergency room again?"

"I went to the emergency room *one* time when I was sixteen," says Eliana, glaring at her mother. "*Nine* years ago."

Conchita shrugs. "You know your father will be very sad if you're not with us for fish tacos tonight." She smiles at Naomi. "It's our family tradition. Fish tacos on Saturday night. We get three orders from *Dos Hermanas*. Their salsa is so good and the fish is so fresh. Sometimes I make them myself, but I'm so busy right now, you know." She looks at Eliana. "Maybe you change your mind." She looks at her phone. "I have to go. Call me if you're not coming home. I hope you do."

"Always love seeing you," says Naomi, accompanying Conchita to the front door. "I will never forget the day your grandmother, who was nanny to Jean and Healing, brought you here to meet us. You were two-months-old and already promising to be one of Mercy's great beauties."

"I should come visit more often," says Conchita, hugging Naomi. "I love you guys."

"Don't go yet," says Healing, coming in from the garden with a basket brimming with vegetables. "We have a vast surplus of zukes and cukes and lettuce. You probably do, too, Conchita, but if not..."

"I'd *love* some of your vegetables, Healing," says Conchita, flirtatiously. "Zeke didn't plant a garden this year. Too busy with his new studio."

"Then I shall burden you with a bag of goodies," says Healing, winking at Eliana. "Please say hi to Zeke for me."

*

When Conchita is gone, Maahiah says to Eliana, "The children will be here soon. Can you tell me now why your family never speaks of

Isabella Remembers? I saw it five times when it came out in France, and I have the DVD now. I *love* this movie."

"The short answer," says Eliana, slicing mushrooms, "is that Papa didn't want me to be in the movie and Mama did. When she overrode Papa's objections, he was very hurt. And now he says if I hadn't been in the movie I wouldn't have my anxiety problems, and Mama says I'm this way because I was traumatized by Papa being so furious about my being in the movie. And for as long as I can remember whenever someone at a family gathering mentions the movie, or when I get a letter or a phone call from my Uncle Fernando, they start raging at each other. So we never speak of it."

"I'm so sorry," says Maahiah, nodding in understanding.

Eliana bows her head and Jahera comforts her with a hug.

"Your parents are misguided in their beliefs about you," says Healing, setting a big pot of water on the stove for the spaghetti. "There is nothing wrong with you. Nothing. What's wrong is that they are trapped in the past and insist on keeping you trapped with them. They are not doing this out of malice, but because they can't escape their old dynamic. I think you are very wise to move away from them."

"I would just add," says Naomi, opening the front door in anticipation of the arrival of Raaz and Oz and Tova, "that though we should always be grateful to our parents for bringing us into this world, gratitude should never be conflated with what the Buddha called Idiot Compassion. Which is to say, staying with your parents would be a colossal waste of your life."

"Sometimes we have no choice but to run away," says Maahiah, taking her turn to embrace Eliana. "Be brave, dear. We will help you."

Now the children come rushing up the stairs and into the house.

"What are you talking about?" asks Oz, sensing the gravity of the moment.

"Life," says Naomi, hugging him. "Our favorite subject."

*

The next morning over waffles, Darby and Marjorie on hand as usual, Naomi taps her teacup with a spoon to get everyone's attention.

"I am happy to announce," says Naomi with a twinkle in her eyes, "that Eliana will be spending several afternoons and evenings with us every week and bivouacking with me on those nights."

"Mazel tov!" says Healing, raising his mug of coffee.

"Mazel tov!" says Oz, raising his glass of orange juice.

"Mazel tov!" says Raaz, raising her glass of milk.

"To celebrate this fortuitous turn of events," says Naomi, resting a hand on Eliana's shoulder, "Healing and Eliana have agreed to perform for us at meal's end."

"Oh how grand," says Darby, raising his mug of coffee. "I was just saying to Marjorie how much I miss hearing live music now that all the shows in Mercy start after we've gone to bed."

"You should come to Eliana's lessons," says Raaz, nodding encouragingly. "Oz and I come and so does Mama and Maahiah and Jadda and Naomi."

"They're in the daytime," adds Oz, his mouth full of waffle.

"We'd love to come," says Marjorie, smiling hopefully at Eliana. "If you wouldn't mind."

"Oh we'd love to play for you," says Eliana, aching with happiness.

*

After Sunday supper, Eliana goes home to her parents, Tova and the kids retire to their house across the street, and Naomi, Jahera, Healing, and Maahiah gather in the living room with the dogs and cats to talk about Eliana.

"I'm still in shock that Eliana is the little girl in *Isabella Remembers*," says Maahiah, sharing the sofa with Naomi. "She's astonishing in that movie. To think she never acted again. What a terrible waste of her genius."

"She's only twenty-five," says Healing with an affable shrug. "She's only just begun to be in the world."

"We must help her make the transition away from her parents," says Naomi, exchanging looks with Maahiah. "I'm sure they will resist the change, but we shall bolster Eliana's defenses."

"I think it's important to remember," says Healing, putting a log on the fire, "that Eliana's performance in that wonderful movie was the result of her parents nurturing her and loving her and allowing her to bloom so brilliantly at such an early age. And also that *not* allowing her to be in more movies sprang from a desire to give her the best life they could. And look at the results. Could there be a more marvelous person than Eliana?"

"And maybe if her parents had allowed her to be in more movies," says Jahera, taking pictures of the four cats assembled on Naomi and Maahiah's conjoined laps, "she wouldn't have become a musician and might never have taken accordion lessons from Shafi and become such a big part of our life."

"She reminds me of when I was a teenager in Marseilles," says Maahiah, thinking back to her own beginnings. "How I wanted so much to leave home, yet I was terrified to go. Then one day my yearning became so strong I just packed a few things and ran to the train station and bought a ticket to Paris. Then I stood there for what seemed like forever expecting my father and brothers to come and drag me home. But finally the train came and I got on and sat by the window still expecting them to come and capture me. Then the train began to move and go faster and faster, and when we reached Lyon a woman got on and sat beside me and asked where I was going. I said I was going to Paris to start a new life, and she said, 'You can stay with me until you find a place to live.' Her name was Marie and she was a pastry chef. I slept on her sofa for two months until I found a job and moved into a flat with five other people. That was how my new life began."

"The unseen ones filled you with the strength to flee," says Naomi, her eyes sparkling with tears, "and sent an angel to guide you on your way."

Ω

8. Ernst and Jolene

After four weeks of kindergarten, on a cloudy Sunday morning in mid-September, the collective gathers for waffles in the little old house, and when the first round of waffles are arrayed on various plates, Oz clinks his glass of orange juice with a spoon to gain the group's attention.

"Me and Raaz," he says with his usual confidence, "have decided not to go to kindergarten anymore."

"We might go *some* days," clarifies Raaz. "Just not *every* day."

Healing, Jahera, Maahiah, Tova, Naomi, Darby, and Marjorie ponder this surprising announcement in silence while the children, satisfied the issue has been resolved, anoint their waffles with yogurt, strawberries, blueberries, and honey.

Naomi breaks the silence by asking, "May we know *why* you don't want to go to kindergarten anymore?"

"One day a week is enough," says Raaz, savoring her waffle. "Maybe... Tuesday."

"Or Thursday," says Oz, nodding thoughtfully.

"We like recess," says Raaz, pausing between mouthfuls. "Singing is fun, only we always sing the same songs and it gets *very* boring so Oz and I sing harmony until Isadora tells us not to because it confuses the other kids."

"Doing art projects with Jadda and Maahiah is much better than doing art projects at school," adds Oz. "*Much* better."

"Everything is better here," says Raaz, addressing her remarks to Darby and Marjorie. "We have the dogs and cats and the garden and the pond and Shafi and Mama and Maahiah tell *much* better stories than the ones Isadora reads to us."

"Here we get to help you make bread and cookies," says Oz, speaking to Maahiah. "They don't even *have* an oven in kindergarten."

"And we *never* go on adventures like we do with Shafi and Jadda and you, Mama," says Raaz, looking at Tova. "It's just better here."

"We need to give school a little more time," says Tova, who had no idea her children weren't thrilled with kindergarten. "School can take a little while to get used to."

"Oh we *got* used to it," says Oz, nodding assuredly. "It's the same every day."

"Tell me again how old you are?" asks Darby, squinting at Oz.

"We're four and a half," says Oz, munching on a blueberry. "Raaz is five minutes older than me because she came out first."

"I didn't reach their level of sophistication until I was in me twenties," says Darby, turning to Tova. "My *late* twenties. Now if memory serves me, you were every bit as advanced as these two when you were four."

"And I *loved* kindergarten," says Tova, flabbergasted by this latest turn of events. "Didn't I Pa-pa?"

"You were madly in love with your teacher," says Healing, nodding. "Mrs. Lowenstein. So much so that when you found out she wasn't going to be your First Grade teacher you vowed never to go to school again. Your grandmother and I finally cajoled you into giving First Grade a try and you immediately fell in love with Miss Dempsey and all was well. Until Second Grade."

"We love Isadora," says Oz, thoughtfully pursing his lips. "Just not kindergarten."

"Let's give it another week," says Tova, her tone suggesting this is non-negotiable.

"See?" says Raaz, giving Oz a look to say *I told you she'd say that.*

"Okay," says Oz with a mighty sigh. "One more week and *then* we'll stop going."

*

When the dishes are done, Healing, Jahera, Tova, and the children accompany Darby and Marjorie on a slow stroll across town to Darby and Marjorie's house.

"You know," says Darby, walking with the children, "when I was a child I attended a Catholic school in Dublin taught by the nuns. Some were sweet and some were sour and we had no choice in the matter."

"What's a nunes?" asks Raaz, smiling curiously at Darby.

"A nun," says Darby, doing his best to pronounce the word as Americans do, "is a woman who... em..." He frowns. "What happens you see is she marries Jesus and wears a long gown that covers every square inch of her body except for her hands and face. The gown is white or black depending on the order she belongs to, and she lives in a big house with other nuns. They teach school and do various things to help the community, and they spend a good deal of time every day praying."

"Who's Jesus?" asks Oz, the name vaguely familiar to him. "Does *he* live in the big house with the other nuns, too?"

"You know," says Darby, chuckling, "the whole thing is rather more complicated than I realized and needs revisiting when you're a bit older."

"When we're five?" suggests Raaz.

"I'm thinking six," says Darby, winking at Tova. "When you're six we'll discuss nuns for days on end."

*

Returning from Darby and Marjorie's house, Healing and Jahera find Naomi and Maahiah on the deck, Maahiah knitting and Naomi perusing a book of Jahera's photographs.

"There was a call for you, dear," says Naomi, looking up from the book. "Dog problem. I left the number by the phone. Someone named Ernst Wagner. He says you're old friends, though I don't recognize the name."

"Oh Ernst," says Healing, lifting the teapot lid to see if freshening is needed. "A singer songwriter. I played accordion on some of his songs while you were in England. He and his wife Lorna moved to Nashville some years ago and I haven't heard from him since."

"Mamon," says Jahera to Maahiah, "we're having supper over at your house tonight. Tova's making fish and potatoes and we'll bring the salad."

"I'll go over soon," says Maahiah, who much prefers the little old house to her digs across the street. "We've been discussing the children being bored in kindergarten after they looked forward all summer to going."

"If they're bored with kindergarten," says Naomi, looking over the tops of her glasses at Healing, "First Grade will be torture for them."

"Often a problem with bright children," says Healing, thinking of his tedious years in school. "It's why so many people home-school their kids now."

"If they have the time and patience and necessary skills," says Jahera, going to put the kettle on for more tea. "It's a tremendous amount of work."

"I haven't found it so," says Healing, shaking his head. "We've been home-schooling Raaz and Oz since they were born. I'd be happy to home-school them for another ten years. They're beginning to read and write and add and subtract, and soon they'll be dividing and multiplying. They're excellent artists, they're fast becoming fluent in French and Spanish, know hundreds of Arabic words, can identify countless plants and insects and birds, and they speak better English than most adult English speakers. And they're not yet five."

"I'm soon to be ninety-three," says Naomi with a twinkle in her eyes. "Yet even I will be happy to volunteer for an hour or so a day to home-school Raaz and Oz should we choose to go that route."

"*We*?" says Healing, arching an eyebrow. "The choice is Tova's, and she is currently ecstatic to have her mornings free of the munchkins."

*

A short time later, Healing settles at the kitchen table and calls Ernst Wagner.

"Healing," says Ernst, his voice deep and rumbly. "How the heck are you?"

"I'm well," says Healing, writing in his notebook *Ernst has a southern accent now.*

"Been eleven years. You believe it? What you been up to since I been gone?"

"Well... since I last saw you, I married Jahera, my mother moved back from England and lives with us now, my daughter had twins and lives across the street, and I recently turned seventy."

"Still playing your squeeze box?"

"Yes," says Healing, writing *sounds sad*. "My quartet Mercy Me plays at *Big Goose* once a month, we play a few weddings a year, and I give seven accordion lessons a week. Are you still in Nashville?"

"No. Thank God. Moved back to Mercy two months ago. Shoulda never left. Only smart thing I ever did in the last eleven years was not selling this place. I had the vacation rental folks manage it while I was gone and that paid for most of my Nashville nightmare. Lorna dumped me two years after we got there and I was pretty wrecked until I met Flo and then she dumped me after three years. Then out of the blue Toby Rafferty had a hit with my song *I Ain't No Loser*, one you played accordion on. Only problem was Toby claimed *he* wrote my song and when I talked to an entertainment lawyer about suing for plagiarism, the lawyer said if I sued Toby, nobody in the business would ever talk to me again. That was three years ago and if I hadn't met Jolene I would have killed myself."

"But you *did* meet Jolene," says Healing, jotting *Nightmare in Nashville*.

"Thank God I did," says Ernst, sniffling. "Angel from heaven."

"Now you're back in Mercy and have a dog problem, so sayeth my mother."

"The thing is," says Ernst, clearing his throat, "we're done with city life and I want to get a couple dogs. Problem is Jolene's been terrified of dogs since she was a kid in Arkansas. It's a deep fear, Healing. We were in town yesterday and she wouldn't walk by a pickup with a friendly old dog in the back wagging his tail. Jolene was shaking like a leaf. I'm hoping you can help her."

"Fear of dogs is a tough one, Ernst. Not insurmountable, but not easy. As it happens, we recently got two sweet puppies. Meeting them might be a good way to begin acclimating Jolene to dogs. Are you free tomorrow?"

"Absolutely. We're here all the time. I'm in the middle of upgrading the recording studio. Jolene's got a voice. Oh my God. You wanna talk about soul."

"I do," says Healing, laughing. "One of my favorite subjects. Shall we come to you at ten tomorrow?"

"How about eleven? Jo likes to sleep in."

"Eleven it is."

*

When supper is served, Healing asks the children if he might borrow Flora and Max tomorrow to help a woman overcome her fear of dogs.

"Can we come with you?" asks Raaz, gazing longingly at Healing.

"This will be while you're in school," he says apologetically.

"See?" says Oz, glaring at Tova. "If we didn't have school we could help Shafi."

"In this case," says Healing, winking at Tova, "even if you weren't in school I would want to do this without you because this is a private lesson like my accordions lessons. As I have explained to you, when

I'm giving a lesson I need to focus entirely on the person having the lesson."

"Except for Eliana's lessons," says Raaz, confidently. "Because she likes us there."

"Eliana is an exception to the rule," says Healing, looking from Raaz to Oz and back to Raaz. "She's not so much a student as my musical peer."

"Pier," says Oz, wrinkling his nose at the homonym. "We go fishing on a pier."

"Sounds the same but spelled differently," says Healing, who loves defining words for the children. "This kind of peer is someone who is your equal, as Eliana is as good as I on the accordion. Thus she is my musical peer."

"Oh," says Oz, pondering this. "Then why does she need lessons?"

"To be continued," says Tova, pointing at the children's plates. "For now let us focus on eating our supper. Shall we?"

*

The next morning Healing and Jahera walk the kids to school, take the adult dogs for a ramble on the beach, and then drive up curvy Big Oak Road in Healing's old truck with the puppies Flora and Max sitting between them. A mile inland from the ocean they enter Big Oak Valley where apple farms flourished from the 1800s to the late 1900s when the farms were subdivided into five-acre parcels.

"Ernst built one of the first houses here after the farms were sold to developers," says Healing, driving slowly on the narrow two-lane road that bisects the valley. "He was an electrician in San Francisco before moving here to pursue his dream of making it big as a song writer."

"What is his genre?" asks Jahera, gazing out the window at deer grazing on the sunlit meadows.

"Country," says Healing, slowing down for a doe and fawn crossing the road. "Though the difference between Country and Folk seems to be more about the *way* the songs are sung than about the chord structures or lyrics. Lorna, Ernst's wife at the time I knew him, was fond of saying, "Ya gotta make it more kickass, Ernie. If it ain't kickass, it might as well be a folk song."

Jahera laughs. "Was Lorna from the South?"

"She wished she was, as did Ernst. Alas they were both born in California, Ernst to German parents in Los Angeles, Lorna to Minnesota Swedes living in Sacramento."

*

Ernst is waiting in front of his house, his wavy gray hair falling to his shoulders, his baggy jeans held up by suspenders, his black T-shirt decorated with big white letters declaring *IF IT AIN'T COUNTRY WHO NEEDS IT?*

"Holy Moly," says Ernst, bear-hugging Healing. "You haven't changed a bit. Seventy? Get outta here. I'm sixty-seven and I could pass as your father."

"Hardly," says Healing, laughing. "This is my wife Jahera."

"Well hello," says Ernst, leering at her. "Aren't *you* gorgeous?"

"Lovely place," she says, looking around to evade his leer.

"Not as lovely as you," says Ernst, continuing to ogle her.

"We have two puppies in the truck," says Healing, dismayed by Ernst's behavior. "Shall we bring them out?"

"Lemme talk to Jolene first," says Ernst, glancing anxiously at the front door. "You won't believe how scared she is of dogs."

"Fine," says Healing, wishing they hadn't come. "We'll await your return."

"Back in a few," says Ernst, heading for the house with a noticeable hitch in his git-along. "Don't let those dogs out yet."

When Ernst disappears into the house, Healing says, "So sorry about that, Ja. He wasn't like this when I knew him eleven years ago. We don't have to stay."

"It's fine, Shafi," she says with a little shrug. "I'll be okay."

Now Ernst returns with Jolene, a striking young woman wearing a blue calico dress, her long black hair in an elaborate braid.

"You brought puppies?" she asks, her face expressionless, her accent mildly southern.

"We did," says Healing, struck by her lack of affect.

"They're both very sweet," says Jahera, smiling at Jolene. "We'll leash them so there's nothing to be afraid of."

"Where I grew up everybody had guard dogs," says Jolene, her voice monotone. "I got attacked bunches a times when I was a kid so they terrify me."

Healing opens the door of his truck, leashes the pups, gives them each a chewy treat, and sets them on the ground.

"Flora is the big one, Max the small," says Healing, leading the puppies to Jolene.

"Oh," she says, smiling a little. "They're like dolls."

*

The humans sit at the big kitchen table having coffee and carrot cake. Jolene holds Max on her lap and Jahera holds Flora.

When Ernst pauses in his lengthy discourse on the virtues of his new recording software, Healing says to Jolene, "Now that you're comfortable with the pups, perhaps you'd like to come to our house and meet our friendly adult dogs."

"Would you find us puppies?" asks Jolene, speaking to Jahera. "Like yours?"

"We'll be happy to help you find puppies," says Jahera, knowing Healing would say the same, "though Max and Flora were chosen by our four-year-old grandson."

"Bring him along, too," says Ernst, with forced good cheer. "More the merrier."

"Once you have the puppies," explains Healing, "it's very important you train them so they won't be difficult to control. I'll be happy to help you with that."

"We'll pay whatever it costs," says Jolene, continuing to address Jahera.

"That won't be necessary," says Healing, taking Flora from Jahera. "I enjoy helping people with their dogs. And now if you will excuse us, we must run. Please call us if you'd like to come meet our dogs."

"Will do," says Ernst, grinning at Jolene. "I'm stoked, babe."

"Thanks for coming," says Jolene, handing Max to Jahera. "I feel better about dogs now. Puppies anyway."

*

"Oh my God," says Healing, sighing with relief as they drive away from Ernst and Jolene's place. "If we'd stayed another minute I'd have gone mad."

"She obviously detests him," says Jahera, holding the puppies on her lap. "Do you think she was on something? She seemed sedated."

"Hard to believe they've been together for three years." Healing grimaces. "She couldn't be more than twenty-two. How is this even possible?"

"All things are possible in a big city like Nashville," says Jahera, petting the pups. "I'm sure she had a life apart from him with lovers and friends he knew nothing about. But she can't have such a life here, so... she won't stay."

"How sad for both of them," says Healing, as they leave Big Oak Valley and descend through the forest to the coast highway. "He seemed completely oblivious to how she feels about him."

"He doesn't know her. He may not know anyone except what he imagines about them. Lots of people are like that. They only see the surface of things. That's why he's only comfortable with very young women. He's immature. Stuck in adolescence. Like Lucien."

"But why is *she* with him?" says Healing, slowing on a hairpin curve. "He's sixty-seven and she can't stand the sight of him. How could she stay with him for an hour, let alone three years?"

"Money," says Jahera, stating the obvious. "He gives her lots of money, and she numbs herself when she has to be with him for more than a little while, and he imagines she loves him because he's seen lots of movies about beautiful young women falling in love with men they meet in bars, and though he's an old man now he still imagines he's one of those young men he saw in the movies and he thinks Jolene just looked at him and fell in love with him, when nothing could be further from the truth."

*

Three days later, no call from Ernst yet, Healing's sister Jean arrives from England for her annual visit, and as September unfurls the children continue to lobby for a cessation of their daily ordeal of attending kindergarten.

"Especially with Auntie Jeanie here," says Raaz to Jahera one afternoon while the two of them are harvesting vegetables. "She's only here for a little while and *every* morning we don't get to be with her. It isn't fair."

"You know, darling," says Jahera, pulling a carrot, "going to school isn't just about having fun. It's about learning new things, too."

"But we already *know* everything Isadora tells us," says Raaz, pouting. "We already learned it from you and Shafi and Mama and Maahiah and Naomi."

"I think we've talked about this enough for now," says Jahera, giving Raaz a kiss. "Shall we sing *Pirouette, cacahuète*?"

"Oui," says Raaz, always eager to sing.

So they sing the sweet French song and take turns singing harmony, and their singing brings Jean out onto the deck to listen and marvel at the beauty of the scene.

*

On the penultimate day of September, Healing arrives home from the Montessori with the kids and finds his mother on the phone.

"Oh here he is now," says Naomi, covering the mouthpiece with her hand. "It's your friend Ernst. His wife left him and he's terribly upset."

"Ernst," says Healing, taking the phone. "What's going on?"

"Oh Healing," says Ernst, his anguish profound. "Two days after you brought the puppies over, Jolene went to San Francisco to visit a friend and the next thing I know I get a text saying she's back in Nashville and wants a divorce. So I fly back there and beg her to come home and she says she doesn't want to live in the country. So I say I'll sell the place and get us a house anywhere she wants and she says she doesn't want to be with me anymore no matter where I get a house. I can't believe it. We were *so* in love."

"I'm very sorry, Ernst. Where are you now?"

"Back in Mercy. Picking up the pieces. I tell ya, Healing, I gotta stop hooking up with women who don't like dogs."

"Good thinking. Get yourself an adorable pup and see what kind of honey *that* attracts. So to speak."

"You should write Country songs, Healing."

"Why do you say that?" he asks, laughing.

"Walk that pup round town every day," sings Ernst in his gravelly voice, "see what comes to the honey. What you want, you can take it from me, is a gal who loves dogs more than money."

"I think you've got a hit on your hands, Ernst."

"They're all hits, Healing. The trick is keeping people from stealing them."

*

In bed that night Jahera asks, "Did you suggest he seek a partner more his age instead of women who could be his granddaughters?"

"I did not. His sexual predilections are none of my business."

"Do you *like* Ernst?" she asks, her tone suggesting she does *not* like Ernst.

"I do. I admire his devotion to writing songs and I very much enjoyed playing accordion for him. He's a fan of minor keys, as am I. If I'd only experienced him as you did when we visited him, I probably wouldn't like him either. But I know him as funny and self-effacing and generous, so... yes, I do like him."

"What are his songs about?"

"Oh... sorrow and confusion and longing for love and hoping for a better day."

"I will try to think more kindly of him."

"You know... when I knew him all those years ago he had a German Shepherd named Lester who was by far the sweetest German Shepherd I've ever known, which in my view speaks volumes about Ernst and gives me hope for him."

"Are you going to help him find his new dog?"

"The children and I are meeting him at the animal shelter tomorrow afternoon."

"Shall I come, too, and take pictures?"

"He might leer at you."

"It's okay. I love taking pictures of the children with all those dogs yearning for love, and I will think of Ernst as one of the children."

Ω

9. Marianne and Philippe

Family and friends celebrate Naomi's 93rd birthday on a sunny Sunday afternoon in October – thirty people gathered on the deck of the little old house for food and drink and pumpkin pie.

Darvin stands with Tova and Jean on the path in the vegetable garden from where they're keeping their eyes on their children running back and forth from the garden up onto the deck to dip chips in guacamole and carry the laden chips back to the garden to eat them. Raaz is wearing a blue skirt, burgundy blouse, and a big purple ribbon in her hair because purple is Naomi's favorite color. Oz is wearing brown trousers and a green shirt, and Esther is wearing a pink party dress.

"Tova tells me you're a pianist," says Jean, dressed in her usual attire of trousers and a long-sleeved Madras shirt, her curly gray hair quite short. "Do you compose?"

"I do," says Darvin, feeling a bit under-dressed in jeans and T-shirt, his longish brown hair going every which way.

"What kind of music?" asks Jean, genuinely interested.

"Jazz, for lack of a better word," says Darvin, beckoning Esther who is gobbling yet another chip heaped high with guacamole. "Though not *classical* jazz, if you know what I mean. It's more... inventions."

"I finally got him to play for me last week," says Tova looking svelte in a burgundy blouse and turquoise pedal pushers, her brown hair in a bun skewered with black chopsticks. "I swooned."

"I'd love to hear you play while I'm here," says Jean, nodding hopefully. "I'm not a musician like Tova and my brother, but I adore piano music."

"Hold that thought," says Darvin, leaning down to tell Esther to save room for an enchilada.

Jean moves close to Tova and whispers, "He's marvelous, and he's just the right height for you."

"I've been gently throwing myself at him," Tova whispers in reply. "To no avail."

"Mama," says Raaz, running up to Tova. "Shafi wants you to sing with him on the deck now."

"Oh joy," says Jean, holding out her hand to Raaz. "Will you take me to a good place to listen?"

"The best place," says Raaz, taking Jean's hand, "is in front of everyone else."

*

When Tova and Healing have wowed the guests with splendiferous renditions of *Summertime* and *Feeling Good*, Naomi says to the gathering, "I'm so pleased you all came today. We have a tradition in our family of asking the person whose birthday it is to share their thoughts about being a year older, and when Healing asked me at breakfast if any such thoughts had occurred to me, I said, 'No, but I had a marvelous dream last night,' and he suggested I share it with you."

"Would you like to sit, Mum?" asks Healing, sensing she is weary of standing.

"A chair would be lovely," she says, nodding.

A chair is brought and Naomi sits and closes her eyes.

"I am walking on the beach at the mouth of the Mercy River when out of the mist emerges a beautiful naked woman. She is neither young nor old, nor is she self-conscious about her lack of clothing. 'Where are you going?' she asks, taking my hand. 'To the end of the beach and then home for tea,' I reply, finding her delightful. 'May I come with you?' she asks with a twinkle in her eye. And I reply, 'I would love you to.' And then I awoke and felt so very glad to be alive."

*

The next morning, Healing, Jean, and Coosi accompany Oz and Raaz on their fifteen-minute walk to school.

"The morning is the best time for everything," says Oz, as they leave Nasturtium Road and enter the awakening downtown. "Only *we* have to miss the *whole* morning in boring kindergarten."

"So much happens in the morning," says Raaz, nodding in agreement. "And Auntie Jeanie is only here for a little while. It isn't fair."

Healing does not reply, having informed the children on several previous occasions that their educational fate is up to their mother.

"I'm so sorry you're not enjoying kindergarten," says Jean for whom the children's complaints are new. "Surely they give you lots of play time."

"Not enough," says Oz, forlornly. "Every time we start having fun the bell rings and we have to go in."

"I remember that happening to me, too," says Jean with a faraway look in her eyes. "Just dreadful."

Healing gives Jean a look to say *Please don't encourage them.*

"Just dreadful," says Raaz, seizing on Auntie Jeanie's expression.

"Just dreadful," echoes Oz.

And the rest of the way to school, Oz and Raaz say *Just dreadful* several more times.

*

When Jean and Healing get home from walking the kids to school, the adults gather around the kitchen table for pumpkin pie left over from yesterday's birthday party, and as Jean pours the first round of tea, Socrates growls at footfalls on the front stairs and Healing goes to see who it is.

He opens the door to a plump woman with frizzy white hair accompanied by a broad-shouldered man with curly brown hair going gray.

"Ahlo," says the woman, her accent distinctly French. "Monsieur Weintraub? I am Marianne Savoy and this is my grandson Philippe. I'm so sorry we didn't call you before we came, but I lost your phone number because everything is in chaos. So we decided just to come here and see if we can film you with your dog now."

"Please come in," says Healing, thinking of Raaz saying *So much happens in the morning*. "We're just sitting down to tea and pie. Won't you join us?"

"You see, Philippe," says Marianne, speaking French to her grandson. "Tea and pie. Everything will be okay now."

"I *love* pie," says Philippe, eagerly. "What *kind* of pie?"

"Pumpkin," says Healing, gesturing for them to enter.

"Pumpkin pie, Grandma," says Philippe, his eyes growing wide with excitement. "I prefer coffee with my pie, but I will drink tea, though I prefer coffee."

"Coffee you shall have," says Healing, bowing to him.

"Merci," says Philippe, returning Healing's bow.

"Such a lovely home," says Marianne, gazing at the four dogs sprawled on the living room floor, three cats snoozing on the sofa, a fire blazing in the hearth. "Of course you would have many pets. May I take off my coat?"

"Please," says Healing, helping her out of her coat and gesturing to everyone at the dining table. "This is my wife Jahera, my mother Naomi, Jahera's mother Maahiah, my daughter Tova, and my sister Jean."

"I know you," says Marianne, pointing at Tova. "From Daniel's movies. He calls you his lucky charm, and for good reason. You are a superb actor. I can't wait to see his new movie with you. Finally he gives you a big part."

"I don't know what to say," says Tova, flabbergasted to be praised so highly by the legendary filmmaker.

"If I ever make another movie I hope you will be in it," says Marianne, matter-of-factly. "But first we must survive the chaos."

"I would love to be in your next movie," says Tova, giving her father a look to say *Can you believe this*?

"I've seen all your movies many times," says Maahiah, coming to greet Marianne. "You are my great hero. Your movie *La Marchande de Fleurs* inspired me to leave Marseilles and go to Paris when I was sixteen and my life changed forever. Please. Come sit down."

"You are Algerian," says Marianne, taking Maahiah's hands in hers. "How beautiful you are."

"Come sit," says Maahiah, leading her to the table. "Tell us about the chaos."

"Oh you don't want to know," says Marianne, sitting next to Naomi.

"Hello," says Naomi, taking Marianne's hand. "A pleasure to meet you. When we heard you were going to put Healing in your movie, Maahiah curated a Marianne Savoy film festival for us, and though I hadn't watched a movie in twenty years, I took peeks at the first two and then was entranced from beginning to end by *Le Moment Intérieur*. When it was over, I declared I need never see another movie in this lifetime."

"This is the best review I have ever had," says Marianne, kissing Naomi's hand.

"Grandma?" says Philippe, pointing at the table and scratching his head. "There are two empty chairs. Which one is for me?"

"Either is fine," says Jahera, gesturing to the chairs.

Philippe frowns. "I'm sorry but I can't decide."

"Sit here," says Tova, indicating the chair next to her.

Philippe sits down and glances shyly at Tova. "You remind me of Margot, our housekeeper in Toulouse. She's from Spain. Are you from Spain?"

"No, I'm from here," says Tova, smiling. "From Mercy."

"I'm from France," says Philippe, proudly. "From Toulouse."

"We flew from Paris to New York and then to San Francisco and came straight here," says Marianne, sighing dramatically. "I am no longer speaking to Robert Engle so I couldn't call him to get your number. I knew you lived in Mercy so we just drove here. Oof. Such a long way! But we had to come, and Philippe likes to drive, so... When we got here we asked the first person we met if he knew where Healing Weintraub lived."

"He was a very tall man," says Philippe, looking around at everyone. "One of the tallest men I ever saw."

"He was sweeping the sidewalk in front of *The Big Goose*," says Marianne, laughing at the name of the pub. "He said he knew you and told us how to get here."

"The one and only Justin Oglethorpe," says Healing, bringing two more cups to the table and a piece of pie for Philippe. "Pie for you, Marianne?"

"Petit, merci," she says, gazing at him. "You have the most wonderful voice, Monsieur Weintraub. So warm and kind." She winks at Jahera. "How lucky you are."

"Oui," says Jahera, smiling at Healing.

"May I ask why you aren't speaking to Robert Engle anymore?" says Healing, fetching Marianne a piece of pie. "I thought he was producing your movie."

"This is our chaos," says Marianne, looking skyward in dismay. "We need more money to finish the movie and he won't give me another penny because he thinks the movie is doomed. So now I must find someone to buy the project from him and give me enough to finish." She shrugs. "Two million. That's all I need to buy him out and finish editing and add the music. Then we take the movie to Cannes. Three million would be better, but I can do it for two. A pittance by today's standards, but this is how things are for me now."

"Grandma," says Philippe, gasping. "You must taste the pie. It is the best pie I have ever had, and I have had lots of pie."

*

After two more hours of delightful gabbing, Marianne and Philippe retire to the nearby East Cove Hotel to recover from jet lag.

At noon, Healing and Tova walk with Socrates and Coosi to the Montessori School where they find Raaz and Oz waiting with their friend Gustav who is coming home with them and staying until his mother gets off work at five.

The children are uncharacteristically quiet on the way home until Gustav blurts, "Sara showed us some bad things on her phone."

Tova stops and says, "She's not supposed to have a phone at school."

"They were hitting a man with sticks and kicking him and he was bleeding," says Oz, bursting into tears.

"It's okay, Oz," says Healing, kneeling beside the little boy and holding him close. "It wasn't real. Just some nonsense on her phone."

"But it *was* real, Shafi," says Raaz, her jaw trembling. "We saw the men kicking him and hitting him and he was bleeding and they wouldn't stop hitting him."

"Did you tell Isadora?" asks Tova, putting her arm around Raaz.

"*I* didn't," says Gustav, shaking his head. "Because I have a phone for emergencies. But Oz told on Sara so Isadora took her phone away and Sara was screaming and crying."

"We'll talk more about this after lunch," says Tova, taking a deep breath.

"Ride on my shoulders, Oz?" asks Healing, nodding encouragingly.

"Okay," he says, sniffling.

"Then me next," says Raaz, defiantly.

"You will have a ride after your brother," says Healing, squatting down so Oz can climb on. "And after you have a turn, Gustav will have one, after which I'll go directly to the chiropractor."

"No, you won't," says Oz, chortling as Healing stands up so the little boy is as tall as Justin Oglethorpe. "You always say that and you never go."

*

The kids have lunch in their house across the street from the little old house, after which they go outside to play with the pups and Healing stays with Tova while she calls the Montessori School to speak to Isadora.

"Are you calling about the phone incident?" asks Carol, the school secretary, sounding beleaguered.

"Yes," says Tova, trying to remain calm. "Sara Covington brought a phone to school and showed things to my children that were very upsetting to them."

"We're having a staff meeting about it this afternoon," says Carol, hurriedly. "I'm sorry, Tova. We've spoken to Sara's mother and she promises it won't happen again."

"But why did it happen *this* time? We signed enrollment agreements stating our children would under *no* circumstances bring phones to school. But Gustav says *lots* of kids have phones at school."

"For emergencies," says Carol, tersely. "They're not allowed to take them out during school hours."

"Take them *out*?" says Tova, outraged. "Take them out of *what*? They are categorically not allowed to bring them to school."

"Can you hold on a sec?" says Carol, putting Tova on hold.

"I can't believe this is happening," says Tova, shaking her head to dispel the horror.

"Hi Tova. Rebecca here. I'm so sorry about what happened with the phone. We've made it very clear to parents that the children *must* leave their phones in their backpacks and not use them at school. They're strictly for after school use."

"Rebecca, we all signed enrollment agreements, and I quote, 'Under no circumstances will my child bring mobile phones or video games to school.' There is nothing in what we signed saying they can bring phones to school and keep them in their backpacks."

"That's the *wording,* Tova, but some of these kids need to call their parents when school gets out to arrange for a ride or to tell their folks where they're going before they come home. Or their parents need to give them an update. We have several children with single parents and this is how they stay connected to each other. We just have to make sure in the future the phones aren't used during school hours."

"*Kinder*gartners have to call their parents to tell them it's time to pick them up? If they have phones in their backpacks and have access to those packs during school, how can you *possibly* keep this from happening again?"

"We'll be discussing this at the faculty meeting today," says Rebecca, who has been the principal at Mercy Montessori for three years. "I'm very sorry this happened. We'll do everything we can to make sure it doesn't happen again."

Tova sets her cell phone on the counter and looks at her father. "Brave new world. Cell phones at the Montessori. Makes me want to throw mine away."

"I suppose if those things could only be used for making phone calls this would be a non-issue," says Healing, despairing of the situation. "But they're all hooked up to the great imagistic spew, and what curious child can resist taking a peek? And then another peek and another and so on."

*

Healing wakes at midnight to the phone ringing in the kitchen and the dogs whining and barking. He jumps out of bed and hurries down the hall to answer.

"Pa-pa," says Tova, urgently. "Can you come over, please? Oz woke up screaming and I can't get him to calm down."

"We'll be right over," says Healing, hanging up and rushing to get dressed.

*

Oz clings to Healing, weeping convulsively, and nothing will calm the little boy until Jahera says, "Let's go across the street and have cocoa by the fire. You and Raaz and Tova can sleep in the guest room."

"No more school this week," says Tova, holding Raaz close. "Tomorrow you can come with us and watch Marianne and Philippe make their movie."

"Oh... oh... okay," says Oz, at last relaxing in his grandfather's arms.

*

At breakfast the next morning Oz asks Tova, "Is that man in the hospital now? The man those other men were hitting and kicking?"

"We don't know what you saw, sweetheart," says Tova, speaking quietly. "It might have been a scene from a movie made a long time ago or it might have been something on the news that happened far away in another country. We just don't know what you saw, so we can't answer your question."

"But why were they hitting him?" asks Oz, starting to cry again. "He was just lying on the ground and they were hitting him and kicking him and he couldn't get up."

"He was all bloody, too," says Raaz, looking at Jean. "And the men with round hats kept hitting him with big black sticks and kicking him."

"I'm sorry you saw that," says Jean, grimacing. "Terrible."

"It was a movie," says Healing, firmly. "When you come with us this morning you'll see how movies are made and you'll understand that what you saw on Sara's phone is *not* real. We don't know which movie you saw, so we can't tell you what it was about, but after you see how Marianne and Philippe make a movie you'll understand that what you saw was not real."

"I think it *was* real, Shafi," says Oz, sniffling back his tears. "Even if it was a movie, I think it was real."

*

Dressed warmly for the cold overcast day, Healing, Jahera, Maahiah, Jean, Tova, Raaz, and Oz bid Naomi adieu and walk with Coosi and Mendelssohn from the little old house to the East Cove Hotel where Marianne and Philippe await them.

Philippe is wearing a large pack frame on which he has secured a heavy old 35-millimeter movie camera and a sturdy tripod. He also has a large aluminum suitcase containing camera lenses, filters, and film canisters, which Healing volunteers to carry.

Oz holds Jahera's hand, and Raaz holds Jean's hand as the group descends the steep stairs from the hotel garden to the beach at the mouth of the Mercy River.

When everyone has made their way down to the sand, Healing says to Marianne, "There is a vantage point just north of here I think will be ideal for your purposes."

"I trust you, Healing," says Marianne, enthralled by the huge breakers rolling into Mercy Bay. "I only hope it is not too far. I'm eighty-six, and though I still walk two miles every day for my exercise, I do not often walk on sand."

"A quarter-mile that way," says Healing, pointing north. "And well worth the trek."

With Oz and Raaz leading the way, people and dogs head north, and Philippe begins to sing a children's song in French about walking in the wind, a song Jahera and Maahiah know very well, and they add their voices to the singing.

"A lovely soundtrack, no?" says Marianne, confiding in Healing. "To take us back to our younger years."

"So beautiful," says Healing, moved to tears. "I'll never forget this."

*

A quarter-mile along, they arrive at a large sand dune where Oz and Raaz run to the top and wave to the adults below.

"I thought you might like to shoot from up there," says Healing, pointing at the children atop the dune. "It's about twenty feet higher than the rest of the beach and gives spectacular views of the shoreline a long way in either direction."

"We must climb and see," says Marianne, turning to Philippe. "Stay here for now. If I like the view up there then you will come."

"Oui Grandma," says Philippe, gazing around in wonder. "This is the biggest beach I have ever seen, and no one else is here but us."

"That's because it's early yet," says Jean, explaining to Philippe. "Later on more people will come with their dogs."

"But not many more," says Tova, glad to see the children happy again after yesterday's trauma. "It's the off-season so there will only be a few locals."

Maahiah stays below with Philippe while everyone else trudges up the dune, Jean lending Marianne a hand.

"Magnifique," says Marianne, out of breath when she reaches the top. "May I hold onto you, Healing, while I catch my breath?"

"Of course," he says, offering her his arm.

When she catches her breath, Marianne says to the children, "Now run down to Philippe and tell him to come up with the camera."

"Philippe! Philippe!" shout the children racing down the dune. "Come up now! Bring the camera!"

"Healing," says Marianne, gazing intently at him. "I want you to take your dogs far to the south and stay close to the shore. When you hear us calling, come back this way so the incoming waves are dying at your feet. When you get back here you will continue walking north and we will track you until we run out of film." She kisses his cheek. "You found the perfect place. Now we must hurry before the clouds go away and too much sun ruins the light." She steps back and looks him over. "I like your purple shirt and the black trousers. Barefoot, please, and roll up your trousers to your knees. No ear warmer. We want to see your whole face. If you catch pneumonia I will visit you in the hospital." She laughs. "And bring you chicken soup."

"As you wish," says Healing, removing his shoes and socks. "What is my pace?"

"You are a man walking along the shore thinking over his life and remembering when you were young and in love. We have film for eight minutes without stopping. Now go quickly, please."

"I shall endeavor," says Healing, striding down the dune with Mendelssohn and Coosi at his heels.

*

When Marianne and Philippe have affixed the camera to the tripod, Philippe says to Raaz and Oz, "Now for the lens and the viewfinder and the film."

The children watch intently as Philippe opens the suitcase and brings forth a large camera lens and a viewfinder, both of which he expertly attaches to the camera. Now he inserts a film canister into a slot atop the camera and beckons Marianne to come have a look through the viewfinder.

"Fabulous," she says, focusing the lens on Healing and the dogs striding south along the shore. "I will need you to sharpen the focus, Philippe."

Philippe looks through the viewfinder, adjusts the focus, and says to the children, "Would you like to see?"

The children nod and Philippe lifts Raaz up to look through the viewfinder.

"What do you see?" whispers Philippe.

"I see Shafi and the dogs," says Raaz, excitedly. "Like a telescope."

"You are very smart, Raaz," says Marianne, nodding. "It looks that way because we have zoomed closer with the telescopic lens."

Philippe sets Raaz down and picks up Oz so he can look.

"What do you see?" whispers Philippe again.

"I see Shafi and Moosh and Coosi," says Oz, gasping. "They look so close."

"Now we must tell your grandfather to turn around and come back this way," says Marianne, waving to Healing. "Shout with me and wave so he will see us."

Everyone waves and shouts *Shafi! Come back!*

Healing and the dogs hear the shouting and reverse direction.

"A movie," says Healing to Mendelssohn and Coosi as they walk against the strong northerly wind, the waves lapping at Healing's feet. "I always wanted to be in a movie, and now I am."

*

"I am very happy about today," says Marianne at supper that night in the little old house. "Of course we must get the film developed to be sure, but I think we captured something splendid. Now we must record Shafi speaking his lines, and for this I will need a quiet room."

"We have a friend with a recording studio," says Tova, thinking of Darvin.

"Perfect," says Marianne, nodding. "Can you call him now and see if we can come tomorrow?"

"I will," says Tova, getting up to go outside with her phone. "What time would be ideal?"

"Just after breakfast," says Marianne, exchanging glances with Healing to affirm this will work. "Then Philippe and I will go back to San Francisco and fly home to France and see if money can be found to finish the movie."

"I would think many people would be eager to produce your movies," says Maahiah, gazing solemnly at Marianne. "In Europe you are a god."

"You are kind to say so," says Marianne, smiling at Maahiah. "But I had my great success in the 1970s and 80s, and the last three films I made were not successful, so... yes, my movies are shown in film classes all over the world, but finding money for even a low-budget film is now very difficult for me. For many years I directed television shows to pay my bills, but now they don't want me for that because I am slow and require too many takes, so... perhaps I am done. We shall see."

*

The next morning in Darvin's recording studio, Marianne and Philippe deploy an old Nagra tape recorder to record Healing's performance of his monologue for the movie, and Darvin records him digitally. Tova and Jean and Maahiah sit in the control room with Darvin and watch through the soundproof glass as Philippe and Marianne sit very still a few feet away from Healing – the reels of the old Nagra turning slowly as Healing recites the seven-minute speech.

When Healing finishes, Marianne says, "This was perfection. Exactly what I want. You have tied all the pieces together for me, Shafi."

"Fantastic!" says Darvin, hurrying into the performance room. "Did you write that, Marianne?"

"I wrote the words," she says, pointing at Healing, "but he gave them life. I never dreamed they could sound so good. Would you burn me a CD, please?"

"Many as you want," says Darvin, nodding. "I'm... I'm blown away."

"Before we go, Marianne," says Healing, feeling a bit lightheaded, "perhaps you will prevail upon Darvin to play us a tune or two. I think you will find his music very much to your liking."

"Would you, please?" says Marianne, nodding to Darvin.

Darvin sits at his grand piano, muses for a moment, and plays an exquisite waltz, by turns ebullient and melancholy and joyful and sad, and joyful again at the end.

When Darvin finishes and turns to Marianne, she gazes at him for a long moment before speaking.

"This is the music I've been looking for my whole life," she says, her eyes full of tears. "Will you compose the music for my movie?"

"I would love to," says Darvin, stunned by her request.

"If I can find the money I will call you," she says, getting up to go. "I'm not just saying that, Darvin. Your music is *exactly* what I want for my movie. It is the very feeling I want. Spacious and nostalgic and romantic. So beautiful."

"What about an accordion/piano duet as part of the score?" says Darvin, bouncing his eyebrows at Healing.

"Yes, of course," says Marianne, nodding emphatically. "For the café scenes."

*

A few hours later, Marianne and Philippe stop by the little old house to say goodbye to everyone, and Maahiah asks to speak to Marianne in private.

"Of course," says Marianne, taking Maahiah's hand. "Where shall we go?"

"To the pond," says Maahiah, leading the way.

They sit on the old wooden bench near the water and hold hands – Mendelssohn and Socrates snuffling around nearby.

"As I told you," says Maahiah, looking into Marianne's eyes, "it was your movie that inspired me to leave Marseilles when I was sixteen and go to Paris where I became an illustrator and met my husband Caspar Dahl. He was a writer who had one great success, a book I illustrated called *Décollé*."

"I know this book," says Marianne, nodding. "I especially like your drawings. The writing is a bit trite for me, forgive me for saying so, but I'm an old cynic, so..."

"A bit trite for me, too," says Maahiah, taking a deep breath. "But lucrative. When Caspar died five years ago he left me four million dollars and I would like to give you the money you need to buy your movie from Robert Engle and finish it as you want."

Marianne gasps. "How can this be?"

"You gave me courage when I was longing to be free," says Maahiah, her eyes sparkling with tears, "and now I want to share the harvest with you."

*

Falling into bed that night, Healing lies on his side watching Jahera read *The People*.

"Read to me?" he says, too agitated to sleep.

"I'm too distracted," she says, closing her book and turning off her light.

"You know what just occurred to me?" he says, taking her in his arms.

"Tell me," she whispers.

"You are now the daughter of a movie mogul."

"And you are a movie star."

"I slept my way to the top," he says, kissing her.

"Well don't rest on your laurels now, Shafi. Show me."

Ω

10. Roxy and Böllwinkle

As October draws to a close, Raaz and Oz cease to attend Kindergarten at Mercy Montessori, and a few days before Halloween the collective and four other families launch Nasturtium School, so named by Raaz and Oz.

The first session of Nasturtium School takes place at Darvin and Esther's house and features Darvin and Tova and Myra Liebowitz presiding over six youngsters preparing and consuming pancakes and smoothies, doing the dishes, cleaning the kitchen, playing in the backyard, walking to the library where the librarian reads them a story, and returning to Darvin and Esther's house for singing.

Home for lunch on the deck of the little old house, Oz and Raaz recount the glories of the momentous first session of home school kindergarten, to which Jean responds, "What fun. How could Day Two possibly top that?"

"Oh didn't Tova tell you?" says Healing, smiling at his sister. "You and Jahera and I have the kids from nine until one tomorrow for Art, Gardening, Recess, Snacks, a walk to the beach for a sandcastle intensive followed by lunch and cleanup here. I was thinking tacos with lots of fixings."

"Rather messy," says Naomi, looking over the tops of her glasses at Healing. "Don't you think?"

"Perhaps," says Healing, his tone professorial. "However, assembling tacos teaches both manual dexterity and proportional distribution such that the sum of the parts does not exceed the carrying capacity of the tortilla."

"And the next day," says Maahiah, laughing, "Myra and I have the children across the street for making Halloween costumes, should anyone care to assist us or take pictures of the artists at work."

"I'm going to be a witch," says Raaz, proudly. "With a pointy hat."

"I'm going to be a pirate with a red bandana," says Oz, who isn't entirely sure what a pirate is.

"Goodness," says Naomi, bringing the teapot to the table. "Once word gets out, your school will be besieged by applicants."

"We already are," says Healing, enjoying the last bite of his quesadilla. "However, in defense of the faculty we have frozen the student body at six."

*

After lunch, Healing and Jahera and Jean take Coosi, Mendelssohn, Socrates, and Puccini for a beach walk, the afternoon blustery and cold.

"What news from Albert?" asks Healing as they trudge north against the wind.

"Oh the usual," says Jean, sighing despondently. "Hates being alone. Says his coffee tastes bitter when he makes it himself. Says Connie's food is bland, so he eats at the pub most nights and goes to the college cafeteria for lunch. Says he feels betrayed by me and doesn't understand why I'm torturing him by coming here."

"I'm sorry, Sis," says Healing, pulling Puccini away from an enticing tangle of seaweed. "I thought he was okay with you coming to spend time with Mum."

"Not for the last several years," says Jean, bitterly. "It's my fault. I catered to his every whim for fifty years and he never learned to fend for himself except as a slow-moving creature of academia where his secretaries cater to him as I do or he fires them until he gets one who will." She makes a face of distaste. "He's a dreadful person. There's no way around it."

"Doesn't he have friends he can spend time with?" asks Jahera, who loves Jean and wishes she were not so burdened by Albert's complaints.

"None," says Jean, shaking her head. "He's mean and critical and contemptuous of everyone. And he drives Fred and Connie crazy insisting they come visit him without their spouses or children."

"I shall not inquire about him again," says Healing, resisting the urge to shout *Leave him for god sake! Run for your life!*

*

Naomi greets the returning beach-walkers with news of a phone call for Healing.

"Do tell," says Healing, loving the sight of his mother sitting on the sofa perusing *The Flattering Light*, Jahera's latest book of photographs with poems by Helen Morningstar, Mercy's unofficial poet laureate and Healing's lifelong friend.

"Charming fellow," says Naomi, looking up from a photograph of Oz having a heart-to-heart with Mendelssohn. "He and his wife Susan recently bought a house in Seascape Villas and actually *live* there. They moved up from Los Angeles four months ago, a year to the day after the youngest of their two children graduated from university."

"You and Paul had quite the chat," says Healing, arching his eyebrow. "What else should I know?"

"Their dogs are acting strangely and the Cheshires cannot discern the cause. Roxy and Böllwinkle are three-year-old German Shepherd siblings, both good-natured and happy since puppyhood, yet they have been in a state of constant anxiety since moving from Los Angeles to Seascape Villas. Maria Castañeda cleans the Cheshires' house, and it was she who told Paul and Susan about your way with dogs and suggested they call you."

"How kind of Maria to recommend me," says Healing, who gives accordion lessons to Maria's grandson Pepe. "Anything else?"

"Paul is second generation Irish from Boston, Susan Chinese from Hong Kong. They've been married for twenty-seven years and owned an art gallery in Los Angeles called *Susan Paul*. They'll soon be opening a new iteration of *Susan Paul* in Mercy. I told Paul you prefer to meet dogs here first and he said that would be fine."

Healing sits on the sofa and takes his mother's hand. "Tell me true, Mum. Have you already solved the case?"

"I have a strong inkling," she says playfully. "However, I'd like to meet Roxy and Böllwinkle before I share my hunch with you. For the sake of fun, I will write my guess down and place it in a sealed envelope to be opened at the conclusion of the case."

"I shall do the same," says Healing, ever delighted by his mother. "Did Paul say *where* in Los Angeles they lived before moving here?"

"Echo Park," says Naomi, frowning thoughtfully. "My knowledge of the interstices of that vast urban sprawl verges on nil. Thus I have no idea where Echo Park is except somewhere south of Santa Barbara."

"I have a vague idea," says Healing, getting up to put a log on the fire. "I shall give Paul a call and arrange for them to come visit."

*

The next morning at the little old house is taken up with six excited children making crayon drawings on butcher paper, playing Hide and Seek in the backyard, enjoying muffins and fruit juice on the deck, weeding the chard and digging potatoes, walking to the beach to build sandcastles, and returning to the little old house to make avocado and refried bean tacos for lunch, after which the children help do the dishes.

When the four non-resident scholars depart, Jahera and Maahiah walk Raaz and Oz across the street to their mother who spent a luxurious morning doing very little.

Meanwhile, Healing and Jean collapse on the living room sofa.

"I am so exhausted I'm tempted to cancel this afternoon's meeting with Roxy and Böllwinkle," says Healing, pulling himself up into a sitting position. "However, since they're not due for another hour, I will take a twenty-minute nap and soldier on."

"So shall I," says Jean, rising from the sofa with a melodramatic groan. "I'll be in the cottage. Do alert me when they arrive."

"Will do," says Healing, stretching out on the sofa. "Would you set the kitchen timer for thirty minutes, please?"

"Didn't you just say *twenty* minutes?" she asks, sauntering into the kitchen.

"I have reconsidered," he says, closing his eyes.

"Well you should," she says, fondly. "You're a fine teacher and the kids adore you."

"As are you and so do they adore you," he says, immediately falling asleep.

*

Healing dreams he is in a play.

Alone on the stage he feels the electricity of the invisible watchers.

"You think I'm afraid, don't you?" he says, speaking to the audience. "Well you're right. I am. You are the ever-present monster in my dreams."

"Who are you talking to?" says a beautiful woman entering from the wings. "There's nobody here but you and me, and I'm no monster."

"Monstrosity is in the eye of the beholder," he says gesturing to the invisible audience. "They are the monster I fear."

She smiles alluringly. "Even so you should kiss me."

He takes her in his arms and...

The timer beeps and he wakes.

*

Revived by their naps, Healing and Jean are waiting on the front porch when Susan and Paul and their German Shepherds Roxy and Böllwinkle arrive in a silver sedan – Roxy medium-sized, Böllwinkle large, both dogs tan-colored and very friendly. Susan and Paul are both friendly, too – Susan petite and bubbly with black hair cut a la

Prince Valiant, Paul husky and bespectacled with remnants of gray hair.

"Of course we'd get here and you'd stop being anxious," says Paul, rolling his eyes at the dogs. "What's up with you guys?"

Roxy and Böllwinkle look at Paul to say *We like these new people. They've got a wonderful vibe and we* really *want to meet their dogs!*

"Sometimes I think they're clueless," says Paul, shaking his head. "And sometimes I think they're geniuses." He looks at Healing. "What do you think they are?"

"The latter," says Healing, laughing as both dogs push their heads under his hands to be petted. "Shall we introduce them to the resident hounds? We've got one very old dog, two elders, and one youngster. And four more across the street, but we'll just meet the four on this side of the street today."

"Böllwinkle gets growly around other males," says Susan, apologetically. "I think he wants to be the alpha."

"Don't we all," says Paul with a little shrug.

"Actually dogs don't want to be alphas," says Healing, exchanging loving looks with Roxy and Böllwinkle as he pets them. "We humans tend to anthropomorphize animal behavior, but I assure you being the alpha isn't something dogs aspire to. They either are the alpha or they aren't. In any case, no matter who turns out to be the alpha, all will be well. My dogs are accustomed to meeting client dogs and enjoy the experience. May I take their leashes?"

"So then how *do* dogs decide who the alpha is?" asks Paul, handing the dogs over to Healing.

"The hierarchic order of a group of dogs is known to all the dogs within a few seconds of meeting each other," says Healing, giving Roxy and Böllwinkle chewy treats. "This knowing comes from an instantaneous analysis of countless streams of information received by their nervous systems, nearly all of which is unknowable to humans."

"You make them sound smarter than we are," says Susan, laughing. "Maybe they are. We give them everything they want."

"Dogs have an entirely different *kind* of intelligence than humans," says Jean, opening the backyard gate. "For instance, your dogs were aware of our dogs the moment you got here, whereas you won't become aware of our dogs until you *see* them."

"Yet your dogs could never run an art gallery," says Healing, leading the dogs through the gate.

"Which *proves* they're smarter than we are," says Paul, laughing.

Mendelssohn, Coosi, Socrates, and Tabinda are waiting on the edge of the vegetable garden and remain there until Healing signals for them to approach. And though Böllwinkle does bristle and growl a little during the mixing and sniffing, he soon knows his place, as does Roxy, after which the resident dogs lead the visitors on a tour of the premises.

"Marvelous dogs," says Healing, standing on the garden path with Susan and Paul watching Böllwinkle and Roxy pee where Mendelssohn pees. "I applaud you for taking such good care of them. They exhibit none of the anxiety you spoke of on the phone, so we will assume they're disquiet is associated with where you live."

"But what could it be?" asks Paul, dismayed. "The house is great. We're right on the edge of the dunes, they've got a big yard, and we love them to death. Yet they're both anxious *all* the time now and hardly sleep."

"They were never like this in LA," says Susan, sadly. "Breaks my heart. We love it here *so* much, and they are so unhappy."

"We'll need to visit them at your place," says Healing, watching Roxy and Böllwinkle approach the spindly fence of the chicken run, which causes the hens to scurry into their coop. "However, before you leave today we would like to introduce you and Roxy and Böllwinkle to our mother with whom you spoke on the phone. She is highly attuned to dogs. As luck would have it, she's in the kitchen preparing tea and coffee to go with my wife's just baked cookies. We'll get out of the cold, leave the kitchen door ajar, and the dogs will come in when they're done exploring."

"We don't like to leave them outside unless we're with them," says Susan, watching the gang of dogs disappear into a copse of Japanese maples.

"If you'd rather follow them, please do," says Healing, going up onto the deck, "though I assure you they'll come back with our dogs in just a few minutes. The yard is well-fenced so they can't wander off, and they have accepted Mendelssohn as the resident alpha and will go wherever he goes."

"Shall we take a leap of faith?" says Paul, holding out his hand to Susan.

"What else is new?" she says, taking his hand.

*

In the toasty kitchen, Susan has tea, Paul coffee, and while Jean and Naomi are asking them about life in Beverly Hills where the previous *Susan Paul* gallery was, the dogs enter en masse and gather in the living room where Healing gives them chewy treats and tells them how marvelous they are.

"You say they are anxious," says Naomi, looking over the tops of her glasses at Paul and Susan. "Do they whimper?"

"No," says Susan, trying to think how best to describe Roxy and Böllwinkle's behavior. "It's sort of like when we lived in Los Angeles and they would hear a delivery truck. Bölly would growl and Roxy would be very tense and alert until the package was delivered and the truck drove away. The difference now is Bölly doesn't growl and they're both on high alert *all* the time."

"They seem worried about something," says Paul, chewing anxiously on his lower lip. "They've never been like this. It's baffling."

"Yet here at our house," says Naomi, gesturing to Roxy flirting with Socrates, "they seem void of anxiety."

"More tea or coffee?" asks Healing, smiling around the table.

"I would love more coffee," says Paul, nodding. "And to know where you get your beans."

"None for me," says Susan, beaming at Healing. "But I'd love to get the recipe for these cookies. They're fantastic."

"I will bring you the recipe when we come to your place," says Healing, getting up to jot a note to Jahera about the cookie recipe. "The beans are the *East Cove Hotel Blend* available at *Good Groceries* where long ago I was the manager."

"The good news," says Jean, nodding to Healing to refill her coffee mug, "is that Roxy and Böllwinkle's anxiety isn't a permanent condition as evidenced by how they are behaving here."

"Not *yet* permanent" says Naomi, with a warning in her voice. "However, I think it behooves us to nip this in the bud before it becomes a less tractable habit."

"I feel like an idiot," says Paul, red-faced, "but I never asked how much you charge."

"My reward is the satisfaction of helping you," says Healing, nodding graciously. "And getting to know you and your wonderful dogs."

*

The next day is Halloween and a home school holiday. Jahera and Tova and Maahiah and the costumed children leave after breakfast to go trick-or-treating at the homes of various friends and classmates, with a festive lunch to follow at the Guptas' house, five-year-old Arjun Gupta the oldest of the homeschoolers.

Healing and Jean do the breakfast dishes, take the dogs for a long walk, and when the pooches are sprawled contentedly by the fire, Healing and Jean bid Naomi adieu and leave for Seascape Villas, a development of opulent homes on the headlands three miles north of Mercy where only a few of those houses are occupied year-round.

"There is nothing I love so much as going on cases with you," says Jean, as they cruise along the coast highway, the sky dotted with puffy white clouds, a strong wind blowing from the north. "Feels so..." She frowns as the right word eludes her.

"Natural?" suggests Healing, who dearly loves his sister.

"Certainly that," she says, nodding. "I would even say *elemental.* As if this is what I was born to do."

"I know what you mean," says Healing, gazing to the west where huge waves are breaking on the shore. "I always feel like I'm on a quest to find a point of connection, a moment in space and time where the puzzle pieces fall into place and the conundrum is revealed to be an answer to a question far greater than the one that initiated the quest." He laughs. "If I may mix my metaphors."

"Oh please do," says Jean, laughing with him. "What else are metaphors for?"

*

Susan and Paul's place is a sprawling one-story house on a large lot adjoining spectacular dunes, beyond which is a beach teeming with shorebirds. Roxy and Böllwinkle are delighted to see Healing and Jean again, yet after a few minutes of visiting they retreat to the darkest corner of the kitchen, their faces drawn with worry.

"This is how they are now," says Paul, anguished. "And nothing we do helps them relax for more than a few minutes."

"Come here Bölly. Come on Roxy," says Healing, kneeling on the floor. "Show me what's troubling you."

They come to him and he pets them, and they both glance furtively at the sliding glass door that opens onto a large deck overlooking the backyard and the dunes beyond.

Healing gets up and goes to the door while the dogs slink back into the kitchen.

"They must love walking on the beach here," says Jean, joining Healing at the sliding glass door.

"Well..." says Susan, exchanging glances with Paul, "we've only taken them to the beach here a few times because it's *so* hard to get over the dunes. The sand is really deep and soft, and it's always windy out there so we mostly walk them in town."

"As I suspected," says Healing, going to visit the dogs in the kitchen.

"What do you mean?" asks Paul, frowning at Healing. "You think our not walking them on the beach here is the problem? That's ridiculous."

"I will explain after we take the dogs to the beach," says Healing, giving both Roxy and Böllwinkle vigorous rubs to dispel their disquiet.

"I need to change my shoes," says Susan, hurrying to get ready.

"Me, too," says Paul, following Susan. "Cold out there, Honey. Bundle up."

*

When Paul and Susan are ready to go and the dogs are leashed, Healing dons a small knapsack containing a jug of water and a plastic bowl.

"To be totally honest," says Paul, leading the dogs to the door, "we've only tried this once and we didn't get very far because the dogs *hated* it."

"May I take their leashes?" asks Healing, giving the dogs a wide-eyed look to say *Fun awaits!*

Paul relinquishes the leashes and starts to open the sliding glass door when Susan asks, "Why are we making them do this when they don't want to? It seems cruel."

"How do you know they don't want to?" asks Healing, smiling curiously at her.

"Because they *hated* it when we went before," says Paul, glaring at Healing. "Can't you see they don't want to go?"

"I only see that *you* don't want to go," says Healing, looking from Paul to Susan. "If you'd rather not come with us, though we wish you would, Jean and I will go with the dogs and you can stay here. If they're not happy out there, we'll bring them right back. But I'll bet you all the tea in India they'll have the time of their lives out there."

*

After slogging through deep sand and being buffeted by a powerful wind, the four humans and two dogs at last surmount the dunes and cross the wide beach to where the waves have firmed the sand.

Healing and Jean unleash the dogs and they race away a short distance, come back, race away again a little further, and return once more. Healing and Jean re-leash the dogs and the group walks north against the wind until Susan and Paul can go no further.

"Reverse course!" shouts Healing, and everyone turns around and heads for home with the wind at their backs.

"What a relief," shouts Paul, overjoyed by how easy it is to walk with the wind pushing him. "I was done for."

"Me, too," says Susan, ecstatically. "No wonder we never do this."

"When we get closer to home," says Healing, handing Böllwinkle's leash to Paul and nodding for Jean to give Roxy's leash to Susan, "we'll let them off their leashes again."

This time when the dogs are freed, they race to the edge of the sea and bark at the crashing waves and chase each other up and down the shore, their speed miraculous.

"Now let's us humans hunker down and wait for the speedsters to return," says Healing, sitting cross-legged in the sand facing north.

Susan sits facing Healing with her back to the wind, Paul sits facing west with a view of the crashing waves, and Jean sits facing east with a view of the dunes.

Some minutes later the dogs join the humans and Healing brings out the water bottle and bowl so the dogs can whet their whistles.

"Look at *you*," says Paul, hugging Böllwinkle. "You're you again."

"I think they'll be happy in the house now, too," says Healing, laughing as Roxy licks his face in thanks for the water. "They were troubled because they had no context for the sounds they were hearing and the vibrations they were feeling in this new place that is so very different from where they spent the first three years of their lives."

Roxy flops down and offers her tummy to be rubbed, and Susan obliges.

"I know this was quite a workout," says Jean, petting Böllwinkle, "but it would be highly efficacious if you brought them out here at least every other day for the next few weeks so they come to know in their bones that this..." She gestures around at the beach and sky and roaring waves. "... is their home now and not to be feared."

"If such an effort is beyond you," says Healing, petting Roxy, "we will be happy to bring them out here for you with one or another of our dogs, and possibly my grandchildren, too."

*

After supper that night in the little old house, when the scary witch and swashbuckling pirate and their mother have gone home to bed, Healing and Naomi exchange envelopes and read aloud the other's surmise concerning *The Bewildering Case of Roxy and Böllwinkle.*

Naomi's note reads *Something they hear and feel but cannot see is terrifying them.*

Healing's note says *The roar of the waves, the strong winds, and the earth vibrating in response to the incessant waves crashing on the shore at Seascape Villas must be demystified for them, or Roxy and Böllwinkle will never let their guards down.*

*

Healing kneels on his yoga mat and uses the bed as a desk for writing.

"Are you writing a poem, Shafi?" asks Jahera, looking up from her book.

"Seem to be," he says, writing the last word. "Inspired by our walk on the beach with Susan and Paul and Roxy and Böllwinkle."

"I love your poems," she says tenderly. "You haven't written one in a long time."

"They seem to want to come again," he says, smiling shyly. "Who knows why?"

"Read to me?"

"There comes a moment when our strength departs and we can no longer walk against the ferocious wind. So we change direction, and our nemesis becomes our loving friend, the great obstacle now a source of joy. Everything we fought so hard against turns out to be what we wanted all along."

Ω

11. Bongo

Eleven days into November, no rain since May, many wells in Mercy have gone dry and water is being trucked in from afar at great expense.

"It's downright depressing," Darby proclaims over Sunday waffles. "Freezing cold here and fires raging inland. Not like any November I've ever known." He gazes at Raaz and Oz happily eating their waffles. "What a world we're leaving these two."

"Don't go there, Dar," says Majorie, giving him a warning look.

Raaz looks up from her waffle. "Where are you going, Darby?"

"I'm not going anywhere, dear," says Darby, smiling at her.

"But you just said you were leaving us," she says, frowning at him.

"I did," says Darby, abashed. "But Margy convinced me not to go where I was going so now I'm not."

"Where were you going?" asks Oz, his mouth full of waffle.

"I was sinking into sadness," says Darby, sighing, "and Margy pulled me out."

"I get sad, too, sometimes," says Oz, nodding. "Mama and Raaz and Jadda try to cheer me up and I don't want to, but then I do."

"Life is full of sorrow," says Naomi, speaking to her great grandchildren. "Which is why we sometimes feel sad. It's natural to feel sad, just as it's natural to feel happy. These feelings come and go and change into other feelings. Just like the weather changes. How dull life would be if the weather was always the same."

"I had a dream last night it was raining," says Raaz, dolloping yogurt onto her waffle. "And Flora and Max ran around the house barking because they didn't know what rain was."

"May your dream prove prophetic," says Healing, manning the waffle iron. "In the meantime, I salute all of you for conserving water.

Our wells remain viable and the pond is nearly full, which is not the case with several of our neighbors."

"Esther and Darvin ran out of water," says Oz, matter-of-factly. "For school tomorrow we're going to watch the water truck come and fill their tank."

"How is *your* well holding up?" asks Tova, inquiring of Marjorie.

"Oh we've got lots of water," says Marjorie, nodding. "We stopped watering the garden in August when the drought was declared, and we don't use much water at the best of times, having been through droughts before."

"In non-drought news," says Healing, bringing a waffle to the table to be divided among the needy, "there's a big minus tide later this morning, and Jahera and Jean and I are going to the beach with the dogs should anyone care to accompany us."

"Can we bring Max and Flora?" asks Oz, excitedly. "They might be big enough to go to the beach now."

"Yes, bring them," says Healing, smiling at the thought of the pups running on the sand. "They'll get as far as they get and then we'll carry them."

*

Two days later, Jahera and Tova have massages at the spa at the East Cove Hotel, Jahera's treat, and after their massages they share a hot tub.

"Darvin kissed me," says Tova, looking down at the water. "Well... I kissed him and he went along with it." She looks at Jahera. "I wanted to tell you because even though I know you're okay with me flinging myself at Darvin, I *am* still officially married to your son who is the father of my children who are your grandchildren. I guess I want your blessing to move out of widowhood, so to speak, not that Lucien is dead, but... you know what I mean. I feel *so* awkward trying to start over with a new person, and the last thing I want is to feel self-conscious around you while I'm at it."

"Sweetheart," says Jahera embracing her. "You have my blessing a thousand times over. I'm glad you kissed Darvin. He's wonderful."

"I tried to contact Lucien three weeks ago," says Tova, relaxing in Jahera's arms. "But he's changed his phone number and email address. So I sent him a letter asking how to contact him should anything happen to the children, and the letter came back unopened and stamped *Return To Sender*."

"The last time I spoke to him was in August and he asked me not to call him anymore." Jahera sighs. "So I don't have his new numbers either. Nor do I want them. I'm done trying to force my way into his life."

"It's such a mystery," says Tova, moving apart from Jahera. "Not that he left, but that he became such a different person. He had such a good sense of humor until the children were born, and then it completely disappeared and never came back."

"He's a chameleon," says Jahera, solemnly. "He becomes whatever he thinks he must be to survive."

*

"The children grow by leaps and bounds," says Healing to Jean as they walk across Mercy with Mendelssohn and Coosi to meet a dog named Bongo and his owner Darla Rosenfeld. "Life speeds apace."

"Certainly does," says Jean, sighing. "Soon it will be Thanksgiving, and a few days later I go back to England, though I don't want to." She shrugs hopelessly. "I am so engaged here in so many wonderful ways. I love going on cases with you and helping with home school and..." She shrugs again. "What can I do? Divorce Albert after fifty-three years of marriage? Every time I get home from Mercy, the first thing he says to me is, 'Don't *ever* go again. My life is hell without you,' which isn't true. He just hates not having a live-in maid to cook and clean and do his laundry."

"Come sooner next year, Sis, and stay longer," says Healing, putting his arm around her. "If he won't come with you, that's his doing, not yours."

"Oh let's change the subject. Tell me about the case."

"Darla Rosenfeld is a painter and performance artist. She moved here from Los Angeles three months ago to be near her close friends the Cheshires, Susan and Paul, who show Darla's work in their gallery. Darla has a five-year-old Foxhound Airedale with a touch of Boxer named Bongo. When Susan and Paul regaled Darla with tales of how we helped Roxy and Böllwinkle overcome their anxiety, Darla decided to call me about Bongo who is having a difficult time adjusting to life far from the madding crowd, otherwise known as Los Angeles."

"You intrigue me, Holmes," says Jean, arching her eyebrow. "Tell me more."

"Darla is an age peer of Susan and Paul," says Healing, imitating Basil Rathbone as Sherlock Holmes. "Which is to say sixtyish. She bought the old Castellano place, which was the Baptist church when you and I were children. Then Luigi Castellano and his wife Bambi bought the church and turned the front half into a pottery studio and the back half into their home." Healing nudges Jean. "If memory serves, in high school you had a mighty crush on their son Philip?"

"More than a crush," says Jean, wistfully. "When I was sixteen, not long before the family went on that fateful trip to England, Philip and I would meet on weekends in the blackberry jungle behind their house to kiss and so forth until we were on the verge of no return. And I'm sure if he hadn't thrown me over for Tanya Vogelsang because I wouldn't go all the way and Tanya would, I never would have stayed in England. But he *did* throw me over for Tanya, and I did stay in England, and the rest is history."

"And here we are," says Healing, stopping in front of the former church, a large two-story building with a red-tile roof and white walls and a front yard bristling with agave plants thriving despite the bitter cold.

A dog barks from within and the big red front door swings open to reveal Bongo, a handsome pooch, and Darla, a striking olive-skinned brunette wearing a billowy orange and yellow blouse, turquoise jeans, and red sandals, her long hair unfurled, her toenails painted turquoise to match her jeans.

Bongo bumps noses with Mendelssohn and Coosi, and all is immediately well among the dogs.

"Come in, come in," says Darla, a Jewish Los Angeleno. "I'm *thrilled* you came. Susan says you're both absolute *geniuses* with dogs. God knows I'm not. Am I, Bongo?"

Bongo looks at Healing to say *I dig your dogs. Come in. Come in.*

"I've been here three months and I'm still not unpacked," says Darla, leading them through the cluttered living room to a big sunny kitchen. "I'm *madly* in love with Mercy, or I was until everybody left for the off-season. Do you call it the off-season?"

"We call it heaven," says Healing, chuckling.

"Seriously?" says Darla, aghast. "When I got here in August the town was like a mini Santa Monica and I just *loved* it. By the end of September... I won't use the word *dead*, but I will use *comatose*. Even so, I really do love it here. Bongo and I went walking in the forest yesterday and I couldn't believe how *wild* it is here. The trees! My god! So huge. Incredible. And the beach? Whales and seals and *so* many birds. Unbelievable! Who knew? Coffee? I have scones from *Café Brava*. Blackberry. Have you had them? Of course you have. In LA their baker would be a celebrity. Thank God for *Café Brava* and *Big Goose*. Don't you just love they didn't put a *The* in front of *Big Goose*? Genius. Do you live here year round? I don't know if I can handle the solitude *and* the cold. I sold my house in LA but kept my condo in

Santa Barbara for when I need a fix of southern California. I mean... what do you *do* here in the off-season? There's like *no* traffic and *no* lines at the movie theatre and *no* wait to get a table in the café. Is a hurricane coming and no one told me? Verges on dystopian. And you know the *weirdest* thing? No one here is ever in a hurry. And everyone is so nice. And they don't seem to be just pretending to be nice. They really are. Are you aware of this? In LA *every*one is in a hurry and everyone is surly. Even small children." She laughs. "I'm babbling. Forgive me. I haven't spoken to an actual person since I had lunch with Susan yesterday. She says *Hi* by the way."

"Coffee would be lovely," says Healing, delighted by Darla.

"Sit. Sit," she says, gesturing to the stools at her kitchen counter. "I'll grind some beans and ignite Mr. Coffee." She beams at Jean. "Susan says you're visiting from England. I *love* England. Where in England do you live?"

"Exeter," says Jean, chuckling at Darla calling her dazzling Italian coffee machine Mr. Coffee. "In Devon. Do you know where that is?"

"Do *I* know where Devon is?" says Darla, filling her grinder with coffee beans. "My second husband was from Devon. Arthur Meisner. We were married for two disastrous years and might still be married if Arthur hadn't been so confused about the concept of fidelity. Otherwise we were perfect for each other. That was thirty years ago. He still calls me on my birthday and I still only understand every third word he says."

"Arthur Meisner the actor?" asks Jean, intrigued.

Darla nods. "They love him on the telly in England, but he was a total bust in Hollywood. *Way* too nuanced for American audiences."

"Speaking of nuance," says Healing, observing Bongo showing Mendelssohn and Coosi around the place, "your dog seems fine."

"Yes and no," says Darla, gazing fondly at Bongo. "Let me get Mr. Coffee going and I'll show you Exhibit A. Plug your ears. I'm grinding."

*

When Signor Caffè is burbling away, Darla leads Healing and Jean upstairs to her studio, an enormous room with high ceilings and seven big skylights, one of the walls hung with two very large canvases, one blank, one a nearly-finished painting, the rest of the room a jumble of furniture and crates and boxes, some open, some yet to be opened.

"I *love* this," says Healing, standing before the painting – an abstract of three people, two interacting and one standing apart. "I love the black and gray figures and the splashes of red behind them, those touches of green, and the marvelous feeling of movement. Those two figures seem to be dancing with each other while the other waits and watches."

"I *so* identify with the woman apart from the other two," says Jean, marveling at the painting. "She evokes *such* a response in me. Her longing to belong."

"Oh my God," says Darla, putting a hand on her heart. "I can't tell you how happy you've made me. Who cares about my dog? Let's be friends."

"Speaking of your dog," says Healing, looking around the studio. "Is he not allowed up here?"

"No, he's *supposed* to be up here," says Darla, nodding emphatically. "That's Exhibit A. He follows me everywhere, but he absolutely refuses to come up here. He came up once when we first got here and never again. I *love* having him with me when I'm painting, though I haven't done much painting since I got here, which I attribute to culture shock."

"May I call my dogs to join us?" asks Healing, wondering what could be keeping Bongo below.

"Yeah yeah," says Darla, nodding emphatically. "Maybe Bongo will follow them."

Healing makes the barest whistling sound, and Mendelssohn and Coosi trot up the stairs, enter the room, stop abruptly, and give Healing looks to say *Not good up here.*

"Come on Moosh," says Healing, wondering what the dogs could be sensing. "Come on Coosi."

The dogs cross the room with obvious trepidation, look at Healing to say *Please don't make us stay here,* and Coosi hurries back to the top of the stairs from where he gazes worriedly at Mendelssohn.

"What's going on, Moosh?" asks Healing, petting Mendelssohn. "Show me."

Mendelssohn looks toward a jumble of boxes behind which is a closed door Healing assumes is a closet.

"Darla?" asks Healing, pointing at the door. "What's in there?"

"A little stairwell," she says, nodding. "Goes up to the roof. Your dogs don't like it up here either, do they?"

"They sense something we don't," says Healing, approaching the door.

Mendelssohn growls and Healing stops.

"Have you been up on the roof since you moved here?" asks Jean, eyeing the door suspiciously.

"No," says Darla, shaking her head. "Those stairs come out at the peak of the roof. For making repairs I think. It's a very steep roof. I looked in there when the realtor was showing me around and there was nothing except the stairs, and I haven't opened that door since."

Healing steps over a cardboard box and presses his ear against the door for a moment before returning to Darla and Jean.

"And?" asks Darla, giving Healing a quizzical look

"Do you work up here at night?" asks Healing, speaking quietly.

"I wish. But as I said, I've hardly done any painting since I got here. Why do you ask?"

"Because if you were up here at night," he says, pointing at the door, "I think you would hear what Bongo and my dogs know is behind the door."

"What?" she asks, horrified.

"Your stairwell is home to a family of nocturnal animals," he says, petting Mendelssohn and giving him a chewy treat. "Animals that most dogs would be reluctant to confront, especially this many of them. It's a good thing you never opened that door or you might have been seriously injured."

"Jesus, what is it?" says Darla, backing away. "Giant rats?"

"No," says Healing, laughing. "Raccoons."

"Are you serious?" says Darla, gasping. "Why didn't Bongo bark at them?"

"He may have barked at them when you first moved here. Or he may have immediately sensed he was hopelessly outnumbered, as did my dogs. In any case, we shall summon our excellent wildlife rescue people to come relocate these raccoons, after which repairs must be made to prevent their return."

"You never heard skittering sounds on the roof at night?" asks Jean, giggling. "As the bandits came and went?"

"Oh my God," says Darla, looking from Jean to Healing. "I thought it was ravens. They land on the roof every day so I thought it was them at night, too."

"Probably these guys," says Healing, pointing at the door. "Bongo doesn't bark at the skittering sounds?"

"He growls," says Darla, flabbergasted. "And I always say, 'Chill, buddy, it's just the big black birds' and he stops."

"Case solved," says Healing, strolling with Darla and Jean to the top of the stairs. "Shall we have some of that marvelous coffee I can smell from up here?"

"Wait a minute," says Darla, before they start down. "Wouldn't *I* have smelled the raccoons? Or smelled their poop?"

"If we'd had *any* rain these last few months you might have," says Healing, nodding. "But we haven't had a drop since you've lived here. Humans can smell *wet* raccoons, but dry raccoons are odorless to us, though not to dogs. Had they pissed or pooped in the stairwell you definitely would have smelled that, but they rarely foul their own nests, unlike rats."

"They have a *nest* in there?" says Darla, covering her mouth with her hand. "But I had the place inspected before I bought it. Wouldn't they have found a raccoon nest?"

"I would guess the raccoons moved in after the place was inspected," says Healing, starting down the stairs. "Doesn't take them long to get established once they find a good niche. May we assume you have a tree or trees in your backyard close to the roof?"

"Overhanging the roof," says Darla, glumly. "Two gorgeous old maples."

"Raccoon highways," says Jean, tittering.

*

Beyond Darla's kitchen is a large sunroom with French Doors opening onto a terrazzo bordered by a high wooden fence separating Darla's backyard from the neighboring yards and from the vacant lot on the next street over.

"I bought this lot, too," says Darla, leading Healing and Jean through a gate onto the vacant lot covered with wild mustard. "It was completely overgrown with gigantic blackberry bushes. My realtor suggested I have them removed because they were a fire hazard. So I hired some guys to do that a few days after I moved in and they hauled away three big truckloads."

"The legendary blackberry jungle of Battersea Lane," says Healing, wistfully. "It was there our whole lives and long before we were born." He gives his sister a knowing look. "Remember Jen?" He smiles at Darla. "I call her Jean now, but she was Jen and I was Helios until she was ten and I was eight. Jen was how I pronounced her name when I was a baby and she called me Helios and we kept those names until we didn't."

"Marvelous view with the blackberry jungle gone," says Jean, gazing at Mercy Bay in the distance. "End of an era."

"I love this view," says Darla, impulsively taking Jean's hand. "I was afraid somebody might build a big house here and block it, so I'm gonna build a cottage with a flat roof where my friends can stay when they come to visit."

"The raccoons lived in the blackberry jungle for generations," says Healing, having harvested hundreds of buckets of blackberries here over the years. "And when their thorny haven was removed, they found new lodgings in your stairwell."

"Is that why Bongo won't come out here?" asks Darla, who never for a moment thought anything lived in those blackberry brambles. "He smells raccoons?"

"No," says Healing, scanning the lot. "Their scent isn't concentrated here as it is in your belfry, so to speak."

"Raccoons in my belfry," says Darla, pointing at Healing. "Genius. I'm gonna use that in my new monologue." She bows grandiloquently. "I'm a performance artist, too."

Healing whistles for his dogs and they come trotting through the gate from the terrazzo where they were hanging out with Bongo who does not accompany them.

"Come with me," says Healing, beckoning the dogs to follow him down the gently sloping lot to the street below – Battersea Lane – where the dogs do some pissing and Healing reminds himself who lives on the street now.

"I was just telling Darla," says Jean, when Healing and the dogs return from their reconnaissance, "about my torrid foreplay with Philip Castellano under the canopy of blackberry vines."

"I never would have had them cut down if I'd known they were of such historic significance," says Darla, laughing with Jean. "I'm a hopeless romantic and I love blackberries."

"Fear not," says Healing, glad to see Jean having so much fun. "The blackberries will return with great vigor. In the meantime, have you met your neighbors across the street on Battersea Lane? Terrence and Jackie Witherspoon?"

"No," says Darla, looking across the street at the Witherspoon's blue house with an old wooden rowboat in front full of cacti. "But I've seen their dog. He's as big as a horse."

"Ajax," says Healing, nodding. "He marks this lot and Bongo read the notice and wants nothing to do with such a behemoth, though Ajax is a sweetheart. I will be happy to introduce you and Bongo to Ajax and the wonderful Witherspoons who have lived here for forty years. I'm confident once the dogs are familiar with each other, Bongo will gladly come out here with you."

"I would love to meet them," says Darla, her eyes sparkling as she looks from Healing to Jean. "And I wasn't kidding about us being friends. I would love that, too."

*

"You should have seen Jean and Darla laughing together," says Healing, kneeling on his yoga mat and using the bed as his desk. "I haven't seen Jean so happy since we were kids. She and Darla are crazy about each other, and I don't mean sexually."

"I know what you mean, Shafi," says Jahera, putting her book away. "Are you writing a poem about them?"

"Might be a poem," he says, looking at his notebook. "At this point I think it's more of a synopsis."

"I'd love to hear," she says, closing her eyes.

He reads his scrawl to himself and makes a few changes before reading aloud.

"The women stand together where the blackberry jungle used to be, the jungle where one of the women nearly lost her virginity fifty years ago. And though the women barely know each other, the woman who nearly lost her virginity in the jungle tells the other woman about the boy she was naked with under the canopy of vines and how she wouldn't let him inside her because she was afraid, so the boy found someone else. And the other woman says *The same thing happened to me on the beach in Malibu when I was fourteen.* And then she says she would never have had the blackberry jungle removed had she known it was of such historical significance. Now they laugh together and embrace and feel a bond stretching back a million years."

*

Ten days later, Thanksgiving two days away, Healing and Jahera and Jean walk with the six homeschoolers from the little old house on Nasturtium Road to the library where Olive Ingersol reads them a story about a brave baby bird who saves her know-it-all father from a fox.

From the library they walk to the brand new *Susan Paul* gallery on Main Street to see five of Darla's big paintings.

Darla and Susan and Paul are on hand for the viewing, and when the children have looked at Darla's paintings for several minutes, Jean asks them if they have any questions for the artist.

"Why don't you use a camera so it looks real?" asks Reggie Chan, pointing at Darla's big abstract of a person dancing with an animal that might be a dog or a lion.

"Very good question," says Darla, smiling at Reggie. "The thing is... when you take a picture of something with a camera you're trying to capture what you *see*. Right? But when I paint, I'm trying to capture what I *imagine*, which is different than what I see. Do you know what I mean?"

"Like you can imagine a blue person," says Sheila Liebowitz, looking to Jean for approval. "Even if people aren't really blue?"

"Why do you make them so big?" asks Esther, wrinkling her nose "We couldn't even get them in our house."

"That's another great question," says Darla, charmed by the children. "A big part of being an artist is allowing yourself to try whatever you want to try. So after many years of making smaller paintings, I wanted to see what it felt like to make *big* paintings. So that's what I did."

"How did it feel?" asks Raaz, who covets Darla's shimmery green blouse and cherry red pants.

"Fantastic," says Darla, beaming at Raaz. "Better than I ever felt before."

Ω

12. Phyllis and Carya

Early in the morning on the second of December, the collective gathers in the little old house to spend time with Jean, as she makes ready to depart for San Francisco from where she will fly home to England.

"Every human society has some sort of ritual for saying goodbye to friends and family who are going on a long journey," explains Naomi, sitting on the living room sofa with Oz on her lap and Raaz close beside her. "My favorite is the Russian tradition of everyone sitting quietly together before the person leaves."

"Why do they sit quietly?" asks Oz, considering the tradition. "Why don't they just talk to the person before they leave?"

"I believe it's a kind of group prayer," says Naomi, smiling at Jean standing arm-in-arm with Tova and Eliana. "A time to think fondly of each other."

"Shall we?" says Healing, about to make a fresh pot of tea.

"Oh let's not," says Jean, laughing. "I'll just sob."

So they don't sit quietly, Healing makes more tea, and they have slices of Maahiah's just-baked bread with butter and blackberry jam and talk excitedly about things they'll do with Jean when she returns in the spring.

And shortly before Justin and Helen are due to arrive to transport Jean to San Francisco, Naomi asks Jean and Healing to join her in the guest room where they will be out of earshot of the children.

When the door is closed, Naomi smiles at Healing and Jean and says, "I have decided how I wish to end my life, barring accident or illness overtaking me first. I wanted to share this with you before you leave, Jean, should my decision figure into how you order your life henceforth."

"I need to sit down," says Healing, sitting on the bed.

"Me, too," says Jean, sitting beside him and holding his hand.

"While your ancient mother remains standing," says Naomi, chuckling. "I am not ill, nor is my mind less sharp than when I was young, and I still very much enjoy being alive. However, I am weary much of the time, and because I want to depart on my own terms before time renders me helpless to make such a choice, I have decided that when Raaz and Oz are seven and I am ninety-six, I will cease to eat and drink until I die. I have been blessed beyond telling to have you for my lifelong friends. I hope you know how grateful I am to both of you."

Jean and Healing embrace their mother and they have a good long cry together.

*

The next morning during the Sunday waffle feast, Darby opines, "Just not the same without Jean here. She's such a dear."

"She's coming back in April for our birthday," says Oz, nodding assuredly.

"A few days *before* our birthday," adds Raaz. "So she'll already be here."

"How old will you be in April?" asks Darby, squinting at the children. "Seventeen?"

Oz laughs. "Not seventeen, Darby. Five. We're still four until April."

Thunder booms and Coosi runs to hide under Healing and Jahera's bed.

"May this thunder presage the end of the drought," says Healing, bringing the first waffle to the table for Jahera to divide among the ravenous. "A morning of indoor activities ahead of us with a walk this afternoon, rain or shine."

"Arjun and his mother are coming to our house today," says Oz, speaking to Darby and Marjorie. "Her name is Kashvi. We're going to see who can build the tallest block tower before they fall over."

"Kashvi is teaching Mama how to cook Indian food," says Raaz, heaping blackberry jam on her waffle. "Because they're from India."

"Vegetable samosas and vegetable pakoras, specifically," says Tova, stretching her arms and yawning. "I'll ring you around three to come over for the tasting. Kashvi's husband Rajiv, and Darvin and Esther are coming, too."

"Speaking of Darvin," says Darby, smiling at Tova, "was it my imagination on Thanksgiving or are you two..."

"We're investigating the possibility," says Tova, blushing.

"Well you have my blessing," says Darby, raising his mug to her. "Not only does the man bear a striking resemblance to Clark Gable, he made me laugh like I haven't laughed in years."

"You *must* hear him play the piano," says Healing, lifting the lid of the waffle iron to check for doneness. "I'll take you to his studio one day and beg him to play for us. He's brilliant."

"We might take piano lessons from Darvin," says Oz, looking at Tova. "Huh Mama?"

"And get a piano to practice on," says Raaz, taking her first bite of waffle. "Only we still want accordions for Christmas."

"The two disciplines will support each other nicely," says Healing, bringing the next waffle to the table. "By the way, Helen and Justin are picking up your accordions at an accordion shop in Berkeley tomorrow on their way home from Helen's poetry reading in San Francisco. Which means you'll be getting your squeeze boxes for Hanukkah instead of Christmas, with Hanukkah coming first this year."

"I begged me mum for a fiddle when I was a boy," says Darby, thinking back to his childhood in Ireland.

"*Fiddle* is another word for violin," interjects Marjorie, anticipating Oz's question.

"Timothy Redgrave was learning the fiddle," continues Darby with a faraway look in his eyes. "He'd take the magical thing out into the field behind the flats where we lived so as not to drive his mum and the neighbors batty with his practicing, and I'd sit with him by the hour watching him play. Now and then he'd let me try. He'd show me where to put my fingers and how to work the bow, and I loved it more than anything. But we were too poor to buy me a fiddle so I never got one." He looks at the children. "I hope you know how lucky you are to get to play an instrument. Not every child gets the chance."

"Why were you poor?" asks Oz, frowning. "Didn't your mother have money?"

"Not enough to buy me a fiddle," says Darby, remembering his dear mum and her gnarled hands. "She cleaned houses every day but Sunday and raised three ungrateful boys without a husband. Every cent she made went for food and rent until we were old enough to work after school and give her the little we made."

"*We* could buy you a fiddle," says Raaz, looking at Tova. "Can we, Mama?"

"Oh I've the money now, dear," says Darby, gazing fondly at Raaz. "You're very generous to offer. But you see, by the time I had enough money for a fiddle I was saving every penny to come to America, so I never got around to buying one." He sighs. "In any case, I'm looking forward to your first accordion concert."

"First we have to learn to play," says Oz, his mouth full of waffle. "*Then* we'll give a concert."

*

The next morning, Raaz and Oz go with Tova to Arjun's house where they and their fellow scholars paint the little wooden boxes they made with Kashvi and Rajiv's help, the boxes to be Christmas Hanukkah Solstice presents for family and friends.

Healing and Jahera take the dogs for a walk in the blessed rain and return home to find Naomi making tea, Maahiah knitting by the fire, and Eliana at the kitchen table writing out a melody that came to her as she fled her parents' house this morning.

"You had a call from Genevieve at the East Cove Hotel," says Naomi, looking over the tops of her glasses at Healing. "Something about a dog who hates *her* dog and the disarray at the hotel arising from said hatred, or so I understood given Genevieve's strong French accent and the fact that she was whispering to not be overheard."

"I shall ring her after we dry the dogs and have our tea," says Healing, bowing to his mother. "The cold has arrived with a vengeance."

"It's deliciously toasty in here," says Eliana, setting down her pencil. "We had a freeze at our house and there was an inch of ice on the pond this morning."

"New song?" asks Healing, pointing at Eliana's staff paper.

"Might be a tango," she says, handing him her music. "Might be a waltz. I hear the violin part, but the chords are still mostly a mystery."

"Shall we play around with it after tea?" asks Healing, thrilled by the prospect.

"I was hoping you'd say that," says Eliana, still feeling somewhat trepidatious about dropping by whenever she feels the need, which is almost every day now.

*

Over tea and cookies, the humans discuss dogs who don't like other dogs.

"Of the hundreds of pooches I've known in my life," says Healing, sharing the sofa with his mother, "I can only think of a few who harbored a general dislike for other dogs. And though certainly many dogs are ultra-protective of their humans and their territory, in my experience only dogs who have been abused manifest behavior comparable to hatred. Which is to say, Genevieve's predicament has all the hallmarks of my least favorite kind of case because the human part of the equation often proves intractable."

"Genevieve's dog Phyllis is the sweetest dog in the world," says Jahera, standing by the fire. "When Mamon and I went to lunch at the hotel a few months ago to discuss the new menus with Genevieve, Phyllis was sweeter than ever. How could any dog hate her?"

"Sweet dogs, as some sweet humans," says Healing, wistfully, "often inspire enmity in those who are *not* so sweet. And even the sweetest dog can be ferocious when threatened."

"When we moved back to England," says Naomi, nodding her thanks to Maahiah for putting the kettle on, "we had a dog named Serena, half Golden Retriever, half little mutt, and sweet beyond sweet. All humans adored her, and most dogs despised her, though she longed to be loved by them. The clearest case of canine jealousy I've ever seen. Ezra doted on her, which made our otherwise congenial mutt Matilda growl and snap at Serena. The poor dear had no idea why she was so reviled. I've known marvelous people, too, who inspire enmity in other people, and it's always quite obviously jealousy."

"Which is why Jahera and I make it our practice to give each of our dogs special attention every day." Healing smiles as Tabinda and Mendelssohn come to him, for they know he's thinking about them.

"No wonder your pack is so peaceful," says Eliana, who always had a dog until her last one died when she was twenty-two and she vowed not to get another until she moved away from her parents. "They all know you love them."

"And they expect this kind of attention from us now," says Jahera, petting Socrates when he comes to her. "A few weeks ago, I forgot to tell Socrates I loved him before I left for the day. Didn't I, Socrates? And when I got home in the evening, you followed me everywhere until I petted you and told you I loved you, and then you were content. Weren't you?"

Socrates gazes into Jahera's loving eyes to say *I love it when you talk to me.*

*

Teatime at end, Healing carries the old phone to the guest room and calls Genevieve.

"Who is calling, please?" says Genevieve, sixty-two, her French accent still pronounced after thirty-five years in America.

"Bon jour, Genevieve. It's Healing. You called about dogs in conflict. I trust one of them is not sweet Phyllis."

"Oh Healing, she *is* one of them," says Genevieve, despondently. "Arno's mother Janet moved here from New York six weeks ago with Carya, a hideous Chow Chow who terrorizes Phyllis and growls and snaps at our guests and their dogs. When I protest to Arno, he says not to worry, that Carya will stop behaving this way once she gets used to being here. But the truth is he's afraid to confront his mother because she loaned us the money to buy the hotel thirty years ago. And though we paid her back every penny plus interest, he still feels beholden to her. Now she's living with us and meddling in our business, berating our staff and complaining about our food. We are world renowned for our food and Janet can't boil a potato! She's ruining us, Healing. Guests are complaining and people who have come here for many years say they will never come again until Janet and her horrible dog are gone, yet Arno will do nothing."

"How does Janet feel about *you*?" asks Healing, who has known Genevieve for thirty years and considers her a paragon of compassion and kindness.

"She hates me," says Genevieve, crying. "She only speaks to me to order me around, and her dog growls and snaps at me all the time. She's destroying our life's work and Arno will do nothing about it."

"I am tempted to say this is beyond my scope," says Healing, speaking quietly. "However, out of loyalty to you, I will drop by at an appropriate time today and give you my opinion about what might be done to improve the dog situation. Tell me the Chow Chow's name again, please."

"Carya," says Genevieve, tersely.

"I'm so sorry to hear of your trouble. What would be the best time for me to visit?"

"Lunch is served until two and overnight guests begin to arrive around three. Shall we say three-thirty this afternoon? Perhaps you could bring Jahera so it won't appear I called you about the dogs. Janet would be enraged if she knew."

"Jahera and I, purely by chance, will arrive at three-thirty," says Healing, hoping to interject a bit of levity into the conversation.

"If you can solve this problem," says Genevieve, pausing momentously, "I will give you carte blanche here for the rest of your life."

"Talk about incentive," says Healing, laughing. "Didn't you just get another Michelin star?"

"We had one star for fifteen years," says Genevieve, plaintively. "And now we have two. But all that will be for naught if Janet has her way."

*

Promptly at three-thirty, Healing and Jahera and Mendelssohn arrive at the sprawling East Cove Hotel where Genevieve, a tall broad-shouldered beauty with graying brown hair, greets them in the grand foyer with her dog Phyllis who is immediately smitten with Mendelssohn and vice-versa.

"Arno is in the dining room with Rajiv and a new table and chairs," says Genevieve, exchanging kisses with Healing and Jahera. "We are remaking the dining room one table and four chairs at a time. Come say hello."

Humans and dogs proceed down a wide hallway, the walls adorned with Jahera's stunning black and white photographs of Genevieve and Arno and their cooks toiling in the hotel's famous kitchen.

"We are sold out of your photos," says Genevieve, locking arms with Jahera. "Arno called you, didn't he? With Christmas coming we want the gift shop overflowing with your photos and books."

"I never got his call," says Jahera, dismayed by the news. "I can make prints for you this week."

"He didn't call you?" says Genevieve, switching to French. "The idiot! He waits on his mother hand and foot and neglects the hotel. We wanted four times as many prints as you made for us last year. How could he have forgotten?"

They enter the grand dining room and find Arno, short and stout with curly gray hair, rejoicing over the exquisite table and four chairs Rajiv just delivered.

"Look at what the Guptas made for us," says Arno, who has the accent of one who grew up in Babylon Village on Long Island. "Aren't they exquisite?"

"I'm so glad you like them," says Rajiv, tall and slender with wavy black hair. "Twenty more tables and eighty more chairs to go."

"Magnificent," says Healing, shaking Rajiv's hand. "Congrats."

"I'm hoping to apprentice Ozan as soon as possible," says Rajiv, exchanging kisses with Jahera. "He's already an excellent sander."

"About time he started earning his keep," says Healing, sitting in one of the new chairs and bouncing his eyebrows at Genevieve. "One could get used to sitting in a chair like this. Fits me like a glove."

Genevieve arches an eyebrow to imply *So it shall be if you solve the dog problem.*

Now Arno's mother Janet limps into the dining room. Short and plump, her silver hair stylishly short, her pants suit gray silk, Janet is accompanied by Carya, a large brown Chow Chow who snarls at

Phyllis, which causes Mendelssohn to return the snarl and prepare to defend Phyllis.

"Oh your damn dog," shouts Janet, waving her arms at Genevieve. "She ruins everything. I just wanted to meet these people and now I can't."

"Your dog needs to be leashed," says Healing, stepping between Phyllis and the menacing Chow Chow. "She is the aggressor and needs to learn that her behavior will not be tolerated."

"Who are you?" says Janet, shocked by Healing's intervention. "A dog expert?"

"I am," says Healing, bowing to her. "Healing Weintraub at your service. You must be Janet. Pleased to meet you. My wife Jahera creates the hotel's menus and took the photographs adorning the walls here. And when fortune shines upon us, my band plays weddings here. I would be happy to help resolve the conflict between your dog and Phyllis if you will allow me."

"There's nothing you can do!" snarls Janet. "They hate each other."

"On the contrary," says Healing, slipping Carya a chewy treat that mollifies her for a moment. "The problem is Phyllis and Carya don't yet know each other in a salutary way. Once they do, the conflict will be at end. Carya's aggression toward other dogs and their humans is another matter and may take longer to resolve. With your permission, I will leash Carya, Phyllis, and Mendelssohn and take them for a stroll to get acquainted."

"I don't have a leash with me," says Janet, glaring at Arno to show her displeasure with this brash interloper. "Some other time."

"I have leashes galore," says Healing, quickly leashing the three pliant dogs and leading them out of the dining room and down the hall to the foyer as the rain conveniently abates.

*

Making their way through the hotel garden to the stairway descending to the beach, Carya growls at Phyllis.

"What's the problem, Carya?" says Healing, speaking soothingly as he brings the dogs to a halt. "Phyllis is a love. If you'll be nice to her we'll have some chewy treats I made fresh just this morning."

He kneels between the warring females, massages their chests, praises them lavishly, gives them each a delicious treat, and encourages them to touch noses and sniff each other, which further diminishes the animosity between them.

Now the four descend the stairs to the beach where Mendelssohn leads Carya and Phyllis on a merry chase that leaves Carya winded and docile and free of animosity toward anyone.

*

A half-hour later, Healing and the sandy dogs climb the stairs from the beach and walk through the garden to the hotel entrance.

"You're as sweet as Phyllis, aren't you, Carya?" says Healing, stopping with the dogs in front of the hotel.

Carya gives Healing a look of love as he pets her, and when Phyllis comes close to get a pet, too, Carya nuzzles Phyllis, and Healing says, "How nice of you Carya," and gives her a chewy treat.

Now Genevieve, Jahera, Arno, and Janet come hurrying out to see how things have progressed.

"We have made the leap," says Healing, rising to greet the humans. "Moosh and I will return tomorrow and work with the girls again. I think you will find relations between them much improved. As for Carya's habit of aggressing hotel guests and their dogs, I recommend she be kept on leash, and when in the presence of guests she should be rewarded for kindly behavior and vigorously restrained when inappropriately aggressive until she learns such behavior toward guests and their dogs won't be tolerated."

Arno embraces Healing and whispers, "You saved my life."

"Carya is a lovely dog," says Healing to Janet. "For some reason she's on the defensive around strangers, and this tendency on her part needs to be addressed by lovingly introducing her to any guests and their dogs you encounter when she's with you. Given her sweet nature, I am confident she will soon adjust to life here and be every bit as welcoming as Phyllis. As you see, the enmity between her and Phyllis is gone and should not recur so long as their presiding humans are civil to each other."

"I'm surprised," says Janet, doing battle with her scowl. "What time are you coming tomorrow?"

*

The next day after lunch, Healing and Mendelssohn return to the hotel with Raaz and Oz, the skies clear after a morning of rain.

Janet is so taken with the children she follows them through the garden to the top of the stairway to the beach.

"I so hoped Arno and Genevieve would have children," she confides in Healing. "But they never did, so no grandchildren for me. What a joy they are."

"Have you forgiven Arno and Genevieve?" asks Healing, taking Janet's hand.

"For what?" she yelps, yanking her hand away.

"For not having children," he says, calmly meeting her angry gaze. "I'm sure they feel your pain in this regard, though there's nothing they can do about it now because they are past the age for making babies. They gave those years to creating this Shangri-La that is Mercy's treasure. Genevieve told me you loaned them the money for the down payment. How good and generous of you, Janet."

Now he takes her hand again and she does not resist him.

"I... I suppose I should forgive them," she says, smiling at the sight of Raaz touching noses with Carya. "Who knows how much longer I have to live?"

"Long enough to spend many more happy days here," says Healing, gently squeezing Janet's hand.

"This morning at breakfast," she says, nodding in agreement, "Genevieve and I had the first civil conversation we've ever had. We even laughed about something together. I can't remember what it was, but... she seemed to like me."

"Did you like *her*?" he asks, nodding hopefully.

Janet looks away. "I resisted."

"No time to waste," he whispers, giving her hand another squeeze.

"You're right," she says, smiling girlishly. "I know you're right."

*

That night after doing his stretching exercises, Healing climbs into bed and inquires, "How go things with the people of the Kalahari?"

"The men just killed an eland," says Jahera, her eyes sparkling, "so there is great rejoicing in the camp. Ko-wi was producing very little milk for her baby, and now with her portion of the eland meat and fat, and more fat given to her by the others, she may be able to make enough milk so her baby won't die."

"How generous of her friends to help her in this way," says Healing, moved by such sacrifice.

"It's more than generosity," says Jahera, turning off her light. "Everything they do springs from a deep knowing that without each other there is no hope of survival."

Ω

13. Moshe

On the thirteenth of December, the seventh day of Hanukkah, the day dawns sunny in Mercy for the first time this month, and while the homeschoolers spend the morning at Reggie Chan's house making things out of clay, Healing and Tova take the dogs on a beach walk.

With the formidable cold keeping everyone else away from the beach, the dogs are unleashed and Coosi, Puccini, and Flora race away to where the incoming waves touch the shore, while Mendelssohn, Socrates, and little Max stay close to Healing and Tova.

"I woke this morning to the kids playing their accordions in their bedroom," says Tova, smiling at her father. "They took them off to eat breakfast and put them on again until it was time to go to school."

"What were they playing?" asks Healing, having given the children two short lessons every day since they unwrapped their little accordions on the first evening of Hanukkah. "Scales? Chords? Songs?"

"Raaz plays *Itsy Bitsy Spider* over and over again," says Tova, giving her father a doleful look, "while Oz plays random notes to accompany *Itsy Bitsy Spider*. And, yes, I have resorted to earplugs."

"I would say I'm sorry," says Healing, laughing, "but I'm thrilled."

"Speaking of thrilled," says Tova, taking a deep breath, "Daniel called this morning from France to tell me he is now calling his movie *Delphine and the Conjurer*."

"Which means you are now the title character," says Healing, pleasantly surprised.

"*If* I go back to France and film the scenes Daniel wrote *after* he watched the rough cut and felt the movie should be about Delphine and not about Andre."

"Have you read the new scenes?" asks Healing, marveling at Tova's good fortune.

"Yes," she says, shivering with excitement. "They're wonderful. It's much more a comedy now. And when I told Daniel I wouldn't do it if Lucien was involved, he said he will never work with Lucien again, so... I would be gone for five weeks, possibly six. I was hoping the accordion players could stay with you while I'm gone."

"We will be delighted to host them in your absence," he says, bowing to her. "When will you go?"

"Mid-January. And just so you know... Darvin and I are no longer kissing, so things are a bit raw between us now."

"Drat. I thought Darvin was perfect for you."

"Oh maybe he is, Pa-pa. But I haven't recovered from what happened with Lucien, and that colors everything. When the kids unwrapped their accordions and were so happy, all I could think of was how incredibly selfish Lucien is. Yet I *married* him and had children with him."

"For which I will be eternally grateful," says Healing, who cannot imagine life without Raaz and Oz.

"I was an idiot to even *consider* moving them away from you," says Tova, bowing her head. "Thank God they have you for their father."

"Thank God they have you for their mother," he says, embracing her. "And Jahera and Maahiah and Naomi and Eliana and Darby and Marjorie, and the cats and dogs. They do not lack for love."

"Nor do I," she says, relaxing in his arms. "Thank you, Pa-pa. Forever and ever thank you."

*

Home from the beach, Healing and Tova find Naomi and Jahera and Maahiah at the kitchen table in the thrall of momentous news.

"What happened?" asks Healing, holding his breath. "The kids okay?"

"The kids are fine," says Naomi, clearly upset. "I suggest you both sit down."

Healing sits next to Jahera, Tova next to Maahiah.

"Yesterday morning," says Naomi, clearing her throat, "Jean told Albert she wanted to return to Mercy in March and Albert flew into a rage and assaulted her. She ran into the backyard where Albert exhausted himself chasing her. He then went back in the house and called Connie and Fred to come over."

"Is Jean okay?" asks Healing, stunned by the news.

"Yes, but there's more," says Jahera, getting up to put a kettle on. "When Fred and Connie arrived, they joined Albert in demanding Jean see a neurologist because Albert claims Jean is suffering from dementia and wants her declared incompetent to make decisions for herself."

"Are they in*sane*?" says Tova, outraged. "Jean is the least demented person in the entire world."

"They *are* insane," says Naomi, nodding wearily. "I knew Jean wanted to return here sooner than later to spend more time with me, and I knew Albert would protest, but I never imagined he would stoop to anything so insidious as this."

"I'll go to England," says Healing, jumping up. "I hate to fly, but I will for Jean."

"Not necessary, Shafi," says Jahera, going to him. "She mollified them by saying she'd changed her mind about coming here, and they believed her. Then last night she escaped to London and flew to New York. She called from La Guardia a little while ago to tell us she'll be arriving in San Francisco this afternoon."

"We'll go pick her up," says Tova, excitedly. "If we leave now we'll be there when she lands."

"Also not necessary," says Naomi, taking Tova's hand. "Darla Rosenfeld, Jean's new friend who had raccoons in her belfry is on her way to San Francisco even as we speak."

"Thank God Jean's safe," says Healing, collapsing on the sofa. "What a nightmare. How could Connie and Fred have gone along with this?"

"Albert has poisoned them with lies about Jean since they were children," says Naomi, wearily. "Now they are middle-aged, and his lies, as the neurologists would say, are hardwired into their psyches." She smiles wanly. "By the way, you had a call from a man named Joel Schlesinger about his dog Moshe. A large mixed breed. I was on *our* phone with Joel when Jahera got the call from Jean on *her* phone, so I did little more than write down Joel's name and number. Referred by Rabbi Feinberg. Joel and his wife Irene recently moved here from Los Angeles and are hopeful you can discover the source of Moshe's sadness."

*

Oz and Raaz successfully lobby their mother into letting them stay up to greet Jean, but by eight-thirty the little ones are fast asleep in the guest room and do not stir when Jean and Darla arrive at eleven.

After Darla departs, the collective convenes in the living room – Naomi and Tova sitting with Jean on the sofa, Healing sitting on the floor with the dogs, Maahiah sitting in the rocking chair knitting, and Jahera standing with her back to the fire.

"The day I got home to Exeter," says Jean, holding Tova's hand, "which seems like the distant past, though it was only eleven days ago, Albert threw a huge tantrum and said if I ever went away again he would divorce me and make sure I didn't get a dime in the settlement. This has been his favorite declaration since I began coming to Mercy after Mum moved back here, so I thought little of it and asked him, 'What if Mum falls ill and I want to be with her?' And he said, 'You were just there. Don't you remember? This *proves* you have dementia.'"

"*Albert* sounds demented, not you," says Healing, pained to think of what Jean has endured for most of her life.

"He first accused me of having dementia when I started raising schnauzers forty years ago," says Jean, wincing at a sharp pain in her neck. "And he said it so many times since then I ceased to take notice. But this time the veil was lifted and I saw how deeply deranged he is."

"Horrid man," says Naomi, who almost never speaks ill of anyone. "Forgive me for saying so, but that's what he is."

"Then what happened?" asks Tova, who met Albert once when she was a teenager and once again in her twenties, and both times found him vile.

"Well when I first got home he said to me, 'Connie and Fred and I think you need to see a neurologist to measure the severity of your dementia.' And when I said, 'Don't be ridiculous,' and went out into the garden to get some air, he ran after me shouting, 'It's freezing cold out here. Do you want to catch pneumonia? This *proves* you have dementia.'" She shrugs. "I saw there was no reasoning with him, so..." She looks at Healing. "...using the tone of voice we employ when speaking to angry dogs I said, 'You need a good cup of tea, dear. I'll make a pot and we'll calm down and get things back to the way you like them. How does that sound?' And in a twinkling he was a big blubbering baby saying he only wanted things to be the way they were before I started going away. I petted him and reassured him, and when we'd had our tea he was back to being snide and bossy and critical, along with a new habit of muttering in unintelligible sing song."

"Oh Jean," says Healing, aching in sympathy. "I'm so sorry."

"Don't be," she says, shaking her head. "No one *made* me throw my life away. I did so voluntarily, and Albert was happy to take advantage. It was only when I started coming here every year after Mum moved back that he became unhinged." She turns to her mother. "I think if I had realized how incapable he was of adjusting to anything even slightly new, I would have trained a replacement to do the thousand

and one things I did for him every day since we wed fifty-three years ago. Yet it never occurred to me that he would feel so helpless without me because he'd called me an idiot so many times I'd come to believe I *was* an idiot and couldn't survive without *him*, which I disproved every time I came home to Mercy." She looks at Tova. "He knew I thrived here and hated that I did."

"You slaved for that monster from the moment you married him," says Naomi, seething with anger. "Ezra and I found it unbearable to be in the presence of him abusing you, which is why we only came to visit you in Exeter once after we moved back to England, and why we insisted you come alone when you visited us in Oxford."

"So what did you do when you realized Albert was insane?" asks Jahera, who grew up with a severely abusive father.

"I began preparing to escape," says Jean, fighting her tears. "In the event he and Connie and Fred tried to prevent me from leaving."

"But why would Connie and Fred think there was anything wrong with you?" asks Tova, baffled. "Surely they could see Albert was the crazy one, not you."

"Sadly they couldn't," says Jean, shaking her head. "When they're with Albert they become his sycophants. It's really quite horrifying to watch them groveling to him."

"Oh Jean," says Tova, putting her arm around her. "You were trapped in an existential horror movie."

"Funny you should say that," says Jean, laughing a little, "because I kept thinking of those Hitchcock films where the sane person is the victim of a madman, and everyone thinks the madman is sane and the sane person is mad."

"How did you prepare to escape?" asks Healing, awed by his sister's resilience in the face of such horror.

"Well the first thing I did was throw myself into the role of obsequious wife to lull Albert into believing I was content in my role as his servant, and then whenever he would go to the university I would pack my most precious things in two suitcases I kept hidden where I knew Albert would never look."

"What about money?" asks Maahiah, looking up from her knitting. "If you used a credit card they'd be able to track you."

"I thought of that," says Jean, nodding. "So I withdrew ten thousand pounds in cash from one of our accounts to pay for travel expenses. I've always handled our finances because Albert is inept with money, so I knew he would be unaware of my withdrawing those funds as well as my transferring fifty thousand pounds to Mum's account at Mercy Savings."

"But if Albert was clueless about what you were doing, why did he attack you?" asks Tova, mystified.

"Because yesterday afternoon I made a grievous error," says Jean, closing her eyes. "Seems like a lifetime ago, but it was only yesterday. After ten days of playing the part of submissive slave and thinking Albert was his old self again, I brought up the subject of coming to visit Mum."

"And he freaked out," says Tova, holding her breath.

"He struck me without warning," says Jean, wincing as she recalls the blow. "He tried to punch me in the face, but he's rather clumsy and I was able to dodge and he only struck my shoulder. Even so, he outweighs me by seven stone and the blow knocked me down. Then as I was crawling away he kicked my leg so hard I thought he'd broken it. Thank God he didn't and I was able to scramble out the door into the garden where he chased me around the goldfish pond until he thought he was having a heart attack and stopped. I'm in far better shape than he, so I had no difficulty eluding him, though his rage was terrifying. Then he went back inside and called Fred and Connie. I could hear him shouting that *I* had attacked *him* and he needed help subduing me."

"Did he let you back inside?" asks Jahera, horrified. "It must have been freezing."

"It was," says Jean, crying a little. "I considered running down the road to our nearest neighbors, but they loathe us because Albert is always so hideous to them, and dusk was falling and I knew if I involved the neighbors there would be a huge mess that might take months to extricate myself from. So instead I called through the open door, 'I'm so sorry, dear. I didn't mean to upset you. What will Connie and Fred think if they find me out here freezing to death? I'm sure they won't like the look of that.' And he let me back in."

"You weren't afraid he'd attack you again?" asks Healing, wishing he'd been there to protect her.

"No because I armed myself with a large weeding knife from the garden shed and stood just inside the kitchen door waiting for Connie and Fred to arrive. I didn't think they'd side with Albert once they saw how deranged he was. But when they got there, they listened to him as if he was a holy sage and joined him in demanding I see a neurologist to gauge the depth of my affliction."

"How could they not see how crazy he was?" asks Tova, irate with disbelief.

"Why do we allow psychopaths to rule the world?" says Naomi, putting her hand on Jean's arm. "Tell us how you finally escaped."

"I thought of the make-believe games Healing and I played when we were children," says Jean, gazing fondly at her brother. "How we would transform ourselves into characters we imagined ourselves to be. Then I blinked at Connie and Fred as if I was waking from a trance and said, 'Oh my God. All this time I've been under the spell of my past life in Mercy and was powerless to escape. But now that you've shown me how much you love me and care for me, the spell has been broken and I will gladly spend the rest of my life here with you.' And miracle of miracles, Connie softened and gave me a hug, which is *so* unlike her, and then Fred ordered takeout Chinese to celebrate. We opened a bottle of champagne and they all got nicely drunk while I only pretended to drink. I laughed at their inanities and thanked them again and again for saving me, and they were reassured, and Fred kept saying, 'So good to have you back, Mum. We thought we'd lost you. We really did.'"

"How cunning you were," says Maahiah, nodding approvingly.

"I felt cunning," says Jean, her eyes narrowing. "And that night, *last* night, Albert allowed me to prepare his sleeping potion as I always do, and I gave him four times his usual dose. And while he slept I got a taxi to the train station, caught the evening train to London, transferred to a train to Heathrow, and now I'm here, and here I'll stay." She kisses her mother's cheek. "Oh and one other thing. Before I got in the taxi to go to the train station, I threw my mobile phone into the gorse bushes so no one could track me."

*

The next morning after breakfast, the children play their accordions for Jean before leaving with Tova and Jahera to walk to Arjun's house for school.

Healing builds up the faltering fire, fetches the old landline phone from the kitchen counter, settles on the sofa with various cats settling on him, and calls Joel Schlesinger.

"Oh Mr. Weintraub," says Joel, his second language Yiddish. "Thank you so much for calling. Rabbi Feinberg praises you to the heavens."

"I'm glad. Please call me Healing. How may I help you?"

"From Los Angeles a year ago my wife Irene and I moved to Mercy. We knew the winters were cold here, but Siberia? This we didn't expect. I'm a golfer and not a good one, but I love to play. This is why we bought a house on the golf course here in Southport instead of buying the house next door to our daughter Judy and her husband Jeff and their daughter Sara who is seven and the reason we moved here. They live at the north end of Mercy."

"Next door to the Guptas," says Healing, laughing. "I've met Judy and Jeff and Sara several times. Charming people with delightful dachshunds."

"Phoebe and Dexter," says Joel, his tone revealing his love for the little dogs. "We should have gotten little ones, too, but this we didn't know six years ago when Irene came home with Moshe who was small and sweet because he was a baby. Now he is the opposite of small, though still very sweet. Our vet in Los Angeles thinks Moshe is part Great Dane and part some other large dog or dogs. Whatever he is, we love him, all one hundred pounds of him. And until six months ago he was happy. Now he mopes. All the time. We took him to the Mercy vet and she suggested we give him more exercise. More than three miles every morning? I'm eighty-one, Irene is eighty, but okay, a two-mile walk we added in the afternoon. Still he mopes. What could it be?"

"When next you come to see Sara and Judy and Jeff, please bring Moshe to our house and I'll give you my opinion. Today is good and so is tomorrow."

"Both good for us, too. Rabbi told me you do this kind of work as a mitzvah, which is admirable, but I would like to pay you for your trouble. God made me rich. May I?"

"If I'm able to help you with Moshe," says Healing, enjoying the way Joel arranges his words, "you may pay me whatever makes you happy."

"Excellent," says Joel, laughing. "Happiness is what we're after here. How does two o'clock this afternoon sound?"

"Perfect," says Healing, smiling as Jean comes in from the garden with the dogs. "We look forward to meeting Moshe."

"Dog case?" asks Jean as Healing returns the phone to its cradle.

"Dog case," says Healing, giving her a hug. "How you doing, Sis?"

"Everything is new," she says, gazing around in wonder. "I feel light as air, as if I've been living under the gravity of Jupiter my whole life, and now moving about is effortless." She smiles incredulously. "There's nothing holding me down now so I can do anything I want."

*

At two, the sky dark with rain clouds, Joel and Irene Schlesinger arrive at the little old house with their enormous hound Moshe. Healing greets them out front with a hearty *Shalom,* and after a brief interaction with Moshe, Healing knows why the big dog mopes.

Which is why he is not the least surprised when he unleashes Moshe in the backyard and the big hound rushes to meet the resident hounds, his joy unbounded.

"You have a dog park in your backyard," says Irene, pointing at Moshe mixing with the friendly pooches. "Are *all* those dogs yours?"

"Three of them live across the street with another elderly dog," says Healing, pleased to see Moshe being so gentle with the puppies Flora and Max, "but they are all members of the Weintraub collective."

"Maybe *this* is what Moshe needs," says Joel, taking Irene's arm as they follow Healing. "More dogs. We could get another one but as I mentioned on the phone, I'm eighty-one and Irene is eighty and Moshe is strong as Hercules, so..."

"Come inside and get warm," says Healing ushering them up the stairs onto the deck. "The dogs will be in shortly."

"If you say so," says Irene, watching Moshe chase Coosi and Puccini. "Look how happy the big lunk is. We'll just bring him *here* every day." She laughs. "I'm kidding. Of course we won't. We make jokes, Joel and I. We're impossible."

*

Over cookies and tea and coffee, Joel and Irene tell Healing, Jahera, Jean, and Naomi about their life in Los Angeles where Joel made a fortune in the jewelry business and Irene was a movie makeup artist.

"When Judy and Jeff moved to Mercy from Los Angeles and had the *nerve* to take Sara with them," explains Irene, "we had no choice but to move here, too."

"Judy is our only child," says Joel, dipping his cookie in his coffee. "A big surprise when we were in our late forties. And I mean big. She weighed nine pounds."

"According to Judy, Sara will be our only grandchild," says Irene, looking skyward. "We hope not, but time is running out." She shrugs and laughs. "Oh well. But listen to this. In Los Angeles where Joel and I were both born, we developed breathing problems when Joel was seventy-three and I was seventy-two."

"We took every lung medicine known to man, but our lungs did not improve," says Joel, shaking his head.

"The doctors were not optimistic," says Irene, shaking her head, too.

"We were both on a waiting list for lung transplants," says Joel, remembering how frightened he was of surgery.

"Still... when Judy and Jeff and Sara moved here, we had to come even if it meant being far-away from the nearest lung specialist." Irene raises her arms to supplicate God. "Because why go on living if we can't see our Sara every day?"

"Then three months after we moved here," says Joel, raising a knowing finger, "we were walking on the beach with Moshe and I said, 'I don't know about you, ziskeit, but I'm breathing better than I have since we met in high school.' And Irene said..."

"Me, too," says Irene, grinning at Naomi. "Lo and behold our breathing problems were gone. Who knew? Not the doctors. I feel fifty-seven again."

"And how's this for ironic?" says Joel, winking at Jahera. "My grandfather was living in Detroit in 1922 and developed lung problems, so his doctor suggested he move to... wait for it... Los Angeles, in those days famous for clean air."

"True we'd like it warmer here," says Irene, shrugging, "but where it's warm all the people go and the air is lousy."

"Now we live here with our dog who mopes," says Joel, sighing audibly. "Or he *did* mope until he came to your dog park."

"Look how happy he is," says Irene, smiling as Moshe enters the kitchen with the mob of dogs. "Who knew?"

"Kum da Moshe," says Joel speaking Yiddish to the big happy hound. "Is this the problem? You've been missing your own kind?"

Moshe smiles and wags his tail and rests his big snout on Joel's lap.

"May we assume you took Moshe to dog parks in Los Angeles?" asks Jean, giving Moshe a kiss when he presents himself to her.

"Are rabbis Jewish?" says Joel, sipping his coffee. "Every day we took him. Sometimes twice."

"When my friends would ask me what I'd been doing since I retired," says Irene, laughing, "I would say, 'Sara and Moshe. Moshe and Sara. What else do I have time for?'"

"I'm pleased to tell you that you have correctly diagnosed the source of Moshe's moping," says Healing, gladdened by the love shown between Moshe and his people. "Given there are no dog parks here in Mercy, and since getting another dog is not a viable option for you..."

"The solution is obvious," continues Naomi. "You can bring Moshe here whenever you come to town and he can spend time with our dogs."

"If he's here when we walk our dogs," says Jahera, refilling Irene's coffee cup, "we'll take him with us."

"Are you serious?" says Joel, incredulously. "We come to town every day. You want we should bring him every day?"

"As often as you like," says Naomi, getting up to put the kettle on. "We like Moshe very much, and we like you, too."

"I think I'm too happy now," says Irene, getting a handkerchief out of her purse.

"Happiness is what we're after here," says Healing, winking at Joel.

"Happiness is what we've found," says Joel, putting his arm around Irene. "Rabbi said this guy was a mensch, and about this she was not mistaken."

*

After supper, Healing answers the phone and is delighted to hear the voice of his cousin Norman calling from Oxford.

"Healing," says Norman, his tone grave, "I hate to be the bearer of bad news but Jean disappeared from her house in Exeter two days ago and a massive search is underway to find her. Albert told the police Jean is suffering from advanced dementia. I had no idea. The police found her mobile phone in the gorse and fear she may have fallen into the hands of those who might harm her. Her picture is all over the news here."

"Hold that thought, Norman," says Healing, covering the mouthpiece with his hand. "Jean. It's Cousin Norman. He says all of England has been alerted to your disappearance *and* your dementia."

"Norman is just the person I wanted to talk to," says Jean, rising from the sofa to take the phone from Healing. "I shall engage him to handle my divorce."

"Norman is a renowned solicitor and a doppelganger of the late Michael Redgrave," explains Naomi, looking over the tops of her glasses at Jahera. "My brother Joshua's son."

"Norman darling," says Jean, cheerfully. "It's Cousin Jean. I'm so glad you called. I'm fit as a fiddle and sharp as a tack. Living with Mum and Healing and the family here in Mercy. What a terrible bunch of twaddle Albert has concocted. I wonder why he would do such a thing? And speaking of twaddle, is this a good time to speak about my plans to divorce him?"

Ω

14. Miguelito

Five days before Christmas, the new *Susan Paul* gallery hosts a holiday variety show attended by two hundred people. Admission is twenty dollars, proceeds to benefit the Mercy Food Bank, and Sherriff Higuera is on hand to oversee the festivities and keep an eye on several young men in the audience who play for opposing soccer teams notorious for their off-field skirmishes.

Darla Rosenfeld opens the show with a hilarious monologue comparing her previous life in Los Angeles to her current life in Mercy, and accompanies her spiel with juxtaposed photographs illustrating these two realities projected on a large screen – the audience roaring with laughter throughout.

Helen Morningstar follows with five poems full of references to people and places in Mercy, and her rhyming poem *The Mercy Post Office* brings the house down.

Act One closes with Darvin and Healing performing one of the songs Darvin has composed for Marianne Savoy's movie *Essentiel*, Darvin tickling the ivories of the gallery's Steinway grand, Healing playing accordion, the audience loving every note.

Following a lengthy intermission featuring fabulous finger food and excellent wine, Healing's band Mercy Me performs two jazzy instrumentals and backs Tova singing Dietz and Schwartz's *You and the Night and the Music* followed by a sultry rendition of Sam Cooke's *You Send Me* that inspires cheering and whistling and cries of, "You send me, too, honey!" and "Cásate conmigo!"

And lastly the show's headliner takes the stage: Guillermo Ontiveros, a burly Mexicano with wavy black hair wearing a San Francisco Giants T-shirt, a Giants baseball cap on backwards, baggy trousers, and a flaming red guitar slung around his neck. Star of the hit television show *Hermanos Hermanas y Dolores*, Guillermo was born and raised in Mercy and comes home several times a year to hang out with family and friends.

When the shouts of *Guillo!* and *Arriba!* and *Andale!* die down, Guillermo takes the microphone off the stand and gazes lovingly at the audience.

"For the seven of you who aren't my cousins or married to my cousins or *about* to marry my cousins, my name is Guillermo Ontiveros. Everybody around here calls me Guillo. But in Los Angeles where I live now, nobody knows who I am. I'm just one of five million Mexican guys who needs to lose weight." He laughs along with the audience. "As most of you know I went to Mercy High with Tova. She was cute back then, you know, pero ahora ella es deliciosa caliente increíble! Que paso, mujer?"

The crowd roars and Guillermo puts the microphone back on the stand to free his hands to play an impeccable flamenco flourish on his guitar.

"Tova and I were in a play together in high school," says Guillermo, taking the microphone off its stand again. "It's true. I played the part of un tonto who was madly in love with her. She was the princess and I was the court jester." He makes a face to say *You know what I'm talking about.* "Type casting."

The audience roars again, and so begins Guillermo's hour-long monologue about growing up in Mercy and his early days in show biz interspersed with dazzling guitar riffs – everyone laughing until they cry.

*

In the ebullient chaos at show's end, Tova approaches Darvin and says, "If it were possible to get pregnant from listening to music, I would now be pregnant from listening to you play the piano."

"If men could get pregnant," says Darvin, smiling wistfully, "I would now be pregnant from listening to you sing."

"So..." she says, expectantly. "We're friends again?"

"Friends," he says, embracing her. "Mutually musically impregnating friends with children home-schooling together."

"What could be better than that?" she says, immediately regretting her choice of words. "I mean... you know what I mean. Better to be musically impregnating friends than not friends at all."

"Much better," he says, letting her go. "And just so you know, I don't regret for a moment exploring the possibility of a romantic liaison with you. God knows I need the practice."

"Me, too," she says, mystified by her decision to stop kissing him.

And she very well might have resumed kissing him right then and there had not Jean and Darla come to spirit her away to celebrate at *Big Goose*.

*

Over pancakes the next morning, Oz and Raaz want to hear all about the variety show they missed.

"We *would* have gone," says Oz, explaining to Darby and Marjorie, "only they started right at our bed time. So we couldn't go."

"The show was too late for me, too," says Naomi, nodding sympathetically. "I shall have to speak to the gallery people about hosting daytime variety shows."

"Too late for us, too," says Darby, giving Marjorie's hand a squeeze. "Not for Margy, but for me. I'm out like a light by nine."

"We can always host variety shows here," says Healing, flipping pancakes while Jean tends the bacon. "In the living room or on the deck when the weather's good."

"Maybe we could have a variety show for our birthday," suggests Raaz, looking at Tova. "Can we, Mama?"

"I don't see why not," says Tova, yawning. "We'll have it at our house with a piano for Darvin in our much bigger living room so more people can come."

Oz and Raaz exchange wide-eyed looks.

"Are we *really* getting a piano?" asks Oz, gaping at his mother.

"We really are," says Tova, yawning again. "As soon as I get back from France we'll go piano shopping with Darvin and Esther."

"I can't *wait* for you to get back from France," says Raaz, pouting. "Why do you have to *be* in that movie?"

"It's my job," says Tova, holding out her arms to Raaz. "It's how I make money to buy the piano and all those shoes you grow out of a week after we buy them."

"Okay," says Raaz, climbing onto her mother's lap.

"Okay," croaks Bogart from his cage in the corner.

Everyone turns to look at the elderly parrot who hasn't spoken since Bacall, his partner of twenty-eight years, died some weeks ago. He bobs up and down on his perch to ask for a treat, and Maahiah obliges by bringing him a piece of dried apricot.

"Are we getting a new parrot?" asks Oz, looking at Healing. "So Bogart won't be lonely?"

"No we are not," says Healing, turning to look at Bogart in his cage. "The era of parrots in this house will end with Humphrey Bogart."

"Why?" asks Oz, frowning. "Don't you like parrots anymore?"

"I love parrots," says Healing, smiling at his grandson. "But I no longer want to keep birds in cages. Better they should live in the wild or in a spacious coop with access to a large scratch yard."

"We might get a kitten when Mama gets back from France," says Raaz, sliding off her mother's lap to go visit Bogart. "We only have two cats at our house now and four dogs, and one of them is Kadan who might die from arthritis."

"Two cats are plenty for now," says Tova, giving Jean a look to say *More coffee, please?* "As are four dogs."

"I was at Darla's yesterday," says Jean, bringing the coffee pot to the table, "and she had *so* many little birds in her yard it made me wonder why *we* have so few birds, and then I realized Darla doesn't have a cat."

"Cats do wreak havoc on the bird population," says Naomi, resigned to the truth. "Not to mention catching lizards and snakes. This is the onus of owning cats."

"Reggie has two cats," says Oz, joining Raaz at the parrot cage to watch Maahiah give Bogart a cracker. "Only they never go outside, so they have lots of birds on their bird feeders."

"Oh I would never keep a cat indoors all the time," says Naomi, shaking her head. "It's torture for them not to be able to go outside. Better not to have a cat at all."

"I once went five years without a cat when Mum was living in England," says Healing, distributing pancakes to the various plates. "The backyard bird population exploded and the Japanese maples were full of nests. There were lizards sunning on the garden path and beautiful snakes who caught all the gophers. We even had a family of goldfinches nesting in the oak at the northeast corner of the yard. Then I got two cats and they quickly dispatched the snakes and lizards and most of the little birds."

"But we *love* cats," says Oz with dismay. "What should we do?"

"We make a choice," says Jean, gazing out the window at the garden. "That's what life is *all* about, Oz. The choices we make."

*

After breakfast the children return to their house with Tova to await the arrival of Sheila Liebowitz and Carlos Rodriguez for a play date, Maahiah puts five loaves of bread in the oven and goes upstairs with Jahera to work on the new menus for the East Cove Hotel, Healing builds up the fire, and Naomi settles on the sofa to watch Healing and Jean give the dogs a good brushing.

"I so love the smell of bread baking," says Naomi, watching Jean snip Mendelssohn's broken toenail while Healing brushes Socrates.

"There's nothing better than that first warm slice with a bit of butter. Nothing."

"I baked bread every week when Fred and Connie were little," says Jean, remembering her sweet children before they became surly teenagers and snooty adults. "They loved to drizzle honey on their bread, and by the time they'd had their fill they were gloriously sticky. I'd put them in the tub, and while they turned the bathroom into a swamp, I'd clean the kitchen." Her smile fades. "Then Albert convinced them grocery store bread was superior to mine and thereafter they refused to eat my bread. So I stopped baking." She muses. "I think I may take it up again. My sourdough was quite good and my challah was good, too, though not as good as Papa's."

"I *love* a good sour dough," says Healing, nodding emphatically. "I hope you do resume your baking."

"I never baked," says Naomi, lying down. "Ezra did all our baking, as you know. He learned from his grandmother. He made rye and buckwheat for our daily bread, and challah for special occasions."

"Making bread teaches kindness," says Healing, brushing Socrates's legs. "Papa said that every time he put his loaves in the oven, and again when he took them out. I didn't know what he meant until I started making bread after you moved back to England. And then I understood. Unless we are kind to the ingredients, the bread never turns out well."

"Making bread was a holy act for Ezra," says Naomi, smiling at the thought of her husband. "He said he could feel angels gathering around him as he took the loaves from the oven and set them on the table to cool. Then he would cut a slice for us to share and we would taste it unadorned and say the first thing that came to mind, usually *Oh my God* or *Can this be true?* or simply *Yum*, and then we'd have the next piece slathered with butter, and then we'd start the water boiling for tea."

"Maahiah learned to bake from her mother," says Healing, looking into Coosi's eyes as he brushes him. "Every time she begins, she says a prayer in Arabic to thank her mother for teaching her to treat the dough as a beloved friend. I think that's what Papa meant by kindness. The more loving we are to the dough, the better the bread will be."

"I love Maahiah," says Naomi, snuggling under the blue afghan Maahiah knitted. "And I love both of you more than I can ever say."

*

Later than morning, Healing gets a phone call from Guillermo Ontiveros.

"Hola Healing," says Guillermo, his voice raspy this morning. "Como ahora?"

"Bien Guillo," says Healing, who worked with Guillermo at *Good Groceries* when Guillermo was a teenager. "You had the audience in the palm of your hand last night."

"How could I not?" says Guillermo, laughing. "Half the audience was my cousins and the other half was my aunts and uncles. Hey man, I love your band. Y *Tova*. What a voice. This a good time to talk?"

"Perfecto," says Healing, carrying the phone to the dining table.

"I got a dog problem. Conchita said to call you. You know my grandfather Marco died five years ago and my grandmother Julia stayed in her house all by herself. I didn't want her to be lonely so I got her a dog. A Chihuahua Pug. Miguelito. Grandma loves him, but she's eighty-eight and a couple months ago she moved in with my mother and my sister and my sister's three kids and my sister's boyfriend who has two big dogs who want to kill Miguelito. That's no joke. They would kill him if they could catch him, but he hides under the bed and they can't get under there. So I've been trying to find him a new home, you know, before we go back to LA, and so far the only cousin I can find to take him is Jaime who already has seven dogs and lives in a dump. Any ideas?"

"Can you bring Miguelito by today? I think I know someone who may want him."

"In a half-hour?"

"Perfecto."

*

Healing and Jean are waiting in front of the little old house when Guillermo and his wife Feliz arrive in a big white Tesla with Miguelito, a small brown cutie pie with pointy ears. Guillermo isn't wearing his baseball cap this morning, but Feliz is, her long black hair in a ponytail.

Feliz sets Miguelito on the ground and he trots up to Healing and Jean as if he's known them his whole life.

"Aren't you a darling," says Jean, reaching down to pet Miguelito, which causes the little dog to rise up on his hind legs.

"He does that to help you pick him up," says Feliz, pointing at Miguelito. "He learned to do that when Abuelita couldn't bend over so far anymore."

"I was at your show last night," says Jean to Guillermo as she picks up Miguelito. "I haven't laughed so hard maybe ever in my life."

"Gracias," says Guillermo, bowing to her. "You know... we would take Miggy to LA with us but we're not home much during the day and we travel a lot, so..."

"May we introduce him to our dogs?" asks Healing, taking Miguelito from Jean and touching noses with him before setting him on the ground. "The folks we know who might want him have a big friendly dog and we'd like to see how Miguelito behaves with our bigger dogs."

"He likes other dogs," says Feliz, exchanging looks with Guillermo. "If they don't try to kill him."

"Yeah," says Guillermo, resignedly. "Like I told you, my sister's boyfriend has these two grande macho dogs, you know. Fighting dogs. So it's no good for Miggy over there."

"I can assure you our dogs will not try to kill him," says Jean, dismayed by humans who encourage dogs to fight each other.

"However," says Healing, leading the way to the backyard gate, "since Miguelito may fear larger dogs after living with those grande macho dogs, I will keep hold of him for the initial introductions."

"He's brave," says Feliz, contemplating Miguelito. "But those two dogs are huge and all they want to do is kill other dogs."

"I'm sorry to hear that," says Healing, opening the gate. "Please don't tell me your sister's boyfriend pits them against other dogs or I'll be compelled to report him."

"We won't tell you," says Guillermo, shaking his head. "We know nothing."

*

Miguelito is ecstatic to meet the friendly resident dogs and follows Mendelssohn around the yard peeing where Mendelssohn pees.

"We'll take him," says Healing, enamored of the little pooch. "If our friends don't want him, we'll keep him."

"You *will*?" says Guillermo, grinning at Healing. "Are you sure?"

"Positive," says Jean, laughing as Miguelito chases after Coosi. "He's our kind of dog."

"I'm blown away," says Guillermo, red-faced with pleasure. "Let us give you some money. This is so good of you."

"No need," says Healing, making a faint whistling sound to summon the dogs. "You've given us a great gift."

"Okay then I'll give your mother some money," says Guillermo, nodding assuredly. "*She* won't say no. You know why? Because when I was a kid I borrowed money from her to buy a skateboard and I never paid her back, and now I finally can."

"She'll be tickled," says Jean, tittering.

"That's what I do for a living," says Guillermo, winking at Healing. "I tickle people."

*

That afternoon, despite Oz and Raaz begging to keep Miguelito, Healing, Jean, Tova, and the children bundle up and walk across town with Miguelito to introduce him to Darvin and Esther and their big friendly dog Joe.

And though Joe and Miguelito greet each other cordially, the chemistry between the two dogs is zilch.

"I don't like little dogs," says Esther, wrinkling her nose at Miguelito. "I want another one like Joe."

Healing and Tova exchange looks to say *Well that's that*.

"Come in," says Darvin, beckoning. "We're making coffee and cocoa."

The adults gather at the kitchen table, Joe exits through his dog door into the backyard, the children go into the living room to play with Esther's wooden train set, and Miguelito sits contentedly on Jean's lap.

"He's a love," says Darvin, filling mugs with coffee. "We'll take him. Joe will get used to him and so will Esther, despite her initial response."

"I will *not* get used to him," says Esther, calling from the living room. "I hate little dogs."

"Max is little," says Oz, frowning at Esther. "You like *him*."

"Max is cute," says Esther, haughtily. "Migatito isn't cute at all."

"Not Miga*tito*," says Raaz, giggling. "Migue*lito*. It means *little Miguel*. I think he's very cute *and* very smart."

"I hate him," says Esther, shaking her head.

Oz's frown deepens. "Why do you hate him? He's a wonderful dog."

"I don't *want* him," shouts Esther, running down the hall to her bedroom. "He's ugly and stupid."

"Excuse me," says Darvin, with a congenial shrug. "I'll be right back."

"I'll distribute the coffee and stir the cocoa," says Tova, going into the kitchen.

Raaz climbs onto Healing's lap while Oz follows Tova into the kitchen.

"Mama?" says Oz, frowning gravely, "I think Esther is in a very bad mood."

"Happens to all of us now and then," says Tova, picking him up and holding him on her hip. "I used to make terrible fusses when I was little, didn't I Pa-pa?"

"You?" says Healing, feigning surprise. "Never. You were always a perfect angel."

"I used to get mad a lot," says Oz, nodding solemnly. "Remember when I wouldn't wear clothes?"

"Vaguely," says Tova, kissing him and setting him down. "A more poignant memory for me is when you were twenty pounds lighter."

"Such a curious thing about age and time," says Jean, who grows fonder of Miguelito with every passing minute. "It seemed I was ten-years-old forever, and now I'm just getting used to being the age I am when it's my birthday again."

Darvin returns with Esther.

"Your dog is nice," says Esther, taking her thumb out of her mouth, "but I don't want him."

"That's fine, dear," says Jean, smiling at her. "Thank you for telling us."

"You're welcome," says Esther, popping her thumb back into her mouth.

"Sit thyself," says Tova to Darvin. "I will serve the children their cocoa now."

Darvin sits and lifts Esther onto his lap, which inspires Oz to join his sister on Healing's lap.

"Nothing better than a good lap to sit on," opines Healing, gazing around at everyone.

"Nothing better," says Jean, looking down at Miguelito who gazes up at her with love in his eyes.

*

On Christmas morning, clear and cold, Darby, Marjorie, Eliana, and Darla join the collective for a waffle feast – Darby and Marjorie having brought along Pierre, their Jack Russell Terrier, who is instantly smitten with Miguelito and vice-versa.

When the last waffle has disappeared, the company moves into the living room where Healing and Eliana play *Jingle Bells* and *Hark the Herald Angels Sing* on their big accordions, and everyone sings along while Oz and Raaz noodle on their little accordions. For the finale, Tova, Jahera, Eliana, and Maahiah sing an exquisite four-part harmony version of The Beatles' *Blackbird*.

As the festivities draw to a close, Darby inquires of Healing, "You wouldn't happen to be looking for a home for Miggy, would you? He and Pierre get along so well, we'd love to have him."

"A few days ago we would have gladly given him to you," says Healing, smiling at Darby. "But since then Miggy has become the darling of the household and the lap dog we've been longing for since Benito departed all those years ago."

"Well in any case," says Darby, pleased to see Pierre and Miguelito communing by the fire, "they'll be great pals from here on out."

*

Healing and Jahera retire to their bedroom at the end of the long day of visiting with friends, and Healing does some stretching on his yoga mat while Jahera sits up in bed reading *The People*.

"What news from the Kalahari?" asks Healing, rolling up his mat and stowing it under the bed.

"The people have just met eight new people, a little band of two young families descended from people Ha-wi remembers from when she was a girl. So now there are twenty-two people camped around the giant old Baobab tree, and everyone knows there is not enough water here to sustain so many people for much longer."

"A joyful time as I recall," says Healing, having read the Kalahari trilogy some years ago. "The men kill a gemsbok so there's lots of meat, and the new people have a boy and a girl who are good matches for a girl and boy among the people, so it's a difficult decision about who will stay and who will leave."

"If only it would rain they could stay together a while longer," says Jahera, closing the book and turning off her light. "I'm exhausted. Let's not do anything tomorrow."

"Good idea," says Healing, crawling into bed. "I'll let you break the news to the children in the morning while I get the fire going, feed the cats, and make breakfast for the collective and Clement and his mother and Justin and Helen as prelude to a beach walk and lunch with Diego and Teresa and their mothers."

"What about the day after?" murmurs Jahera, drifting off to sleep.

"The day after is far in the future," says Healing, closing his eyes and imagining rain falling on the desert. "Who knows what might happen?"

Ω

15. Kadan and Zoya

On January seventh, the morning cold and rainy, Isabella Cisneros drives across town from her veterinary clinic to Tova and Maahiah's house on a mission of mercy to end the life of Maahiah's old dog Kadan who can no longer get up to go outside and relieve himself.

Oz and Raaz have been visiting the old dog every day, petting him and talking to him, but despite Healing urging her to allow them to be there when Kadan dies, Tova decided *not* to involve the children in the end-of-life proceedings.

"They're only four," explained Tova, who is terribly conflicted about leaving her children for six weeks to go to France to star in the movie *Delphine and the Sorcerer*. "I'm not ready for them to watch their beloved friend die. I'm sorry, Pa-pa, but I can't deal with how upset they might be. We'll be at Arjun's for school when Isabella comes."

*

The sad deed done, Healing and Jahera lift the heavy body into a garden cart and pull the cart through the rain to the south end of the property where Healing spent several hours yesterday digging a deep hole to receive the body.

Jahera and Healing lower the body into the grave with the aid of Kadan's old blanket that will stay with the body, and Jean sprinkles in a handful of tasty chewies.

"Dear Kadan," says Healing, gazing at the corpse. "Stalwart companion. Thank you for sharing your life with us."

"Lovely soul," says Jean, placing her hands together and bowing to the corpse. "Come back soon."

"I love you Kadan," says Jahera, crying.

"Goodbye my love," says Maahiah, throwing the first handful of soil into the grave.

*

When the mourners return to the little old house, they find Naomi having tea with Sheriff Higuera, the rakishly handsome and unflappable Sheriff of Mercy, known to the members of the Weintraub collective as Ruben.

"Mi hermano," says Healing, always glad to see his good friend. "What brings you here on this stormy morning?"

"Please get dry first," says Ruben, smiling at everyone. "I'm here on official business, but there's no hurry."

Everyone sheds their raincoats, Healing builds up the fire, Jahera mollifies the dogs with treats, Jean grinds coffee beans for a fresh pot, and Maahiah busies herself making cookies.

"Now we are ready," says Healing, taking the chair next to Ruben.

"As I was telling your mother," says Ruben, nodding to Naomi, "we got a call this morning from a woman named Angela Sutherland, she's an assistant to the Vice-Consul of the British consulate in San Francisco inquiring about Jean."

"Oh dear," says Jean, pressing down the plunger of the French Press. "I was afraid something like this might happen."

Ruben nods. "I told Ms. Sutherland I spoke to you recently at the variety show and assured her you were in full command of your senses and not being held here against your wishes. Even so, she requested I interview you and videotape the interview for her to see. I said I would do so if you were amenable. We can do this at the station or here if you prefer. I'm sorry for the inconvenience, but this should keep them from sending somebody up here to bother you."

"We can make the video in my studio," says Jahera, pointing at the ceiling. "I have a little stage and my camera shoots excellent video with good sound." She gives Jean a wide-eyed look. "We'll light you like a movie star."

"Oh in that case," says Jean, affecting a haughty air, "I'll have to get all gussied up."

"Perfect," says Ruben, rising to go. "You get gussied up while I take a spin around town. I'll be back in an hour."

"We'll be ready," says Jahera, accompanying Ruben to the door. "But why not stay for coffee and my mother's cookies?"

"Oh do stay, Ruben," says Naomi, pointing out the window. "Look at the rain coming down. Stay cozy with us."

"Alas we are shorthanded today," says Ruben, putting on his raincoat and hat. "Otherwise I would. See you in an hour."

*

For her interview Jean sits in an armless chair on a little stage, the backdrop a blowup of one of Jahera's photographs of the beach at the mouth of the Mercy River with Jean and Healing small in the distance walking the dogs.

Wearing a teal dress shirt, her curly gray hair swept back from her face, Jean answers Ruben's questions about who she is, how she's feeling, and how she came to be in Mercy. Her answers amount to a brilliantly told autobiography beginning with her birth in this very house seventy-three years ago and culminating with her dramatic escape from Exeter a few weeks ago.

Having asked the requisite questions, Ruben says, "Is there anything else you'd like to add?"

"Yes," says Jean, somberly. "While I appreciate the consulate's concern for my well being, I want to make it perfectly clear that my husband Albert and my son and daughter did *not* request this investigation out of any real concern for me, but as part of their scheme to portray me as incompetent so they can deprive me of half the assets accrued by my husband and me over the course of our fifty-three years of marriage, assets I should be awarded through divorce. I do hope you will order them to desist in their harassment of me and my loving family here in Mercy."

Ruben signals Jahera to cease recording. "That was great, Jean."

"Thank you, Ruben," she says, standing up. "I appreciate the opportunity to say all that. Gives me a feeling of completion."

"A pleasure for me to hear," he says, shaking her hand. "Inspiring."

*

When Raaz and Oz get home from school, the first thing they do is hurry to Maahiah's cottage to visit Kadan as they have every day since he became too weak to do anything more than go outside to relieve himself.

Finding their old friend gone, they run back to the house shouting, "Mama! Kadan is gone. Where is he?"

"He died," says Tova, standing in the kitchen, trembling with fatigue and sorrow. "I'm so sorry."

"Where is he?" asks Oz, anxiously. "Where did they put him?"

"They buried him," says Tova, crying. "By the little pine forest."

"Can we go see?" asks Raaz, urgently.

"Yes," says Tova, sobbing. "I'll get my raincoat on."

So the children and Tova walk with Puccini and Flora and Max through the vegetable garden and take the path across the meadow to where Kadan is buried on the edge of a little stand of coastal pines.

"I wish we could see him," says Oz, gazing at the mound of soil.

"Me, too," says Raaz, nodding sadly.

"Maybe he'll hear you if you say goodbye now," says Tova, glad to see the children aren't more upset.

"Kadan," says Oz, standing near the grave. "We're going to plant a tree for you like they do at Shafi and Jadda's house. To make shade in the summer."

"With your name on a sign," says Raaz, standing next to her brother. "On a stick."

Puccini and Flora and Max sniff around the grave and Max lifts his leg and pees.

"He's telling Kadan he's here," says Raaz, turning to her mother. "Isn't he, Mama?"

"Yes," says Tova, crying some more. "Let's get out of the rain. We'll come again when it stops."

*

After supper at the little old house, the collective gathers in the living room and Jahera and Healing tell the story of how they and their big dog Carla found the starving newborn pups Kadan and Tabinda in an abandoned den in the forest near Harold and Shirley Silverstein's house.

"We rushed them to the veterinary clinic," says Jahera, sharing the sofa with Tova and Oz, "and Isabella wrapped the puppies in warm blankets and gave them puppy milk replacer. Then she kept them at the clinic for two days to make sure they were strong enough for us to bring home."

"Then they lived here for six months with Carla as their doting mother," says Healing, sitting in the rocking chair with Raaz on his lap. "After which Tabinda stayed with us and Kadan went to live with Maahiah."

Tabinda hears her name and gets up from her place by the fire to come get pets from Healing.

"I like having a dog sleep with me in my cottage," says Maahiah, sitting in the rocking chair knitting. "I was hoping Puccini would want to, but he prefers to stay in the house with Flora and Max. So I will get another dog, perhaps a small one like Miguelito and Max."

"We could go to the animal shelter tomorrow," says Raaz, jumping down from Healing's lap and running to Maahiah.

"What a good idea," says Maahiah, setting down her knitting to give Raaz a hug. "Only I want to wait a little longer until I'm not so sad about Kadan being gone. We'll go in a week or so."

"I'm very good at choosing puppies," says Oz, getting down from the sofa and climbing onto Healing's lap. "Aren't I, Shafi? I picked out Flora and Max, didn't I?"

"Yes, you did," says Healing, hugging Oz. "I'm sure you will prove most valuable in choosing Maahiah's new companion."

*

So on January sixteenth, three days after Tova left for France to make her movie, the children and adults of the collective, minus Naomi, walk across town to the Mercy Animal Shelter where they find dozens of dogs, young and old, in need of homes.

Oz and Raaz hurry from pen to pen searching for a likely little dog while Jahera takes pictures and Jean communes with an elderly Schnauzer.

"Choose for me, Shafi," says Maahiah, standing next to Healing. "She can be any size."

And in that moment, Healing sees a young dog sitting in the far corner of a pen she's sharing with four other young dogs. She feels Healing's gaze, looks at him, and raises a paw to beckon him.

"Here she is," says Healing, his heart pounding as he goes to her. "With golden brown hair like Moosh."

*

Emilia Martinez, who has worked at the Mercy Animal Shelter for thirty years, informs the collective that the young dog was found by a man and woman hunting for mushrooms in a forest a few miles south of Mercy.

"They said she followed them out of the woods to their car," says Emilia, overseeing Maahiah filling out the adoption papers. "They said they would have kept her but they live in a studio apartment in San Francisco and didn't have any room for her. She's been here nine days. We think she had some obedience training because she likes to be on a leash and she obeys pretty well. We think she's six-months-old, half Rhodesian Ridgeback, part Golden Labrador, part Dalmatian."

"My surmise differs slightly from yours," says Healing, clipping a leash to the young dog's collar and giving her a treat. "I think she's four-months-old, quarter-Ridgeback, quarter Golden Retriever, quarter Golden Lab, and quarter Harrier. Her down-hanging ear flaps are classic Harrier, as is the white splotch on her flank."

"I wondered about her ears," says Emilia, smiling at Healing. "When you take her to Isabella for her next round of shots, have them do a DNA test and tell them to put it on our bill. I'm curious to see if you're right."

"So am I," says Healing, petting the happy dog. "Not that it matters."

*

In the living room of the little old house, Maahiah keeps the young dog on a leash for her initial meeting with the dogs from both households – Puccini, Flora, Max, Mendelssohn, Socrates, Coosi, Miguelito, and Tabinda.

Watching the pup happily mingling with the other dogs, Maahiah says, "I'm going to call her Zoya."

"What does Zoya mean, Mamon?" asks Jahera, taking pictures of the excited dogs.

"*Loving*," says Maahiah, unleashing the pup.

"Now," says Healing, speaking to Oz and Raaz, "for the next several weeks Maahiah will do most of the handling and feeding of Zoya until she understands that Maahiah is her primary human."

"I'll keep her in my cottage with me at night," says Maahiah, laughing as Zoya plays with Flora and Max who are just her size. "Until she learns she lives there."

"But we can still play with her, can't we?" asks Oz, wrinkling his nose.

"Of course you can," says Healing, nodding. "Speaking of which, let's give her a bath to start her new life with us."

"I must say I was expecting another little dog," says Naomi, sitting on the sofa with Miguelito on her lap. "Judging by Zoya's paws and stature, she may eventually be bigger than Socrates."

"I think you're right, Mum," says Healing, heading down the hall to the bathroom to start the bath. "No Chihuahua she."

*

That evening when the children finally succumb to sleep in the guest room, and Healing returns from walking Maahiah and Zoya to Maahiah's cottage, a game of Scrabble ensues with Jahera taking an early lead by spelling REFLEX with her X on a Triple Letter square.

"Quite a pack we've got here now," says Jean, glancing at the eight pooches slumbering by the fire.

"Remember," says Healing, pondering his rack of letters, "three of those dogs are visiting from across the street, though I agree the entirety does verge on overwhelming."

"I remember when we had *twelve* dogs," says Naomi, chuckling as she spells the word OXEN. "You were nine, Jean, and Healing was seven. Our three dogs were spending their nights in the woodshop because we had people sleeping in the living room and several more camping in the backyard. One of those campers had a beautiful black female hound named Ophelia who was not yet spayed. She mated with our two resident males, Thorstein and Veblen, and had a litter of eight. Thus we went from four dogs to twelve overnight."

"God we loved those puppies," says Healing, grinning at Jean. "A varied lot to say the least. Big ones and small ones, longhaired and shorthaired. We kept Caroline, a small black and white, and the others were taken by people responding to our ad in the *Mercy Messenger*."

"I remember Caroline," says Jean, fondly. "Her whole body shimmied when she wagged her tail."

"After Ophelia littered," says Naomi, studying her rack of letters, "we became more vigilant about making sure any dogs on the premises were spayed or neutered, though I must say those fuzzy newborns were a daily delight."

"While I just wanted all those people to go away," says Jean, placing her squares on the board to spell EPIC, "so it would only be our family and the dogs and cats and a few good friends."

"Your father and I often wished the same," says Naomi, wistfully. "Yet we also wanted to be a haven for our friends. The problem was, our friends had friends who had friends and we didn't have the heart to turn anyone away."

"It's fine, Mum," says Jean, selecting new letters. "I'm just currently in the throes of regretting staying in England and marrying Albert."

"Ezra begged you not to stay in England," says Naomi, recalling her husband's anguish about being parted from Jean, "but you were adamant about staying and argued that since *I* had left home at seventeen to come to America, you should be allowed to do the same, only in reverse. So we let you decide for yourself."

"Or did it only *seem* she was making the decision?" says Healing, placing his letters to spell QUEST. "Do we really make our own choices? Or are we merely pawns of fate?"

"I never thought I had a choice about anything until I was in my forties," says Jahera, brooding over the six vowels and one consonant on her rack. "I definitely felt I was a pawn of fate, though I see now I made the choices that shaped my life."

"What about Zoya?" says Healing, selecting his new letters. "Why out of all those wonderful dogs at the shelter did I choose her to come live with us?"

"She's one very lucky dog," says Naomi, prepared to use all her letters to spell QUIXOTIC if only Jahera doesn't spoil the board. "But did *you* choose her? Or did *she* choose you?"

"Come to think of it," says Healing, recalling the moment Zoya beckoned to him, "*she* made the choice and I was powerless to refuse her."

Ω

16. Darling

On February 2nd, the day marvelously sunny, Nasturtium School is thrown into turmoil when Reggie Chan's parents inform Tova they are switching Reggie back to the Montessori kindergarten so "he will have a more normal education."

On February 5th, cold and rainy, Sheila Liebowitz's parents inform Jahera they have re-enrolled Sheila at the Montessori kindergarten to "keep her on track for college."

On February 7th, sunny again, the four remaining members of the Nasturtium School student body – Raaz, Oz, Esther, and Arjun – come down with nasty colds necessitating a hiatus from the rigors of formal education.

On February 10th, an icy cold Saturday, Jean departs with Darla and Darla's dog Bongo for a two-day drive to Darla's condominium in Santa Barbara where they will spend a week seeing the sights of southern California.

*

On February 13th, snow in the forecast, Nasturtium School resumes at the little old house with Naomi presiding over the four scholars while Jahera and Jean go shopping for groceries and art supplies, and Healing and Maahiah take the three pups to the vet for vaccinations.

"This is a true story about Healing, whom you call Shafi," says Naomi, sitting on the living room sofa with Miguelito on her lap.

Oz, Raaz, Arjun, and Esther are sitting on the floor amidst the dogs, the fire crackling, the windows white with frost.

"Have we heard this story before?" asks Oz, who much prefers new stories to ones he's already heard."

"I rather doubt it," says Naomi, thoughtfully.

"Are we making valentines today?" asks Esther, who hasn't made any valentines yet and tomorrow is Valentines Day.

"Yes you are," says Naomi, looking over the tops of her glasses at Esther. "As soon as Jean and Jahera get home from the store. In the meantime... a story."

"How old was Shafi when this happened?" asks Arjun, who turned five in September.

"He was twenty-two," says Naomi, recalling her handsome young son. "Working as a landscaper, acting in plays at the local theater, and playing accordion in a trio with Buster Gomez and a beautiful woman named Darling Chamora."

"Was this before Mama was born?" asks Raaz, who has been feeling sad about her mother being away for so long.

"Yes," says Naomi, nodding. "Several years before."

"Is this story about a dog?" asks Oz, hopefully.

"It is," says Naomi, who would be happy to go on answering their questions and never tell the story.

"I think we should let her tell the story now," says Arjun with his Hindi accent and usual tone of authority.

"How about *one* more question before she starts?" asks Raaz, giving Arjun a mischievous smile.

"Oh-kay," says Arjun, with a sigh of surrender.

"What instrument did Darling play?" asks Raaz, getting up from the floor and sitting next to Naomi.

"She played the violin and sang like an angel," says Naomi, putting her arm around Raaz. "Just like Eliana. Buster played guitar in those days. He was twenty-three and had yet to take up the bass."

"How old was Darling?' asks Esther, who loves the name *Darling* and thinks she might change her name to *Darling*.

"I believe she was twenty-five," says Naomi, remembering Healing's beautiful lover. "We can ask Healing when he gets back from the vet with the pups."

"They might have fevers," says Oz, making a sad face. "From the shots."

"Can we *please* hear the story?" asks Arjun, impatiently.

"So..." says Naomi before more questions arise. "One day in early summer, Healing and Rodrigo Sandoval were building a wall to encircle a large garden at Marcus Dalrymple's house on the edge of the forest. Marcus was a renowned horticulturalist and this walled garden was to be his ultimate showcase."

"What's a horkitulcherist?" asks Oz, baffled by the word.

"A horticulturalist is one who studies agriculture," says Naomi, clearing her throat. "Otherwise known as the science of gardening."

"Was it a wooden wall?" asks Esther, wrinkling her nose as she often does when asking a question.

"Stone," says Naomi, nodding.

"So there they were," says Arjun, folding his arms. "Building a wall. Then what happened?"

"Thank you for keeping us on point, Arjun," says Naomi, winking at him. "So... in the forest not far from where Healing and Rodrigo were building the wall, there lived..."

"A bear?" guesses Oz.

"*Two* bears," says Esther, who has a habit of enlarging on the other kids' guesses.

"Certainly possible," says Naomi, chuckling. "Even probable. But that's not what this story is about, though it *is* one of the reasons Healing and Rodrigo were building the wall. To keep the bears out."

"A fox?" guesses Raaz.

"A mountain lion?" gasps Arjun.

"Also likely," says Naomi, who wishes the other adults were here to enjoy the children guessing. "But those are not the kind of animal I am about to name."

"Raccoons?" says Oz, thoughtfully pursing his lips. "Skunks?"

"The forest was home to all the animals you just named," says Naomi, smiling at the children. "As well as owls and hawks and deer and elk and ravens. But the animals in question were coyotes."

"Excuse me," says Arjun with wrinkled brow. "Didn't just you say this story was about a dog?"

"I did," says Naomi, restraining herself from guffawing, "and it is."

"Go on," says Oz, crawling over Socrates and Tabinda to get closer to Naomi. "So Shafi and Rodrigo were building the wall. Then what happened?"

"Well," says Naomi, pausing for dramatic effect, "a month or so *before* they began building the wall, a female coyote who lived nearby gave birth to two pups."

"Pups?" says Esther, wrinkling her nose. "I thought they were coyotes?"

"Baby coyotes are called pups," says Naomi, nodding to confirm this. "As are baby dogs. And one afternoon when those coyote pups were about seven weeks old, they followed their mother from their den to the edge of the forest. And that is when Healing and Rodrigo looked up from building the wall and saw the mother coyote and her two pups gazing at them from across the meadow. Healing counted the pups, one and two. And the next day at dusk, the mother and her pups came again, and Healing counted the pups again, one and two. But on the third day when the coyote mother and her pups arrived, Healing counted one and two and *three*, though he noticed something a little different about the third pup, so he got his binoculars from his truck..."

"He keeps them in the glove compartment," explains Raaz to Arjun and Esther, "only he doesn't have gloves in the glove compartment."

"Why does he call it a glove compartment if it doesn't have gloves?" asks Esther, wrinkling her nose yet again.

"He said people *used* to keep gloves in the glove compartment," says Raaz, shrugging. "But they don't anymore."

"So Healing looked through his binoculars," says Naomi, continuing, "and he saw that the *ears* of this third pup did not point up like the other two pups, but were floppy!"

The children gasp.

"Then Healing handed the binoculars to Rodrigo and asked, 'What do you make of this?' And Rodrigo studied the pups and said, 'I see two baby coyotes and a baby dog,' which was, indeed, the case. So they decided to catch the baby dog and bring her home to live with us." Naomi stifles a yawn. "And that's just what they did."

"How did they catch him?" asks Oz, excitedly.

"She was a her," says Raaz, looking at Naomi. "Wasn't she?"

"Yes, she was. And I'm sorry to say I'm very tired all of a sudden, so Healing will have to tell you the rest of the story when he gets back from the vet. Now here are Jahera and Jean home from the store to help you make valentines while I take a little nap. What wonderful questions you asked, and what fun I had telling the story."

"What did you name the puppy?" asks Esther, who is currently obsessed with names.

"Healing named her Darling," says Naomi, closing her eyes. "After Darling Chamora who he was passionately in love with."

"What's *passionately*?" asks Oz, frowning at yet another unfamiliar word.

"When one is passionately in love with someone," says Naomi, opening her eyes, "one is very *very* interested in that person."

"Oh," says Arjun, raising an eyebrow in imitation of his father. "I see."

*

When Healing and Maahiah return from the vet with Max, Flora, and Zoya, they find the children and Jahera and Jean arrayed around the dining table making valentines, while Naomi, bedecked with cats, dozes on the sofa.

"Shafi?" asks Oz, looking up from drawing a big heart. "How did you catch the puppy who lived with the coyotes?"

"Ah," says Healing, smiling at his slumbering mother. "Mum told you the story of Darling."

"Only she didn't tell us how you saved the puppy from the coyotes," says Arjun, busily gluing little red hearts inside a big purple heart Jahera helped him draw.

"I wouldn't say we *saved* her," says Healing, settling the pups on a blanket in the living room. "She was quite happy living with the coyotes. However, we knew it was likely the mother coyote and her pups would eventually meet up with other coyotes, and then the dog pup would have been in danger. So Rodrigo and I decided to catch the dog pup by leaving tasty treats on the edge of the forest to entice the pups and their mother."

"Cookies?" asks Esther, looking forward to dessert after lunch.

"Not cookies," says Healing, laughing. "Though I'm sure they would have enjoyed those. We put out slices of turkey and they gobbled those right up. The next day when they returned hoping for more turkey, Rodrigo and I jumped out from our hiding places and Rodrigo caught the dog puppy while the coyotes ran away."

"Did the dog puppy try to bite Rodrigo?" asks Raaz, drawing a heart inside a heart.

"No," says Healing, remembering Rodrigo diving headlong into a mass of ferns in pursuit of the puppy. "She wiggled and whimpered and tried to get away, but she didn't bite him. She was only two months old and sweet as could be. A mix of German Shepherd and Golden Lab. We brought her home and our dog Gypsy took care of her. We named her Darling and kept her for three months until she went to live with Rodrigo and his family for the rest of her life. She was a wonderful dog and nearly as smart as Moosh."

"What if she had stayed with the coyotes?" asks Arjun, fearing the worst. "Would they have *eaten* her?"

"The mother coyote and her pups would *never* have eaten Darling," says Healing, shaking his head. "But a pack of coyotes who didn't know Darling might have. The more intriguing question is: *how* did that puppy come to be with the coyotes?"

"Maybe the mother coyote stole Darling from a mother dog who had puppies," says Oz, drizzling glue on his valentine to ready the page for glitter.

"Maybe Darling got lost and the mother coyote found her," says Raaz, getting down from her chair to go sit on Jean's lap.

"That's what I think happened," says Jean, imagining some heartless human disposing of a litter of puppies in the forest. "I think the mother coyote had just given birth to her pups and decided to add Darling to her little brood."

"Time to put our art supplies away," says Jahera, getting up from the table. "Then we'll wash our hands, please, and we will assemble our burritos."

"And after burritos we'll have dessert," says Esther, emphatically.

"Yes," says Jahera, nodding to Esther. "And after dessert we will finish making our valentines and put them in envelopes for the people we're giving them to."

*

When Esther and Arjun go home, Rico Silveira, Dominique Tremblay, and Buster Gomez join Healing in the living room for their last rehearsal after thirty-five years of playing music together as the band Mercy Me.

Jahera sets up two cameras on tripods to film the rehearsal, while Jean, Maahiah, Oz, Raaz, and Naomi sit at the kitchen table to listen.

Tomorrow night the band will perform at *Big Goose* as they have every Valentine's Day since they first got together, and then Mercy Me will disband forever. Rico the guitarist is moving to Portland, Oregon with his wife Sally, and Dominique, clarinet and saxophone, is moving to Vancouver, British Columbia with her partner Sheila, both couples having sold their Mercy homes for millions of dollars they hope will sustain them for the rest of their lives.

When the band takes a break after playing a half dozen tunes, Buster sets down his standup bass and asks the children what they've been up to.

"Today," says Oz, "Shafi told us how he got the puppy from the coyotes and named her Darling."

"Oh Darling," says Buster with big sigh. "Named after Darling Chamora who we had a trio with before she went to LA to make it big."

"She was a genius," says Dominique, sighing at memories of the brilliant Darling. "But she didn't make it big."

"I was doing studio work in LA a couple years after she moved down there," says Rico, changing a string on his guitar, "and I told my producer he should get Darling to play violin on his project. And he said, 'She doesn't play anymore. She's working as a cocktail waitress in Studio City and married some deadbeat actor.'"

"It was Darling who got me playing bass," says Buster, feeling he might cry. "One night after a gig at *the Goose* she said, 'Buster you're good on guitar, but Healing's got the chords covered. Why not play bass?' And the very next day I was in Darby's shop and he'd just traded a grandfather clock for a big old black bass he sold me for a hundred bucks, though it was worth much more."

"You played that bass for our last few gigs with Darling," says Healing, remembering beautiful Darling as he saw her fifty years ago, a red rose in her long black hair.

"She loved you, man," says Buster, nodding solemnly. "But you wouldn't go to LA, so that was that, and you were sad for a long time after."

"How could she give up a gift like that?" says Rico, shaking his head. "I'll never understand."

"Maybe she needed a break," says Healing, picking up his accordion. "Maybe she's playing again now. I hope so."

"When Sheila and I get settled in Vancouver," says Dominique gazing at her three compadres, "we'll come visit and you'll come down from Portland, Rico, and we'll gig at *the Goose*. Okay?"

"Sounds good," says Rico, unconvincingly.

"In the meantime..." says Healing, playing the opening chords of *My Funny Valentine*. "... the farewell concert."

*

That night Jahera sits on the edge of the bed brushing her hair and watching Healing lying on his back on his yoga mat hugging his knees.

"Tell me about Darling," she says quietly.

"You and she might have been taken for sisters," says Healing, smiling up at his beloved, "though she was not as tall as you."

"She was Mexican?" asks Jahera, wishing she could see her.

Healing releases his knees and sits up. "Her *father* was Mexican and her mother was Chinese. She was born in Guadalajara where her father played violin in a Mariachi band and her mother was a cook. The family moved here when I was twenty-one and Darling was twenty-four."

"How did you meet her?"

"On the beach," he says, vividly remembering the first time he saw Darling. "I was walking our dogs and she was standing near the water singing."

"What was she wearing?"

"A black skirt and a blue down jacket, and her feet were bare."

"How romantic," says Jahera, smiling. "Was it love at first sight?"

"I would say *love at first listen*. I loved her voice. She was a tenor with a bell-like tone, very much like your voice, and when we discovered we were both musicians we became friends. My folks got to know her folks, and our families occasionally had meals together. Her mother was an excellent cook and her father was a wonderful storyteller. She had two brothers, one younger and one older, the younger a trumpet player, the older a guitarist, both of them eager to go to Los Angeles."

"What was the name of the band you had with her?"

"Los Tres," says Healing, wistfully.

"When did you become lovers?"

"A few months after we started gigging."

"Were you heartbroken when she left?"

"Not really. I missed playing music with her and missed having a lover, but I was mostly relieved when she left. She was sad and angry most of the time, except when she played music, and she had no interest in my family and friends."

"Why was she angry?"

"She would never talk about her feelings with me, and she refused to talk about her life before she came to Mercy, though from what her father and mother told me their life in Mexico was very hard." He muses for a moment. "I'll never forget the last rehearsal we had here. She was amazing as always, and Papa praised her to the moon, and Darling said, 'What good is it if nobody hears me?' And Papa said in his kindly way, 'You may not be aware of this, Darling, but the universe is always listening to you and responding in ways beyond your knowing.'"

"What did she say to that?"

"She said, 'No, Ezra. That's not how it works. You have to show the people in power that you have something they want. And people in power don't care about what goes on in Mercy. You could be Jesus Christ, but if you're not preaching in LA or New York, nobody cares."

"What did your father say to that?"

"He said, 'Be that as it may, I will be front and center at *Big Goose* for your performance tomorrow night. I wouldn't miss it for the world.'"

Ω

17. Bonita

"How ironic," says Healing, hanging up the phone and putting a kettle on for tea. "Or perhaps the machinations of the universe are simply too complex for my little brain to compass, and everything makes perfect sense."

"Tell me," says Jahera, just returned from driving Tova and the children to Darvin and Esther's house for school, a cold rain falling as winter hangs on into March – the collective hugely relieved to have Tova home from her movie-making in France.

"Genevieve wants Mercy Me to play two weddings and a big party at the hotel in April, and *five* weddings and two parties in May," says Healing, putting a log on the fire. "And lots more weddings after that. When I told her Mercy Me is no more, and Dominique and Rico live far-away now, she said if I'll put together another band she'll pay us *three* times what she paid us the last time we played there, which would be a thousand dollars each per gig. A staggering sum."

"Doesn't sound ironic to me," says Jahera, coming into the kitchen. "Sounds lucrative."

"I say *ironic*," he says, with a sigh, "because if Rico and Sheila had known they could make several thousand dollars a month playing weddings here, they might not have moved away. But we only had two wedding gigs last year because everybody wants string quartets or DJs, not jazzy accordion bands. Yet unbeknownst to us, Genevieve and Arno have been aggressively pushing a new wedding package at the East Cove Hotel featuring a video of Mercy Me playing a wedding there and wowing the crowd."

"Do you *want* to play all those weddings?" she asks, surprised by his angst.

"If I had a good band, yeah," he says, quelling the whistling kettle. "We need the money now that the residuals from your father's book have slowed to a trickle, and Maahiah gave all her money to Marianne Savoy to finish her movie, and Mum has finally outlived her savings."

"Don't worry, Shafi. I have plenty of work right now and we have money in the bank. We're fine."

"Yes but *Right Now* has the annoying habit of becoming the future, and the future is what happened to Rico and Dominique and why they had to move away. Besides... it could be fun making a new band."

"Will you still call yourself Mercy Me?"

"No, my love," he says, kissing her. "Mercy Me is history now."

*

In the afternoon when the rain becomes a drizzle, Healing and Mendelssohn walk across town to Buster and Carmen's house on the west side of Mercy – Buster a retired grocery clerk, Carmen a retired high school Spanish teacher.

Over coffee and carrot cake, Healing proposes to Buster that they start a new band to take advantage of the tsunami of wedding gigs on offer at the East Cove Hotel.

"Lo siento, hermano," says Buster, shaking his head. "I'm done."

"Done?" says Healing, shocked. "Done playing music?"

"I only kept going because I love you guys," says Buster, nodding. "But it's too hard on my back now and I got bad arthritis in my fingers. They ache for days after a gig. I'm an old man, Healing. You stay young and I'll come hear you play."

"Are you guys okay financially?" asks Healing, fearing the worst.

"We're fine," says Carmen, fetching more coffee. "We don't owe anything on the house and I have a good pension and Buster gets pretty good Social Security, and Celia is doing okay in San Diego, so... yeah. We're fine."

"She really gonna pay *three* times what we got last time for a wedding?" says Buster, marveling at the sum. "Hombre! That's crazy good money."

"That's what she offered," says Healing, wistfully. "And she's always true to her word. So... I guess I'll try to find somebody else to play with me."

"What about Eliana?" says Buster, feigning sincerity. "You're always talking about what a genius she is."

"Y ella es muy bonita like her mother," says Carmen, laughing, too. "Un poquito loco, pero..."

"I take exception to the word *loco*," says Healing, aware that Carmen and Buster are not the only ones in town who think Eliana is a bit cuckoo. "I will grant you *eccentric* and *volatile* and *dramatic*, and it's true she hasn't performed in public since she was eleven." He smiles slyly. "But she's a consummate musician and I'm sure she'd love to make her living playing music. I shall inquire. Thanks for the suggestion."

"How old is she now?" asks Carmen, filling Healing's mug. "She still working as a gardener and living at home?"

"She's twenty-five," says Healing, nodding in thanks for the coffee. "Still working as a gardener and still living at home, though now she's spending a few nights a week at our house as companion to my mother."

"I was kidding about Eliana," says Buster, giving Healing a worried look. "You don't want to start a band with a dramatic volatile eccentric, do you?"

"I've been playing accordion with Eliana since she was nine," says Healing, remembering how the little girl insisted on playing a full-sized accordion from the get-go and how she conquered the big squeezebox with ease. "She was already an excellent violinist and she surpassed me on the accordion by thirteen. She still comes for a so-called lesson every week and we have a fabulous time playing."

"I think *you* might be the loco one, hermano," says Buster, wishing it didn't hurt so much to play his bass now. "You can call your band Los Locos."

"Probably not the best name for a wedding band," says Healing, laughing. "Or maybe it's a perfect name. Los Locos."

*

On the way home from Buster and Carmen's, Healing and Mendelssohn visit *Found Wood*, the cavernous warehouse full of salvaged wood from old houses and fallen trees. Hal Gustafsson opened *Found Wood* fifty years ago with his wife Miyoshi Nakadate, a wood sculptor. Eighty-two now, his snow-white hair in a ponytail, Hal has a deep growly voice and beautiful blue eyes inherited from his Swedish parents.

"As I live and breathe," says Hal, giving Healing a hearty hug.

"You're looking well, Hal," says Healing, giving the least of tugs on Mendelssohn's leash to have him sit.

"Tayo and I were just talking about your farewell concert at *the Goose* and what a shame nobody recorded it," says Hal, shaking his head. "You and Buster gonna put together another group?"

"Yes," says Healing, nodding. "Well… *I* am. Buster has arthritis in his fingers now and his back is giving him trouble. So… is Tayo around?"

"He's out on a job right now," says Hal, frowning. "You know he doesn't play bass anymore. Hasn't played bass since he went to prison. That's fifteen years ago now."

"I thought maybe I could convince him to come out of retirement," says Healing, smiling hopefully. "Would you have him call me?"

"I will, but…" Hal grimaces. "He's pretty inward now, Healing. You know? I mean… he's fine, but… I'll tell him you came in."

"He's the best bass player I've ever heard," says Healing, remembering Tayo as a boy coming to the little old house for reading lessons with Naomi. "In any genre. Seems a shame he doesn't play anymore."

"He's got a little piano now. And he's got a girlfriend for the first time since he got out. Sheila Nuñez. You know Sheila. Works at the bank." Hal grimaces again. "It's none of my business, Healing, but why stir up those old feelings? You know what I mean? That rock star life and all that shit that went with it got him put away for three years."

"Of course it's your business," says Healing, who considers Hal a saint for hiring people no one else will. "But I'm not asking him to tour the world with an electronic fusion band. I'm just putting together an acoustic trio to play weddings at the East Cove Hotel. That's all."

"I get it," says Hal, relaxing. "I'll tell him."

"Merci," says Healing, bowing gratefully. "How's business?"

"Good," says Hal, gazing around the warehouse. "Last week a guy came all the way from Berkeley with a huge flatbed truck to pick up nine massive pieces of oak. He's carving Jesus and the Twelve Disciples for an installation at the Museum of Modern Art. Wrote a check for nine thousand dollars and it didn't bounce. He's coming back for more next week, probably from this tree Tayo and Pepe are salvaging right now. Crazy, huh?"

"Fantastic," says Healing, applauding.

"I'll tell Tayo to call you," says Hal, smiling. "Who knows? Maybe he'll *want* to play with you. He loved Mercy Me."

*

As dusk descends on Mercy, Maahiah and Tova drink good red wine and speak French while preparing supper together, Maahiah always more animated when conversing in French. Jean and Jahera and the children and the dogs are in the garden harvesting chard, and Naomi is in the rocking chair reading Helen Morningstar's new book of poems *Now Why*.

Healing carries the old landline phone to the sofa where Gracie the old calico cat settles on Healing's lap while he calls Eliana to see if she'll be in his new band.

Eliana's father Zeke answers. "Healing? I was just about to call you."

"About...?" asks Healing, who has known Zeke since Zeke was born fifty-five years ago when Zeke's father was the Weintraub's dentist and Zeke's mother visited Naomi every Monday morning to have a Tarot reading.

"Our dogs chased a young feral cat under my studio this morning," says Zeke, anxiously. "I want to rescue him and keep him as my studio cat. Or her. I have no idea what sex she is. My problem is she's *way* under the building where the dogs can't get to her, and neither can I because the crawl space is only eight-inches-high. She's *so* skinny I think she must be starving to death. I called Animal Control and gave Lucas a hypothetical and he said if she's feral and sickly they have to assume rabies and they'll just catch and kill. He says they have no choice with the shelter so full."

"I'll come out tomorrow morning," says Healing, excited by the prospect of rescuing a feral kitten. "In the meantime, leave a small bowl of milk and a bowl of water under your studio as far as you can reach. Keep your dogs away and we'll hope she's still there in the morning."

"Thanks, Healing. I appreciate it. Here's Eliana."

"Shafi?" says Eliana, excitedly. "I had the most *amazing* dream about you last night. We were dressed as Gypsies and playing accordions for hundreds of people. I was wearing a purple skirt and a white blouse and a red scarf, and you were wearing a white shirt and black pants and a red bandana, and the audience *loved* us."

"Remarkable. That's what I'm calling about."

She gasps. "You had the same dream?"

He laughs. "Not exactly. I'm wondering if you'd like to form a band with me to play weddings at the East Cove Hotel."

"Oh I'd love to," she says anxiously. "But I don't think I can because I'd be too afraid to play in front of all those people."

"We won't often be in *front* of people at wedding gigs," says Healing, reassuringly. "We'll mostly be off to the side playing the processional and recessional, and then after the ceremony we provide background music for the reception. Sometimes people dance to our music, but we're not so much concertizing as providing ambience."

"Oh I want to," she says fervently. "But I think I'll be too anxious."

"Tell you what. I'll scare up another player or two and we'll get together and see what happens."

"Okay Shafi," she says, her voice trembling. "I want to. I really do."

*

The next morning after breakfast, Healing drives two miles inland on Baskerville Road to Zeke and Conchita's beautiful home on twenty acres of meadow and forest.

"Thanks for coming," says Zeke, giving Healing a hearty hug. "I set out milk as you suggested and she drank it all. Now what do we do?"

"Are we sure she's still there?" asks Healing, waving to Conchita who is pacing up and down on the front porch talking on her phone.

"She's still there," says Zeke, leading Healing to his studio, a beautiful little redwood cabin in a clearing fifty yards from the house. "I think she's afraid to leave."

"If she's still a kitten she'll be easy to tame," says Healing, approaching the cabin. "Where'd you get this exquisite little house? Did you build it?"

"No. Dino Andrini's daughters built it on Dino's farm when they were teenagers and learning to be carpenters and architects." Zeke gazes morosely at the cabin. "Dino sold it to me last year for five hundred bucks right before he sold his place for three million and bought a house in Bellingham right on the water with a private pier for his fishing boat. For only five hundred grand."

"Did Conchita sell his place for him?" asks Healing, remembering when Zeke was a gardener and Conchita was a barmaid and they were always scrambling to pay their bills.

"Who else?" says Zeke, disdainfully. "She's the go-to realtor for all the old timers selling out and moving away."

"She sold Rico and Sally's little house for two million, and Dominique and Sheila's place for four million," says Healing, shaking his head in wonder. "They're set for life now, only just not here."

"I think it's sickening so many of our friends have to leave," says Zeke, who grew up in Mercy when most of the population was working class.

"Sad," says Healing, nodding in agreement. "So here's the plan. I brought you a big cage trap. Tonight you'll put the bowls just barely under the cabin, and again not very much milk, and we'll leave the cage a few feet out from the side of the cabin. Tomorrow night you'll place the cage a foot away from the cabin with the cage door open. Set the bowls between the cabin and the cage. Always use the same bowls. The third night, place the bowls *just* outside the open door of the cage, and just a little milk. We want her to stay hungry. On the fourth night put the bowls a foot *inside* the cage. I'll show you how to set the trigger pad so when she's all the way inside, the door will close. Once you've caught her, or him, bring the cage inside the cabin, put a litter box in there and give her plenty of milk. If you decide you don't want to keep her, I'll take her."

"Oh I want her," says Zeke, longingly. "I'm hoping she'll be my muse and get me writing again."

*

Two days later on an unexpectedly sunny Friday, Maahiah and Jean walk the kids to school at Arjun's house while Tova and Jahera do the breakfast dishes, and Naomi luxuriates at the dining table with coffee and crossword puzzle.

Healing builds up the fire, straps on his gorgeous old Weltmeister accordion, and strolls around the living room playing one of Naomi's favorite songs, Billy Taylor's *I Wish I Knew How It Would Feel To Be Free*.

Mid-song the front door opens and Eliana enters with a violin case on her back and an accordion case in hand. She sets down her cases, Healing nods to her, and she sings the words of the song, her voice a warm lyric contralto inspiring Tova and Jahera and Naomi to sing along with her.

At song's end, Naomi gives Eliana a hug and says, "Singing with you is my idea of heaven."

"Mine, too," says Eliana, hugging Tova and Jahera.

"You look fantastic," says Tova, wishing the kids could see Eliana in her long purple skirt and billowy white blouse, her long brown hair in a ponytail tied with a crimson bandana.

"I'm the luckiest person in the world," says Eliana, dancing into the living room. "What shall I play first? Violin or accordion?"

"Let's begin with violin," says Healing, laughing as the dogs mill around Eliana vying for her caresses.

"I'm determined not to be afraid," she says, getting out her violin.

"Just imagine you're in a movie," says Healing, playing a G for her to tune to. "Imagine your character has been playing music for weddings since she was a little girl, having learned from her parents who learned from their parents, Gypsies all."

"Oh I can do *that*," she says, excitedly. "And the wedding guests will find us exotic and mysterious and wish they were Gypsies, too."

"As in your dream," says Healing, playing a series of Gypsy-like chords.

"And I am your cinematographer," says Jahera, affixing her camera to a tripod. "Making a movie to show Genevieve and Arno."

"If I'm not mistaken," says Healing, going to the front door, "those footfalls presage the arrival of our bass player Tayo Garcia."

The collective breath is held as Tayo enters with his big standup bass in a black canvas case, the doorway seeming too small for him.

"Hello," says Tayo, six-foot-seven, his head shaved, his accent a mix of his mother's Nigerian British and his father's Mexican Spanish. "I don't know if this will work, Healing, but here I am."

"Welcome," says Healing, ushering Tayo into the room. "Anybody here you don't know?"

He looks at the women gathered in the kitchen, and a smile dispels his somber mien. "I know everybody here. Naomi who taught me to read, Jahera who always takes pictures, Tova who went to high school with me, and my cousin Eliana." He nods to Eliana. "Though I never can remember which kind of cousin we are."

"Second I think," says Eliana, dazzled by him. "Or third. I never can remember either."

"You are well?" asks Naomi, taking one of Tayo's enormous hands in both of hers.

"I'm okay," he says lovingly. "How are you, Naomi?"

"I'm well," she says, sensing his deep sorrow. "I'm so looking forward to hearing you play."

"They didn't let me bring my bass to prison," he says quietly. "And when I got back home nobody wanted to play with me, so I let it go." He shrugs. "We'll see if my fingers remember what to do."

"I'm sure they will," says Naomi, encouragingly.

"How long were you in prison?" asks Jahera, setting up a second camera.

"Three years," says Tayo, bringing his bass out of its case. "I've been out for twelve years and I still wake up sometimes thinking I'm there."

"You are not there," says Naomi, resuming her place at the table. "And you will never be there again."

"Gracias, Naomi," he says, plucking a string on his bass. "Gracias Healing for inviting me to try."

*

An hour later, having played through a dozen songs, the trio rests.

"I love this more than anything," says Eliana, putting her violin away. "I think we sound fantastic."

"I do, too," says Healing, grinning. "What thinkest thou, Tayo?"

"Could work," he says, setting his bass down. "Her violin makes me want to use more bow. Give us a string section sometimes."

"Please do," says Healing, shedding his accordion. "Now all we need is a name and some tea."

"I would call you Désir," says Jahera, continuing to film the newborn band.

"Perfect for wedding gigs," says Tova, putting a kettle on. "Désir. Genevieve will love it."

"Désir," says Healing, trying out the name. "Seems good."

Tayo muses for a moment. "Why not Deseo? Since two of us are Mexicano."

"Deseo," says Naomi, savoring the word. "A song in itself."

"Deseo," says Eliana, softly. "I love it."

*

The next morning during the pancake breakfast Healing gets a call from Zeke.

"I caught her," says Zeke, breathless with excitement. "She's a beautiful tabby. Golden brown with black stripes. Can you come take a look?"

"I'll be there in an hour," says Healing, eagerly. "How's she behaving?"

"She devoured a bowl of milk and now she's cowering in a corner of the cage. I'd give her more milk, but you cautioned me not to."

"Give her more water, but no more milk until I get there. Does she appear to be ill?"

"Not sure. She's favoring her back left leg and one of her eyes is encrusted with crud, but she seems pretty good otherwise."

"Make that a half-hour. Can't wait to meet her. Or him."

"Can we come with you?" asks Oz, his eyes wide with excitement. "To see the wild kitten?"

"With your mother's permission," says Healing, returning the phone to its cradle. "And if we may take her car so you will be safely belted in your special seats, then yes."

"Can we go with Shafi, Mama?" asks Raaz, urgently. "Please?"

"On one condition," says Tova, pausing portentously. "I come, too."

*

"I'd guess she's ten-weeks-old," says Healing, squatting beside the cage on the floor in Zeke's cabin. "Shouldn't take long to tame her. What a beauty."

"You're guessing female?" says Zeke, on the verge of tears.

"Yes," says Healing, gazing at the little tabby sitting sphinxlike in the far corner of the cage watching the humans. "Though we won't know for certain until we pick her up. What do you think, Tove?"

"I don't like the look of her eye," says Tova, who was a veterinarian's assistant for nineteen years. "I know it will be traumatic for her, but I think we should take her to the vet as soon as possible and get her shots and have her eye taken care of. I'll be happy to help you with that, Zeke. We'll wear the requisite gloves and get her into a little travel cage."

"I agree," says Healing, standing up. "A day or two being handled by the folks at the clinic will hasten her getting used to humans. Then when you get her home you mustn't let her out of the cabin for several weeks until she considers this her home."

"When shall we take her in?" asks Zeke, looking at Tova.

"I'll call the clinic when they open on Monday and set up a time," says Tova, smiling at the adorable kitten. "Then I'll bring the travel cage and we'll take her in."

"Can we talk to her now?" asks Oz, looking up at Zeke.

"Yeah, go ahead," says Zeke, smiling down at Oz.

Raaz and Oz kneel beside the cage.

"Don't be afraid," says Raaz, speaking quietly to the little cat. "Zeke loves you, and we love you, too."

"When you come home from the vet," says Oz, matching his sister's tone of voice, "we'll come play with you. Okay?"

Entranced by the children's voices, the wild kitten takes a tiny step toward the little humans and makes a plaintive mewing sound.

*

Two weeks later in the early afternoon, Healing, Tayo, and Eliana get together at Eliana's house for their seventh rehearsal, their inaugural wedding gig just a week away.

During a break, Healing goes to see how things are progressing with the kitten.

"Come in, come in," says Zeke, ushering Healing into the cabin where the little cat is sitting on the sofa.

"She's still skittish," says Zeke, gently picking up the kitten. "When it's just the two of us, she's on my lap all the time now. And she likes Eliana and Conchita, so..." He smiles at Healing. "Thanks so much for helping me. And thanks for asking Eliana to be in your band. She's over the moon."

"My pleasure," says Healing, offering his fingertips for the kitten to sniff.

"I got her into the little harness Tova gave me and took her outside on a leash a couple days ago," says Zeke, nuzzling the kitten. "She tiptoed around for a minute and then ran back inside. I took her out again yesterday and she roamed a bit further until a dog barked and she raced back in and hid under the sofa. Then this morning we walked all the way around the outside of the cabin, and then she sat on the porch for a while before coming back in."

"Have you named her?"

"Not yet," says Zeke, laughing to keep from crying. "Writer's block. Haven't written anything in three years. I was going great guns there for a while and then everything just stopped." He shrugs hopelessly. "Don't know why. Now I can't even think of a name for my cat."

"May I?" asks Healing, holding out his hands for the kitten.

"She might not want to come to you," says Zeke, shaking his head.

"Let's try," says Healing, whispering.

Zeke hands the kitten to Healing and she immediately begins to purr.

"Hello sweetheart," says Healing, stroking the kitten's head. "When you look at her, Zeke, what's the first word that comes to you?"

"Bonita," he says, smiling through his tears. "Bonita."

*

"I've never known *you* to suffer from *photographer's* block," says Healing, climbing into bed at the end of another momentous day. "Have you ever?"

"Not since I met you," says Jahera, awaiting him. "But before... many times."

"What was it like? Being blocked?"

She muses for a moment. "Nothing stood out from anything else. I think it was a symptom of my sorrow. I was blind to inspiration because everything was muted and unclear and chaotic. When one is sad, life is a blur."

"What would end the blurriness?"

"In the fall or in the spring the light would change, and the shadows of things would attract my eye and I would get my camera. And once I began shooting, my curiosity would take hold and I would keep shooting."

"I wonder what could change the light for Zeke. Not the literal light, but the light inside him."

"I think he is dealing with something more than sorrow."

"What do you think it is?"

"I think when he read the first draft of his thousand-page novel, he knew enough to know he would have to write a second draft, but he also realized he didn't know how to do that. He is a writer of rough drafts, not an accomplished writer. He was a gardener for forty years and in that time he became a master gardener, but not a master writer. And he knows it would take him many years to become a masterful writer, maybe the rest of his life, with no promise of success. So he's stuck in indecision while his wife madly sells houses and amasses a fortune, and his daughter, his companion in stuckness, is about to fly away."

"I want to help him," says Healing, thinking of how Zeke cried as he said the name of his cat. *Bonita*. "But I'm no editor except of my little poems."

"Just be his friend," she says simply. "He chose a path that requires constant isolation, when what he needs is the opposite. I did the same thing until I was forty-two and felt like a failure, though I was not a failure. I just couldn't see the truth, which was I needed to stop being so alone in my life."

"What happened when you were forty-two? I don't think you ever told me."

"When I was forty-two, after twenty years of striving to sell my photographs, someone at the Borenstein Gallery in London agreed to look at my portfolio, a woman named Anna Duval. She was twenty-seven and everything I was not. She was gregarious and funny and happy in her work, while I was frozen in sadness and despair. My appointment with her was supposed to last fifteen minutes, but she spent an hour looking at my photos, something that had never happened to me before at a major gallery. And when she was done looking at my photos she said, 'I would crop most of these differently than you have. I think your photos are masterpieces obscured by what's around them, and in some cases by what you have taken away.

Would you like to work with me and see what we can create together?' And I was so insulted, I grabbed my portfolio and walked out the door, and she came running after me and said, 'I hope you'll come back one day. I think we could learn so much together.'"

"Did you go back?" he whispers.

"After three days of not eating or drinking or sleeping, I went back to her and she helped me take the next great leap in my art."

Ω

18. Harpo and Dumont

April gets off to an eventful start with Raaz and Oz turning five, followed by a ferocious windstorm that knocks out the electricity in Mercy for three days, followed by the death of Bogart and the subsequent removal of the parrot cage from the sunniest corner of the kitchen where parrot cages have stood for seventy years – the kitchen suddenly enormous.

And late this morning, April eleventh, a sunny Saturday, Jean gets a call from her cousin Norman who is representing Jean in her divorce from Albert. After a bit of friendly banter, Norman says something that causes Jean to go blank for a moment.

"Excuse me," she says, coming to her senses. "Did you just say Albert intends to remarry and is no longer contesting the settlement we proposed? Or did I mishear you?"

"You did not mishear me," says Norman, speaking more slowly. "He grants you two million pounds, plus my fee. The law is crystal clear that you should get much more, but per your wishes he will keep the house in Exeter, the holiday cottage in France, and bonds and annuities currently valued at three million pounds. As I told you, he'll be retaining five times what you're getting, but you are a generous soul and he is not."

"Do we know whom he intends to marry?" asks Jean, stupefied by the news.

"His solicitor would not divulge that information," says Norman, taking a deep breath. "However, Constance called yesterday and asked if I would help her and Frederick file suit against Albert for changing his will such that his new wife gets everything and Constance and Frederick get nothing. I told her I could not represent her because it would be a conflict of interest since I'm representing you in the divorce, and I referred her to another solicitor. In the course of our conversation, Constance revealed that Albert is marrying a woman named Angela Morrison. She also informed me that Ms. Morrison is three months pregnant and Albert is the purported father."

Jean gasps. "Angela Morrison? Albert's secretary at the university? She's not yet thirty. *Pregnant*? By *Albert*? Impossible."

"Be that as it may," says Norman, his tone consoling, "the advent of Ms. Morrison has sped the plough, so to speak, and we should be able to wrap things up quite soon. A few months hence the settlement monies will be transferred to your account in Mercy and you will be free of this unpleasant imbroglio. Constance asked me to tell you she's terribly sorry for doubting you and hopes you will forgive her."

Conversation at end, Jean returns the phone to its cradle and goes out into the backyard where Healing, Jahera, Maahiah, Oz, Raaz, and Tova are in the vegetable garden preparing beds for the first planting of spring. Naomi is sitting in a wicker armchair on the garden path observing the goings on, while Mendelssohn, Coosi, and Miguelito wander about nearby.

"You all right, Jean?" asks Healing, looking up from overseeing the children planting chard seeds.

"I'm..." Jean frowns. "I'm in shock. When you have a moment, I'd like to speak to you and Mum. I'll be in the living room."

*

Healing and Naomi join Jean on the sofa, and after Jean shares the news of Albert and his pregnant fiancé, Naomi says, "Thank goodness you escaped him. I'm sorry you had to hear the sordid details of his continuance, but I am overjoyed you are free of such a terrible encumbrance."

"I hope to be overjoyed, too, Mum," says Jean, trembling. "At the moment I feel like I've been hit by a truck."

"Come get your fingers in the dirt, Sis," says Healing, putting his arm around her. "Then we'll take the dogs to the beach and get our feet in the sand."

"The hardest thing," says Jean, allowing Healing to help her up, "is knowing Albert never loved me, yet I stayed with him all those decades without a whiff of love." She winces at a pain in her neck. "The only thing I ever did for myself was raise my schnauzers, and he never let a day go by without lecturing me on what a terrible imposition the dogs were on his life."

"Never again will he wound you," says Naomi, following her children to the garden. "Let us rejoice."

*

The following Saturday, April eighteenth, Deseo plays their first wedding gig at the East Cove Hotel, rain causing the wedding and reception to be moved from the hotel garden into the banquet room where the seventy wedding guests thrill to Deseo's opening song, a luscious rendition of *Deep Purple* to which the bridal party and the handsome young groom enter. And when the bride begins her stroll to the altar, Deseo swings into a dazzling *The Girl From Ipanema,* and the blushing beauty arrives at the altar to cheers and applause - the doorway of the banquet room crowded with hotel guests eager to see who could be playing such glorious music.

At ceremony's end, the newlyweds sashay down the aisle to a jazzy *You Send Me,* and the crowd goes wild when the bride and groom stop midway to laugh and kiss.

In the ensuing hubbub, while the hotel staff readies the banquet room for the reception, Deseo relocates to a small stage in a corner of the room and are about to launch into their wedding-reception repertoire when an excited young woman rushes up to them.

"Would you be willing to come to Los Angeles and play at my wedding?" she gushes. "We'll pay for your travel, of course, and put you up at the Beverly Wilshire and pay you whatever you want. I'll do *any*thing to have you play at my wedding."

"We are flattered," says Healing, bowing to her. "However we only play weddings in Mercy. So if you'd like us to play at your wedding you will have to be married here." He waves to Genevieve. "The wedding maven herself will be glad to give you the particulars, and again let me say how glad we are you dig our music."

Now Healing plays the iconic opening chords of the Beatles' *Norwegian Wood*, Tayo adds a tasty bass line, and Eliana plays the melody on her violin and simultaneously sings the words, her self-harmonizing so compelling that everyone within earshot stops whatever they're doing to listen.

*

Three evenings later, as a Scrabble game rages in the living room of the little old house, Jean comes home from accompanying Darla to the Mercy Players Theatre where Darla tried out for a part in the comedy classic *Ellen Is the Problem*, a staple of small town theatre companies everywhere.

"You'll never guess what just happened," says Jean, standing by the fire.

"Darla got the leading role?" says Healing, looking up from his rack of letters.

"We won't know about that until Friday," says Jean, shaking her head. "Callbacks are Thursday. She'll surely get a part. The question is will she be cast as Ellen? She hopes so, and I hope so, too, though Maureen McGillicutty read brilliantly and is thirty years younger than Darla, so it's more likely Darla will be cast as Ellen's mother and Maureen will get the part of Ellen." She smiles dreamily. "Who knows what might happen?"

Naomi looks over the tops of her glasses at Jean and declares, "You've met someone."

Jean nods timidly.

"Who is he?" asks Naomi, breathlessly.

"His name is William Charlton," says Jean, blushing. "He was there to try out for the play and sat next to me and asked what part I was hoping to get, and I said I wasn't trying out and just came to support my friend, and he said, 'Drat. I was hoping we'd be in the play together so we could get to know each other.' And before I could stop myself I said, 'Well we could get to know each other anyway.' And he said, 'Splendid.' Then after the audition he asked if I'd like to go for coffee tomorrow and I said *Yes*." She blinks to dispel her disbelief. "We're meeting at *Café Brava* at ten."

"Wonderful," says Jahera, joining Jean by the fire. "What do you know about him?"

"I know he has beautiful gray blue eyes and wavy gray hair going white, and he's new in town and a very good actor and..." She laughs. "I can't believe this is happening."

"What's Darla's take on him?" asks Healing, tickled to think of his sister going on a date after fifty years of enslavement to Albert.

"Darla says he's a hunk," says Jean, blushing. "Though he's not at all fat. I think he's terribly good looking and Darla thinks so, too, and... he really seems to like me, though I have no idea why."

"He likes you because you're a beautiful charming person," says Jahera, giving Jean a hug. "I'm so happy for you."

"Nothing may come of it," says Jean, hardly knowing what to do with her feelings. "I'm just... amazed."

*

The following day at noon, Healing and Jahera return from a long beach walk with Coosi and Mendelssohn and Puccini to find Jean and Naomi sitting on the deck having tea, Jean looking radiant and Naomi grinning from ear to ear.

"How was your date?" asks Jahera, gazing expectantly at Jean.

"Fun," says Jean, shrugging.

"Fun?" says Healing, arching an eyebrow. "Elaborate, please."

"Well... Will is joining us for waffles on Sunday," says Jean, blushing brightly.

"Oh it's *Will* now, is it?" says Healing, taking off his shoes. "The romance moves apace."

"Tell them more, dear," says Naomi, nodding encouragingly. "I don't mind hearing everything again."

"I'll make more tea and bring crackers and cheese," says Jahera, picking up the empty teapot and carrying it away. "Don't start until I come back."

Healing whistles for the sandy dogs to join him at the corner of the woodshed for a shower, and they come without hesitation knowing the humans will give them marvelous massages with big towels after the sand is washed away.

Jean and Healing are in the midst of drying the dogs when menacing gray clouds move in from the ocean, the temperature plummets, and humans and dogs hurry inside where Healing builds up the fire and Jahera fetches her camera to take advantage of the beautifully muted light.

When the dogs are content by the fire and the humans are settled around the kitchen table, Jean resumes her report of her first date with William.

"So I got to *Café Brava* promptly at ten. You know me. Chronically on time. And William... Will... was already there and had gotten us a window table and... he brought me a rose from his garden." She gestures to a spectacular yellow rose in a blue vase on the kitchen counter. "He was wearing a burgundy wool sweater over a teal dress shirt, and..."

"Brown corduroy trousers," adds Naomi, approvingly. "I think it's always a good sign when a man wears corduroy *and* favors teal."

"What about his shoes and socks?" asks Healing, feigning deep interest in such things. "Handmade leather and argyle?"

"Sandals," says Jean, laughing. "No socks."

"How does he take his coffee?" asks Jahera, joining in the laughter.

"He has his first few sips black," says Jean, sighing as one in love. "Then he adds a little cream. No sugar."

"Good to know in advance of the waffle soiree," says Healing, winking at Jahera. "To which Darby and Marjorie and Eliana are coming, too."

"Then what happened?" asks Jahera, taking pictures of Jean.

"Then we talked about the audition and told each other about our lives, and then it got so crowded and noisy we walked to Will's house and I got to meet his marvelous dogs and cats."

"Where does he live?" asks Healing, dizzied by the volume of news.

"He bought Agnes Wagner's house, two doors down from Buster and Carmen," says Naomi, thrilled for her daughter. "I *adore* that house."

"He must be rich," says Healing, hoping to sound factual rather than judgmental. "One has to be, doesn't one, to buy a house in Mercy now?"

"Well he's not rich," says Jean, shaking her head. "Or he wasn't. He was a high school Drama teacher in Palo Alto for forty years. Bought a house there forty-three years ago for eighty thousand dollars and sold it last year for five million. He paid two million for Agnes's house, so I suppose he *is* rich now, though that never entered my mind."

"Does he have children?" asks Jahera, guessing he does. "Grandchildren?"

"He has two daughters and two granddaughters, one from each daughter," says Jean, thinking of William's refrigerator crowded with photos. "He was married to the mother of his daughters for twenty years. The marriage ended when the girls went to university. He married again five years later and that marriage lasted four years. He retired from teaching when he was sixty-three and was an actor in San Francisco and Berkeley and Palo Alto until he was seventy-two and sold his house and moved here. He's seventy-three now, nine weeks older than I."

"Well you've always had a thing for older men," says Healing, frowning gravely. "Now about his dogs and cats."

"His cats are Beatrice and Juliet, Beatrice a Persian Siamese amalgam, Juliet dark brown, both sleek and shorthaired and friendly and talkative. Harpo and Dumont are Golden Doodles, delightful three-year-old siblings, Harpo the male, Dumont the female."

"William is a Marx Brothers fan?" asks Healing, delighted by the names.

"Devout," says Jean, bursting with love for William. "He has an enormous black and white photo of Groucho, Harpo, Chico, and Margaret Dumont from *A Night At the Opera* framed in gold on the wall over his piano. And he's *steeped* in Shakespeare. Knows the comedies and *Hamlet* and *Lear* by heart. You're going to love him, Helios!"

"Goodness," says Naomi, her eyes filling with tears. "I haven't heard you call your brother Helios since you were children and he called you Jen."

"I *feel* like a child again," says Jean, her eyes sparkling. "Well... a teenager anyway."

"Did he play his piano for you?" asks Healing, who knows a good deal of Shakespeare by heart, though not nearly as much as William claims to know.

"No," says Jean, blushing anew. "I was too shy to ask. He said he's not very good but loves to play. He had Mendelssohn's *Songs Without Words* on the piano along with Chopin's *Nocturnes* and some Cole Porter."

"Does he have a garden?" asks Healing, expectantly. "Agnes had fabulous roses out front and brambles in the back."

"He's got the front yard in good shape now," says Jean, imagining cutting roses from William's bushes and putting them in a vase she's going to give him as a gift. "He's in the midst of clearing the backyard for a pond and raised beds, and he's going to plant fruit trees and build a small greenhouse."

"He sounds ideal," says Healing, exchanging looks with Naomi and Jahera. "As if he was *made* for you."

"Yes, I think he was," says Jean, complacently. "He checks all the boxes, as they say. And then some."

*

On Sunday morning, the day overcast, William arrives with flowers for the household and Groucho Marx glasses for Raaz and Oz, spindly plastic frames with mustaches and noses attached. The children love the silly things so much they insist on wearing them during breakfast, which prompts Jahera to get her camera, ostensibly to take pictures of the children, but really to photograph Jean with her new beau.

William, charming and chatty, laughs heartily at Darby's quips and Naomi's droll comments, which inspires both of them to greater heights of verbal fancy.

At meal's end, Jean and William go with Oz and Raaz on a tour of the property with a multitude of dogs while everyone else stay inside to gab about William.

"Isn't he *fabulous*?" says Tova, doing the dishes with Eliana. "Wasn't it *so* wonderful how he hung on Jean's every word?"

"He *adores* her," says Eliana, exchanging looks with Tova. "Restores my faith in..." She can't think of the word she's looking for.

"Fate?" suggests Tova, nodding.

"Angelic intervention," says Marjorie, sitting in the rocking chair by the fire with Miguelito on her lap.

"He's what we call *easy to laugh*," says Darby, sharing the sofa with Maahiah, both of them bedecked with cats. "God bless him."

“There was a moment during breakfast,” says Healing, adding a log to the fire, “when amidst the din of laughter I murmured a line from *Much Ado About Nothing* in response to something you said, Darby, and William winked at me and recited the answering line. I was stunned. Pleasantly so.”

“Which lines, Pa-pa?” asks Tova, taking off her apron and sitting down with Naomi to study the crossword puzzle, Maahiah sitting nearby knitting.

“I said ‘What pace is this thy tongue keeps?’ and William replied, ‘Not at a fast gallop.’”

“Imagine knowing Shakespeare so well,” says Jahera, putting a kettle on for tea. “How good that must be for the brain.”

“I’ve got to read more Shakespeare,” says Eliana, going to sit amongst the dogs near the fire. “I’ve been mired in Jane Austen for months now.”

“They will get married,” says Maahiah, looking at Eliana. “Soon.”

“How do you know?” asks Eliana, meeting Maahiah’s gaze.

“There are no barriers between them,” says Maahiah, resuming her knitting. “Nothing to keep their souls apart.”

“Love looks not with the eyes, but with the mind,” says Healing, reciting his favorite lines from *A Midsummer Night’s Dream*. “And therefore is wing’d Cupid painted blind. Nor hath love’s mind of any judgment taste; wings and no eyes figure unheedy haste: And therefore is love said to be a child, because in choice he is so oft beguiled.”

“I couldn’t have said it better meself,” says Darby, winking at Healing. “Forsooth, I couldn’t have said it at all.”

*

In their bedroom that night, Healing kneels on his yoga mat and uses the bed as his desk while Jahera sits up reading *The Children*, sequel to *The People*.

"The moment Albert ceased to contest the divorce," says Healing, putting his pen down, "the universe arranged for Jean and William to meet."

"Are you making a poem about it?" asks Jahera, looking up from her book.

"Doggerel," says Healing, perusing his scrawl. "No doubt inspired by my after-breakfast recitation from Shakespeare."

"Read to me," says Jahera, closing her eyes to listen.

Healing smiles at his scrawl and reads, "The attic is full of things we've fooled ourselves into keeping. Food for ghosts who come to stay and haunt us while we're sleeping. Through God's good grace one lucky day that useless junk gets thrown away, and ghosts depart and now we hear for joy the angels weeping."

Ω

19. Zubina

On a warm Saturday afternoon in early May, while Healing, Eliana, Tayo, and Tova are performing for a hundred wedding celebrants at the East Cove Hotel, Jahera and Jean are toiling in the vegetable garden while keeping tabs on Oz, Raaz, and Arjun who have ventured to the edge of the maple copse where they are doing battle with murderous aliens, a game Arjun learned from his cousins who play video games about such things.

The younger dogs Coosi, Flora, Max, and Zoya are with the children while Mendelssohn, Tabinda, and Puccini sprawl on the deck, knackered from their long walk this morning.

Inside the little old house, Naomi is drowsing on the sofa while Socrates and Miguelito are in the kitchen hoping for morsels to fall as Maahiah make bread.

Socrates gives a little growl at the sound of someone coming up the front stairs and goes to see who's there. Maahiah dries her hands and hurries to the door, and here is a pretty young woman in blue jeans and a sleeveless red T-shirt, her hair short and blonde, holding a slumbering baby.

"Ahlo," says the young woman, her accent profoundly French. "My name is Jennifer Badeaux. Is Jahera here?"

"She's in the backyard," says Maahiah, knowing Jennifer is Lucien's partner. "Please come in. The dogs are friendly."

"Merci," says Jennifer, her manner of speaking reminiscent of a little girl's. "Lucien *said* there would be dogs and cats here. I would have a cat but Lucien doesn't like cats."

"Is Lucien with you?" asks Maahiah, switching to French. "I'm Lucien's grandmother."

"I recognize you from Lucien's photos," says Jennifer, replying in French. "He thought it would be best for me to come without him, so he stayed in Santa Rosa."

"I'll get Jahera," says Maahiah, hurrying away.

Naomi sits up and looks over the tops of her glasses at Jennifer.

"Hello. I'm Naomi, Tova's grandmother," she says in English. "My French is not spectacular. Do come sit with me, dear. "

Jennifer sits beside Naomi and shows her the baby. "Her name is Zubina. She'll be three months in four days. She was born in Zurich on February ninth. I required no drugs and the birth was not difficult for me."

"She's a beautiful child," says Naomi, gazing at the sleeping babe. "Unquestionably your daughter."

"I think she looks more like Lucien," says Jennifer, giggling.

"Where are you living now, dear?" asks Naomi, sensing something missing in Jennifer, some important dimension of personality.

"We live most of the time now in Zurich," says Jennifer, standing up as Maahiah returns with Jahera.

"Hello," says Jahera, her voice shaking. "I'm Jahera. Lucien's mother."

"Hello," says Jennifer, nodding politely. "I'm Jennifer Badeaux, Lucien's wife. I recognize you from his pictures of you."

"Where is Lucien?" asks Jahera, trying to remain calm.

"In Santa Rosa," says Jennifer, nodding to affirm this. "We flew from Los Angeles early this morning and Lucien hired a car and driver to bring me here. This is your granddaughter. Her name is Zubina. We are going to put her up for adoption, but before we do we wondered if you would like to have her."

"Why are you giving her away?" asks Jahera, trembling with anger.

"Well..." says Jennifer, with a disconcerting lack of emotion, "we had her because Lucien thought it would be good for him to have a child. But once we had the baby, he didn't want her. And then he had to go to Los Angeles for a job, so we decided to see if you would take her."

"How old is she?" asks Jahera, crying.

"She'll be three months in four days," says Jennifer in her little girl voice. "If you want to keep her I brought her medical records and birth certificate and a notarized letter from Lucien saying she is your biological granddaughter. I've been weaning her onto formula so she won't miss my milk."

"Was this *your* idea?" asks Jahera, taking the baby from Jennifer. "Or Lucien's? Please tell me the truth."

"Oh it was my idea," says Jennifer, cheerfully. "I thought it would be nice for her to grow up with her sister and brother. Lucien said *No* at first because he always says *No* at first, but a few days later he said *Maybe so*, and then he got a job in Los Angeles and said we could bring the baby to see if you would take her."

"Of course we will," says Maahiah, taking the baby from Jahera.

"Good," says Jennifer, going to the door. "If you'll follow me I'll give you her clothes and medical records and the letter saying she is your granddaughter, and then I must get back to Santa Rosa because we have to be in Los Angeles tomorrow."

Naomi and Jahera beseech Jennifer to stay until Tova and Healing get home, but she leaves before Jean and the children can even catch a glimpse of her.

*

So the guest room in the little old house becomes the nursery, and Maahiah volunteers to spend her nights in the bed next to Zubina's crib. All the adults of the collective share baby-tending duties throughout the day, and Raaz and Oz hold Zubina and feed her and play with her whenever the adults will allow them to.

Much to everyone's relief and delight, Zubina is a happy baby and seems entirely untroubled by the disappearance of her mother. She sleeps through the night without waking, has a hearty appetite, naps for three hours from late morning until early afternoon, and goes to sleep right after supper.

The first time Healing held Zubina he called her Zubu, and now everyone calls her Zubu, including the pediatrician who declared her to be in excellent health and possessed of advanced motor skills for one so young.

*

For the first few days after Zubu arrived, Oz and Raaz were perplexed by everyone referring to Zubu as their sister, so Healing drew a family tree with MAAHIAH, CASPAR, NAOMI, and EZRA on the top line, JAHERA, HEALING, and JEAN on the next line down, TOVA, LUCIEN and JENNIFER on the next line down, and RAAZIYAH, OZAN and ZUBINA on the bottom line, with appropriate connecting lines showing who came from who. This genealogical diagram is of great interest to Raaz and Oz, so Healing affixes it to the kitchen wall where the parrot cage used to be.

Naomi adores Zubu and speaks to her as if she can understand adult vocabulary.

Jean is gaga over Zubu and frequently totes her to William's house from where she and William promenade around town with Zubu riding in a front-facing baby carrier.

Jahera and Maahiah were initially distraught about *how* Zubu came to them, but they are both so in love with her, the *how* of Zubu's arrival no longer impinges on their joy of having her in the family.

For Tova, sadly, the coming of Zubu has rekindled her rage about Lucien abandoning Raaz and Oz, and she rarely takes care of Zubu, though when she does, she and the baby get along splendidly.

Raaz and Oz are thrilled beyond telling to have Zubu in their midst and never tire of being with her.

And Eliana takes care of Zubu every chance she gets, singing to her, and imagining having a baby of her own.

Of the dogs, Mendelssohn is by far the most attentive to Zubu, though Healing makes sure to present the baby girl to each of the dogs every day so they become accustomed to her, and she to them.

*

On the evening of May fourteenth, eleven days after Zubu arrived at the little old house, Healing puts Raaz and Oz to bed in the guest room and tells them a story about their fictional selves and their fictional little sister solving The Mystery of the Missing Cookies (Socrates and Mendelssohn the culprits.)

When the children are asleep, Healing joins Naomi, Jean, Jahera, Maahiah, and Tova in the living room to discuss their favorite subject these days: Zubina.

"This morning" says Tova, sipping her wine, "Raaz asked me, 'If Zubu is our sister, why doesn't she live at *our* house?' and I didn't know what to say."

"Maybe she *should* live over there with us," says Maahiah, who intends to sleep with the baby at night no matter which side of the street they live on. "It might feel odd in a year or so for Zubu to be living here and Raaz and Oz to be living over there."

"For now you can tell Raaz that Zubu will come live with you when she's a little older," says Jahera, who never wants Zubu to live anywhere but with her and Healing.

"But *will* she live over there when she's older?" asks Healing, looking at Tova. "Do you want a third child in your house, Tove?"

"I don't know," says Tova, torn. "I love her, but she's a constant reminder of what Lucien did to us. I know I'm being petty, but there it is."

"You're not being petty," says Jean, who struggles every day with her anger about Albert abusing her for so many years. "I don't see why you should have to play the part of her mother if you don't want to. Oz and Raaz don't care where she sleeps at night. They're just happy to have a sister."

"She has Lucien's genes," says Healing, gazing solemnly at Tova. "But he is not her father in any other way. She is a newborn and needs love, endless love, as we all did when we were babies, and as we all do now. I pray you will cease to conflate her with your relationship with Lucien. She was born as you were born, through a confluence of a hundred million miracles. *How* we arrive here in these bodies ceases to matter once we are here. All that matters now is that she be loved and cared for and allowed to grow into her fullness."

*

On the last Sunday in May, the morning hot and sunny, copious waffles consumed, Raaz and Oz enjoy cocoa with marshmallows on top while the adults have coffee and tea.

Jahera passes Zubu to William who makes a silly face that causes Zubu to gurgle with pleasure.

"You know, *I* didn't come to live with my parents until I was five-months-old," says William to Raaz and Oz. "And when I was thirteen-years-old, I asked my mother Mamie why my father Fred and my much older brother Ted were both so tall, when I was *not* tall and not *going* to be tall. That's when Mamie told me that Ted had an older sister named Virginia, and *Virginia* was my mother and gave me to Mamie and Fred when I was a baby. Which meant my parents were really my grandparents, and my brother was really my uncle. And though I thought I should be sad about this, I wasn't sad because my grandmother and grandfather and uncle were such good parents to me."

"Did you ever get to see Virginia again?" asks Raaz, who wonders if she'll ever see her father Lucien again.

"I did," says William, recalling the magic moment. "Eight years ago. I was in a play in San Francisco, and after the play I was coming out of the theatre when a man and woman approached me and asked me to sign their programs. And as I was signing them, the woman said, 'I was so proud of you because... you are my son.' Their names were Via and Jeff. My mother had changed her name from Virginia to Via. They were visiting from Minnesota, and a year later I went to Minnesota to visit them. After that we exchanged Christmas cards until my mother died three years ago. She was a sweet person and I was her only child. She said she didn't know who my father was."

"Why didn't she keep you when you were a baby?" asks Oz, mystified.

"Well... she was very young when she had me," says William, gazing down at Zubu. "She ran away from home when she was fifteen and had me when she was sixteen, and because she was having such a hard time taking care of me she thought it would be better to give me to Mamie and Fred, so that's what she did."

"We never know what may happen in life," says Darby, smiling at the children. "Look at me. I was alone and lonely for most of me life, and then out of the blue Marjorie came along to keep me company. You just never know what might happen, so you want to be ready for anything."

William passes Zubu to Healing.

"Most of you will remember Carla, the biggest dog we've ever had," says Healing, holding Zubu so she has a view of everyone around the table. "Carla died a few years before Raaz and Oz were born. She was by far the best mother dog we've ever had."

"Did she have puppies?" asks Raaz, frowning. "I thought all our dogs got fixed so they don't have babies because there are too many dogs."

"Carla never gave birth," says Healing, remembering the day he and Jahera and Carla found the pups Tabinda and Kadan in a nest in the forest, their mother having abandoned them. "But she was a loving mother to every pup and dog who came to live with us while she was alive, including Tabinda and Kadan and Socrates."

"Oh Carla," says Tova, taking Zubu from Healing. "She even loved the cats."

Zubu makes a humming sound to say she'd like some goat's milk, and when Maahiah goes to warm the baby bottle, Jahera comes to take Zubu from Tova.

"I'll nurse her," says Tova, nuzzling the baby. "I'm falling in love."

"May I have some goat milk, too?" asks Oz, watching his mother nuzzle the baby.

"I didn't think you liked goat's milk, Oz," says Naomi, looking over the tops of her glasses at him. "You always make such a sour face when I drink mine."

"Well now I do like it," says Oz, matter-of-factly. "Because it's very nutritious."

"Indeed it is," says Healing, looking at William. "You know, I'm sorely tempted to quote The Bard at this moment. Can you guess which lines?"

"From *Hamlet,*" says William, nodding. "I was thinking the same thing."

"Shall we?" says Healing, smiling expectantly.

So William and Healing speak as one, William's voice a little deeper than Healing's.

"Our wills and fates do so contrary run, that our devices still are overthrown; our thoughts are ours, their ends none of our own."

*

That night, Jahera looks up from reading *The Children* and asks Healing, "Are you writing a new poem?"

"Gibberish," says Healing, closing his notebook. "Time for bed. Read to me of the Kalahari?"

She waits for him to get in bed before she begins to read.

"'Her stomach full of meat for the first time in five moons, Oh-Ni is filled with hope she will have the strength to dig tubers tomorrow and gather nuts so her bag will be full when they set out a few days from now for Always Water Here. Mahn holds their baby Kuah and sings to him about hunting antelope and bringing home meat. Oh-Ni listens to Mahn singing and knows that tonight she will not wake in the dark fearing for her baby's life.'"

Healing lies on his back and gazes at the knotholes in the ceiling and thinks back to the beginning of the day when he carried Zubu outside to help him oversee the dogs, after which he made waffles and presided over the children for the morning before changing into his wedding togs to play a four-hour gig at the East Cove Hotel as prelude to walking the dogs before supper, doing the dishes after supper, and partaking of an epic game of Scrabble.

"You missed your nap today, Shafi," says Jahera, putting her book away and turning off her light. "You must be exhausted."

"And now I'll lie awake worrying about Oh-Ni and her baby," says Healing, embracing his wife. "As I recall it's a long way to Always Water Here."

"Don't worry," says Jahera, kissing him. "They lived thirty thousand years ago and helped our species survive so you and I could be together now."

"So Zubu would be born and come live with us."

"Sometimes when I hold her I imagine she is our child we made together and I gave birth to her. I don't know why I feel this way, but sometimes I do."

"Maybe because you're her mum now and I'm her papa."

"Or maybe because we both wished we could have a child together, so the universe gave us Zubu."

Ω

20. Marzipan

On a sunny Monday morning in early June, the day after Healing's seventy-first birthday, Tova walks Raaz and Oz to Esther and Darvin's for the last day of school, and when she returns to the little old house she finds the elders of the collective gathered on the deck having tea and being entertained by Zubu – the dogs waiting with varying degrees of impatience to go on their first walk of the day.

Healing holds Zubu upright so she can freely practice the motions of walking.

"I have an announcement," says Tova, sitting down next to Naomi.

"Oh good," says Naomi, taking Tova's hand. "We love announcements."

"I have been offered a role in a movie to be filmed in Portland in September, directed by Morris Goodman. A five-week shoot. I told Morris if I took the part I would need to come home every ten days, and he said he would arrange the shooting schedule accordingly. So... if I take the part, may I leave Oz and Raaz in your care while I'm in Portland? I need to let Morris know yay or nay by tomorrow."

"Of course we'll take the children," says Jahera, thrilled for Tova. "Who is Morris Goodman and how does he know of you?"

"Morris Goodman's most recent film *The Dabbler* made boatloads of money and was nominated for two Oscars. Morris saw me in *Her Eloquent Refusal* two years ago, liked my performance, and when Morris was in France two weeks ago, Daniel showed him a rough cut of *Delphine and the Sorcerer*. Morris called me the next day and asked if I would read his script for a movie called *With Cream Or Black*, and I said I would. The script came the next day via special courier, with a cover letter offering me a dizzying sum to play the lead."

"Might we know the dimensions of *dizzying*?" asks Naomi, looking over the tops of her glasses at Tova.

"Two hundred thousand dollars," says Tova, frowning at the ridiculous sum. "Ten times what Daniel paid me for *Delphine*."

"Good God," says Healing, handing Zubu to Jean. "What's the movie about? I hope you don't have to kill anyone."

"No killing, Pa-pa. It's a comedy about a woman named Anna, played by me if I take the part, who owns a food truck in Portland with two zany friends. The three of them have culinary romantic adventures and plumb the depths of the human psyche."

"A food movie," says Jean, bouncing Zubu. "Some of my favorite movies are food movies."

"Mine, too," says Maahiah, marveling at Tova's good fortune. "What kind of food will you make in your truck?"

"Nouvelle Tex-Mex," says Tova, laughing. "One of my zany friends is Mexican, the other French."

"I'm so happy for you," says Jahera, embracing Tova. "The children will be fine, especially if you come home a time or two during your adventure."

"What a remarkable life you've had," says Naomi, gazing in wonder at Tova. "When you were nine-years-old you said you were going to be a movie actor, and now, despite a thousand detours, you are."

Tova turns to Healing. "Do you think I should do it, Pa-pa?"

"If you like the script," he says, nodding. "Then yes."

"I do like it," she says sincerely. "I can see why he chose me for Anna. She's a hopeless romantic masquerading as a cynic with a relentlessly ironic sense of humor."

"Then by all means do it," says Healing, embracing her. "You'll be great."

*

At noon, Healing and Jahera leash Coosi and Miguelito and walk across town to Darvin and Esther's house where Jahera poses the four scholars with Darvin, Healing, Kashvi and Rajiv, everyone wearing

Nasturtium School T-shirts, the photos to memorialize Year One of Nasturtium School.

*

"I'll miss our school," says Raaz as they walk home. "Maybe we could have summer school like at the Montessori."

"With field trips to the beach and Darla's art gallery," says Oz, in charge of Miguelito. "Arjun and Esther could come, too."

"Field trips are a splendid idea," says Healing, keeping Coosi on a short leash. "Along with frequent play dates, or as we used to call them *playing with our friends*."

"Can we go to *Café Brava* now?" asks Oz, hopefully. "To celebrate the end of school with scones?"

"Lunch awaits at home," says Jahera, tousling Oz's hair. "We'll go to the café soon, but not today."

"Is First Grade harder than Kindergarten?" asks Raaz, frowning at Healing.

"Not harder," says Healing, shaking his head. "Different. You'll learn to read and write even better than you already do, we'll put on plays, Kashvi and Rajiv will teach you Mathematics and Advanced Box Building, Maahiah and Jahera will teach Art and French and cooking, and every day we'll work on translating *Moby Dick* into Latin. But it won't be hard. Just *very* interesting."

"He's being silly again," says Oz, exchanging looks with Raaz.

"I know," she replies. "He pretends to be serious when he's not."

"They've found me out," says Healing, forlornly.

"You'll just have to up your game, Shafi," says Jahera, laughing.

"What's *up your game*?" asks Oz, pursing his lips in anticipation of learning something new.

"It means to improve your technique," says Healing as they turn onto Nasturtium Road. "To get better at something."

"Are you being silly again?" asks Raaz, suspiciously.

"No. *Up your game* really means to get better at something," says Healing, solemnly. "I'll never be silly again."

"Yes you *will*," says Oz, rolling his eyes. "You can't help it."

*

"Look! A dog," cries Raaz as they arrive home and find a small brown shorthaired mutt standing at the bottom of the stairs with no attendant human in sight.

"Hello there," says Healing, kneeling to pet the friendly pooch. "Who are you?"

"I've never seen him before," says Oz, petting the dog. "Are you lost?"

Healing reads aloud the name on the pooch's well-worn collar. "*Marzipan*. Sweet name for a sweet pooch."

"Is there a phone number?" asks Jahera, taking pictures of Miguelito and Coosi greeting Marzipan, the mood congenial.

"There is a number," says Healing, unclipping the leash from Miguelito's collar and clipping it to Marzipan's collar. "With a Los Angeles area code."

*

While Marzipan enjoys the company of the resident hounds in the backyard, Healing calls the number on the dog tag.

A woman answers with a hushed, "Hello?"

"Hi. My name is Healing Weintraub and I'm calling regarding a small brown dog named Marzipan. He just showed up at our house and I dialed the number on his dog tag. Is he your dog?"

"You have Marzipan?" says the woman, urgently. "Where are you calling from?"

"Mercy," says Healing, excited by the woman's excitement. "Do you know where that is? On the far north coast of California."

"Just a minute," says the woman, muffling her phone.

A man comes on the line, his voice a growl. "Is there a girl with the dog? Slender. Dark brown hair?"

"No. Only the dog. A four-year-old mix of Jack Russell and Spaniel."

The woman comes on the line again.

"Hello?" she says, her voice shaking. "Are you still there?"

"Still here," says Healing, guessing they're having the call traced. "Still Healing Weintraub calling from Mercy. Am I correct in assuming Marzipan is your dog?"

"Yes," says the woman. "Do you... do you know who we are?"

"I do not," says Healing, quietly. "The tag reveals only the name *Marzipan* and the number I called. That's all I know, along with what I have deduced from what the man said, which is that a girl and Marzipan went missing at the same time, though when that was I have no idea."

"Okay," says the woman, clearly stalling for time. "Um... where did you say you were calling from?"

"Mercy, California," says Healing, growing impatient. "If you're having this call traced, I can save you the trouble by giving you our address and turning the dog over to the Sheriff of Mercy who is our good friend. Would you prefer I do that?"

"I'm sorry," says the woman, starting to cry. "Here's Melvin again."

"Here's the situation," says Melvin, gruffly. "Our daughter Rachel disappeared three years ago with her dog. We're gonna fly up there right now. I see there's an airport in Mercy."

"Rather small," says Healing, guessing he's speaking to someone wealthy. "I don't think they handle jets."

"Where is this place? Siberia? Okay. I see the listing. No jets. We'll fly to Santa Rosa and drive from there. We should be there in about six hours. Can you keep the dog until we get there?"

"Long as you like," says Healing, calmly. "We have several other dogs and Marzipan seems quite happy here. I recommend you stay at the East Cove Hotel."

*

So that evening after supper, Melvin and Melanie Berkholtz, stars of the long-running sit-com *Mel & Mel,* arrive at the little old house with their stunning Romanian assistant Tara and their imposing Israeli bodyguard Alan, their arrival causing Marzipan to cower in the kitchen rather than joining the humans in the living room.

Sheriff Higuera is on hand along with Raaz and Oz who successfully lobbied to stay up to meet Marzipan's owners, and when Healing is done introducing the members of the collective to the visitors, Tova, Maahiah, and the children depart for their house across the street, and Naomi and Jean retire to Naomi's cottage.

When the remaining humans are seated, Melvin, a burly fellow with a Brooklyn accent, his baldness disguised by an expensive toupee of gray hair, takes over the proceedings.

"Rachel disappeared three years ago when she was sixteen and she could pass for twenty-one," he says, sounding as if he's spoiling for a fight. "We're talking serious eye candy. Okay? Get the picture?"

"The love of our life," says Melanie, a buxom brunette from New Jersey. "She was..."

"Now listen," says Melvin, interrupting his wife and pointing at Sheriff Higuera. "We *know* she was kidnapped even though the idiot police classified her a runaway. Just because we never got a ransom note doesn't mean she wasn't kidnapped. There's *no* way she would have left on her own. She just got accepted to Yale. She was happy."

"Rachel and Marzipan were inseparable," says Melanie, crying. "We're hoping she's somewhere nearby."

"The report LAPD sent me says Rachel is now twenty," says Sheriff Higuera, who watches *Mel & Mel* every week with his wife. "Which means should we make contact with her we cannot legally compel her to return to you."

"What are you? A moron?" says Melvin, sneering at Sheriff Higuera. "You know *nothing* about our daughter. When I say she didn't leave on her own, she didn't leave on her own. Okay? Don't give me this *compel* crap. If you find her, she's coming home."

"I am compelled to inform you of the law," says Sheriff Higuera in his unflappable way. "Now that we have photos of her, we'll be on the lookout."

"Whatever," says Melvin, dismissively. "We've got a private investigator coming here to handle things. We'll take the dog now."

"May I make a suggestion?" says Healing, nodding to Melvin and Melanie.

"Make it quick," says Melvin, scowling. "I'm exhausted."

"I suggest we keep Marzipan here with our dogs for the time being and put up notices around town saying we've found him and are looking for his owner. If for some reason your daughter is avoiding discovery, she would be much more likely to contact locals than your private eye whose presence will be known far and wide within minutes of his arrival, just as *your* presence was known to everyone in Mercy mere moments after you checked into the East Cove Hotel."

"Who are you? The town idiot?" says Melvin, getting up and heading for the door. "Tara. Get the dog."

But before Tara and Alan can corner Marzipan, the wily pooch escapes out the ever-ajar kitchen door and hides somewhere in the backyard where Tara and Alan cannot find him in the dark. Their failure to secure the pooch inspires Melvin to heap abuse on Ruben and Healing for aiding and abetting the kidnappers, after which the television stars and their assistants leave for the East Cove Hotel vowing to return on the morrow to collect Marzipan.

*

In the morning, Sheriff Higuera joins the collective for the Saturday pancake feast while Marzipan explores the backyard with Mendelssohn and Miguelito. The adults refrain from speaking of last night's unpleasantness, and the usual gaiety prevails until Socrates growls at visitors coming up the front stairs: Melanie, Tara, and Jack Fielding, a stout fellow with glossy black hair. Melvin has remained at the hotel with a debilitating headache, and Alan has stayed with him to stand guard.

Tova and Jahera take the children out to the garden, which leaves Jean, Naomi, and Maahiah to eavesdrop while doing the breakfast dishes.

When Sheriff Higuera and Healing and the three visitors are settled in the living room, Jack introduces himself as a private investigator and Melanie says, "I want to apologize for Melvin's behavior last night. This is all very upsetting for him, as you can imagine. I hope you will forgive him."

Healing and Sheriff Higuera make no response to Melanie's pleas for forgiveness, and Jack says, "So... we like your idea of putting up a homey local notice about Rachel's dog. If and when Rachel calls, you'll arrange a time for her to come here, you'll call me, and I'll be here when she arrives."

"That I won't do," says Healing, shaking his head. "I will be glad to put up a notice and meet with her, but I won't be party to entrapment."

"You are aware, aren't you, there's a substantial reward if you help us find Rachel?" Jack smirks at Healing. "As in fifty thousand dollars."

"I want no reward," says Healing, standing up. "I must ask you to leave now."

"If I may intercede," says Sheriff Higuera, giving Healing a look to say *Sit down, my friend. I'll handle this.*

"Please," says Melanie, beseeching Healing. "We don't want to trap Rachel. We just want to make sure she's safe and not being held captive by some crazy person."

"I understand," says Healing, sitting down. "This must be very difficult for you."

"A nightmare that never ends," says Melanie, bowing her head. "This is the first glimmer of hope we've had since she disappeared."

"Here is what I suggest," says Sheriff Higuera, speaking slowly. "If by some miracle your daughter is in the vicinity and sees a notice about her dog and comes to get him, Healing will encourage her to communicate with you. He will then give me a full report, which I will relay to you. I suggest you leave Marzipan with Healing, return to Los Angeles, and keep making my wife's favorite television show. If your daughter makes contact with Healing, you will know shortly after I do."

*

Heeding Sheriff Higuera suggestions, Melanie, Melvin, Tara, and Alan return to Los Angeles, leaving Jack in Mercy for another week during which no one responds to the eye-catching poster featuring a darling photo of Marzipan – the poster stapled to dozens of telephone poles and fences around town.

*

On the morning of the Summer Solstice, a week after Jack Fielding leaves town, Jean answers the phone on the kitchen counter.

"Weintraub enclave. Jean speaking."

"Hi Jean," says a woman with a cheerful voice. "It's Trudy Honolulu. From *Café Brava* and *Big Goose*. You come to the café with William."

"Oh Trudy," says Jean, smiling at the thought of the charming young woman who always wears polka-dot clothes and red-framed glasses, her bleached blonde hair streaked with blue. "How nice to hear from you."

"I'm calling about Marzipan," says Trudy, growing serious. "Do you still have him?"

"We do," says Jean, beckoning to Healing. "Let me give you Healing."

"Trudy," says Healing, having expected an intermediary to call on behalf of Rachel Berkholtz, though certainly not the flamboyant Trudy Honolulu. "You're calling about Marzipan? Wonderful dog. He's chasing squirrels in the backyard even as we speak. How do you know him?"

"I got him..." She hesitates. "A year or so ago. I live up Wiley Creek Road and I don't usually bring him into town, but I did last week and he ran away. And you found him. So... I'll come get him whenever it's convenient for you."

"Now is good," says Healing, eager to learn how Trudy came to own Marzipan. "We're just doing the breakfast dishes as prelude to taking the dogs for a walk. Do you know where we are?"

"Who doesn't?" says Trudy, cheerful again. "I'm not working today and I'm in town, so... I'll be there in a few."

Healings hangs up the phone and announces, "Trudy Honolulu will be here shortly to get Marzipan and shed some light, we hope, on the whereabouts of Rachel Berkholtz."

"I *love* Trudy!" says Raaz, standing on a footstool helping Maahiah do the dishes.

"Me, too," says Oz, ensconced on the sofa reading *The Cat In the Hat Comes Back* for the umpteenth time. "She loves polka dots."

Naomi looks up from the crossword puzzle. "Might *Trudy* be Rachel Berkholtz with an ersatz name?"

"Doubtful," says Healing, looking at the photograph of Rachel when last seen three years ago – an exceedingly slender woman with long brown hair. "Unless she's gained sixty or seventy pounds."

"Gaining sixty pounds would be a good disguise," says Jahera, sitting at the table with Zubu on her lap. "It would change her face as well as her body."

"Rachel is now twenty," says Healing, frowning at the photo of the young woman. "Our Trudy has been tending bar at *Big Goose* for at least two years when not working at *Café Brava*, which means she's at least twenty-three."

"Unless she has a false ID," says Maahiah, looking up from her knitting. "I got one when I was sixteen and needed to be eighteen."

"To be continued," says Healing, hearing Trudy on the stairs.

*

Trudy, her sweatshirt red with black polka dots, her trousers black with red polka dots, is in the middle of saying *Hi* to everyone when Marzipan comes racing in from the backyard and leaps into Trudy's arms.

"You little escape artist," she says, laughing as Marzipan licks her face. "I was *worried* about you."

"Definitely your dog," says Healing, judging from Marzipan's adoration of Trudy. "You've only had him a year?"

"Or so," says Trudy, crying. "I think we knew each other in a former life."

"Speaking of which," says Healing, giving a nod toward the kitchen door, "may I speak to you in private? We'll walk the dogs to the pond."

*

Healing and Trudy sit on the old wooden bench a few feet from the water's edge while Marzipan and Coosi and Mendelssohn snuffle around nearby.

"So..." says Healing, looking at Trudy. "As you may imagine, I called the Los Angeles phone number on Marzipan's tag, and Melanie Berkholtz answered."

"Oh boy," says Trudy, closing her eyes. "I should have changed the tag when I got Marz from Rachel. Silly me."

"As a result of my calling them," says Healing, certain now that Trudy is Rachel, "Melanie and her husband Melvin came here looking for Rachel."

"I heard about that," says Trudy, nodding. "Crazy, huh? Television stars descending on Mercy. I'm really sorry you got dragged into this mess, Healing."

"Better me than anyone else in Mercy," says Healing, dispensing chewy treats to the dogs. "So let me ask you this, Trudy. From what you know of Rachel, do you think she'll ever communicate with her parents again? They really are suffering not knowing if she's alive or not."

"I'm sorry her mother is suffering," says Trudy, stoically. "But from what Rachel told me, her father never cared about her except that she fulfill his idea of *beautiful* even if it meant starving herself to death. As for communicating with her mother, maybe Rachel will send her a letter through a friend in Europe so they can't trace who sent it."

"I support Rachel in all of this," says Healing, clearing his throat. "There's just one problem. Her parents will want to know who claimed Marzipan. If I report that no one did, they will want to come get him. If I tell them *you* claimed him, Jack will return to have a close look at you."

"I thought of that," says Trudy, making a clucking sound that prompts Marzipan to hop up on the bench. "I think the best thing would be for Marzipan to escape from your yard and be transformed into a new dog with a new tag and a new name. I'm sure your fence is riddled with holes through which a wily dog might escape."

"Riddled," says Healing, nodding in agreement. "What will his new name be?"

"Boo Boo," says Trudy, laughing. "Like it?"

"Love it," says Healing, laughing with her. "I will wait a few days to inform Sheriff Higuera of Marzipan's disappearance, after which the good sheriff will communicate the news to Rachel's parents."

"Have you ever seen their show?" asks Trudy, as they walk back to the house, the dogs trotting ahead of them.

"Never have," says Healing, shaking his head.

"Every episode begins with Melvin doing something hurtful to someone. Then Melanie spends the rest of the show going to incredible lengths to make amends for what Melvin did, so that by the end of the show Melvin actually believes he did something good by being hurtful. For some reason millions of people never tire of this device."

"Art imitating life?" asks Healing, aching in sympathy with her.

"A woman enabling a horrible man," says Trudy, nodding. "America's favorite pastime."

"Thank goodness Boo Boo came to *us* and not someone else," says Healing, smiling as Raaz and Oz come rushing out the kitchen door to be with Trudy.

"Thank goodness," says Trudy, opening her arms to the children.

Ω

21. Bart

On the last day of June, the dogs come in for supper, and Tabinda is missing from the pack, so Jean and the children go looking for her and find her body near the pond.

Three evenings later, Socrates lies down in the living room with the other dogs and never wakes again.

*

On July seventeenth, Tova, Raaz, and Oz leave with Jean and William for a seven-day trip to Berkeley, San Francisco, and Palo Alto. Their itinerary includes wandering around North Beach and Golden Gate Park, visiting museums, spending time with William's daughters and their families, meeting some of William's friends, riding on trains and ferry boats, going to a baseball game, staying in motels, and having Thai food, Indian food, and Japanese food.

*

On the morning of July twenty-second, Naomi is sitting at the kitchen table pondering the crossword puzzle, Healing is doing the dishes, Jahera is carrying Zubu around singing to her, and Maahiah is warming a baby bottle of goat's milk.

"I have an announcement," says Naomi, clasping her hands. "As I told you some months ago, my intention was to live until Oz and Raaz are seven. However, forces beyond my control are now making my life difficult, and I don't think I'll be able to live much longer without medical assistance. Since I do not wish to prolong my life in that way, I am going to leave you sooner than I had hoped by ceasing to eat and drink. My fast will begin on the first of August, ten days from today. As you know, I visited Dr. Hardy yesterday and he has agreed to prescribe morphine should I experience unbearable pain in the latter stages of the process. I'm sorry to bring you this news so soon after Socrates and Tabinda died, but I wanted to tell you before the children return from their trip."

"Oh Mum," says Healing, going to her.

"I have one request, dear," she says, clinging to him. "I would like to have a party before I depart at which you and Eliana and Tayo and Tova perform my favorite songs. A barbecue for our close friends."

*

An hour later, Healing and Jahera walk with Mendelssohn across town to visit Darby and Marjorie.

"I'm afraid to tell Darby," says Healing, gazing forlornly at Jahera. "He'll be devastated."

"Don't be afraid," she says quietly. "I'll tell them."

Healing starts to cry, which moves Mendelssohn to nudge Healing's hand to say *Don't be sad, Shafi. I'm here with you.*

*

"I was certain your mother would outlive me," says Darby after he and Marjorie have a good long cry.

"I'm not prepared for her to die," says Healing, shaking his head. "She's slowed down some, but otherwise she's all here. I just... I'm in shock."

"Ah God, my boy, it's hard," says Darby, putting his hand on Healing's shoulder. "There's no way to prepare except to love her and be with her until she goes."

Healing bows his head and weeps and Darby keeps his hand on Healing's shoulder.

"We will come every day to help you," says Marjorie, holding Jahera's hand.

Healing looks up at Marjorie. "She'll be glad you're there."

"My mum died when I was twenty-seven," says Darby, sighing. "With nothing to keep me in Ireland I came to America in search of the Beatniks. I found none in New York so I took the train to Chicago. No luck there, I got on a Greyhound bus to San Francisco where I found a few old Beats hanging on in North Beach, but they were jaded and unfriendly and the women were hard, so I hitchhiked north and got a ride with Jim Young in his old brown pickup. He brought me to Mercy and let me sleep on his living room sofa until I got my bearings. And it was on my second day here I was walking down Main Street when who should come walking toward me but Naomi and Ezra and you, Healing, fourteen you were, each of you with a friendly dog. I said, 'Top of the morning to you,' and your father smiled his beautiful smile and said, 'You must be the Irish fellow sleeping on Jim Young's sofa.' And Naomi said, "Do come for supper. We are perishing from a lack of interesting guests.' And that was how I began to wiggle my way into your good graces."

*

Returning from Darby and Marjorie's, Healing and Jahera find Naomi and Maahiah sitting on the sofa laughing.

"May we know the cause of your mirth?" asks Healing, laughing, too, despite his sorrow.

"You had a call about a dog," says Naomi, chuckling. "When I got off the phone I said to Maahiah, 'I must teach you how to probe for salient details when taking calls for Healing.' Why this struck us as funny we don't know, but it did."

"Have you the strength to fill me in on the details of the case?" asks Healing, sitting beside his mother.

"I do," says Naomi, her eyes sparkling. "The caller was Elvis Oglethorpe, Justin's nephew. Works at the lumberyard. He and his wife Didi have a new baby, Fiona, three-months-old. Their dog Bart, a large Husky Lab, has taken to growling at Fiona, and Didi is terrified he might hurt the baby. Thus Bart has been exiled to the backyard, and Elvis and Didi are considering finding a new home for him, possibly with Justin and Helen."

"Curious," says Healing, getting up and wandering into the kitchen. "I gave Didi and Bart weekly lessons for five months starting when Bart was three-months-old. Three years ago. He's a splendid dog. I can't imagine him growling at the baby. Let's hope it's not too late to fix the problem. But if we can't, I'm sure Helen and Justin and their dog Pushkin would love to have Bart come live with them."

"Or *we* could take him," says Jahera, putting a kettle on for tea.

"I suppose we could," says Healing, starting to cry again. "Didn't occur to me."

*

The next morning as breakfast is ending, Healing answers the ringing phone.

"Hi Pa-pa," says Tova, joyfully. "I'm calling from Palo Alto to let you know we're extending our trip three more days to visit William's friends in Santa Cruz and Monterey. We're having *so* much fun."

"Oh Tove, I think it would be better if you didn't extend the trip" says Healing, anxiously. "Mum is..."

"Let me speak to her," says Naomi, taking the phone from Healing. "Hello Tova. The fates have conspired to make it necessary for me to depart sooner than I had planned. We're going to have a party next week at which I hope you will sing with your father and Eliana and Tayo, after which I'll settle down in my cottage to make the transition. I'd very much appreciate you and Jean and the children coming home sooner than later so we can have more time together before I go."

"We'll come home tomorrow," says Tova, bursting into tears.

"Thank you, dear," says Naomi, sighing with relief. "No need to tell the children about my plans. I will tell them when you get home. How does that sound?"

"Okay," says Tova, sobbing. "See you tomorrow."

"I wonder if we might make a trip to the beach today," says Naomi as she returns the phone to its cradle. "We could drive to the end of Gulley Road where I can walk out a little way on the sand. I'm not so good walking on sand anymore but I'm longing to go to the beach and could certainly go a little way with your assistance."

"I'll call Justin and Diego," says Healing, picking up the phone. "See if they'll meet us there and carry you close to the water in your Adirondack chair."

"Good thinking, dear," says Naomi, having a sip of her tea. "I haven't seen Justin and Helen in weeks and I've been wanting to tell Helen how much I love her new poems. And I've been missing Diego terribly, but he's been so busy with his photography I haven't wanted to bother him." She looks over the tops of her glasses at Jahera and Maahiah. "Diego is one of our great achievements, don't you think?"

"Yes," says Jahera on her way out the door to have another cry in the garden.

"Shall we take a picnic?" says Naomi, nodding to Maahiah. "Your hummus and flat bread and olives, please. And you'll come with us, won't you, dear?"

"Yes," says Maahiah, finishing the breakfast dishes. "I will prepare a pique-nique."

*

Shortly after midday, the sky free of clouds, Jahera and Maahiah with Zubu in her stroller walk to Gulley Road while Healing and Naomi drive there in Healing's little old pickup with Mendelssohn and Coosi and Naomi's Adirondack chair riding in the back.

Waiting for them where Gulley Road ends at the beach are Justin and Helen and Diego Rodriguez, the formidably strong photography instructor at the community college. When Naomi is settled securely in her sturdy wooden chair, Diego and Justin carry her across the sand to the shore of Mercy Bay where hundreds of pelicans are fishing in the shallows.

Two big beach blankets are unfurled and the humans gather around a feast of hummus and flat bread, olives, cheese, and sautéed vegetables, along with fish and chips and wine and lemonade courtesy of *Big Goose*, Helen and Justin's pub.

"Oh the glory of this place," says Naomi, holding Zubu on her lap. "For the first ten years we lived here, Ezra and I brought Healing and Jean to the beach every day, save for the stormiest of days." She turns to Healing. "Remember? The pull was irresistible."

"Still is, Mum," says Healing, nodding in thanks to her.

"Like the tide going out," says Diego, who just now learned Naomi is going to die soon. "I'm gonna come see you every day, Naomi. Okay? Teresa will want to come, too."

"I was hoping you'd say that," she says, handing Zubu to Maahiah.

"Remember when I used to think there was nothing to do here?" says Diego, grinning at Healing. "I was gonna move to LA where all the action is." He laughs. "I didn't know *any*thing when I started working for you. Nothing."

"In the Sixties," says Naomi, gazing upon the shining sea, "when our house was a haven for those seeking an alternative to the status quo, Ezra and I divided our visitors into two camps: those who found Mercy entirely lacking, and those who found Mercy overflowing with riches. And though I know it is simplistic to divide humanity in this way, I still do."

"How could anyone not be inspired here?" says Helen, entranced by the waves arising again and again from the tumult.

"Whenever I take a group of new students out to shoot pictures for the first time," says Diego, smiling at Helen, "some of them take pictures on the way, but most of them wait until we get where we're going. Then they look around and say, 'Why did you bring us here? What is there to see? What do you want me to take a picture of?' And I always remember what you told me, Healing, about not criticizing people, so I don't argue with them or tell them they're blind, you know, because I was blind, too, until Jahera taught me a great picture doesn't have to be something fantastic. It's about the light and shadows and the way the forms relate to each other, and the thousand details that make everything so compelling."

"When I hear you speak, Diego," says Naomi, holding out her hand to him, "I am so very glad I got to watch you grow into your brilliance."

"Gracias, Naomi," he says, feeling blessed by her. "You helped me so much."

*

The next morning, Healing and Jahera go to visit Elvis, Didi, and Fiona Oglethorpe, and their dog Bart.

Elvis is forty-four, a very tall redhead who works at the lumberyard. Didi is thirty-nine, a petite brunette who worked as a secretary at the hospital until Fiona, chubby and rosy-cheeked with her father's red hair, was born three months ago. Bart is three-and-a-half, an eighty-pound mix of Husky and Lab, extremely intelligent and all about love.

Didi invites Healing and Jahera into the cluttered little house where Elvis is standing in the living room holding Fiona who is in a very fussy mood.

"May I?" asks Jahera, offering to take the baby from Elvis.

"For sure," says Elvis, handing Fiona to Jahera. "She's being a total pill this morning."

"Because *I'm* being a total pill," says Didi, wandering into the disastrous kitchen. "I haven't slept in forever and I've only had one cup of coffee today."

"Fiona's usually pretty mellow," says Elvis, yawning. "But last night she woke up like seven times so we're kinda groggy this morning."

"Welcome to my life," says Didi, yawning, too. "You guys want coffee?"

"No, thank you," says Healing, noting Fiona ceased to fuss the moment Jahera took her from Elvis. "We just had some. Where is the marvelous Bart?"

"In the backyard," says Elvis, wincing as he says so. "Like I said on the phone, he acts weird around the baby so we're keeping him outside until we figure out what to do."

"How does he act weird?" asks Healing, frowning curiously.

"He growls at her," says Didi, grimly. "Scares the crap outta me."

"Shall we go see him?" asks Healing, looking at Elvis.

"Yeah," says Elvis, gesturing for Healing to follow him.

So while Jahera stays with Didi and Fiona, Elvis leads Healing out the kitchen door into the unkempt backyard where Bart rushes up to Healing, tail wagging.

"Hello big boy," says Healing, petting the affable pooch. "What's this I hear about you growling at Fiona?"

Bart spins in a circle and grins wide-eyed at Elvis.

"He thinks we're going on a walk," says Elvis, shaking his head at Bart. "I haven't had much time for him since I started working fifty hours a week to make up for Didi not working, and Didi only has time to walk him when my mom or Helen come to watch the baby, and then she usually just crashes, so..." He smiles sadly at Bart. "Sorry guy. We'll go on a walk later."

"I'd like to see how he behaves in the house," says Healing, giving Bart a chewy treat. "May we?"

"Yeah," says Elvis, despondently. "It'll freak Didi out, but... lemme tell her we're bringing him in."

"Before you do, may I ask you a few questions?"

"Sure," says Elvis, wearily. "He's such a good dog I'd hate to lose him. But Didi says he's a monster around the baby. I haven't actually seen him act that way, but she says he growls at her, so..."

Bart drops a soggy tennis ball at Healing's feet.

"What changes have you made in Bart's life since Fiona arrived?" asks Healing, throwing the ball across the scraggly lawn and watching Bart give chase.

"Well like I said, we don't walk him enough now." Elvis shoves his hands in his pockets. "And Didi keeps the hall door closed now whenever he's in the house. Or she did until we moved him outside."

"He used to go down the hall?"

"Oh for sure. He slept on the bed with us." Elvis yawns. "But when Didi started getting up four times a night to nurse Fiona she said Bart was in the way so we moved him out to the living room, and now he's outside. If we still have him when it gets real cold we'll keep him in the garage."

"Any other changes?"

"Not really," says Elvis, shrugging. "Except he's not allowed on the couch anymore."

"Because?"

"That's where Didi sits to nurse the baby and she doesn't want Bart bugging her."

"Was Bart often on the sofa before Fiona arrived?"

"All the time. He sat with us when we watched television, took naps there, and when he'd get in the way in the kitchen we'd say, 'Go to the couch, Barty.'"

"So the sofa was his comfort zone."

"For sure," says Elvis, nodding.

"Any other changes you can think of before he was exiled to the backyard?"

"No." Elvis frowns. "He was fine before I had to go back to work. That's when he started growling at the baby. Like I told you, I haven't actually *heard* him growl at her, but Didi says he does and it scares her to death."

"Lastly," says Healing, petting Bart, "would you say Didi and Bart were on good terms before Fiona arrived?"

"You serious?" says Elvis, taken aback. "They were like best friends. She picked him from the litter, trained him, walked him every day, and she took him to you for lessons. Remember? That's what makes this so sad. She used to love him more than anything and now she hates him because she thinks he's gonna hurt the baby." He grimaces. "You think maybe he's jealous of Fiona? Why else would he growl at her?"

"I don't know," says Healing, petting Bart again. "If you will forewarn Didi, we'll bring the pooch inside and see what develops."

*

When Healing and Elvis and Bart enter the house they find Didi at the dining table drinking coffee and texting someone on her phone, while Jahera sits on the sofa with Fiona on her lap, the little girl fast asleep.

Bart trots over to Jahera to say hello and Didi jumps up shouting, "Get away from her Bart! Get away."

Fiona wakes up startled and begins to cry, and Bart slinks away to the far corner of the living room.

"Why did you do that?" asks Healing, mystified by Didi's behavior. "Bart was just being friendly."

"Because he growls at her," says Didi, glaring at Healing. "Maybe not then, but he usually does, and then Fiona starts crying and I freak out. I can't handle this anymore. We're gonna have to get rid of him."

Jahera rocks Fiona and coos to her, and the baby girl relaxes and ceases to cry.

"I certainly don't want to endanger Fiona," says Healing, exchanging looks with Jahera, "but I'm confident I can teach Bart not to growl at her. I'm also very sure he would never intentionally harm her. If you will allow me to try a little experiment."

"Okay," says Didi, starting to cry. "But keep hold of him. Okay?"

"I will," says Healing, holding out his hand to Didi. "Come sit on the sofa and we'll start anew."

"I'm sorry," she says, allowing him to lead her to the sofa. "I haven't had much sleep since the baby was born so I'm kinda raggedy."

"I understand," says Healing, seating her next to Jahera. "Now take Fiona from Jahera and I will introduce Bart to her."

Jahera hands Fiona to Didi, and the baby girl immediately begins to fuss.

Healing sits next to Didi and says to Bart, "Come here good boy. Come meet your sister. Come on now."

Bart gives Didi a fearful look and stays in the corner.

"You will need to invite him," says Healing, speaking quietly to Didi. "Last he heard from you, he wasn't supposed to come near her."

"Come on Barty," says Didi, tearfully. "Come say hi to Fiona."

Bart crosses the room, and Healing takes hold of Bart's collar and encourages him to smell the baby.

Fiona continues to fuss and whimper, and Bart expresses his sympathy for her with a low moaning sound.

"See?" says Didi, pointing fearfully at Bart. "He's growling at her."

"Quite the opposite," says Healing, petting Bart. "He senses her distress and he's saying he wants to be of assistance to you."

"He *is*?" says Didi, gazing at Bart in disbelief. "He's not growling?"

"That's not a growl," says Healing, looking at Bart. "Is it, Barty?"

Bart wags his tail and makes the low moaning sound again.

"Oh my God," says Didi, bursting into tears. "I'm so sorry, B. I didn't understand."

"I would also suggest you invite Bart to avail himself of the sofa again," says Healing, standing up. "This has been his favorite place since he was a puppy and it is now where you sit with the *new* puppy, so to speak, and Bart would like to be here with you. If you don't want him in your bedroom at night, I suggest you make the sofa his nighttime bed and train him to sleep here. No need to keep the hall door closed. He's very smart and you've trained him well."

"I slept very little in the weeks after my son was born," says Jahera, gazing at the baby. "Such a difficult time. Even so, you've done a marvelous job with Fiona."

"Oh thanks," says Didi, smiling through her tears. "I feel like such an idiot for screaming at Bart."

"Not at all," says Jahera, petting Didi. "You're doing fine."

"Come take my place, Elvis," says Healing, getting up.

Elvis sits beside Didi, and she hands him Fiona.

"Now invite Bart up on the sofa with you," says Healing, nodding encouragingly.

"Okay B," says Elvis, petting Bart. "Come on up. Be gentle now."

Bart hops up on the sofa and gazes bashfully at the baby.

"You can be up here now," says Elvis, continuing to pet Bart. "Just gotta be gentle when the baby's close."

Bart looks at Fiona and wags his tail.

"You can give her a kiss," says Elvis, presenting Fiona to Bart. "Be gentle."

Bart looks at Didi.

"It's okay, B," says Didi, crying for joy. "I just didn't understand what you were saying. Go on."

Bart gently touches his nose to Fiona's cheek and she makes a sweet humming sound that causes Bart to grin and wag his tail.

*

The next day in the garden, a glorious summer day, Tova, Healing, and Jahera are pulling weeds and watering the thirsty plants while Naomi sits in a wicker armchair on the garden path watching Oz and Raaz pull carrots and wash them with the garden hose.

"Would you bring me a carrot, please?" asks Naomi, beckoning the children. "And tell me more about your fantastic journey."

Oz pulls a carrot for Naomi and another for himself, washes them, and goes with Raaz to tell Naomi about their ferryboat ride from San Francisco to Larkspur and back to San Francisco again.

When the exciting nautical tale has been told, Naomi says, "Now I have something to tell *you*."

"What happened?" asks Raaz, gazing expectantly at her great grandmother.

"Well it hasn't happened yet," says Naomi, putting her arm around Raaz, "but after the party next week, I will be at the *very* end of my life. So then I'll rest in my cottage until I die. I hope you'll come visit me while I'm resting because I won't be coming into the house anymore or going across the street. But that won't be until after the party."

"Maybe you just have a cold," says Oz, climbing onto Naomi's lap. "Maybe you *won't* die."

"Everything and everyone has to die one day," says Naomi, putting her arms around him. "Like these carrots. Remember when they were tiny seeds and you planted them and covered them with soil and they didn't sprout for a long time. But then they did sprout and they became seedlings and we thinned them so some would get big. And now you've pulled the big ones at the end of their lives. I started as a tiny seed, too, as you did, and I grew for ninety-four years, which is a very long time. Now I'm at the end of my life. It's just how life is."

"But I don't want you to die *ever*," says Raaz, anxiously. "I love you."

"I know, dear," says Naomi, caressing her. "But I *have* to die. It's how the universe works. Things are born and die, and then more things are born and more things die. On and on forever."

Raaz shakes her head and runs to her mother.

"But you won't die until *after* the party," says Oz, remaining on Naomi's lap. "And that won't be until next week."

"That's right, dear," she says, kissing him.

"Will we bury you in the maple forest and plant a maple tree for you?"

"I would love that," says Naomi, crying a little. "However, it is more likely I will be cremated and you will spread my ashes in the trees."

"What's *cremated*?" asks Oz, snuggling with her.

"Ask Healing, dear," says Naomi, closing her eyes. "Time for my nap."

So Oz goes to Healing and asks what *cremated* is, and after Healing explains as best he can, Oz and he agree it would be preferable to bury Naomi in the forest of Japanese maples.

"We'll ask Ruben if we can," says Healing, his vision blurred by tears.

"Why do we have to ask Ruben?" asks Oz, frowning. "We bury the dogs and cats there and don't ask him."

"True," says Healing, holding Oz close. "I just thought it would be good to ask Ruben because he will know the rules for burying people, which are different than the rules for burying dogs and cats."

"Is Ruben coming to the party?" asks Oz, growing sleepy in Healing's arms.

"Of course he is," whispers Healing. "He wouldn't miss it for the world."

*

"I may never sleep again," says Healing, still awake at midnight.

Jahera does not stir, her breathing slow and steady, so Healing slips out of bed and goes down the hall to the living room where Mendelssohn is waiting to go out with him.

They walk to the pond, the sky a glimmering mass of stars, the crickets making their songs over the sound of the distant surf.

Mendelssohn nudges Healing's hand and Healing kneels beside him.

"Life is sad, Moosh," says Healing, petting his old friend.

Mendelssohn touches his nose to Healing's nose to say *We always have each other*.

"Until we don't," says Healing, shivering as he rises to go back inside.

No says Mendelssohn, nudging Healing's hand. *We* always *have each other*. *We always do.*

Ω

22. Freedom

Three days before Naomi's party, the morning fog in no hurry to depart, Joel and Irene Schlesinger arrive at the little old house with their enormous good-natured hound Moshe, a handsome mix of Great Dane and Rhodesian Ridgeback, his fur short and golden brown.

"So," says Joel as he and Irene stand with Healing on the deck watching Moshe go with Mendelssohn, Miguelito, and Coosi to visit the pond. "We have momentous news and a question for you."

Healing smiles. "We heard from the Guptas that Judy and Jeff and Sara are moving to Honolulu."

"And we are moving with them," says Irene, smiling brightly. "They're leaving in a couple weeks so Sara can start school there in August, and we'll be moving in September. We bought the kids a house in a very nice neighborhood and we bought a townhouse for us three blocks away."

"On the most beautiful golf course I've ever seen," says Joel, with a happy sigh. "No more golfing in a parka. The only problem is..."

"Moshe," says Healing, nodding. "We will be happy to take him."

"Oh thank God," says Joel, raising his arms to the heavens. "We insist on paying for his food. He eats like an elephant."

"If you wish," says Healing, bowing to them. "I hope you'll come to the party on Saturday."

"Of course we will," says Irene, sadly. "We love Naomi. And we love you. We're *so* grateful to you. What can we bring?"

"Just you," says Healing, his tears on the rise. "Would you mind keeping Moshe until a few days before you leave? Things are a bit tumultuous here right now."

"Be happy to," says Joel, nodding emphatically. "The last thing we want to do is be a burden to you."

*

Later that morning, Jean, Healing, Tova, Raaz, and Oz take the dogs for a beach walk and find lots of people and dogs enjoying the sand and the crashing waves.

"I'll miss Irene and Joel," says Jean, holding Moshe close so he is less likely to tug on his leash. "Such charming people."

"I will miss them, too," says Healing, in charge of Miguelito and Coosi and Mendelssohn. "But they'll be happier in Hawaii. They found it unpleasantly cold here and now Joel will be able to play golf in a short-sleeved shirt."

"Where's Hawaii?" asks Oz, who is holding Flora's leash, Flora now as big as Mendelssohn and sweet as can be. "Why is it so warm there?"

"I'll show you in the atlas when we get home," says Jean, recalling the happy hours she and Healing spent as children perusing the atlas with Naomi and Ezra.

"Mama?" asks Raaz, who has charge of little Max. "When will our school start again?"

"In a month or so," says Tova, tugging Puccini away from a pile of delicious seaweed. "When Arjun and Rajiv and Kashvi get back from India."

"Where *is* India?" asks Oz, frowning at his mother.

"We'll look that up in the atlas, too," says Tova, exchanging smiles with Jean. "When we get home."

"We may have a new student," says Jean, antsy to get back to her mother. "Her name is Georgia Fidelio. She's six and just moved here with her mother Lola from Italy. Lola is the new ophthalmologist at the hospital. They live next door to Darla."

"Excitement abounds," says Healing, slowing to a stop. "Shall we turn the hounds around and head home? Who knows what fun they might be having without us."

*

When Joel and Irene return to the little old house in the afternoon to get Moshe, they find Eliana, Tayo, Tova, and Healing performing on the deck for Naomi, Maahiah, Jahera, Oz, Raaz, Zubu, Jean, William, Helen, Justin, and Darla.

"We thought the party was Saturday," says Joel, when the quartet finishes a rousing rendition of Rogers and Hammerstein's *Sunday Sweet Sunday*. "I hope we didn't miss the appetizers."

"No appetizers today," says Naomi, laughing, "but do join us for supper. The resident gourmands are barbecuing corn and fish and vegetable shish kebobs."

"A dress rehearsal," says Jahera, giving Irene and Joel hugs. "Please stay for supper."

"How can we refuse?" says Irene, loving how affectionate Jahera is.

"Unfortunately I have to leave in twenty minutes," says Tayo, smiling at Naomi. "Any requests before I go?"

"Oh I'd love to hear *Deep Purple* again," says Naomi, smiling brightly. "I know you started with that today, but I love it so much."

"So do we," says Tayo, nodding to Healing and Eliana.

Healing plays the lovely chord progression, Tayo adds a heartbeat with his bass, and Eliana and Tova sing the song together, their exquisite harmonizing moving everyone to tears, save for the children who are simply thrilled by the sound of the music.

In the still of the night once again I hold you tight
Though you've gone, your love lives on

*

When the corn and fish and vegetables are sizzling on the barbecue, Naomi and Eliana sit together on the garden bench bathed in the golden light of day's end.

"At breakfast today," says Naomi, gazing fondly at Eliana, "Healing mentioned your wedding gigs have proven so lucrative you are considering moving out of your parents' house and getting a place in town."

"I've wanted to get my own place for years," says Eliana, in her excited way. "Just never had the wherewithal. Or the courage. Now I have both. The trick will be finding a place to rent. There's a terrible shortage of rentals in Mercy these days."

"Would you like to live in my cottage?" asks Naomi, taking Eliana's hand. "After I'm gone? I would love for you to live here to help with Zubu and be auntie to Raaz and Oz. Jean was going to live in my cottage, but now she's shacking up with William." Naomi laughs. "I've always loved that expression. Maahiah has her cottage across the street, so... Healing and Jahera said they'd love for you to live here if you want to." She smiles mischievously. "I promise not to haunt you."

"Oh I wish you would," says Eliana, crying. "Then I won't miss you so much."

"We've known each other since you were born," says Naomi, putting her arms around Eliana. "You were one-and-a-half when Ezra and I moved to England. I remember taking you on a tour of the vegetable garden shortly before we departed and you asked politely, 'May I pick a flower?' I said you could and you proceeded to pick several dozen sweet peas we put in a vase on the kitchen table."

"I've always been greedy for flowers," says Eliana, laughing.

"I'll never forget the moment we met again after I moved back to Mercy," says Naomi, her eyes sparkling. "I'd only been home for a day when you came for your accordion lesson. You were fourteen, charming and beautiful and funny. You deftly assumed my British accent and dazzled me with your intellect, and then you and Healing played a gorgeous accordion duet and I knew without a doubt you were one of the most fully realized people I've ever known."

"Me?" says Eliana, sniffling. "I'm one of the most *un*realized people I've ever known. I'm almost twenty-six and I still live with my parents who would *love* for me to live with them for the rest of my life. I've never even come close to having a lover. Of either gender." She pouts. "What do you mean by fully realized?"

"I mean you are void of false persona," says Naomi, looking into Eliana's eyes. "You speak your feelings without inhibition, you are reflexively loving and kind, and you feel the sufferings of others as your own. As for not having had a lover yet, you are protected, my dear, by your genius and your originality such that most people are incapable of recognizing you as anything but a beautiful eccentric. But do not despair. Though you have yet to meet your future partner, you will. I have inquired of my cards about you many times and there can be no doubt that one day, if you will forgive the cliché, your prince will come."

*

When the feasting subsides and no one is inclined to leave, more wine is poured, tea is brewed, and cocoa is made for the children.

"One of my fondest memories is of a poetry reading at *Crow's Nest Books*," says Naomi, gazing around at her beloved friends, "when Helen read for the first time in public. I remember walking home in the moonlight with Ezra and Healing, and Ezra saying, 'Unless those two poems Helen read were flukes, I believe I have finally found a living poet who speaks to me as do the dead poets I so admire.' And thereafter we never missed one of your readings until we moved back to England, and whenever you published a new volume of poems, Ezra immediately ordered a copy and waited impatiently for it to arrive. Then he would read your poems again and again, sometimes aloud, sometimes to himself." She smiles hopefully at Helen. "Might you recite one for us now? I would love it so."

"Of course," says Helen, who has been crying all day about Naomi dying.

"Ezra called you his Sappho," says Naomi, closing her eyes. "He liked to read your poems while listening to Mendelssohn."

"Do *Sage*, honey," says Justin, prompting her.

"Good idea," says Helen, agreeing with her husband's choice. "When my book *Spin Cycle* came out, Ezra sent me a letter from England saying how much he liked *Sage*, how it reminded him of Graves and Durrell and the questions they ask in their poems."

"Ezra called it *Helen's Prayer*," says Naomi, breathing deeply of her memories of her husband.

Helen closes her eyes and recites, "Dawn brings no relief from the sorrow clinging to me, a heavy shawl of grief. The sage is standing on my kitchen table. She's not much taller than the wine bottle holding a wilted rose, the dishes from last night still not done. 'Oh why do people choose cruelty over love?' I ask her. 'When love is so obviously the better choice?' 'Obvious to you,' says the sage, doing a funny little dance. 'Obvious to those with food in their bellies, to those who were loved by mother and father and friends, but not so obvious to the unloved, the hungry, the ones deeply scarred by fear.' 'And so?' I ask. 'What can we do to change them?' 'Love them,' says the sage, bowing to me. 'Without hope of changing them or being thanked for loving them. Love them without pause without fear without question.'"

"Wow," says Joel, gazing in wonder at Helen. "That's the best poem I've ever heard. Not that I've heard many poems, but after this one I want to get your books."

"Thank you, Joel," says Helen, nodding graciously to him.

"What do you think Helen's poem is about Oz?" asks Tova, looking at her son.

"You should love other people," says Oz, nodding. "Even if you're hungry."

"It's also about a little person named Sage," says Raaz, smiling at Helen. "Who likes to dance on your table."

*

A light rain graces Mercy on the morning of Naomi's party, and by the time the twenty guests arrive in the early afternoon the sun is shining brightly and steam is rising from the deck and rooftops.

At the south end of the deck stand two tables soon to be graced with Algerian and Mexican specialties and Tova's spicy chicken thighs, corn-on-the-cob, vegetable shish kebobs, and broiled cod caught this morning in Mercy Bay.

Naomi is enthroned in the garden in her wicker armchair with another chair and a small table alongside her on which she has her Tarot deck, a jar full of pens, and a stack of postcards featuring Jahera's photos of the Weintraub pooches and kiddies. Guests are invited to sit with Naomi and choose a Tarot card from which Naomi intuits a thing or two for the guest to write on a postcard and take with them as a keepsake.

The first person to sit with Naomi is Darby.

"I thought I'd better do this before I've had too much to drink," he says, fighting his tears. "Before I become maudlin and idiotic and can't stop crying. Going to miss you more than I can say, Naomi. You've been a mainstay of me life and the cause of incalculable joy."

"I will say the same of you, my friend," says Naomi, who is entirely free of doubt about her decision to die. "Please shuffle and choose a card."

Darby fumbles with the deck and draws the Seven of Pentacles.

"How perfect for you," says Naomi, gazing fondly at her old friend. "You have accomplished much in your long life and you are happy with Marjorie now. Sometimes you fret about not having accomplished some great something, and it is time to cease fretting about that and simply enjoy life."

"I'll take that to the bank," says Darby, his eyes full of tears. "I'll think of you always."

*

The next person to sit with Naomi is Tayo, resplendent in white dress shirt and black trousers.

"I wanted to take my turn early," he says quietly. "Before we get caught up playing your favorite songs."

"You're letting your hair grow," says Naomi, gazing at him. "I always loved seeing your curly locks when you were a child and came for your reading and writing lessons."

"You mean my kinky locks," he says, laughing.

"No I mean curls," says Naomi, laughing with him. "Albeit kinky curls."

"I shaved my head for the first time on my twentieth birthday," he says wistfully. "And went on shaving it every week for the next twenty-four years. But when I started playing music with Healing and Eliana, I wanted to let it grow again. And the minute I did, everything in my life changed."

"Tell me," says Naomi, nodding encouragingly. "Your secrets are safe with me."

"No secrets," he says, shaking his head. "After my first few rehearsals with Healing and Eliana, Sheila asked me to quit playing music with them because she wasn't comfortable with me spending so much time with Eliana. So I invited her to come to a rehearsal and she came and saw there was nothing going on with Eliana and me, and things were okay again until we had our first gig and I brought home more money than I make in two weeks working at *Found Wood*. Sheila said it made her feel like a failure that I could make more money in a few hours playing music than she made in a month as a bank teller. I told her my money was *our* money and gave her a thousand dollars to go shopping with her sister. They bought new clothes and new shoes, and Sheila was happy for a while and I was in heaven playing with Healing and Eliana. And then a few weeks later I came home from a gig and raved about Eliana's playing and Tova's singing, and Sheila freaked out and said if I didn't quit the band she would leave me. I told her praising them wasn't criticizing her, and in another month I'd be out of debt for the first time in twenty years, and I wasn't gonna quit. So she moved out. Two weeks ago." He smiles sadly. "I know it's good we broke up, but I miss her so much."

"It *is* good you broke up, Tayo," says Naomi, gazing fondly at him. "Despite your sorrow. She was an impediment to your healing. Your higher self held sway and this is to be celebrated. Now draw a card, though I know what it will be."

"How do you know?" asks Tayo, smiling quizzically.

"A clear image of the card came to me just now," she says, marveling at how small the cards are in his big hands. "When that happens to me, the card invariably appears."

"I choose the top card," he says, shuffling the deck one last time. "What will it be?"

"The Magician," she says as he sets the deck on the table and turns over the top card to reveal the drawing of a man wearing a red robe – The Magician.

"How am I a magician?" he asks humbly.

"With your music, your kindness, and your wisdom," she says, taking his hand. "Wisdom gained from the long and difficult journey you made to arrive at this moment in the continuum the Buddhists call karma."

They gaze at each other for a long loving moment.

"Thank you, Naomi," he says, turning to Helen who has come for her turn.

"Love awaits you, Tayo," says Naomi, smiling at him as he rises to go. "Believe me."

*

An hour later, her Tarot cards returned to the wooden box Ezra made for her seventy years ago, Naomi joins the revelers on the deck where she has a taste of everything and a sip of white wine, after which she says to Healing, "Would you play now, dear? I'm going to lie down in my cottage and have a nap. I'll leave my window open so I can hear you as I drift off to sleep."

"We'll play all the songs again after your nap," says Healing, kissing her. "Love you Mum."

"Love you," she says, kissing Raaz and Oz and Zubu and Maahiah before she has Jean and Jahera help her down the stairs and through the garden to her cottage where she lies down on her bed and closes her eyes as Deseo begins to play *I Wish I Knew How It Would Feel To Be Free.*

*

"This must be a lucid dream," says Naomi, walking on a faint trail through a forest, the air smelling of Algerian spices.

She comes to a clearing and sees someone in the distance she thinks might be Ezra, but now she sees the person is a young woman naked save for a necklace of turquoise stones.

"Here you are," says the young woman, holding out her hand to Naomi.

"Is this my end?" asks Naomi, taking the young woman's hand.

"Nay," whispers the young woman, leading Naomi onto a vast beach, the ocean roaring in the distance. "Your freedom."

Ω

23. Henry and Bianca

On the morning of September seventh, a month after Naomi died, Jean stands in the doorway of Naomi's cottage watching Eliana and her father Zeke put the finishing touches on the new interior paint job, the walls Navajo white, the trim turquoise.

"We'll leave the windows open for the next few days," says Eliana, wearing old jeans and a raggedy T-shirt, her long brown hair in a bun. "Then I'll move in. Can you believe it?"

"I can," says Jean, smiling ecstatically. "Mum would be thrilled."

"Papa sanded and oiled Ezra's gorgeous table," says Eliana, coming to stand with Jean in the doorway. "And Mama and Papa bought me a comfy sleeper sofa and matching armchair and a delicious queen-sized bed." She looks at Zeke on a ladder painting the wall above the kitchen sink. "Thank you, Papa."

"You're welcome," he says, his overalls splattered with white paint, his graying brown hair in a stubby ponytail. "Your mother loves buying furniture."

"Oh and I'm getting the most exquisite rug," says Eliana, holding Jean's hand. "Made by a Hopi woman who spins her own yarn from her very own sheep and then dyes the yarn with dyes she makes from plants she gathers in the desert. She weaves her rugs on a wooden loom and each rug takes months and months to make. Mine is seven-feet by nine-feet with a turquoise border and the most beautiful reds and browns." She gives Jean a worried look. "I might be afraid to walk on it."

"Oh don't be, dear," says Jean, feeling Naomi speaking through her. "A good rug likes nothing better than being walked on."

"Guess what?" says Eliana, shivering with excitement. "I'm taking care of Zubu for *four* hours tomorrow while Jahera and Maahiah and Shafi preside over the scholars."

"Oh do bring her over to William's house, won't you?" says Jean, blushing. "I mean... *our* house. We'd love to have a visit from you and the holy child."

"I will," says Eliana, hugging Jean. "I can't wait for tomorrow."

*

When Jean departs, Zeke comes down from the ladder and slowly washes his brushes in the sink.

"Well I guess that's that," he says, giving Eliana a sorrowful look. "Anything else you need me for?"

"I think we're done," says Eliana, telling herself *I will not succumb to his anguish*. "Want to go to the café, Papa? My treat?"

"No," he says, looking away. "I should go."

At which moment, Healing appears in the doorway carrying Zubu in a front-facing baby carrier – Zubu seven-months-old now, a strawberry blonde with big brown eyes, keenly interested in everything and everyone, her usual expression a smile.

"Stunning job," says Healing, peering into the cottage. "Kudos to the painters. I've come to invite you to join us for a tea party on the deck. Darby and Marjorie procured several of Luisa's ambrosial peach scones from *Café Brava,* Maahiah has just made a big pot of delicious Mazagran, and I have made good black tea."

"Sorry," says Zeke, shaking his head. "I gotta get home."

"Oh come on, Papa," says Eliana, taking his hand. "At least come say hi to everybody."

"Yana," says Zubu, holding out her arms to Eliana.

"Did she just say your name?" asks Zeke, emerging from his sorrow to gaze in wonder at the baby. "Or was that a random sound?"

"That's what she calls me," says Eliana, taking hold of Zubu's foot. "I'm Yana."

"What does she call *you*, Healing?" asks Zeke, remembering when Eliana was a baby and called him *Eek*.

"She calls me Howie," says Healing, resting his hand atop Zubu's head. "It's her way of saying Shafi. So of course now Oz and Raaz call me Howie, too. I don't imagine it will last, but one never knows."

"If ever someone was *not* a Howie," says Zeke, laughing, "that someone is you."

"I thought so, too," says Healing, laughing with him. "But now I rather like it, especially when *Oz* calls me Howie. He puts the emphasis on the *How* and sounds like he's from New Jersey. Tickles me no end. Come have scones."

"I'll come say hi," says Zeke, surrendering. "I can't stay long, but... I'll come say hi."

*

When Raaz and Oz get home from Arjun's house at half past twelve, they sit at the kitchen table with Healing eating carrots and cucumbers and hummus while Zubu sits in her high chair devouring smooshed banana delivered to her mouth on a rubber spoon wielded by Maahiah.

"Exactly ninety minutes from now there will be an extremely rare 2.9 minus tide," says Healing, consulting his tide chart. "Which means we will be able to walk on sand *all* the way to where Mercy Bay meets the greater ocean, something only possible a few days every decade. A trek of about seven miles round trip from the end of Gulley Road. You twins up for such a long walk? Jahera and Jean and William are coming and we shall bring along dates, cookies, apples, and jugs of water."

"Of course we can walk that far," says Raaz, looking at her brother to see if he agrees with her.

"Of course we can," says Oz, who has no idea how far seven miles is.

"Excellent," says Healing, winking at Maahiah. "I think you can, too."

"Can Moosh still walk that far?" asks Oz, knowing Healing sometimes worries about Mendelssohn getting tired on long walks.

"He can, but we won't ask him to come with us today," says Healing, touched by Oz's concern. "Nor will we take the short-legged dogs or Puccini who has a problematic foot. We will take Coosi, Moshe, Flora, and possibly Zoya. What do you think Maahiah? Is Zoya up to seven miles on sand?"

"You might have to carry her the last mile or so," says Maahiah, wiping the smoosh off Zubu's face. "I'm sure she'd love to come."

"No carrying dogs today," says Healing, getting up from the table. "We'll take our three dogs and William's two and leave the rest of the pack to enjoy the sunny backyard."

"How many more days until Mama comes home from Portland?" asks Raaz, sighing. "She *loves* minus tides."

"I believe we noted her first hiatus from movie-making on the Degas calendar," says Healing, pointing to the calendar affixed to the wall where the parrot cage used to be. "If you will find the square with the 7, which is today, and count forward to the square with your mother's name, you will have your answer by subtracting 7 from that number."

Raaz goes to calendar and finds the square with a 7.

"Eight, nine, ten, eleven, twelve, thirteen, fourteen," she counts. "What's fourteen minus seven, Oz?"

"Well," says Oz, pursing his lips, "seven *plus* seven is fourteen, so fourteen *minus* seven is also seven." He looks at Healing. "Right?"

"Brilliant deduction, Oz," says Healing, imagining his mother looking up from her crossword puzzle to gaze in wonder at her great grandson.

*

As the adventurers are about to sally forth, the phone rings and Maahiah shifts Zubu from one hip to the other to answer.

"Weintraub constellation. This is Maahiah." She listens for a moment and gives Healing a look to say *A new case for you.*

"I'll call them back this evening," whispers Healing.

"He's not available right now," says Maahiah, bouncing Zubu as she starts to fuss. "He will be glad to return your call this evening. May I tell him more specifically what you are calling about?" She listens with furrowed brow. "Oh I see. How difficult for you. How long would you say this has been going on?"

"Come on Shafi," says Oz, tugging on Healing's hand. "The minus tide is going out right now!"

"So true," says Healing, waving to Maahiah as he follows the children out the door.

*

The beach at the mouth of the Mercy River is vast even at modest low tides, but when the intrepid explorers arrive at the beach today the expanse of sand is so immense the breakers are barely visible in the distance – the sky crowded with gray and white clouds, the light muted, timelessness holding sway.

And not only do the explorers see dolphins and seals gamboling in the bay, and ospreys and pelicans diving for fish, they come upon a pod of gray whales swimming close to shore, two of whom rise completely out of the water and crash down sending spray high into the air.

*

With two miles yet to go on the return leg, as Healing expected might happen, the children are so knackered Healing and Jahera have no choice but to give them piggyback rides.

"If you could carry me just a *little* way more, Shafi," says Oz, riding on Healing's back, "my legs would be ready to go again."

"Mine will too," says Raaz, riding on Jahera's back. "Just a little way more."

"I'm available for schlepping duty," says William, taking pictures of the children on their grandparents' backs. "Should who would fardels bear need to be relieved of such burdens."

Healing laughs at William's reference to a line from *Hamlet* and retorts, "To grunt and sweat under a weary life seems to be our fate today, and well worth it."

"How much do these giants weigh now?" asks Jean, for whom the days of picking up anything weighing over thirty pounds are over.

"Last time we weighed them," says Healing, striding along, "Oz topped the scale at forty-four pounds and Raaz at forty-six. However, that was two months ago and methinks the poundage has increased considerably since then."

"I'm done," says Jahera, out of breath. "Your turn William."

"I can walk now, Jadda," says Raaz, getting down.

"Could you carry me a *little* more, Shafi?" asks Oz, yawning. "Then I'll be ready to walk. I promise."

"I'll get you as far as that big log looming in the distance," says Healing, guessing that to be another quarter-mile. "From there we're only a mile or so from Gulley Road."

"We'll stop and rest as many times as we need to," says Jahera, feeling light as a feather without Raaz on her back.

"Our first rest stop will be that big log," says Healing, his ankles and calves beginning to sing. "Where we will eat the last cookies to sustain us for the final push."

*

After supper, exhausted from their epic walk, Oz and Raaz lie down among the dogs in the living room and fall fast asleep, and a few minutes later Healing and Jahera carry them to bed.

Maahiah settles on the sofa with her knitting, Jahera goes upstairs to her studio to download the hundreds of photos she took today, and Healing returns the call of the fellow who called this morning about his dog and cat.

"Good evening. This is Healing Weintraub returning Steven Bishop's call."

"Hello," says Steven, his voice warm and songful. "Darla Rosenfeld suggested I consult you. I'm another artist who followed Susan and Paul Cheshire here from Los Angeles. I've been in Mercy a year now and wish I'd moved here twenty years ago."

"Splendid," says Healing, immediately liking Steven. "What is your art, if I may ask?"

"I'm a potter," says Steven, simply. "Bowls and vases and teapots and mugs."

"Wonderful. What seems to be the problem?"

"My dog Henry is three-years-old, a mix of Golden Lab and Mastiff and who knows what else. He's ninety pounds, light brown, shorthaired, very friendly, and there's nothing *physically* wrong with him. But ever since I got my cat Bianca, Henry is much less affectionate, as if he's *afraid* to be affectionate. Or so it seems to me."

"How does this apparent fear manifest?" asks Healing, sitting down at the table and opening his notebook.

"It's hard to explain, but... for instance, he used to love sitting on the sofa with me and now he won't."

"Does Bianca sit on the sofa with you?" asks Healing, writing at the top of the page *Henry dog, Bianca cat*.

"She does. But she and Henry like each other. They get along fine."

"Aside from no longer sitting on the sofa with you, how is Henry less affectionate?"

"Well he used to come to me for pets all the time, and now he never does. He still likes it when I pet him, but he no longer *asks* to be petted."

"And you attribute this change to the coming of Bianca?"

"Well that's when Henry changed, so yes."

"Did you get Bianca when she was a kitten?"

"Yes. Two years ago."

"So Henry was one when you got Bianca?"

"Ten months."

"Are you free tomorrow afternoon?"

"Yeah, I'm here all day," says Steven, eagerly. "I'm three miles up Baskerville Road. One-one-seven-nine-four. On the right side of the road as you're coming from town."

"Oh you bought Dino Andrini's place," says Healing, writing *Dino*.

"Yes, I did," says Steven, surprised. "Did you know Dino?"

"Everyone who has lived in Mercy for more than ten years knew Dino," says Healing, smiling at the thought of good old Dino. "We all bought fish from him right off his boat. I'll tell you more about him when I see you tomorrow. Shall we say two-ish? And may I bring my wife and grandkids? I'm sure they'd love to see your pottery studio."

"Great. A reason to tame the chaos."

"Oh don't go to any trouble. We enjoy chaos."

"Not this much chaos," says Steven, laughing. "Trust me."

*

The next morning after breakfast, two leaves are added to the table to give five students and three teachers ample space for drawing and writing on butcher paper – Raaz, Oz, Esther, Arjun, Jahera, Maahiah, Healing, and the new student Georgia Fidelio who is six.

"Today," says Healing, smiling around at everyone, "we will begin with a session of blabbing. Arjun would you please start things off for us?"

"I will," says Arjun, speaking with the Hindi accent of his parents. "On our way here this morning four wild turkeys crossed the road in front of us and Darvin said this is a good omen. Then Esther asked what an omen is and Darvin said an omen tells us when something is going to happen."

"What if there are only *three* wild turkeys?" asks Raaz, looking at Healing. "Is that a good omen, too?"

"Probably," says Healing, nodding. "A matter of magnitude I would imagine."

"Would seven be even better?" asks Esther, wrinkling her nose.

"Seven is my favorite number," says Jahera, smiling at Esther. "So it would certainly be better for me."

"What's so good about wild turkeys?" asks Oz, pursing his lips. "Mama says if they get in the vegetable garden they'll eat everything."

"When cooked properly," says Healing, who knows firsthand of what he speaks, "Wild Turkey meat is most delicious. One adult wild turkey will provide enough meat for *thirty* people, which is why I think they are considered a good omen. They represent abundance."

"I would like to see a wild turkey," says Georgia, with her charming Italian accent. "Maybe we can go outside and look for one."

"That's a wonderful suggestion for a field trip," says Jahera, nodding to Georgia. "This morning, however, we are going to work on writing letters of the alphabet. Then we'll have a snack and recess, and then we will walk to the library to return our books and check out new ones."

"We might see some wild turkeys on our way to the library," says Raaz, who finds Georgia enchanting.

"Sometimes we see them in the ravine," says Oz, who is considering marrying Georgia when they're both a little older. "We can go see during recess."

"But first," says Jahera, handing around big rectangles of butcher paper, "we are going to practice writing the letters of the alphabet."

"I'm already pretty good at this," says Oz, confiding in Georgia.

"So am I," says Raaz, drawing a capitol A at the top of her page. "See? Now watch me draw the little *a*."

"I know how to make the letters," says Georgia, nodding confidently. "But it's good to keep practicing."

*

When Arjun, Esther, and Georgia depart at noon, the collective has lunch on the deck and Eliana recounts the many things she did with Zubu this morning.

"The high point of the day so far," says Eliana, smiling at Zubu sitting on Jahera's lap, "was when Zubu slapped the water in William's pond and the slapping sound made Harpo bark. So Zubu slapped the water again, and Harpo barked again, and I have no doubt Zubu would still be slapping the water if we'd let her. Wouldn't you Zubu?"

"Yana," says Zubu, beaming at Eliana.

"Further proof of her sophisticated sense of humor," says Healing, knowing his mother would have said something along those lines.

"We're going to visit the new potter in town," says Jahera to Eliana. "Raaz and Oz and Shafi and I. His name is Steven Bishop. He bought Dino Andrini's place a mile past your folks' house on Baskerville Road. Shafi is looking into his dog and cat problem."

"I've met him," says Eliana, nodding approvingly. "My mother had the listing. He's very handsome, forty-eight, and single. He'd be *perfect* for Tova. I'd love to tag along, and on the way back we can stop at my folks' place and pick apples."

*

The rusty boat anchor that for so long marked the entrance to Dino Andrini's place has been replaced by a large golden ceramic Star of David hanging on a rusty steel chain dangling from the branch of an oak tree.

The farmhouse, formerly dingy gray, is now light adobe brown with red trim, the rotting front porch replaced by a spacious deck, and the big barn wherein Dino's four daughters kept their horses has been converted into Steven's pottery studio. Adjacent to the barn is the greenhouse wherein Dino grew marijuana, the always-filthy glass now sparkling clean for Steven's lemon trees and tomato plants and fantastic cacti.

Jahera parks next to a small white pickup, a deep-voiced dog barks briefly, and Steven emerges from the barn with his big hound Henry by his side – Steven tall and broad-shouldered with short brown hair and glasses, Henry broad-chested and friendly.

In his zeal to befriend the visitors, Henry knocks Oz down.

"Sorry about that," says Steven, giving Oz a hand up. "He doesn't know his own strength."

"It's okay," says Raaz, hugging Henry. "Our dog Moshe knocks us over, too."

"Moshe is even bigger than your dog but not so jumpy," says Oz, petting Henry. "Can we see in the barn? Shafi says you make bowls on a wheel."

"You can and I do," says Steven, shaking hands with Jahera and Healing and Eliana. "My son and I spent the morning making order out of the endemic chaos."

"His son being moi," says a young man emerging from the barn, his curly brown hair falling to his shoulders, his accent French, his mien effeminate, his blue satin blouse tucked into purple tights descending into black rubber boots.

"Marcel," says Steven, presenting his son to everyone.

"Visiting from Montreal," says Marcel, bowing absurdly low. "Who are all of you?"

"I'm Oz," says Oz, approaching Marcel and shaking his hand. "Short for Ozan. It means *poet* in Arabic."

"I'm Raaz," says Raaz, shaking Marcel's other hand. "Short for Raaziyah. It means a gift from God." She frowns. "Some people don't believe in God, but Oz and I do and Shafi and Jadda do, too."

"Only God might not be a person," explains Oz. "He might be all the stars and everything."

"I never believed in God until now," says Marcel, blinking at them. "You just converted me."

"I'm Jahera," says Jahera, shaking Marcel's hand. "Oz and Raaz's grandmother. *Jadda* is Arabic for grandma."

"I'm Healing, their grandfather," says Healing, bowing to Marcel. "Also known as Shafi and sometimes Howie."

"I'm Eliana," says Eliana, shaking Marcel's hand. "I live with them and play music with Shafi."

"Eliana," says Marcel, obviously smitten with her. "A pleasure to meet you."

"Come see the studio," says Steven, leading the way into the barn where he keeps his several potter's wheels, kilns, and four big tables displaying bowls and vases and teapots in various stages of completion.

"What instrument do you play?" asks Marcel, hovering near Eliana. "Don't tell me. You play the violin like Stépahne Grappelli, you sing like Eva Cassidy, *and...*" He arches his eyebrow. "You play the accordion like a Gypsy goddess."

"How could you possibly know that?" asks Eliana, squinting suspiciously at him.

Marcel smiles sheepishly. "We had dinner at the East Cove Hotel on Sunday and you and Howie and your gorgeous bass player were playing for a wedding."

"You're a cad," says Eliana, blushing. "Are you a musician?"

"I am," says Marcel, smiling alluringly. "Can you guess my instrument?"

Eliana closes her eyes. "Clarinet."

Marcel's jaw drops. "How did you know?" He turns to Steven. "Did you tell them, Papa?"

"I told them nothing about you," says Steven, shaking his head. "I didn't even tell them you were here."

"Please tell me how you knew," asks Marcel, coming close to Eliana.

"I'm a witch," she says, haughtily. "Your mind is an open book to me. But fear not. I'm a good witch and won't hurt you."

"Can you show us how you make bowls?" asks Oz, looking at Steven. "Please?"

"I thought you might ask," says Steven, winking at Oz. "So I readied a few balls of clay to give you a demonstration, after which I'll help you and your sister make bowls."

"Are you a potter too, Marcel?" asks Jahera, delighted to see Eliana so taken with the young man.

"No," says Marcel, with a dainty shrug. "I'm Second Clarinet in the Orchestre symphonique de Montréal." He looks at Eliana. "But I love it here in Mercy and want to come more often."

"You should," says Eliana, assuredly. "Mercy is the fount."

"I agree," says Steven, sitting down at one of the potter's wheels. "I've thrown the best pots of my life since moving here."

Marcel places chairs on either side of the wheel so Raaz and Oz can stand on them to watch Steven place a ball of clay in the center of the throwing surface and get the wheel spinning with a few powerful kicks. Now he drizzles water atop the spinning ball, places both hands around the moistened orb, and lifts the clay into a cylinder into which he inserts his thumbs at the top and spreads the sides outward to form an exquisite bowl.

"Voila," says Steven, slowing the wheel and beckoning Oz to come sit on his lap. "Now we will set this one aside and affix a fresh bat to the wheel so you and I can make a bowl together. And then Raaz and I will make one."

*

Bowl making at end, Marcel leads the giddy twins and Jahera and Eliana on a tour of the grounds while Healing and Steven and Henry go into the farmhouse to meet Bianca, Steven's big gray tabby who is napping on the sofa in the spacious living room.

When Bianca sees Healing, she jumps down from the sofa to rub against Healing's legs and mark him with her scent, and the moment Healing bends down to pet Bianca, Henry heads for the door.

"Oh don't go Henry," says Healing, picking up Bianca and setting her on the sofa. "I've got a treat for you."

Henry hurries to Healing.

"Where does Henry hang out in the evening when Bianca's on the sofa?" asks Healing, giving Henry a chewy treat and petting him.

"By the fire," says Steven, sadly. "That's where he spends his nights now, too. He used to sleep at the bottom of my bed, but Bianca sleeps there now and Henry rarely goes into the bedroom anymore."

"So this clearly has to do with Bianca," says Healing, continuing to pet Henry. "Though it's not that Henry doesn't like her. And she would be fine with him sleeping on the bed and sharing the sofa with her."

"So why did he stop doing all those things?" asks Steven, anguished by the change in his dog. "And why did he stop approaching me for affection?"

"Shall we sit?" asks Healing, nodding hopefully.

"Of course," says Steven, gesturing to the room. "Anywhere you like."

Healing sits on the sofa, Bianca claims Healing's lap, and Henry heads for the door.

"Henry," says Healing, enticingly. "Please stay."

Henry returns to Healing and accepts another chewy treat while Bianca remains on Healing's lap purring loudly.

"As you can see," says Steven, sitting in an armchair, "they're fine being close to each other, yet Henry... oh I don't know. Maybe it's okay. I just miss him wanting to be with me."

"Did you have another dog or cat when you got Henry?" asks Healing, continuing to pet the happy dog.

"No," says Steven, shaking his head. "In fact, it was one of the rare times in my life I *didn't* have another dog or cat or both, and that's because a few weeks after my last cat died I went to Sweden for a year and then to Japan for a year. Teaching gigs. I got Henry a few months after I got back from Japan, and as I told you on the phone I got Bianca when Henry was ten-months-old."

Healing looks at Henry and says, "Go see Steven now."

Henry goes to Steven and smiles rapturously as Steven pets him.

"I think I know why Henry's behavior changed," says Healing, pleased to see the great love between Steven and Henry.

"You do?" says Steven, gazing intently at Healing.

"Yes, I think if you had waited to get Bianca until Henry was fully grown, I doubt very much his behavior would have changed. However, because you got Bianca before Henry's habits were hardwired into his adult neurological system, and given Henry's extremely cooperative nature, he interpreted your encouraging Bianca to sit and sleep where he sat and slept to mean that you, Steven, the alpha, wanted Bianca to be second in the family hierarchy and Henry third."

"Because he was still a puppy?" asks Steven, watching Henry trot out the door to find Marcel and those interesting visitors. "What if I had insisted he sit on the sofa with us and sleep on my bed? Do you think he'd still be sitting on the sofa and sleeping on the bed and coming to me for pets?"

"I do," says Healing, petting the purring Bianca. "And by the way, it's not too late to train Henry to get on the sofa with you. It would entail putting him beside you and rewarding him, and when he jumps down, repeating the process many times until it became his habit again. But I wouldn't do that if I were you."

"What would you do?" asks Steven, plaintively.

"I would create a new situation for relating to him. Maybe put a small sofa next to where Henry spends his evenings now and invite him to sit with you there while repeatedly referring to the sofa as *Henry's sofa* until it becomes his habit to spend time with you on his sofa. Might take a while, but if you aren't happy with the current situation, that's what I recommend, though the *easiest* solution would be to realize that Henry is perfectly happy with how things are now."

*

On the way home from Steven's house, Oz says, "Steven is going to cook our bowls in his kiln and then we'll come back and glaze them and he'll cook them again and then we can take them home."

"I'm going to glaze *my* bowl red with gold spots," says Raaz, confidently. "And then I'm going to make a vase for the kitchen table."

"I'm going to glaze *my* bowl blue and green," says Oz, excitedly, "and then make a gigantic bowl for salad."

"Steven and Marcel are coming for supper when your mother gets home from Portland in a few days," says Jahera, looking back at the children. "I think she'll like Steven. Don't you?"

"Of course she will," says Oz, nodding assuredly. "He's very nice."

"Well..." says Eliana, sighing dramatically, "I'm madly in love with Marcel. But I'm not moving to Montreal. If we're going to have a relationship, he'll have to move here."

"Good plan," says Healing, laughing.

"I won't be surprised if he *does* move here," says Jahera, looking back at Eliana sitting between Raaz and Oz. "He's crazy about you."

"I already miss him," says Eliana, her jaw trembling.

"Me, too," says Raaz, pouting sympathetically. "He's *so* nice."

"I miss him, too," says Oz, looking at Eliana. "But don't worry. We'll see him again because he's our friend now."

*

That night Jahera snuggles with Healing and says, "Don't you think Steven is just perfect for Tova?"

"No comment. I thought Darvin was perfect for Tova. Still do. And she's indifferent to him."

"That's not true. She loves Darvin. They're just not meant to be married."

"Oh so now Tova and Steven are getting married?"

"If she'll hurry up and get back from Portland before he meets someone else. Yes."

"He *is* good with the kids," says Healing, recalling how encouraging Steven was of the children when he made bowls with them. "And he's great with his dog and cat. And he's a brilliant potter. But who knows what Tova will think of him. She's inscrutable to me now that she's a movie star." He closes his eyes. "I'm ashamed to admit it, but... I never thought she'd succeed as an actor, though I know she's brilliant. I guess I projected my own failure onto her."

"You didn't fail, Shafi. You chose not to pursue an acting career."

"I say that, but the truth is I was afraid to fail, afraid to leave home and the safety of Mercy. I was terrified of the great big world on the other side of the tracks, as the song goes. That's why Eliana and I get along so well. We're both big scaredy cats."

"I fear Marcel will break Eliana's heart. She's such an innocent, and he is not."

"The young heart is trapped in a carapace of childish illusions, and it is the carapace that breaks when those illusions are shattered, not the heart."

"That's from one of Helen's poems. Which one?"

"*The Forge.* About when she got pregnant at sixteen and raised her daughter on her own. *Made molten in the forge of despair, by necessity I pounded myself into a sword.*"

Ω

24. Marcel and Steven

On September ninth, the day after the collective met Steven and Marcel, the little old house is basking in gentle sunlight and Eliana is chopping kindling in front of the woodshed when Marcel emerges from the kitchen onto the deck wearing a turquoise blouse, pink slacks belted with a burgundy sash, red sandals, and a straw hat sporting a peacock feather, his clarinet case in hand.

"I was in the neighborhood and thought I'd drop by and say hello." He bows to Eliana. "I hope you are thrilled."

"I am," says Eliana, blushing brightly. "I was just thinking how nice it would be to have tea with you and hear you play your clarinet."."

"I prefer coffee," he says, plaintively. "Do you like coffee?"

"I love the *smell* of coffee, but I can't drink it," she says, apologetically. "Caffeine is not my friend. Nor is alcohol. Nor can I tolerate cell phones. They give me horrific headaches. However, I've been making coffee for my parents since I was six and I'd be happy to make you some. Maahiah made cookies this morning. She's a fabulous baker."

"I'd love coffee and cookies," he says, frowning at her as she comes up the stairs. "You seem different today."

"So do you," she says, returning his frown. "I wonder why."

*

They sit at a little table on the porch of Eliana's cottage, his mug of coffee and her mug of mint tea steaming in the sunlight.

"I moved out of my parents' house two weeks ago," says Eliana, sighing with relief. "I'll be twenty-six on the fourteenth of October and this is the first time in my life I've lived apart from them."

"We are both Libras," says Marcel, gazing at her. "I will be twenty-seven on the *fifteenth* of October."

"My mother says I'm a double Libra with my moon in Leo, if that means anything to you," says Eliana, sipping her tea. "I wonder if you're a double Libra, too. I don't know anything about astrology. Do you?"

"My mother is an astrologer," says Marcel, sipping his coffee. "She makes charts for people and speaks in vague generalities about their futures. Big change is coming. You're at a crossroads. The next few months will be eventful. Things like that." He peers through the open door of the cottage. "So this is where you live now?"

"I *will* be living here starting day after tomorrow. We just painted inside and I'm waiting one more day for the paint fumes to be gone before I move in. I've been staying in Maahiah's cottage across the street while Maahiah's been sleeping over here in the guest room with Zubu. And Raaz and Oz are staying over here, too, while Tova is in Portland making a movie."

"Tova is not Zubu's mother?" asks Marcel, dipping a cookie in his coffee.

"No. Zubu's mother is Jennifer Badeaux. She's married to Lucien who is Jahera's son and Tova's *ex*-husband. Lucien is the father of Oz and Raaz and also the father of Zubu. Jennifer and Lucien live in Zurich."

"So why is Zubu here and not in Zurich?" asks Marcel, frowning.

"Because Lucien and Jennifer *thought* they wanted a child, but after Zubu was born they decided they didn't, so they gave Zubu to Jahera. Can you imagine? Giving up such a wonderful child?"

"We all get born somehow," says Marcel, shrugging. "My mother left my father when I was two and I didn't see her again until I was nineteen. Now I live three blocks away from her in Montreal and see her every week and only see my father once a year." He shrugs again. "Big change is coming. You're at a crossroads. The next few months will be eventful."

"What different lives we've had," says Eliana, yet to go a day without seeing one or both of her parents.

"Everyone has a different life than everyone else," says Marcel, squinting at her. "Are you in a relationship?"

"Me?" she says, startled by his question. "No. I've *never* been in a relationship. Though I've had lots of crushes and a few sensual adventures that stopped short of the grand finale."

"I'm surprised," he says, sounding disappointed. "When I heard you playing and singing at the wedding I thought *This is a woman who knows about love.*" He frowns. "Are you sexually attracted to women?"

"No," she says, shaking her head. "Though I love women."

"Why do you think your sensual adventures stopped short of the grand finale, as you say?"

"Oh I stopped them," she says matter-of-factly. "Because none of those men wanted to know me except sexually, and I'm not interested in having sex just to have sex. I have girlfriends who like having sex just to have sex, even with people they hardly know, but I'm not comfortable with that."

"Why not?" he asks, his tone implying he *is* comfortable having sex with people he hardly knows.

"Because I want sex to be part of a love bond," she says simply. "Something sacred."

"My father feels the same way," says Marcel, dismissively. "Whereas I am promiscuous and only have sex with men."

"So then yesterday was..."

"A delirious aberration. I have never been attracted to anyone as much as I was attracted to you. *Any*one. But today the frisson is gone and I am once again as I have always been. I think you are lovely, Eliana, but I no longer want to have sex with you."

"The frisson is gone for me, too," she says, baffled. "I wonder what that *was* between us. I was ready to marry you and have your children."

"I know," he says sympathetically. "I hope you are not too disappointed."

"I don't seem to be," she says, wondering why she isn't. "Perhaps it was a glimpse into the future when someday you'll fall in love with a woman."

"I doubt it," he says, waving the idea away. "I've known I was gay since Fourth Grade when Mr. Delaney came into the classroom and I wanted to be naked with him. After that I pursued boys relentlessly, and I still do."

"I was in love with my Fourth Grade teacher, too," she says, feeling she might cry. "Mr. Carlson. When I closed my eyes he sounded exactly like Nat King Cole who I worshiped, and he had the most beautiful eyes."

"I worshiped Nat King Cole, too," says Marcel, amazed. "In fact, it was hearing Nat King Cole singing *But Beautiful* that made me want to become a musician. I was eight-years-old when my father played that song for me."

"I love that song," says Eliana, petting Mendelssohn.

"Shall we play together now?" asks Marcel, with little enthusiasm. "I've been practicing Elgar's *Salut d'Amour* for a recital. You can accompany me."

"Okay," she says, her eyes full of tears.

"I think we can be friends, Eliana," he says, opening his clarinet case. "I would like us to be."

"Me, too," she says quietly. "I'll fetch my accordion."

*

The next morning when Jahera and Healing and the children leave for school at Georgia's house, Eliana joins Maahiah and Zubu on the sofa, the baby girl now able to sit up by herself.

"You seem sad today," says Maahiah, looking at Eliana.

"I *am* sad," she says, righting Zubu before she topples over. "When I met Marcel day before yesterday we were crazy about each other, but when he came to visit yesterday the magic was gone, completely gone, and I didn't even *like* him."

"These things happen," says Maahiah, going into the kitchen. "Bring Zubu and talk to me while I bake."

"Even playing music with him was disappointing," says Eliana, carrying the baby into the kitchen. "He's a big showoff and not the least soulful."

"Your situation reminds me of my dear friend Constantine who died thirteen years ago," says Maahiah, getting out her bowls and bread pans and measuring cups.

"Yana," says Zubu with a little complaint in her voice.

"Are you hungry?" asks Eliana, looking at Zubu. "I'll warm a bottle for you."

"It's time," says Maahiah, glancing at the kitchen clock. "She'll have her milk and then sleep. She's very punctual. I think she will always be on time in her life."

*

After putting Zubu down for her nap, Eliana returns to the kitchen and says to Maahiah, "You were starting to tell me about Constantine."

"Constantine DuPrau," says Maahiah, measuring flour into a big bowl. "I met him when we were living in Paris in 1972. Caspar was the foreman on a hydrology project in Provence and was gone for weeks at a time. Jahera had just started school and I was working as an illustrator. One of the books I was asked to illustrate was a collection of love poems by Constantine, who was a well-known poet and essayist. We met at his editor's office on rue de Gaston Gallimard, and after Constantine looked through my portfolio he asked if I could draw twenty drawings beginning with boys giving flowers to girls, then young men giving flowers to young women, then older men giving flowers to older women, and the last drawing would be an elderly man giving flowers to an elderly woman. I asked if he wanted all the drawings to be the same man and woman throughout their lives and he said, 'No. Make them all different.' We agreed I would show him my first two drawings before I did the rest, and he invited me to lunch at his house."

"What is it about Marcel that reminds you of Constantine?" asks Eliana, putting a kettle on for tea.

"Well... I was not happy in my marriage so I hoped to have a love affair with Constantine," says Maahiah, truthfully. "But when I took the drawings to his house and his wife Gloria led me to the patio where Constantine was waiting for me, I knew at a glance he was homosexual. Yet when I met him at his editor's office I was sure he was a man who loved women." She marvels at her memory of that moment. "It was a great mystery to both of us, for he *had* been attracted to me when we first met, though he never before wanted a woman, and his desire for me did not last but a few hours."

"I'm confused," says Eliana, frowning. "He was married to Gloria?"

"In those days gay men often married women because it was not acceptable to be openly gay. I'm eighty-three, remember. Things were very different for gay people in those days."

"Did he like your drawings?"

"He loved them," says Maahiah, kneading her dough. "The book was a big success and I remained very close to Constantine and Gloria until they died."

"Did Caspar like them?" asks Eliana, remembering Maahiah's deep-voiced husband who died a few months before Oz and Raaz were born.

"No," says Maahiah, shaking her head. "Constantine and Gloria became my friends long before Caspar became famous for his book *Décollé*, so he was very jealous of Constantine's success. They were *my* friends, never his. And they loved Jahera and she loved them. We saw them every week when we lived in Paris, and after we moved to Chambéry, Jahera and I would spend April in Paris with them every year. Then for August, Jahera and I would go to England with them where we rented a house in the Lake District. And for many years we spent January with them in Greece."

"Caspar didn't mind?" asks Eliana, never having imagined Maahiah independent of her husband.

"Oh he hated it. But I told him if he objected, I would leave him. He was a very difficult person, vehemently anti-social, and we needed to get away from him time to time and be with people who loved us." She adds a little water to the dough. "When Caspar was eighty he said he couldn't bear for me to go away anymore. By then Constantine had died and Gloria was quite elderly, so I would only visit her in Paris for a few days every month. And when we moved here, I called her every day until she died."

"Was she your lover?" whispers Eliana.

"Yes," says Maahiah, her tears falling on the dough. "The love of my life."

"How wonderful you got to love each other for so many years," says Eliana, embracing Maahiah.

"I'll tell you something else," Maahiah whispers. "I never thought I would love anyone again as much as I loved Gloria. But then..." She hesitates. "This is only for you to know. Promise?"

"Promise," says Eliana, placing her hand on her heart.

"The moment I met Shafi, I fell in love with him, and I have loved him ever since. He knows it, and Jahera knows, too, though we never speak of it. They don't mind, and I know he loves me, though we will never be lovers. It doesn't matter. What matters is the feeling we share when we cook together and bake together and work in the garden together. And every morning and every evening we embrace and I am filled with his love."

*

Three afternoons later, the day after Tova gets home from Portland, Steven and Marcel arrive at the little old house for a beach walk and supper.

When Tova and Steven first shake hands and look into each other's eyes, Tova knows with every cell in her body she wants to spend the rest of her life with Steven, and he knows the same, and then they both dismiss their feelings as a trick of the mind.

*

After a glorious walk on the beach, the children and Marcel accompany Eliana to her cottage to try out her new sofa and bounce on her new bed and gaze in wonder at her beautiful Navajo rug. Jahera and Maahiah and Healing make supper, William builds up the fire and wrestles with the dogs, and Jean plays with Zubu on the sofa.

And though Tova doesn't invite Steven to walk to the pond, that's where they go.

"So..." says Tova, sitting next to Steven on the old wooden bench. "What's happening between us is unprecedented for me. How about for you?"

"Yes," he says, taking off his glasses and blinking at her. "Unprecedented. Though lust is certainly an ingredient in the enchantment, along with this uncanny feeling of..."

"Please put your glasses back on before I swoon," she says, breathlessly. "Uncanny feeling of...?"

He puts his glasses back on. "Knowing you before now. Intimately."

"Yes," she says, looking away to stop seeing him. "Pre-knowing. Like... when I was seven and my father played Ella Fitzgerald singing *Early Autumn* and I knew I was going to be a singer. And when I was ten and went to Drama camp and went up on the stage for the first time and looked out at where the audience would be and knew I was going to be an actor." She looks at him to make sure he's still there.

"But I've never felt anything like this for another human being. Until now."

"Maybe we made a pact in a previous life to meet again in this lifetime and it's taken us all these years to find each other? Not that I believe in reincarnation. But how else can we explain this?"

"We can't," she says, laughing hysterically. "I only know I want to kiss you, though it might kill me and I need to get back to Portland and finish making a now-entirely-inconsequential movie. I was also hoping to live until my children became adults. Maybe we should wait to kiss until I get back from Portland."

"Nonsense," he says, kissing her.

"How wise of you not to wait," she says, kissing him again.

"I know what this is," he says, sitting back and pointing at her. "This is a lucid dream. This just *seems* to be happening. How long will you be in Portland?"

"Fourteen days," she says, standing up and holding out her hand to him. "Otherwise known as a million years. Will you wait for me?"

"To do what?" he asks, taking her hand and standing up.

"Well I think the first thing we should do when I get back," she says, leading him homeward, "is... have orgasms together, which will calm us down and help us think more clearly about how to proceed."

"I would like that very much," he says earnestly. "But what if I'm already in a relationship?"

"You can't be," she says, dropping his hand as they come in sight of the house. "The question is: why *aren't* you in a relationship?"

"Why do you think I'm not?" he asks, taking her hand again. "And why aren't *you* in a relationship? You're exquisite."

"How do you know I'm not?" she asks, thrilled he isn't afraid of anyone seeing them holding hands. "In a relationship."

"Because," he says, stopping to look at her, "you would never do this with me if you had a partner. Nor would I do this with you if I had one."

"True," she says, nodding in agreement. "So... how shall we proceed?"

"Now? Or when you get back from Portland?"

"For now I think we should restrain ourselves so we don't confuse the children. Then when I get back from Portland we'll be together constantly. How does that sound?"

"When you get back from Portland," he says tenderly, "we will get to know each other and see what happens."

"I went too fast, didn't I?" she says, remorsefully.

"No," he says, laughing. "You're wonderful. And very funny."

"It's the endorphins," she says, her eyelids fluttering. "Those horny little molecules."

"It's more than endorphins," he says, taking her in his arms. "Much more."

*

When Darby and Marjorie arrive for breakfast the next morning they find Healing making waffles, Jahera frying bacon, Eliana making coffee, Raaz playing with Zubu amidst the dogs on the living room floor, Maahiah in the rocking chair knitting with a cat in her lap, and Tova sitting on the sofa with Oz looking at the many drawings he made while Tova was in Portland.

"What a delightful domestic scene," says Darby, as he and Marjorie shed their coats. "The coffee brewing, bacon sizzling, waffles on the rise. The stuff of divinity."

Tova gets up to hug Darby and Marjorie.

"You look fantastic," says Marjorie, smiling inquiringly. "Things must be going well with the movie."

"Wonderfully well," says Tova, who hasn't thought about the movie even once since she met Steven. "The director wants me to be in his next movie, too, and *another* director came to watch the filming for two days and now *she* wants me to be in her next movie. We'll be solvent for decades."

"You look positively radiant," says Darby, giving her a quizzical look. "Don't tell me you're in love. Or *do* tell me."

Tova laughs. "I can't hide anything from you, can I?"

"Who is he?" asks Darby, eager to know.

Tova looks around at everyone and says, "Steven Bishop, the potter. He lives up Baskerville Road. You'll fall madly in love with him. It's impossible not to."

*

"They're perfect for each other," says Jahera, sitting in bed and too excited about Tova and Steven to keep reading. "Don't you think?"

"Insufficient data," says Healing, kneeling on his mat as he scribbles madly in his notebook.

"Are you writing about them?"

"Maybe so," he says, looking at what he's written.

"Read to me?"

"It's very rough."

"Please?"

"I am small and helpless. People carry me and feed me. I learn to walk and follow those people until I am grown. One day we come to a fork in the path. A strong feeling makes me choose the way no one else chooses. I am sad and afraid, but I don't go back. Years pass and my fear and sorrow disappear. I come to a raging river. Many people live here. They never try to cross the torrent. I stay here until I grow restless and try to cross. I am swept downstream and can't get out until the waters slow and leave me on the far shore where there is no path. I wander through a dark forest until I find a faint path, but I cannot decide which way to go, so I build a hut and live next to the path for many years. One morning you come along the path and we like each other and we decide to go on together. We come to a village on a river. The villagers welcome us and help us build a boat. We row across the river and go on. But we miss those people who helped us build our boat, so we row back to them and build a house in the village. This is where we are now.

Ω

25. Healing Shafi Howie

On the evening of October seventeenth, Healing is sitting on the aisle seat in the last row of the Surf Theatre, the exit door a few feet away. He is about to watch the final Mercy showing of Marianne Savoy's movie *Essentiel*, the title appearing in elegant white letters on a black screen, the English subtitle *Heart of the Matter*.

Essentiel has been playing at the Surf for three days now, four shows a day. This is Healing's last chance to see the movie on the big screen. He was going to attend the first screening but was overcome with anxiety and did not go. Then he was going to attend the seventh showing and developed a persistent cough and stayed home.

This morning Jahera begged him to see the movie on the big screen, and though he felt feverish and woozy after an early supper, he allowed Jahera and Tova to take him to the movie and sit with him in the last row, which is as close as he can bear to sit.

The opening credits proclaim the enchanting music for the movie was composed by Darvin Shapiro and performed by Darvin Shapiro and Healing Weintraub. When Healing's name appears on the screen, the audience erupts in applause.

The penultimate credit reads *Produced by Maahiah Dahl*, and the final credit is *Written and Directed by Marianne Savoy*.

As Marianne's name fades away, the blackness dissolves into a spectacular view of the beach at the mouth of the Mercy River, the shore besieged by enormous waves, the vast expanse of sand void of people save for a solitary man in the distance walking north with two dogs trotting ahead of him.

Now Healing's voice fills the theatre.

"I've lived whole lifetimes since I fell in love with Camille forty years ago, though it seems like only yesterday when I first saw her on the Rue de Seine."

Man and dogs grow larger on the screen and someone cries "That's Healing!" and thunderous applause ensues.

"I can't manage this," whispers Healing, and out of the theatre he goes.

*

Tonight being a Tuesday, *Big Goose* is only half-full, the mood mellow. Justin is tending bar tonight and Healing finds a stool between Lisa Moreno who works at the bookstore and Denver Tuttle who owns *Tuttle's Jams and Jellies*.

"On the house, my friend," says Justin, placing a half-pint of stout before Healing. "In honor of your bravura turn in *Essentiel*."

"Many thanks," says Healing, gulping the bitter brew.

"Only French movie I ever saw before yours was in a film class I took in college," says Denver, a burly fellow with sandy blond hair. "Fell asleep ten minutes in because nothing much was happening. When I woke up I couldn't figure out what was going on so I left. But I liked *your* movie. That gal who played Camille? Jesus God. They should put her in a James Bond movie. And every time I'd start to get confused, you'd come on and explain things, and I was like... Hey I can get this."

"It was my first French movie," says Lisa, smiling shyly at Healing. "I loved how when you were young everything was so clear, you know, and when you were old everything was kind of misty like in a dream. I loved how it went back and forth like that. It was very beautiful."

"How was it for you, man?" asks Denver, nudging Healing. "Seeing yourself on the big screen?"

"Overwhelming," says Healing, gulping his beer.

"Music's incredible," says Justin, in awe of Healing. "Darvin's making us some CDs to play here and at home. You guys should win Oscars."

"I'm glad you like it," says Healing, tapping his empty glass. "Love another."

"Did *you* like the movie?" asks Justin, serving Healing a pint this time.

"I only saw the opening credits," says Healing, gulping the brew to quell his pain. "Just caught a glimpse of an old man who might have been an actor if he'd only had the courage to take the leap."

*

Walking home, drunker than he's ever been, Healing stops on the sidewalk in front of the two-story building where Darby's antique shop used to be, the ground floor a snazzy gift shop now, the upstairs luxury apartments.

He remembers the windows of Darby's shop plastered with posters for poetry readings at the bookstore, the latest plays at the Mercy Players Theatre, and music at *Big Goose*, along with notices for garage sales, lost dogs, lost cats, firewood, and hundreds of business cards of local artists and entrepreneurs.

"Now there's only the fence at *Good Groceries*," says Healing, going to see what's posted there.

*

"Does that say *puppies*?" he asks, squinting at a notice tacked to the old fence, the words barely discernible to him in light from a street lamp thirty feet away.

A squad car approaches and slows to a stop.

"Buenas noches, señor actor," says Ruben, gazing out his window at Healing. "We loved your movie. Your voice could tame wild beasts."

"Ruben," says Healing, marveling at how handsome Ruben is. "Might I borrow your flashlight? There's an intriguing notice I can't quite make out. Might be puppies. Tayo's been wanting a dog."

Ruben gives Healing a big flashlight to illuminate the message typed on a small square of paper.

SHEEPDOG BORDER TERRIER PUPS
TWO LEFT OCTOBER 14 NO SHOTS
50$ EACH TONY 771-1944

"Many thanks," says Healing, returning the flashlight to Ruben. "You are a true friend, Ruben."

"Get in, hermano," says Ruben, quietly. "I'll drive you home."

"I will accept your kind offer," says Healing, bowing to Ruben, "if you will lend me paper and a pen to write down Tony's phone number before my memory betrays me."

*

"In all the years I've known you I've never seen you so drunk," says Ruben, driving at the speed of walking. "Que paso?"

"Oh Ruben," says Healing with a heavy sigh, "I miss my mum and Darby's shop and how things used to be before everything changed."

"Everything always changes," says Ruben, smiling at his old friend.

"I tried to watch the movie," says Healing, bowing his head. "I couldn't bear it."

"You don't need to see it," says Ruben, nodding in understanding. "You gave us a gift. That's enough."

*

They pull up in front of the little old house and Ruben turns off his engine.

"I wake up in the middle of the night," says Healing, sobbing, "worrying about Raaz and Oz and Zubu and the terrifying future awaiting them."

"I feel the same way about my daughters," says Ruben, nodding. "And now Juanita is pregnant and soon I'll be a grandfather like you."

"I guess there's nothing we can do but be good to each other," says Healing, looking at Ruben. "What else *can* we do?"

"Nada," says Ruben, shaking his head. "Be good to each other. That's the whole enchilada."

*

In the morning, Healing walks Oz and Raaz to Arjun's house for school and hangs around for a few minutes to visit with Arjun's mother Kashvi before he makes haste to the parking lot at *Walker's* grocery store where a man with a bushy gray beard is waiting by an old brown truck.

"You Healing?" asks the man, his accent betraying his Midwest origins.

"I am he," says Healing, raising his hand in greeting. "You must be Tony."

The man nods and gets a cardboard box out of the truck.

"I'm in love," says Healing, smiling into the box where two adorable puppies are scrabbling at the sides. "How big is the mom?"

"Mini Aussie," says Tony, gruffly. "Got knocked up by my sister's Border Terrier before I could get her fixed. There were seven pups, now there's just these two. Ten-weeks-old. One's a boy, one's a girl."

"Where do you live, Tony?" asks Healing, picking up the male and nuzzling him. "I've lived here my whole life and you are new to me."

"Only been here a couple months," says Tony, nodding. "Me and my wife came out from Wisconsin. We're living up Frog Pond Road at the Wilson's. You know Ruth and John? Ruth is my wife's aunt."

"Ruth and I used to take yoga at the rec center together," says Healing, picking up the female pup. "And Ruth shopped at *Good Groceries* when I was manager there."

"Ruth still goes to yoga," says Tony, grinning. "Still shops at *Good Groceries.* We're helping her with John. He's got dementia and she can't handle him by herself anymore."

"I'm so sorry to hear that," says Healing, pained by the news. "It's good they've got you and your wife to help them."

"We were looking to move anyway." He fishes a card out of his wallet. "I fix appliances if you know anybody needs work done. Washers, dryers, refrigerators."

"You're just the person I've been looking for," says Healing, taking the card. "We have a refrigerator in need of an overhaul. As for the puppies, you said fifty each?"

"How about eighty for the two of'em?" says Tony, hopefully.

"You drive a hard bargain," says Healing, extracting a wad of bills from his pocket. "Two hundred it is. Only I keep the box."

"Serious?" says Tony, frowning at Healing.

"Serious," says Healing, handing him the money.

"Well okay," says Tony, gripping Healing's hand. "Thank you, bro. Big time."

*

Healing takes the puppies directly to Isabella Cisneros who declares them in good health and leaves the vaccinating to her assistant Gwyneth Cumberland who sings to the little darlings as she gives them their shots.

*

Home with the puppies, Healing introduces the baby dogs to the adult dogs while Jahera makes a puppy bed near the fire.

"Have you named them yet, Shafi?" asks Maahiah, holding Zubu while Eliana chops vegetables for minestrone soup.

"No. I'm hoping Tayo will want them," says Healing, petting the pups. "And he'll name them."

*

Tayo arrives a half-hour later wearing a splendid brown and red dashiki, his hair a black frizz peppered with gray. He kneels on the living room floor and gazes down at the pups conked out from their vaccinations.

"I want them," he says quietly. "Can I take them now?"

"You can," says Healing, resting his hand on Tayo's shoulder. "Or you can leave them with us for a few weeks and let them learn a thing or two from the older dogs. Whatever you like."

"You'll house train them for me?" says Tayo, grinning at Healing. "That's a no-brainer. I'll leave them here until you give me the all clear."

"I was hoping you'd say that," says Healing, laughing. "So the kids can play with them for a while. We'll leave the naming to you."

"Oh let the kids name them," says Tayo, standing up.

"Stay for lunch," says Jahera, eager to photograph Tayo holding the puppies.

"Thanks but I'm taking my mother out to lunch for her birthday," he says, bowing to Jahera. "Can I bring her by this afternoon to see the pups?"

"Please," says Jahera, who adores Tayo's mother. "Any time."

*

At noon, Healing and Tova leash Moshe and Coosi and Flora and set off for Arjun's house to get Raaz and Oz.

"I have news, Pa-pa," says Tova, handling the rambunctious Flora. "Multiple headlines."

"Regarding you and Steven?" asks Healing, arching an eyebrow.

"I'm saving that for last."

"Do tell," says Healing, who cannot shed his heavy cloak of sorrow.

"Daniel called from Paris yesterday to tell me *Delphine and the Sorcerer* will have its world premiere in May at Cannes! And Steven and I are going."

"Fantastic," says Healing, hugging her.

"And Morris called this morning to let me know *Cream Or Black* will have a theatrical release in June and start streaming a month later."

"Amazing," says Healing, wishing he felt more excited about Tova's success, yet feeling only grief. "And what, pray tell, is the headline about Steven?"

"Well..." she says, her eyes filling with tears. "He asked me to marry him and I said yes, and we don't want to wait so..."

"You'll be married in the little old house on Thanksgiving."

"How did you know?"

"Might as well," says Healing, shrugging nonchalantly. "The usual suspects will already be there for turkey and pie."

"No. I mean how did you know Steven asked me?"

"Because after waffles on Sunday he asked me for your hand in marriage," says Healing, bowing to her. "And not wanting to disappoint him, I said *Yes*."

*

A short time later, after Healing and Tova have raved sufficiently about the scary papier-mâché masks the kids are making for Halloween, the four humans and three dogs head home with nary a mention of the puppies in the living room.

"I suggest we pick up the pace," says Healing, eyeing the lowering clouds. "A significant downpour is imminent and we foolishly left the house without umbrellas."

They almost make it home before the deluge, but not quite, and when Oz and Raaz rush into the house to take off their wet clothes by the fire, they find the puppies and go wild with joy.

*

Four days later on a cold drizzly Sunday morning, Raaz and Oz and Moshe and Mendelssohn accompany Healing to the hen house to gather eggs for the waffle batter. They find seven eggs, which Healing declares is an excellent haul for late October.

"Shafi?" asks Oz, carrying the basket of eggs to the house. "Why don't hens lay very many eggs in the winter?"

"Because there is less daylight now than in spring and summer," he explains, "and the days are colder, too. So the hens use more energy staying warm, which leaves them less energy for making eggs."

"Why don't you put a heater in the chicken coop?" asks Raaz, who heretofore didn't know chickens got cold.

"I do put a heater in there when it gets *very* cold," says Healing, following the kids up onto the deck. "However, it's more the amount of sunlight that makes a difference when it comes to egg laying. That's why some people put bright lights in their hen houses and keep the lights on throughout the winter, but I don't do that because if I were a chicken I'd enjoy the annual break from making eggs. Fortunately for us, Matilda and Eunice and Bess are Golden Comets, and Golden Comets lay eggs year round."

"Why not have *all* Golden Comets?" asks Oz, thoughtfully pursing his lips.

"Because I like having different kinds of chickens who lay different colored eggs," says Healing, scanning the yard to make sure all the dogs are okay before he follows the children inside.

*

During the waffle fest, as talk of Halloween and the Thanksgiving nuptials reaches a fever pitch, Zubu raises her arms to Healing and cries, "Howie. Howie."

Healing lifts the baby girl out of her high chair and carries her into the living room to visit the puppies in their little pen, and for a moment Healing's sorrow abates.

*

After a good long post-waffles visit by the fire, Healing drives Darby and Marjorie home, a hard rain falling.

At their door, saying goodbye, Marjorie takes Healing's hand and says, "Grieving is how we make room for joy to return."

*

Driving home, the windshield wipers no match for the downpour, Healing pulls over to the side of the road, turns off the engine, and weeps.

*

When at last his tears abate, with the rain drumming loudly on the roof of the little old truck, Healing hears someone scratching on the passenger-side door. Seeing no one at the window, he opens the door and a young female dog, shivering cold and wet, jumps into the truck.

"Now how in the world did you know I had a towel?" asks Healing as he dries the affable pooch who seems entirely unafraid. "Not to mention a chewy treat with your name on it?"

The dog nudges Healing's hand.

"Here you are," he says, feeding her. "I see you have no collar. So... should you decide to live with us, with your permission, I will call you Lucky."

She smiles to say *You can call me anything you want.*

"Lucky it is," says Healing, starting his engine. "Home we go."

So Healing and Lucky drive across town to the little old house on Nasturtium Road where upon their arrival the sun breaks through the clouds and a brilliant rainbow appears over Mercy Bay.

Ω

Author's Note

In Chapter 7 of this novel, Eliana mentions a movie she was in when she was four-years-old – *Isabella Remembers.* The story of Eliana being in that movie is entitled *Many Grandfathers* and is included in my collection of short stories *Why You Are Here.* The stories in that collection take place in Mercy twenty years before the events in *Pooches and Kiddies,* and several of those stories feature Helen Morningstar, Justin Oglethorpe, Eliana and her parents, and Ruben Higuera, the unflappable sheriff of Mercy, all of whom appear in this volume as well as in *Good With Dogs and Cats,* the prequel to *Pooches and Kiddies.*

About the Author

Todd Walton is the author of many volumes of fiction including: *Inside Moves, Forgotten Impulses, Ruby & Spear, Buddha in A Teacup, Under the Table Books, Little Movies, Why You Are Here*, and *Good With Dogs and Cats: the adventures of Healing Weintraub*. His many albums of original songs include *Dream of You, Through the Fire, Lounge Act In Heaven, Mystery Inventions*, and *Ahora Entras Tu*.

His web site and blog are at UnderTheTableBooks.com.

Printed in the USA
CPSIA information can be obtained
at www.ICGtesting.com
LVHW040549240824
789100LV00003B/612

9 781958 892718